# JOSEPHUS

## A NOVEL

# JOSEPHUS

## A NOVEL

# B. MICHAEL ANTLER

*For my Mommas and Winnie.*

# Table of Contents

# Table of Illustrations

Book Cover, Border Frames, Maps & Illustrations
ending with "a" by Tauseef Ahmed

Illustrations ending with "g" by Gora Gorskiy

Illustration XXIV by Tauseef Ahmed
with assistance from Gora Gorskiy

# Author's Note

**THOUGH THIS** is a work of fiction, I have taken great care to accurately depict the historical figures—the accounts of the main characters: Josephus, Titus, Vespasian, Nero, John of Gischala, Ananus, Simon bar Giora, and Eleazar ben Simon, are very close to the historical record.

Furthering a mission of historical accuracy, I followed Josephus' great work, *The Jewish War*, or *Bellum Judaicum*, in researching and writing this book. While many liberties are taken with the detailed descriptions throughout the novel, and Part II (which is mostly fabricated), the crux of the story is honest to Josephus.

My goal in writing this book was to provide a modern narrative that did not exist concerning the Jewish or Judean war against the Romans between 66 and 73 C.E. The last attempt at historical fiction concerning Josephus was undertaken by Lion Feuchtwanger in a trilogy written between 1932 and 1942, which I chose not to read until after my book was published.

While Josephus' work is thorough, many may not find it accessible as it was written nearly two thousand years ago in ancient Greek[1]—it was then translated into Latin and then French before English, making even the modern English translations of Josephus very challenging for any reader.

---

1 Thomas Lodge (b. 1558, d. 1625), an English physician and author first translated Josephus' work into English in 1602, from a French translation.

Throughout Josephus' work there are sections when one could not hope to improve upon his dialogue. From time to time, I believe it is more than appropriate, but advantageous and novel to quote Josephus. You will notice long, multi-paragraph speeches that have a different style, and many are offset, especially Josephus' speeches pleading with the Judeans outside the walls of Jerusalem. After all, Josephus said it first and best, and he even wrote it down for us.

*A note on Israel:* Throughout the book, I refer to the whole of what we today consider the Jewish lands in the Middle East as Judea, Galilee, Idumea, or the Holy Land. It is not appropriate to refer to this area as Palestine as that was an official creation of the 2nd century C.E.,[2] though it had been known colloquially as Syria Palestina since as early as the 5th century B.C.E. Additionally, Israel then was not the Israel we know today, and therefore the name is also inappropriate. Israel is, however, mentioned as the nation of Hebrews or Israelites but not as a reference to boundary lines on a map.

*A note on Herod:* In *The Jewish War,* Josephus spends many chapters describing the Herodian dynasty and its internal power struggles. I have excluded almost all of this part of Josephus' work as it is mostly unimportant to the rebellion of the Judeans and the destruction of Jerusalem in 70 C.E.—the focus of *The Jewish War.*

*A note on sexual violence:* During the entire writing and editing process I struggled with how to, if at all, show the savage truth of what the Romans and Judeans did to the Judean men, women, boys, and girls. This war was filled with unspeakable horrors, many of them sexual. In the end, I believe depicting limited scenes of sexual violence was absolutely necessary to fully appreciate the gravity of the First Roman-Jewish War.

---

2 The Roman Emperor, Hadrian, renamed Judea to Syria Palestina after the Judean revolt of Bar-Kokhba (132-136 C.E.)

Finally, it is my sincere hope that this work inspires the reader to read *The Jewish War* and delve into the study of antiquity. Josephus is so unfamiliar to many in the current generations on this Earth as his work ceased being a primary text for Christians whereas, in the nineteenth century, worshippers of Christ were more likely to own Josephus' complete works than any other book in the world save the *Bible*.

*The Jewish War* is not an easy text, but the important stories it tells far outweigh the challenging nature of its prose.

—BMA

# PART I

"You are gods, sons of the Most High, all of you; nevertheless, like men you shall die, and fall like any prince. Arise, O God, judge the Earth; for you shall inherit all the nations!" *Psalms 82:3*

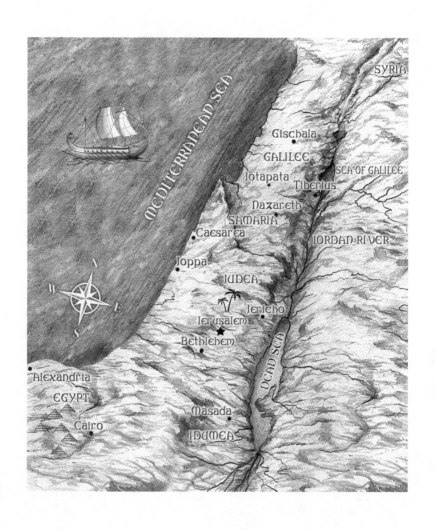

**Map: 1st Century A.D. Holy Land**

# Prologue

**AT THE** beginning of the first century A.D., there was an uneasy peace across the land of Judea. The Roman Empire controlled the whole of countries now known as Israel, Syria, Lebanon, and Egypt. Judeans were forced to live subserviently under their European masters, and all orders came out of Rome.

The Romans were known to harass the Judean population without cause. Many times a blasphemous insult to the Hebrew God or the defilement of His holy house would cause such an uproar among the Judeans that violence would break out. Several times Roman governors were forced to execute one of their own soldiers to avert an uprising. Other times, the spendthrift fiscal behavior on the part of the Romans in Judea stirred up talk of rebellion.

Tiberius ruled the Roman Empire as Caesar. He demanded a proper benediction from his Hebrew subjects as proof of their unwavering obedience. To accomplish this goal, Tiberius had statues of himself, depicted in god-like fashion, placed on the rooftop of the Temple in Jerusalem.

At the sight of Tiberius' heretical 'standards,' the Judeans nearly burnt down their own city. Worshipping these statues of Caesar condemned a Judean in the eyes of God—it constituted the capital crime of idolatry, and any Judean who prayed to them would be inviting instant death by stoning as well as damning their immortal soul. Thus, an impassable conflict was set into motion in which the Judeans were willing to die for their beliefs and the Romans were willing to kill to maintain absolute control over their Judean subjects—compromise on the part of either belligerent was not an option.

Sitting as governor of Judea in Caesarea, the Mediterranean port city from which Roman authority emanated, was Pontius Pilate. Upon the erection of the standards, Judeans throughout all of Judea streamed into Caesarea to demand the standards' immediate removal. Pilate refused. For five days and nights the Judeans camped out all around Pilate's residence. Tensions rose, and Pilate began to fear for his life at the sight of the tens of thousands of outraged Judeans. He countered this threat by inviting the Judeans to the amphitheater so he could hear and redress their complaints.

Once the Judeans had gathered inside the theater, Pilate gave a prearranged signal to the Roman soldiers he commanded. The Judeans were instantly encircled by a ring of Roman swords and spears three rows of men deep. Pilate threatened to slaughter every last one of them if they refused to accept the standards on the Temple and throughout Judea.

The Judeans, though completely surprised by Pilate's treachery, remained intransigent. Outraged at being forced to criminally and irreparably offend God or be put to death, they bent their necks under the Roman blades and dared Pilate to make good on his threat. Upon realizing that there was no compromise to be had with his subjects and again fearing for his life, Pilate balked and agreed to remove the standards.

Soon after the standards fiasco, Pilate enraged the Judeans once again by spending a large portion of the holy treasury from the Temple on an expensive new aqueduct, some fifty miles in length. Pilate's next visit to Jerusalem was met with a rowdy mob incensed by his exorbitant spending projects.

However, Pilate was prepared for this backlash and had his soldiers quickly swing into action. A melee ensued. The Romans used their clubs to beat the Judeans savagely, in many cases fatally. Even more Judeans trampled one another to death. But Pilate did manage, through his chicanery and brutality, to forestall a Judean uprising.

After Tiberius' reign as Caesar ended, Caligula came to power, and the conflict over the standards arose once more. Again the Judeans were threatened with death for refusing to accept Caesar's statues, and again they refused to violate God's commandment against worshipping false idols, even if it meant losing their own lives.

The governor of Judea, now Petronius, was so won over by the courage of the Judean resolve, he agreed to petition Caligula one final time against erecting the standards. But before word could return from Rome in response to Petronius' plea, Caligula had been assassinated and the statues were never erected, averting an insurgency.

And so it was over the course of Roman rule in the last hundred years. Whenever Rome angered the Judeans, rebellion was always a moment away.

Then came the outrage over taxes...

# Chapter 1:

# Roman Taxes Due

**IN 66** Anno Domini, Nero ruled as Caesar over the Roman Empire. The Romans ruled Judea from their stronghold city of Caesarea on the Judean coast. The Roman governor of Judea, now Gessius Florus, sat at his office desk, preparing himself mentally for his eleven o'clock meeting: the monthly tax revenue review of Jerusalem.

He took a long drink of red wine from a goblet in one hand and gnawed away at a green apple held in the other. He wore a Roman tunic, decorated beyond practicality with gold pips and pins.

Titus, son of General Vespasian and currently serving Gessius as his chief of staff, stood by the side wall in his boss' office snacking on dates, attending the meeting but not participating in it.

A meek double knock came from Gessius' office chamber door.

"Come in, damn you!" Gessius yelled out.

Gessius was a short ogre of a man. At nearly sixty years of age, his waistline was big enough to match the largest in Rome—he was so fat he could no longer mount a horse and had to be hauled around in an oversized litter.

Modius, the ancient minister of taxation, entered Gessius' chamber. He bore a scroll in one hand and kept his head low to prevent looking into Gessius' eyes, avoiding accidentally inciting confrontation.

"Yes, yes—give us the scroll," Gessius griped, extending his hand towards the document impatiently.

Modius accelerated his feeble, old-man waddle, presenting the scroll to Gessius' hand.

But before he began reading, Gessius placed the scroll on his desk, picked up his wine, and drank the remains of it. He loudly banged the empty goblet down on his desk. Still, Gessius was not finished drinking—instead of taking up the scroll, he took the carafe of wine on his side table and refilled his goblet.

Gessius' way of dealing with stress was wine. Given the vicissitudes of his position, he drank regularly—he was known to drink a quarter-cask of the stuff daily. Many nights it took the entire Governor's Guard to carry Gessius' passed-out body from his cold office floor to his lambskin-covered bed.

Gessius, finally settled, began reading the scroll.

Modius could immediately sense the governor was becoming displeased. Additionally, small growls could be heard as Gessius punctuated his displeasure with verbal noises.

Modius offered up a bevy of excuses silently in his own mind. It was not his decision to double taxes. That proclamation was Gessius' doing, and it had resulted in the Judeans banding together and refusing *en masse* to pay nearly *all* taxes. The outrage over the increased taxes resulted in smaller tax receipts than had been collected the month prior!

Gessius' face turned bright red like a ripening steak tomato.

"Thirty talents," Gessius muttered slowly. He looked up and irately stared Modius directly in the eyes. "Thirty talents!" he repeated, shouting and beating his desk with a closed fist.

"My lord, the Hebrews…" The old minister started to explain the extremely light receipts from Jerusalem.

"Silence!" Gessius shouted. "You bring me thirty talents from all of Jerusalem! *Two thousand* talents was the quota!" he screamed. "There are two explanations for what is going on here. You are either stealing from me or you are a fool!"

After a moment of looking Modius up and down, scourging him with his eyes, Gessius concluded, "You are too much of a coward to steal from me. Only a fool would fail to collect Caesar's *just* taxes and show his face alive again as you have done—I could collect thirty talents from my brother's whorehouse this minute!" Again Gessius beat on his desk, this time scattering some of his work papers onto the floor.

He then reached for the first object he could grab, which happened to be the browning green apple core, and threw it at Modius with all his might. The minister winced, not because the core caused any great pain, but because Modius *was* a coward and Gessius' every act made him fear for his undeniably pathetic life.

The minister fell to his knees and started to beg.

"My most great and just Lord Governor, I pray you give me but a fortnight more and I promise you will have your two thousand talents. I need just a brief time longer," Modius pleaded.

"Oh, do shut up!" Gessius barked, interrupting the minister's groveling with a backhanded slap to Modius' face.

"Ahhhh!" Modius screamed at the pain of his physical chastisement.

"I tire of you, Modius. Let me do us both a favor," Gessius said, taking a dagger from his waist. He jabbed it directly into Modius' Adam's apple in one precise thrusting motion.

Modius' surprised eyes bulged out of their sockets and spent their final moments silently cursing Gessius, who returned a labored smirk.

Gessius twisted the blade—blood began rushing out of Modius' neck, pooling on Gessius' white marble floor. He quickly fell over dead.

Gessius retrieved his dagger from Modius' throat and cleaned the blood off the blade with the cloth of the departed's robe.

"Titus, get this corpse out of my sight. And put his head on a pike as a message for the Hebrews. I want a sign that reads 'Tax Evader' placed underneath him."

"Yes, my lord—guards!" Titus shouted.

Roman soldiers burst through Gessius' chamber doors, nodding in obedience upon their entrance. They rushed to drag Modius' dead body out of Gessius' office.

"Head," Gessius said to the guards, making a chopping motion to his own neck.

The guards nodded again, this time in acknowledgement of Gessius' order.

Hauling the newly-dead Modius, the guards moved with the regularity of men accustomed and completely desensitized to the most horrid of occupations. A bright red trail of blood streaked the marble as they took Modius away. And of course, the guards closed the office doors softly and respectfully on their way out.

"Thirty talents. A tax collector shows up with *thirty talents!*" Gessius said incredulously, talking in soliloquy.

He turned back to Titus. "I trust you will see Caesar's taxes are collected within a fortnight. You are my right arm, and if you cannot see these taxes collected, who can?" Gessius asked rhetorically.

From beyond Gessius' office, a gladius could be heard loudly hacking off Modius' head.

"I couldn't stand that old dunce," Gessius groused.

Titus, not wanting to insult the dead, moved the conversation along. "But concerning the Hebrews, they are an obstinate people. They could have a hundred thousand gold talents among them, and they would not swear to fifty."

"Yes, they are obstinate, and it will be your job to free them of that trait by *any* means necessary," Gessius said. "You best not fail. If I have to report to Caesar a take of thirty talents, it will mean both our lives. You know Caesar enjoys sadistically executing his failed commanders. The lucky ones only lose their heads—we should be so lucky. They talk of flaying and death by the Brazen Bull. I haven't worked my rump off these forty years last to be cooked alive after my skin is removed."

Gessius, exhausted from the brief debacle, grasped for his goblet full of wine and drank the entire contents in one swallow. He then grabbed the wine carafe to refill his goblet, but the vessel was empty.

"Wine!" Gessius shouted out to his young manservant, who rushed to refill the empty carafe.

Hurrying as if his life depended on his rapid service, the servant placed a refilled carafe on Gessius' desk.

"Are you going to make me pour it too, you little brat?" Gessius barked at his boy.

"You always pour from the carafe, my lord," the young servant replied.

"Insult me in front of my subordinates as well?" Gessius yelled, standing up and making a motion towards the boy like a father about to corporally punish his son. "Get out, you lil' bastard!" he shouted, preferring not to try and chase down his nimble squirrel of a servant.

Sitting back down at his desk, Gessius refilled his goblet from the replenished carafe. After taking a few sips, and with a smile anew on his face, he revealed his cruel solution regarding the unpaid taxes due: "I hear there is an untold fortune inside the Temple. Liberate the Hebrews of it. Have I made myself clear?" he asked.

"Crystal clear, my lord. I will not fail you. Hail, Caesar!" Titus shouted, pounding his chest with a closed fist before turning to walk out of the governor's office.

"Titus!" Gessius added, stopping Titus before he took more than a few steps towards the exit. "Don't forget about Modius' head."

"How could I forget such an order, my lord?" Titus answered and then left the office.

Titus, a tribune and looking to make a name for himself as Gessius' chief of staff, had lobbied his father, General Vespasian, to allow him to spend some time going his own way versus always following in his father's military footsteps.

Though a willing Roman soldier, he took no pleasure in being Gessius' errand boy. And delivering a dead head was obviously a job below Titus' status. Gessius understood this and made Titus do his pedestrian bidding to remind him who was governor and, more importantly, who was not.

Titus walked down the corridor and over to the guards that had carried away Modius.

"Where's the head?" Titus asked curtly.

The highest-ranked of the Roman guards merely pointed to a burlap sack dripping with blood on a table beside himself.

"Caesar thanks you for your service," Titus said facetiously and grabbed the sack.

Titus walked so fast out of the governor's mansion he was nearly running.

"Give me my nag," he demanded of his personal guards, who had been babysitting his horse while he had been meeting with Gessius. Titus took the reins of his white Arabian. "Make sure the sack is closed tight. I don't want his head falling out," he barked to the soldiers assisting him.

He then mounted his beast. Two of his bodyguards followed on their own horses. The three took off at a breakneck pace for Jerusalem.

Titus' eyes were dilated with disgust that he was being made to haul a head that was to be piked and erected for the benefit of Rome's Judean subjects. But he was a loyal officer, always obey-

15

ing commands. He was also ambitious—Titus dreamed of being governor of Judea himself one day.

With regards to his Judean disposition, he did not enjoy slaying Judeans the way other men in the Roman service did, but he understood that at times it was a necessary part of the job.

Physically, Titus was the model of a male Roman specimen. Tall, a few inches over six feet, and at only twenty-five years of age, his body was in its physical prime. He kept it that way—Titus was often exercising when he was not on duty or training with his soldiers.

During the ride, Titus' mind ran through the military scenarios on how he might take the gold from the Temple with the fewest casualties on both sides. He was an intelligent man as well, and as such, he was willing to try to use his guile first to convince the Hebrews to pay the overdue tax balance rather than initiate a mass slaughter.

A cloud of dirt rose from the ground as the trio of Romans rode for two hours before arriving in Jerusalem.

"Bread, water, milk!" vendors cried out at the Damascus gate of the great city.

"Out of the way!" Titus yelled to a crowd of people blocking his path.

One of his bodyguards, seeing Titus' path obstructed, took out a spear and reversed his hold so the bladed end faced him. Then he smacked an old man in Titus' way on the head with the wooden end of the spear. The old man tumbled to the ground, and the remaining people blocking Titus' way quickly dispersed.

The company advanced through the city towards Antonia Fortress, the Romans' military stronghold.

The fortress was named for Mark Antony, a patron of Herod the Great, the builder of the edifice. There a Roman garrison kept order—always reminding the Judeans of their true masters.

Antonia Fortress had been made a quasi-part of the Temple Mount—it was connected to the Mount, being adjacent to the western corner of the Temple complex. A small bridge, no greater than ten feet wide, allowed men direct passage between the two structures.

Four great identical towers rose into the sky from each of the fortress' corners. The towers were fitted with windows large enough to accommodate spear-throwers and archers. The roof of each tower was flat except for the staggered merlons around the edges of the tower tops. The Romans kept large ordnances on each tower roof. Each of the four towers stood over a hundred feet in the air. The towers made all enemies before them cower in the awesome presence of such a well-fortified and tall citadel.

Like the Temple, Antonia had been made with solid blocks of marble. And, like the walls around Jerusalem, no fire, projectile, or ram would be sufficient to easily take or breach its defenses.

Titus dismounted his horse as he approached the fortress entrance. He removed the sack with Modius' head and walked up to the centurion on duty.

"Sound the horn," Titus ordered the centurion at the entrance.

"What's the trouble, my lord?" the centurion asked.

"We're raiding the Temple. Get your men ready." Titus turned to the Roman soldiers in the barracks and yelled, "All able-bodied men—suit up!"

The soldiers of Antonia Fortress all cheerfully grunted together, happy to be put into action.

"Minister Modius needs to be piked," Titus ordered an idle Roman soldier sitting nearby on his bum, and he threw the bloody sack at him.

"Of course, my lord," the soldier obsequiously replied, fumbling about but finally catching Modius' head.

"Oh, and don't forget to nail a sign that says 'Tax Evader' to the pike," Titus commanded.

"Of course, my lord," the soldier acknowledged.

Titus turned his efforts back to the tax collecting. He assumed command of the garrison and readied a band of the fortress's finest soldiers, one thousand strong. The Romans suited up in their steel armor. Gladii of the finest alloyed metals hung in their sheaths from the men's waists. Spears, eight feet in length, were raised to the heavens, reflecting blinding sunlight in all directions. Roman eagle flags stood tall, flowing with the wind. Titus rode his white Arabian horse at a walking pace, leading the way to the Court of Gentiles on the Temple Mount.

As the Romans spread across the Temple Mount, the marketplace grew quiet of voice but loud of military footfall and grunts. Women rushed to carry their children to safety. Merchants closed their stalls, left their goods where they lay, and hid wherever they could.

The Temple was originally built by King Solomon and then rebuilt by Ezra and Nehemiah. King Herod had renovated the Temple several decades earlier.

The Temple contained all of Judean antiquity: Torahs, sacred chalices, holy olive oil, treasures of gold and silver, gemstones, and countless other items of importance and value.

Frankincense, that musky smell created by burning the dried sap of the Boswellia tree, could be detected in the air upon close proximity to the Temple Mount—the Judeans burned it without cessation, as commanded by God.

The innumerable animals in the complex, both living and sacrificed, emanated the stench of a butcher's meat market, which mixed with the tang of horse stables and barnyards. These smells all joined together, creating an unmistakable noxious essence that was the second Temple of David.

The Temple and Antonia Fortress

The Temple complex itself was actually a series of different courts. The first court was the Court of Gentiles, the largest court many times over. It encompassed almost the entirety of the top level of the Temple Mount and was wrapped with a perimeter of colonnades.

All were allowed entry into the Court of Gentiles. It was essentially a grand marketplace. Sheep, goats, rams, bulls, pigeons, and many other forms of livestock were for sale. The Temple's main purpose was to provide a priestly blessing, and that could only be accomplished through ritual animal sacrifice. Choosing an animal depended on one's wealth and the severity of one's sins—the merchants sold livestock that catered to all needs.

Inside the Court of Gentiles was a more exclusive court, the Court of Women, reserved for Judeans only.

"Do *not* enter the Court of Women," Titus sternly ordered his centurions commanding the vanguard of the military train.

Titus, though on a mission of tax collection, still respected the Hebrews' sacred rituals and customs—only Israelites were permitted to enter the inner and holier Temple courts.

The Roman squadron grunted as they finished their formation inside the Court of Gentiles—spears, shields, and swords were readied. Sitting high on his horse, Titus gave the order to his signal man. A clarion horn bellowed for all to hear on the Temple Mount. Slowly the Judean high priests of the Temple and the judges of the Sanhedrin, the tribunal of religious law, came out of the inner courts to see about the Roman call.

The eldest and chief high priest—David *the Wise* led the way, followed by Simon bar Giora, one of the rising power players in the Sanhedrin. Ananus, the second eldest of the high priests followed Simon. Joseph, son of Matthias, and his father, both high priests as well, followed behind Ananus. Bringing up the rear was the youngest high priest, Seth, son of Shem, barely seventeen years of age but still several years now a man by Judean standards. The judges all wore black full-length robes with assorted gold and bejeweled accessories and turbans on their heads. Many had multiple gold rings on each finger, carrying as much gold as possible on their bodies, seemingly the one physical labor they would endure. They walked with an elevated sense of importance, but the judges could not even begin to compete with the opulence of the high priests' livery, gems, and swagger.

The elder high priests moved with a divinely granted, heightened sense of superiority, arrogance, and obstinance. It seemed every inch of their bodies was improved upon. Their facial hair was accented with extra virgin olive oil, giving it an unmistakable shimmer that Sadducee priests enjoyed flaunting.

The priests' clothing was also overly ornate and seemed to grant them extra-human rights. It was more like a multilayered and multicolored series of garments, covered with gold and gem accoutrements. The priests' first garment was a long, plain white garb, nearly touching the toes and with sleeves down to the wrist. But one could hardly see much of this garment except the bottom few inches above the toes and the ends of the sleeves. Directly on top of the white garbs, they wore blue robes of the finest cloth that cut off at the shoulders and hung down to the shins. On the bottom of the robe, alternating small golden bells and little pomegranates hung from the fringes, creating a windchime sound whenever in motion.

On top of their robes, they wore an apron-like garment called the ephod, which covered their front and back. It shouted its own importance with its blue, purple, scarlet, and gold interwoven linen. Two gemstones adorned their shoulders on top of the ephod, each one representing six of the twelve tribes of Israel. They even wore ornamental multicolored linen sashes and large white mitre turbans with a streak of rich blue cloth down the middle, lined with gold. An additional piece of gold attached to the hat was engraved with the Hebrew words, 'Holy to God.'

But all that livery pomp was barely noticeable due to the bejeweled gold breastplate each priest wore. The shimmering square plate was encrusted with twelve different gemstones, one for each of the tribes of Israel. The large gems were displayed on the priestly gold plate like a military badge, three side-by-side columns of four stones each. This was called the 'Oracle' or 'Plate of Decision.'

Interestingly enough, the priests went barefoot as they were walking on holy ground on the Temple premises.

Titus was staring down at the magnificent-looking priests, deciding which one to engage with, when he noticed all Judean eyes now focused on him. He was undeniably grandiose in his sparkling gold, crimson, and silver uniform on top of a magnificent beast.

"I am Titus, tasked by our lord, the great Governor Gessius Florus to collect two thousand talents justly owed to Caesar by you, his Hebrew subjects. What say you, priest?" Titus asked the chief high priest, David *the Wise*.

"I say this is the House of God—not a treasure chest," David said impudently for all around to hear.

Titus looked to his left and his right and saw light laughter among the Judeans. He slowly dismounted his steed and walked up to David *the Wise*.

Titus grabbed his small dagger from his side and pulled it out of its sheath. He quickly and violently slammed the steel into the top of David's head. The priest went limp instantly and collapsed to the ground, lifeless.

Loud cries of women and children rang out. The Judean men shouted with rage.

Blood gushed out of David's head where the blade entered his skull. A small red stream of blood ran between Titus' feet.

Again Titus gave the signal for the horn. The piercing sound of the clarion brought all quickly to attention.

Roman soldiers readied their spears, swords, and shields. The archers all put arrows to their bows and drew them taut.

Titus removed the dagger from the priest's head and held it high in the air. "Hebrews!" he shouted. "I will execute every last man, woman, and child in this damned city until my coffers are full! Caesar demands two thousand gold talents, and two thousand gold talents he shall have!"

Titus focused his gaze on Seth, son of Shem, the youngest of the high priests.

"You there, young priest—what is your name?" Titus asked.

Seth looked up at Titus, nearly in tears at the loss of David *the Wise* and visibly shaking from head to toe. He looked as if he was trying to say something, but no words came out of his mouth. Only the young priest's bladder could open. The Roman soldiers broke into laughter while Seth stood in front of Jerusalem wetting himself.

"Silence!" Titus shouted at his men, and then he turned back to Seth. "I will ask you one last time, boy. What is your name?"

"I… I am Seth, son of Shem," he said nervously.

Titus continued, "Seth, son of Shem, answer me—are there two thousand gold talents in the Temple?"

"Give him what he wants, Seth, and let's be done with the Romans," advised Joseph, son of Matthias.

"Excellent advice, priest," Titus said to Joseph.

Trembling, but done urinating himself, Seth replied with a very soft and muddled, "Yes."

"You answer questions well—if only the old priest could have learned from you," Titus said mockingly.

After a deep breath, Titus walked up close to the young priest and softly said into his ear, "I want you to run into the Temple and bring me two thousand gold talents. *Now go!*"

Quickly the young priest sprinted into the Temple.

The Roman soldiers, now standing at ease, began to gossip among themselves. One moderate-ranking soldier, a legionnaire, had the audacity to grab a small bucket of water from a Judean commoner in the marketplace. He took the bucket and thoroughly drenched a couple of high priests and judges. A great eruption of laughter broke out through the Roman ranks.

Simon bar Giora was hit with a sizable deluge, and his instincts were to head-butt and flog the Roman soldier taunting him. But before Simon could take so much as a full step towards the Roman, Joseph took a firm hold of Simon's arm and ensured a petty insult would not escalate into further bloodshed.

But the Roman soldier who had served up the water-dousing indignity was not done playing.

Next, the soldier placed the bucket down on the ground face up, five feet in front of the high priests and judges. He raised his tunic up from below his knees to above his waist and squatted, taking a long and loud shit for all Jerusalem to hear, see, and smell.

"Argh!" the defecating soldier screeched out as his droppings came thudding down into the bucket. "That's a good one," he said, looking at his putrid creation. Then he picked up the bucket and walked up directly in front of the high priests. He turned the bucket upside down inches from their bare feet, leaving his feces to desecrate the holy ground of the Judean House. He even made a praying motion with his hands, taking the humiliation to the max.

The priests and judges stood frozen and silent, unable to express their outrage. Only their eyes voiced the anger in their hearts.

The regular Roman soldiers could barely control themselves, laughing so hard as to strain their abdominals. Some dropped their spears and shields.

"That's enough. Stand at attention!" Titus ordered, not permitting his soldiers to degenerate into animals during state business.

No more than five minutes later, Seth returned with a coin chest in his arms. He presented Titus with the chest. Titus opened it—his eyes blinked uncontrollably from the blinding, flickering light. There were two thousand gold talents in the chest. Even Titus paused for an extended moment, marveling at the sight of the great Hebrew wealth.

Slamming the chest lid closed, Titus shouted: "Next time, Jerusalem, pay *what* is owed *when* it is owed, and you will not need to lose the life of one of your priests!"

He made the signal to march out. The thunderous sound of Roman feet pounding against the ground once again shook the earth.

The Judeans carried David *the Wise's* body into the Temple to be washed and prepared for burial. Judean men, women, and children were now in mourning. The Hebrew grief chants carried on for what felt like a lifetime. Each word was screamed out with the maddening wail of an inconsolable soul.

"It hasn't yet begun," Simon yelled to the backs of the Romans as they left.

"Fool! Or are you personally fond of Roman crucifixion?" Ananus ridiculed.

"There is nothing foolhardy about fighting an evil like the Roman Empire," Simon challenged Ananus.

"I can see plenty foolhardy about it," Ananus replied.

"Stop!" Joseph yelled out. "David's blood is not yet cold, and you fight like rats by the very spot where he fell? Rome will still be here in the morning and the next. I'm going to bury my friend. Maybe both of you should think about doing the same."

The squabble was silenced by Joseph's wisdom.

"Joseph is right," Matthias said. "We can argue with each other over Rome in the morning and the morning after. They are not going anywhere. David needs us now. Come, let us bless him together as he would have wanted—as friends."

**Titus Slays the Chief High Priest at the Temple**

# Chapter 2:

# The Upper Marketplace Slaughter

**IMMEDIATELY FOLLOWING** the Roman theft from the holy Temple treasury, Jerusalem slid closer yet into a full military confrontation. The Judeans first began to fight using their tongues.

Mostly responsible for instigating the fight with the Romans were Judean youths and children. In the streets they passed around faux collection baskets in front of Roman soldiers, taunting them over their avarice. Many other Judeans hurled insults—referencing sexual acts with Roman soldiers' mothers were the most popular. Throughout the city, women emptied chamber pots on Romans free from accident.

Gessius Florus sat at his desk in his office in Caesarea, drinking wine as usual, nibbling on dates, and reading a scroll presented to him by Tribune Rovis of Antonia Fortress, who had just arrived from Jerusalem. Titus sat off to the side of the office, cutting an apple into slices with the dagger he had only days before used to escalate the Judean conflict.

Gessius' mouth dropped open in disbelief as the scroll read like horrific local headline news:

*\*Two children sought for stealing Roman soldier's coin purse;*
*\*Female Judean jailed for depositing excrement in front of*

*Antonia Fortress;*
*\*Three Judean children seen urinating in Roman cistern;*
*\*Ten Judean women arrested under suspicion of emptying*
*chamber pots on Roman soldiers;*
*\*Over three hundred foul names Judeans allegedly called*
*Romans to their faces.*

"Do the Judeans not realize that I control their very lives?" a furious Gessius growled.

"They seem to have forgotten who rules whom," Rovis said.

"I should execute an entire hippodrome of Hebrews. I want examples! I want examples! I want those responsible on the cross!" Gessius screamed while beating on his desk with closed fists. "We're going to Jerusalem!"

"When do you want to leave, my lord?" Titus asked.

"We're leaving right now—as soon as I finish my wine, that is," Gessius replied and began drinking his goblet quickly. "Fetch my chariot, Titus!"

"I'm surprised he doesn't want to be carried around in his litter," Titus thought to himself, bringing a small smile to his face.

"Rovis, join us?" Gessius offered.

"Of course, my lord. I must return to Antonia Fortress regardless," Rovis answered.

Titus had the horses, bodyguards, and other personal effects readied for travel. Gessius sat on a chair secured to his oversize chariot.

Titus had made the mistake of personally chauffeuring Gessius around once before—now with his seniority, he merely delegated the honor to a younger officer.

The Roman party set out and made haste for Jerusalem.

Gessius, following in the footsteps of his predecessor, Pontius Pilate, decided to call the Judeans to assemble in the great amphitheater. The high priests, including Joseph and his father Matthias, the judges of the Sanhedrin, and leaders representing the Zealots, Essenes, Pharisees, and Sadducees were all in attendance.

The entire Roman garrison from Antonia stood at the ready, keeping Gessius protected against any potential violence that might spawn from his arrival. Immediately, his first edict demanded the Judeans give up all those known to have participated in the insolent behavior. The Judean leaders attempted to explain that the insults were only the result of foolish young children and assured Gessius that Jerusalem was still obedient to its Roman masters. Gessius was enraged by the refusal of the Judeans to name names. He decided to teach the Judeans a lesson in submission.

"Hebrews. I have given you the opportunity to avert punishment, but you continue to deny me. If Caesar himself were before you, would you also deny him? Have you not learned what happens to those conquered peoples that refuse the empire?" Gessius queried the audience from the center platform in the amphitheater.

Simon bar Giora, a Sadducee, as were most judges and priests, stepped forward and attempted to appease Gessius.

"Lord Governor, Jerusalem and all of Judea submits to your will and that of great Caesar. But we know not who hath given offense. Would you punish us all for the transgressions of an unknown few? If so, you would be condemning many more innocent men than guilty ones," Simon argued.

"Deliver those Hebrews responsible for the insults to Caesar and Rome or you will all suffer," Gessius countered.

"We cannot comply, Lord Governor," Simon said humbly.

"Cannot comply or will not?" Gessius asked.

Simon froze, unable to verbalize the proper response.

"Do not trouble yourself, Hebrew. It matters not," Gessius said. Unwilling to play what he considered 'Judean games,' he was done arguing.

Gessius stood up from his dais, raised his arms, and proclaimed, "I will teach a lesson to you Hebrews all of Jerusalem will not soon forget!"

Then he walked out of the amphitheater's rear exit.

The Judeans, seeing Gessius leave, started to cry out frantically, praying for his return. Many other Judeans hurriedly ran from the stadium, unsure if the Romans might slaughter the whole of the Judean population assembled.

The soldiers started to move out. At the sight of the full Roman garrison leaving the amphitheater, the Judeans were somewhat calmed but still feared what horror Gessius' threat might bring.

The Romans were not marching back to the barracks at Antonia. Instead, they headed directly to the Upper Marketplace, a short ten-minute hike away from the amphitheater.

There were maniacal grins on the faces of many of the soldiers. Some seemed so excited about the upcoming melee that they had to restrain their feet from moving too fast, causing disorder in the marching column.

Titus led the legion on his white horse. He knew that this was the beginning of a greater conflict that would shock the entire world, and he was not enthusiastic in the same way his men were. Titus was no stranger to war, serving in several campaigns across the empire before his posting in Judea. He knew the hell that war delivered to both sides. But it was his solemn duty to follow the governor's orders. Though Titus did not approve of Gessius' response to mere insults directed at the Romans by the Judeans, he would follow his directions with complete Roman resolve.

The Roman soldiers approached the Upper Marketplace and caught thousands of Judeans about their daily business.

"Romans!" Titus shouted. "Teach these Judeans what happens to those who refuse Caesar!"

And with that, the Roman columns, standing four men abreast, dispersed in all directions. A thousand swords and spears were raised high, reflecting mesmerizing, flickering white sunlight. The Romans roared with a bone-chilling battle cry the entire marketplace could hear. Deafening screams of mortal terror came in return from the defenseless Judeans.

First the soldiers went after the able-bodied males. Romans would slay with a swing of their swords those that tried to fight. Many Judeans ran, and it took two or three Romans to capture those people attempting to flee. Once in custody, the Romans would hold the Judean steady while another soldier would slice open their throat or impale them through the heart.

Some Judeans grabbed blunt instruments and used them to defend themselves, bludgeoning those Romans they were lucky enough to strike. But Roman swords cut through most of these weapons with one swing of the blade.

There was no mercy given to the Judean males. Even after subduing a Judean, soldiers stuck daggers into their eyes, removing them for trophies. Spears entered lungs and stomachs and intestines. Spiked iron maces were swung so hard they ripped whole jawbones off. Swords severed hands, arms, feet, and legs. Women and children unfortunate enough to be in harm's way were slain without a second thought. They were only lucky if they received a single fatal slice to the neck.

One towering monster of a Roman warrior, named Gigantus, stood a full seven feet tall. His biceps were the size of some men's waists. He was bald with several large scars on the side of his head and face. He wore a long goatee beard that was mud brown. His eyes pierced gray, a color that seemed to turn deep black in the nighttime. He was a natural soldier, and everything he did on the battlefield proved it. He never bestowed the slightest mercy on

## Gigantus in the Upper Marketplace

any enemy he encountered—man, woman, or child. His monstrous roar alone frequently caused men to soil themselves.

Gigantus seized one small Judean girl running terrified in the chaos. She could not have been more than ten years old. He raised her squirming body in one hand up into the air and stared at the girl, directly into her eyes for a long moment, then he grasped his other hand around her head—with one great pull, Gigantus ripped her head clean off. He took the head and punted it fifty yards across the marketplace.

He turned around and saw a young male Judean charging at him with maddened rage for his abominable crime. The young man took a big swing with a wooden baton and hit Gigantus squarely in the face. Gigantus did not even flinch. He punched the Judean back, close-fisted into the chest, sending him flying twenty feet across the marketplace. The young Judean lay motionlessly, wheezing for breath, massive rib fractures torn into his lungs. Gigantus walked towards the young man, his beastly eyes looking up and down upon the helpless body he had broken. Then Gigantus pulled out an obsidian knife from his belt sheath.

"Mommmmaaa!" the Judean youth screamed out as Gigantus cut into his chest, pulling out his heart.

Gigantus raised the still-beating heart high into the air for all to see. "Death to you! Food for me!" Gigantus yelled out, and then bit down on the still-pumping heart, tearing a big chunk of flesh off with his shaved-sharp teeth and swallowed it.

He took the remainder of his bloody food and launched it a hundred yards into the air like he was throwing a discus. It landed in front of a young boy who began screaming uncontrollably at the sight of the beating heart. The boy's dog raced to the meat and had a satisfying supper.

Gigantus continued his ruthlessness. He pulled out his oversized gladius that looked nearly twice as long as a regular-issue blade. He swung with such fury that despite its size, it appeared lighter than a standard Roman gladius. Gigantus aimed for the necks of his enemies with a horizontal chopping motion. With one swing he decapitated man after man. Corpses dropped instantly with blood gushing up a foot or more from their severed necks.

Within a half-hour, the whole of the marketplace ground was covered with blood and flesh. Now that many of the Judean men were dead or bleeding to death, the Roman soldiers turned their attention to the newly-husbandless wives and their daughters.

Soldiers grabbed and brutally beat the Judean women mercilessly into submission. They tore off female clothing from the waist down and savagely took their innocence away. The ground was now covered with dead and dying bodies lying next to Romans mounted on top of their screaming victims. Many soldiers thrust with such anger as to rip the females from the inside out. The cries of the Judean women rose louder than those of the disemboweled men that lay dying in the streets next to them.

A few of the Romans grabbed young boys and anally assaulted them. For in Rome, homosexual acts were not taboo as in Judea. Women, young girls, and boys alike lay crying in the dirt, bleeding from their loins next to one another.

The Romans, having satisfied their carnal desires, turned towards the marketplace looting. Everything of value was taken. A few small fights broke out among the men competing for the gold and silver spoils.

Titus was enraged. His soldiers had permission to kill, rape, and steal to their hearts' content, but infighting was strictly prohibited. He charged over to one of the fist fights and slew both Romans as a warning to the entire garrison. The other men fighting instantly stopped their petty pecuniary squabbles.

Not an hour had passed and over three thousand dead Judean bodies had turned the streets into rivers of blood.

White doves began to gather. The birds began to slurp up the blood from the streets, as did the stray dogs and cats. Soon all the animals were as red as the blood-soaked ground.

"Burn it down!" Titus commanded. "Burn it all down!" And with that order, the soldiers set fire to every last building, tent, and plank of wood in the marketplace.

The air reeked of shit as the disemboweled had spilled their feces all over. Urine could be smelt but not seen as thick red blood obscured the yellow secretions. Then came the stench of all things incinerated.

A great plume of black smoke rose over Jerusalem. Though the Roman slaughter was contained to a relatively small area of the city, every last Judean in Jerusalem could sense the horror, suffering, and outrage this latest Roman offense had brought upon the people.

For this brutalization of innocent Judean civilians, there could be no peace.

# Chapter 3:

# The Temple Gathering

**WORD OF** the savage butchery, rapes, and pilfering of the Upper Marketplace traveled through the streets faster than human feet could run. Before the day's end, all the Judeans of any societal consequence had been summoned and had arrived at the Temple to discuss the proper response to this latest Roman crime beyond crimes. The leaders of the factions in attendance met in the Court of Israelites—only Judean men were allowed in this inner sanctum.

There were four main groups participating in the Temple gathering: the Sadducees (the priestly and plutocratic class), the Pharisees (the moderate and commoner class), the Zealots (religious crusaders that advocated violence to further their cause), and the Essenes (mostly harmless religious fanatics above all else). Also in attendance was a troop of Judean bandits loyal to various lords, most notably the rogue, John of Gischala.

Simon bar Giora rose before all in the court and brought the meeting to a start.

"This assembly of the Grand Council of Jerusalem is now in session." Simon spoke loudly for all to hear. "As we all know, the Romans committed a premeditated massacre in the Upper Marketplace earlier today. We are here to discuss how each faction seeks to respond to this outrage."

In midlife at forty years of age, Simon was a good judge, trusted public servant, and combat veteran who commanded the respect of almost all of the Judeans inside the city walls. He was a wealthy man by birth, not by occupation. His great-grandfather had established reliable trade routes to the Far East and got rich in a few short years moving spice, taking his family from local destitutes and unknowns in one decade, elevating them to landowners and ministers in the next.

Simon's familial wealth was represented by his clothing. When not in his judge's garb, he wore a Roman-style toga, carrying much fine multi-colored cloth on his left shoulder. He also wore several gold rings which were encrusted with quartz and diamonds on his fingers. But what made Simon really unique were the massive emeralds in each of his ears—each one was a whole inch in diameter. Gold bracing secured the stones to his ears, right above the ear canal. Everywhere he went in the city, people recognized him instantly as the 'Green Judge.'

"First, we will hear from the Sadducees," Simon said and nodded to Ananus.

In *de facto* control of the city were the Sadducees. Wanting to protect their property and position, they sought a peaceful response to Rome. They believed there was no path to a military victory against their European overlords. The Sadducees were also the wealthiest and most powerful faction in Jerusalem, holding positions of the greatest prestige and influence. The vast majority of government appointments were held by Sadducees. Most of the high priests were Sadducees, including Ananus, now the chief high priest.

"My brothers, we are gathered tonight for the most solemn of purposes," Ananus began. "We must determine how to best respond to this latest and most horrific Roman atrocity. It would be easy and expedient to curse the Romans and declare open war until only one belligerent remains standing. But that course of action will only lead us to total destruction. Let us use this opportunity to impress upon the Romans the need to change their ways for the betterment of all involved. A fist given to Rome will only come back to us, many times harder. Let us avert our own annihilation and instead create a stronger, more secure peace with the Romans."

Ananus' plea for peace was not well received by any faction in attendance except a staunch section of the Sadducees who had put Ananus up to the task of securing peace at all costs.

After a few moments of scattered chatter rising among the congregation, Simon rose again seeking to keep the meeting moving in a positive direction.

"We will now hear from Eleazar ben Simon, leader of the Zealots," Simon said to the assembly.

Sitting at the back of the congregation hall was the one faction that would always disagree with Ananus, if only on principle: the wild Zealots, led by Eleazar ben Simon.

The Zealots believed that there was only one answer to the Roman injustice: complete and utter destruction of every Roman in all of Judea. No magistrate, no trial, but summary execution of all the Romans they could find. God had granted Israel to the Judeans for all time, and they believed it righteous to slay heathen invaders.

The Zealots were also highly religious, praying morning, midday, and evening. Before food or wine was consumed, a prayer thanking God was always required and strictly enforced. They eschewed all forms of pleasurable vices and thus sought to close all the Roman brothels in the city though Romans, Judeans, and Arabs frequented them regularly.

"Quiet! We cannot decide how to act if we cannot hear one another," Simon shouted above all the commotion in the Temple. "Eleazar, you have our attention."

"Thank you, my Hebrew brother. I come before all of Jerusalem tonight. I come before Almighty God!" Eleazar took a deep breath, closed his eyes, and whispered a prayer as he prepared himself to deliver his diatribe. "They murder us in the streets like rabid dogs. They murder our priests. They rape our women and children. They steal our hard-earned and even harder-saved treasure. They spit on our God, trying to erect their standards on His holy house—our God that hath delivered us out of bondage from Egypt! Don't forget who your God is, my brothers. There is only one way to respond—the way our God hath commanded us to respond. The Roman invaders must all die!" Eleazar yelled to a great cheer from his Zealot followers—many of the Sadducees and Pharisees audibly supported Eleazar's warmongering as well.

With that ovation, Eleazar, contented with himself, sat down, assured he had convinced Jerusalem to side with war.

"Hear me! I shall speak on behalf of the Pharisees," Joseph, son of Matthias, shouted above the crowd. "I grieve today as all Hebrews in Jerusalem grieve. If we take the sword to the Romans, surely we can expel them from our city."

A great cheer erupted in the Temple.

Then Joseph attempted to temper the enthusiasm with the calming motion of his arms and said, "Does any soul present believe that once we kill or force all the Romans out of Jerusalem, they will simply never come back?"

Now a curious whisper circled the congregation.

Joseph continued, "The Romans will come back again and again and again until either they are all dead or we are. That is their nature. That is why they rule half the known world."

A hiss now swelled in the Temple hall, though it was obvious he was speaking truth.

"If the Roman numbers were small, or if ours were large, I would say let them come. But the situation is quite the reverse. They have a million battle-tested soldiers ready at a moment's notice, with millions more that can be conscripted. We have no more than a couple of hundred thousand men capable of bearing arms, with less than ten thousand trained in the art of warfare," Joseph continued to a sobering audience.

"They conquered the Greeks, the great nation of warriors that expelled Xerxes. The Macedonians, once masters of the entire world under Alexander the Great, are now all slaves of Rome. They rule our neighboring states of Egypt and Syria. They have made servants of the tribes of Germania, the strongest and tallest warriors the Earth hath yet seen. Nor are they dissuaded by great seas, venturing into and capturing Britannia. Are you still not convinced?" Joseph said as he looked around at many dejected souls.

"Gessius Florus is the cause of our current predicament, not Rome," Joseph continued. "As Caesars come and go, so will Gessius. We are accustomed to patience, which God hath taught us in the wilderness. For forty years we wandered, praying for salvation daily. Have we forgotten? Let us be wise and stop this madness before countless more innocent Judeans are slaughtered.

"War is the cruelest of human activities, and once started, it does not easily cease—it only ends when one belligerent is destroyed by the other. Many of us are young and cannot remember the horrors of war and are thus overly enthusiastic at our chances of victory. Are we so arrogant, so irresponsible, and so hasty as to strike a blow against Rome only to see it lead all of Jerusalem and Judea to certain destruction?" Joseph concluded to a completely silent assembly.

Then a voice cried out from the crowd as Joseph took his seat. "Coward!" Nathan, a Zealot captain of Eleazar, shouted.

"Leave the personal attacks out of this!" Simon yelled to Nathan. "He's trying to keep the peace, which is his job."

"This doesn't concern you, Giora," Nathan countered.

"It concerns me if I say it does. And I say it does," Simon retorted.

Nathan immediately jumped up out of his seat and charged towards Simon. But before he could accost him, Rafuele, one of Simon's colleagues, stepped in and subdued Nathan. Many others jumped to their feet, their hands by their blades. For a moment, it looked as if blood was going to be spilt in their holiest house.

Then Ananus gave the signal to Seth, the young priest. Seth grabbed the shofar and blew a commanding note that rose above all the chaos and silenced the uproar.

"Stop it! This is God's most holy house!" Ananus yelled out. "Do not forget who we are fighting for. We are fighting for each other, and if we kill ourselves here in God's holy Temple, what chance do we have against the Romans?"

Ananus looked around—the entire hall was quieted. "Good!" Ananus barked.

"Who else wishes to speak?" Simon, regaining control of the gathering, queried the audience.

John of Gischala rose up out of the congregation. John was a man who believed in God as long as he could profit from Him. He saw the current situation as an opportunity to gain great power and wealth among the Judeans. He loathed the Romans but would not hesitate to slay a fellow Judean if the situation required it.

At age fifty, John's waistline was more than healthy, though John was not wealthy. He spent his ill-gotten gains on wine, ale, prostitutes, and games of chance—money disappeared as a result of John's vices faster than he could accumulate it.

As a male specimen, he was repulsive. But he did command respect because he was so naturally terrifying. John's hair was short and greasy, the color of glossed salt and pepper. His graying beard hung long and scraggly. One of his eyes was a faded light blue matte color; he was no stranger to battle, losing his left eye's vision decades earlier.

He was known for his barbaric raids across Judea. He had amassed a following as he promised and delivered great booty to his men from those unfortunate enough to cross his path.

John looked around and grinned at the hundreds of eyes keenly planted on his face. He had been waiting for the perfect moment to increase his following and fracture the Judean factions for his own gain—it had now come.

"Joseph is right! He is right that we will be able to destroy the Roman garrison stationed here. He is right that Rome will come back for Jerusalem. But he is wrong that we will be slaughtered to the last Hebrew soul!

"God will protect us," John continued. "Our walls will be reinforced with the will of the Lord. Our spears will seek out the heretical Roman throats and bellies, guided by the Almighty. We will be victorious for we defend Jerusalem, land given to us by God for all time!"

A thunderous cheer broke out among John's bandit followers, the Zealots, Sadducees, and Pharisees alike. For a moment, it felt as if the entire earth trembled with God's approval.

Hearing the cries of war, Joseph knew there was no way to prevent what would in all probability be the complete destruction of Jerusalem.

A mass of commoners from each allegiance was waiting in the Court of Gentiles for their leaders to return with instructions on how to proceed. But seeing the leaders of the different factions of Israel all celebrating as they came running out of the Court of Israelites, there were no words needed to explain the verdict: it was war.

A mob formed in the middle of the Court of Gentiles. The Zealots and bandits were joined by a large share of Pharisees also keen on an armed resistance against the Romans.

Simon, seeing the rush to war, was alive with such happiness for the future of Jerusalem, he actually started tearing up.

Joseph, depressed, left the Temple for his home. He was teary-eyed for an entirely opposite reason to Simon's. He knew the fate the Judeans had just sealed for themselves.

Once home, he put a pot of water on the fire and grabbed a jar from his kitchen cupboard. He opened the jar and pulled out a handful of tea leaves. At the sight of the water boiling, Joseph took the pot from the fire and filled it full of leaves.

Presenting his father with some evening tea and sipping on his own, Joseph began to confess the looming destruction of the city to Matthias, who was still sitting shiva and had not attended the Temple gathering out of respect for David *the Wise*.

"Father, I know not what can be done to prevent our destruction. The Zealots will seek Roman blood soon, perhaps this very night. They cannot be satisfied by anything less."

"Joseph, my son, have faith in God. He led us across the Red Sea out of Egypt. He saw our return to Jerusalem from the exile of Nebuchadnezzar. We have kept our covenant with God, and God will keep His."

"Father, I believe God will see our people to a great future one day, but how many untold Judeans will have to die because we chose a bloody path instead of a wise path?"

"Relax, my son. God will see you through your journey. I promise you that because I know it. Now forgive me, but I'm old and I tire."

"Goodnight, Father," Joseph said and kissed Matthias on the forehead.

He left Matthias' quarters and sat up all night, unable to sleep.

It was after midnight when he was roused in his chair by a great noise coming from across the city. Joseph stood up and instinctively followed the origin of the sounds through the streets of Jerusalem.

The uprising had begun.

Only hearing screams and not yet seeing from where they emanated, Joseph looked up towards the Temple Mount.

A comet which had not been seen in almost eighty years hovered in the night sky over the Temple. Its shape was almost that of a scimitar, and it was pointing directly down to the Temple's inner sanctum.

"God help us."

# Chapter 4:

# The Uprising

**JOHN'S BANDITS** and Eleazar's Zealots were now united. Upon exiting the Court of Israelites they were already hard at work on conspiratorial efforts. The Judeans wanted the Romans gone from Jerusalem. Striking at the Roman heart in Judea, they agreed on attacking the barracks at Antonia Fortress. But first they needed a place to prepare their stratagems.

Teeming with great rage, the Zealots moved like sheep following Eleazar and John to the city's amphitheater. John's bandits, intermingled, followed with the same zest.

As Eleazar and John marched through the city, the number of their followers swelled. Any commoner that came into contact with the mass of fanatics and bandits immediately saw their soul degenerate into a maddened state caused by the mob's raging energy. Friends laughing began brawling. A couple kissing started yelling at each other. A mother holding her baby at her breast removed the child only to hear it wail in hunger, herself now indifferent to her baby's needs. Judeans that were about the town on their own private business became radicalized by little less than the sights and sounds of the Zealots and bandits marching.

The mass arrived at Herod's amphitheater. John and his bandit followers changed clothes, donning the long dark robes of the Zealots, to great cheers from a united crowd.

Eleazar took the main stage, raising his arms above his head.
"Men, tonight we return Jerusalem to the Judeans!"

A chant broke out among the Judeans: "Yisrael! Yisrael! Yisrael!"

"We will kill every last one of them, sparing no man, woman, or child! The Romans will soon all be where they should be: *in Rome!*" Eleazar said, and more raucous applause rang forth. "We will do more than kill them, we will teach them! We will teach the Romans what happens to the wicked when they battle the children of God. Take their eyes, their noses, and their ears, and any other body parts that are used only for their Roman evil. A hundred silver talents for the man that brings me the heaviest sack of extremities!"

Hearing the bounty now put forth for the cruelest man caused such an uproar that the chants of "Yisrael!" were replaced with those of "Eleazar!"

Eleazar raised his hands to the heavens. "I am not God. Remember that, my Hebrew brothers, but I will show you the path that God hath chosen for us. Now this is what I want you to do…" Eleazar explained his attack plan in detail to a completely attentive audience.

He divided his following into war companies, assigning special tasks to each group, all coalescing into one central goal: the death or expulsion of every Roman in Jerusalem.

As soon as Eleazar finished his mission brief, his followers, now some four thousand strong, began to move out. But unlike the Roman garrison that had shook the earth earlier in the day, the Zealots and bandits were now quiet; the Romans on guard duty at Antonia Fortress were not able to hear a foot touch the ground nor see a single lit torch. Additionally, the blackness of night obscured the Judeans' presence, especially in their dark robes.

They first walked from the amphitheater to a local construction site and commandeered all the ladders. As they closed within a few blocks of Antonia Fortress, they began splitting up into smaller groups, each going a different direction. The ladders were placed along the sides of multi-story buildings. The Zealots looked like floating Grim Reapers as they climbed up onto the rooftops in the night sky—two thousand Zealots now sat crouching low, covered in darkness, waiting. Another two thousand crazed Judeans who had joined the anti-Roman effort hid themselves on the street level, inside the homes and businesses of Jerusalem's residents.

Eleazar and John approached the very entrance of the barracks. The barrack's gates were made out of hardened cast-iron bars and securely closed. One hundred soldiers could be seen standing at the ready, inside the gates. Another eight hundred Romans were about their off-duty business. There were also two soldiers standing guard right outside the gates.

Eleazar stood in the middle of the street and lit his torch from one of the Roman lamps shining upon the barracks' entrance. "Romans!" he shouted. "See what destruction has come to thee by thine own hand!"

And with that, Zealot soldiers materialized from the darkness. A company of twenty fanatics jumped the two Roman guards outside the barrack gates. The Romans were instantly held in custody, frozen by the arms of ten Judeans on each man.

John and Eleazar both held up their swords high above their heads. "God wills it!" John shouted as loud as he could.

Eleazar screamed even louder, "God wills it!"

In view of all the Romans inside the barracks and all the commoner Judeans outside the gates watching the drama unfold, John and Eleazar simultaneously pushed their swords directly in the sternums of their respective Roman hostages, killing them nearly instantaneously.

A great cry arose from the Roman garrison on duty who witnessed the slaying of their comrades. The tirones and legionnaires unconsciously grabbed for their spears, swords, and shields. Rushing towards the fortress entrance without officer instruction, they flung the gates open and charged in fast pursuit of John, Eleazar, and the small company of Zealots that participated in the slaying of the Roman guards.

The Zealots, though they were running away from the barracks seemingly in retreat, were actually leading the Romans directly to their graves.

The off-duty Romans in the barracks furiously sprang up from their doings and quickly followed after the first wave of soldiers in a mad dash to seek vengeance. Now the entire Roman barracks was empty and its soldiers in hot pursuit of the Zealots except for a few non-combatants and officers remaining at Antonia.

Little did the Romans know that thousands of raging Judeans lay in wait on the rooftops of city buildings, armed with stones and bricks and oil and fire. Thousands more were hidden in homes throughout the streets of Jerusalem, wielding swords, daggers, batons, and maces.

John and Eleazar led their company of Judeans into a smaller side street alley, and the Romans pursued. The chase continued until the entire Roman force had been drawn into the alley. John and Eleazar's men ducked into a hidden alcove, disappearing from Roman sight and out of harm's way.

Seth, the priest, standing on the tallest building over the small street, seeing Eleazar, John, and company reach safety, took his cue and blew the shofar. This signaled the Zealots on the tops of buildings to begin hurling stones off the rooftops down upon the Romans. The entire Roman garrison was now caught in the small alley street with rocks raining down upon them.

All the Romans could do was use their shields to cover themselves. Some soldiers were hit instantly on the head with large stones and keeled over dead just as fast. Other Romans were able to protect their heads but were struck in the feet, legs, and torsos by the onslaught of the Judean rocks. The unscathed Roman soldiers attempted to arrange a defense.

"Romans!" yelled one of the Roman commanders. "Defensive positions. Erect the tortoise! Testudo! Testudo!"

Quickly the Romans moved close to one another and raised their shields collectively to create a mobile wall of protection from the raining rocks. Their shields, when combined together, moved like scaly armor and were effective against almost all of the stones thrown upon them.

Seth blew the shofar once more. From the rooftops, the Zealots now heaved buckets of oil upon the main Roman force centered in the street. Then lit torches were tossed down from the buildings, igniting the oil in a great fireball explosion, scorching Roman flesh and earth alike. The Roman shields could not defend against the oily fire, and many soldiers broke position, opening up gaps in the tortoise. More stones were thrown, and the Roman defense began to collapse.

Half of the Romans lay dead on the ground or ran around aimlessly while burning alive. The other half tried to survive by protecting themselves with their shields above their heads.

Seth blew the shofar yet again. The hellfire of stones and oil from above ceased. Then a great echoing scream of John's bandits came roaring back and forth from both ends of the alley. The bandits had entrapped the Romans from opposite ends, joined by two thousand supporting Judean fanatics.

One hundred bandits charged from each direction with their full might, their swords raised to attack the Romans caught in the sealed-off street.

The Judean Uprising

John directed the ground assault, which was swift and merciless. The Romans knew not in which direction to face their enemies as swords came at them from seemingly everywhere.

Blades would not stop entering the Roman bodies, even after they were dead—the Hebrews released over a hundred years of anger at being subjugated by their oppressive European overlords.

The Romans were defeated, with many of their injured bleeding out in the street. The troops centered in the alleyway were now nothing more than a butchered human bonfire. Screams of terror and suffering rang out as the Judean lust for chopping, stabbing, and cutting could not be quenched that night.

John was now going to inflict harsher punishment on those that were unlucky enough to still be breathing. He did not just slay his Roman enemies, for John was cruel. He mutilated alive those Romans that were unfortunate enough to become acquainted with him in the last moments of their lives. Romans soldiers writhed in grave agony as John cut off ears and noses, and gouged out eyes with his long dagger. He even cut off the penises and testicles from living and dead Romans indifferently. John put his trophies in a leather sack which he carried over his shoulder with pride.

Romans being mutilated screamed while John laughed. Many offered surrender and begged for mercy but neither John nor any other bandit or Zealot soul heard their pleas or desisted. Finally, when his victim could please John no more with his suffering, John would slay the soldier.

John's entire tunic, his hands, and his face were covered in a heavy coat of blood before he finished brutalizing the Romans. He walked away from the battle admiring the human trophies he had collected.

*  *  *

**GOVERNOR GESSIUS** was in the process of copulating with his wife's sister during the beginning of the uprising in Jerusalem. He howled like a wolf, safe in his governor's mansion in the town of Caesarea, some forty miles away from Jerusalem. While he ascended towards a climax, his sister-in-law moaned like an otter—an entire garrison of his soldiers had just been destroyed.

The governor's aide-de-camp awkwardly walked into Gessius' bedchamber frightened, as a messenger carrying bad tidings in the Roman service should be.

"A boy comes with news of an uprising in Jerusalem, my lord," the aide said, gulping deeply, fearing Gessius' response.

Gessius, fully hearing his man, continued thrusting into his adulteress.

"Almost, almost, *almost…*" Gessius moaned. "Damn it!" he yelled and threw his sister-in-law off his lap. "You couldn't wait one bloody minute!" he chastised his aide. "Send the messenger boy in," Gessius barked.

The young messenger entered Gessius' sleeping chamber while he was still indecent and only beginning the process of putting on a robe. The messenger tried to avert his eyes as the sight of Gessius' fat naked body caused a gag-like reflex.

Gessius' sister-in-law sat unashamedly naked on the bed, interestedly watching the emergency briefing.

"Lord Governor. I come on behalf of my lord, Titus. He prays I tell you of the great unrest at the Antonia Fortress."

"Out with it, boy! What says Titus?" Gessius asked impatiently.

"He says the Antonia Fortress has been sacked. Overrun completely by various factions of the Judeans. Every Roman the Judeans could get their hands on was put to the sword without mercy."

"My gods. And what of Titus?" Gessius asked solemnly as he began to comprehend the true gravity of the night's events.

"Lord Titus and some of his commanders were not in the barracks at the time of the attack—they were dining at a local Roman public house when the uprising started. But once the trouble commenced, they began slaying the Judeans in rebellion as fast as their swords would permit. Titus attempted to trek from the public house back to the barracks, but for every Hebrew Titus and his men slew, two more took their place. They had no choice but to seek refuge before being ensnared by the insurgents closing in on him and his men from all sides."

"Is Titus alive, boy?" Gessius asked.

"I know not, my lord," the boy replied.

Gessius took a Roman denarius from his person and placed it in the boy's palm. "Run along now," he said.

Gessius walked out to his veranda overlooking Caesarea. He stared into the black horizon.

"Jerusalem sacked!" he yelled hysterically. "My gods, what will Caesar do to me?"

*  *  *

**IT WAS** early in the morning, still black dark, but all of Jerusalem was celebrating the victory over the Roman garrison. Wine was flowing, meat was cooking on the grill, the harlots were awake and soliciting. Merchants brought out their trade goods. Almost no one in the city was asleep.

The Judeans had taken the Antonia Fortress. Eleazar stood in front of the angry crowd of Judeans on top of a rostrum so all could see and hear him. Still drenched in blood, he looked more like the Devil in the torchlight than a defender of Jerusalem. Behind Eleazar were John and his top bandits, also covered in thick blood.

The Zealots held captive a dozen Romans who remained in the otherwise emptied-out barracks. Antonia was seized when the Judeans returned from the side-street massacre of the Roman garrison. There were children, less than half the height of grown men, wives, and a few Roman ministers and old officers now forcibly held at the mercy of Eleazar.

The Judeans pelted the Roman prisoners with rotten apples, heads of wilted cabbage, and bad eggs. Many screamed out obscenities. One young Judean ran up onto the stage and bent his bare ass over and spread his cheeks. He loudly passed gas in the faces of the Roman captives to the overwhelming approval of the mob of Judeans. Raucous laughter, curses, and chants—the crowd was overcome in a murderous craze.

Then Eleazar stepped forward raising his arms up high. The crowd quieted. "Tie them!" Eleazar shouted.

Quickly Zealot disciples, accompanied by a few high-ranking bandits, began to tie the Romans together, forming a large circle of standing bodies.

The Roman children began wailing and screaming—their mothers futilely begged for them to be spared.

One of the captured Roman officers stood weeping pitifully while another shouted at the Judeans for a quick death.

"Get it over with, you Hebrew bastards!" a Roman minister yelled out.

John came over and patted the minister's head.

"You won't have to wait much longer, Roman scum," John said cheerfully and then punched the man in the stomach.

The dozen Romans all stood motionless, barely able to breathe as they were pressed against one another like a bundle of sticks tied tightly together by twine.

Eleazar began to speak again. "Jerusalem! I make a solemn oath to you tonight. Follow our God Yahweh who saw our return to Jerusalem from the exile of Babylon. Follow our holy cause to defend Jerusalem for us, the *chosen people*. Follow me, and I will never permit a Roman to command another Hebrew in the city as long as I draw breath!"

The public erupted with a cheer heard through the entirety of Jerusalem.

"Now watch, my Judean brothers and sisters. Watch the fiery death the Almighty smites down upon the godless invaders of Jerusalem!"

Then Eleazar signaled with his hand, and the Zealots began tossing every stick and plank within reach upon the feet and heads of the captive Romans.

"Give them oil too!" one of the common Judean onlookers called out. "Give them holy oil from the Temple—they would steal it. Now let them burn in it!"

The fanatics on the platform holding the Romans moved to grab large pots from beside the stage and tossed their oily contents onto the bodies of the prisoners. One Zealot, his face cloaked in his robe, held out a chalice towards the crowd. He put the chalice into one of the pots of oil collecting a full cup's worth. Then he walked directly up to a little Roman girl standing in the middle of the hostage pile. The spectral figure poured the entire chalice of black oil atop the little girl's head. She could only cry while her face turned pitch black, clutching onto her mother's hand for comfort.

"See the justice God brings down upon those that steal from His Temple and murder His high priests and innocent children," John yelled.

Then a Zealot grabbed one of the torches from a disciple and tossed it upon the oiled-up Roman captives.

Another great cry burst forth from Jerusalem. It was the terrified Romans starting to cook alive. The oil-covered, burning Roman bodies began to light up the night sky.

The little girl's cries were similar to the screeching and popping sounds of a wet log set ablaze. Her skull exploded in a small fireball.

The majority of the Judeans in attendance cheered at the sight of Romans burning alive. Many others turned their heads and covered their ears. The smells of oil, wood, skin, and hair burning caused many to cough heavily. Nearly everyone began to cover their noses with their clothing. Some Judeans winced as if they were able to taste the burnt flesh. The intense heat was felt on everyone's skin.

The execution was overwhelming to the senses. Screams, overpowering heat, burning human flesh, blinding flames, and a bitter taste in the air caused many women to faint, while even more girls and boys alike vomited their wine and supper.

"There are no more Romans in Jerusalem!" Eleazar shouted, receiving muted cheers which the horrors of the execution had caused.

John stood with a cold smile, mesmerized by the sight of the towering flames. And then, as the fire began to die down, long after the screams of the condemned had ceased, Eleazar, John, and their followers walked off the platform into the darkness of the night and were gone.

▪ ▪ ▪

**SIMON BAR** Giora had not participated in the ruthless uprising, but he was a witness to all the events. He stood atop a nearby rooftop watching the deluge of stones and fiery oil, and the savage street fight.

Once the fight was ended, he moved towards the massing Judean population and witnessed the execution of the captured Romans, as did Joseph, son of Matthias.

Joseph could not sleep that night. He had gotten up and walked towards the chaos. He felt divinely compelled to follow the sounds of the city and witnessed the events of the uprising.

He stood next to Simon bar Giora watching the cooling embers of the execution fire flicker inside Antonia Fortress as the first rays of daylight began to shine.

"How long before Rome returns? What price have we paid forward for one night's childish indulgence?" Joseph asked Simon.

"God is with us, Joseph," Simon replied.

"Is He? I pray God is with us. But I fear He sends us signs from the sky that portend doom." Joseph pointed at the comet. "We will need Him in the coming months more than ever before."

# Chapter 5:

# The Quiet Time

**FOR SEVERAL** months after the Roman garrison at Antonia had been slaughtered by the Zealots, there was no direct response from Rome. Life continued in Jerusalem mostly indifferent from Roman rule. And before long, few going about their daily business even thought of the now-absent and distant Roman invaders.

As Rome had been expelled from Jerusalem a power vacuum now existed. Vying for control of the city were Eleazar's Zealots and the wealthy Sadducee ministers and merchants. Eleazar formed an alliance with Ananus, consolidating his power so much that he and the Zealots now operated out of the Temple Mount.

John of Gischala had returned to his banditry in the countryside, seeing easy spoils due to the withdrawn Roman presence.

But now a savage new Judean sect calling themselves the Sicarii had sprung up.

They were Zealots without ethics or qualms about slaying anyone obstructing their cause. They were a secret society that seemed to be everywhere and nowhere at the same time. The Sicarii would kill their enemies in broad daylight, usually in the middle of busy streets and marketplaces. They hid in plain sight wearing commoner clothes that brought neither attention nor suspicion after they had struck down their victims.

The Sicarii would position themselves next to or behind a target and inflict deadly blows with their small daggers to the heart, throat, and bowels. And before anyone could see or cry murder, the Sicarii had already calmly walked away into another crowd, forever escaping justice.

They were in the business of killing Sadducee Judeans of money or status. They focused their attention on those whom they considered collaborators with Rome. Sometimes they would choose a random target with no connection to wealth or city politics just to instill fear across Jerusalem. Many a day began with a body hanging by a rope around the neck from a bridge or post. The Sicarii always attached a wooden board across the chest of their victim—this one said 'FAUTOR,' Latin for collaborator.

Upon people hearing of or seeing a murdered corpse lying about, the streets would hastily empty for hours, bringing the business of the city to a standstill. Many moderate Judeans were too terrified to go draw water at the fountains or purchase food from the vendors—they stayed holed away in their homes, paying poor orphans to deliver their sustenance.

The Sicarii numbers continued to grow. Their recruitment methods were just as opaque as their murderous techniques. There were vague stories of young men being accosted with knives to their genitals while they slept at night by ghouls wearing masks. The Sicarii were said to threaten death to their recruits and their families if they did not join the ranks. The Sicarii made good on their threats, showcasing the slain corpses for the public to view.

Now that the Romans were gone, the city was left with no policing. More vigilant members of the city and members of the new Judean Free Government formed an all-hours guard to watch over the busiest streets and markets. Across Jerusalem, Judean guards protected the population, sporting bronze armor and carrying steel blades. The Sicarii were not deterred, making these guards targets of priority.

The terror reached such a frenzy that the whole of Jerusa-

# Sicarii Murder a 'Fautor' or Collaborator

lem was frozen in a paralyzing fright. Unable to continue regular daily life, the Judeans were not preparing for the eventual Roman response to the uprising at Antonia.

It had been three months now, and Jerusalem no longer remembered its small uprising against the mightiest nation the world had ever seen. Everyone was preoccupied with the Sicarii threat.

No one in Jerusalem knew what truly befell the Roman government or what their present intentions were. With the Sicarii terrorizing the city, few but Eleazar and Sadducee men of importance and wealth cared.

Simon bar Giora, the minister tasked with Jerusalem's general administration by the new Judean Free Government, also had an eye on Rome. To uncover what the enemy was up to, Simon enlisted spies. He sent scores of men throughout Judea to act as lookouts for a potential Roman reprisal. Some of these spies even made their way to Rome and relayed messages encoded in Hebrew, decipherable only by using a Torah—a text no Roman owned nor understood.

News came in that the Romans appeared to be dealing with greater conflicts across the empire than the revolt of the Judeans. The spies from Rome reported that the empire intended to return in full force to conquer the city, but first they intended to sack other Judean cities across the Holy Land before making their way back to Jerusalem. Cities such as Antioch, Ascalon, Gamala, Gabara, Jotapata, and Acre were repeatedly mentioned. Hundreds of thousands of people from these cities moved into Jerusalem, seeing the large, fortified metropolis as a bastion of safety. Countless others sojourned to small desert towns far away, taking no chance of being caught in the Roman tide they believed would come any day.

Simon knew of the other peoples and countries Rome was currently occupied with subduing. He still believed that once Rome was done with their current enemies, they would return, exacting ruthless retribution over the bloodshed caused by John's bandits and Eleazar's Zealots. He knew the Romans would never forget or forgive an insurrection. How could they? It would mean the beginning of the end of their control over half the known world.

To address the concerns of the Roman return, Simon began to oversee all major defensive aspects in Jerusalem. He hired and trained young men into the soldiery. He collected taxes from the masses. He enlisted countless masons and carpenters to create new fortification walls and gates around the city. By lecturing at schools, the amphitheater, and even marketplaces, he launched a propaganda campaign so that the Judean people would not forget the Roman threat while simultaneously bolstering his own value to the residents.

Simon created the infrastructure to produce armaments including smelting plants and a streamlined blacksmithing operation. He oversaw food distribution, creating a storage facility that could hold ten thousand bushels of grain—the city would come to depend on it during the coming months.

His skill in logistics could not be matched, and he was quickly given oversight of the rest of Judea as well. Only control of the Judean Free Army eluded Simon, making addressing the Sicarii threat nearly impossible.

But he did more with what he had than any other man could have done in Simon's position.

Reports from Judean operatives continued to mention Roman threats looming over Galilee. Simon could not manage a Galilean defense while serving as the head minister of Jerusalem. He needed a qualified, intelligent, and reliable deputy to serve there as governor.

The first person that came to Simon's mind was Joseph, son of Matthias. Simon arranged a meeting to talk about the gubernatorial appointment at Joseph's home.

Meanwhile, Joseph continued his work at the Temple. As one of the preeminent scholars of the priesthood, he was privileged enough to avoid the duties of animal sacrifice, a task nearly every other priest was required to perform. Joseph did not relish providing blessings for sinners as it required him to be up close to the sights, sounds, and smells of animals being constantly slaughtered. He was content to stay in his office which was closer to the Sanhedrin than the Court of Priests. In a small room under the large Temple portico, far enough from the dying screams of helpless beasts, Joseph could work in peace.

He sat at his desk, an old scroll to his left and a fresh scroll to his right. He held a quill and dipped it in ink. But instead of continuing his translation, he sat still, as if in a trance, pondering the future.

Once more he looked over the small note Simon had placed on his desk earlier in the day, before Joseph had arrived to begin his work:

*I'll be stopping by your home this weekend. It's been too long since I've been to visit your family. There is lots to talk about.*

*—Simon BG*

"All I can think of is Rome," Joseph said softly to himself and put down his writing tool. "And I'm certain it's all Simon can think of as well."

# Chapter 6:

# Joseph, Son of Matthias

"**ADONAI, HEAR** my prayers! Tell me how I can serve your glory in this desperate time," Joseph, son of Matthias whispered vigorously to God as he knelt down, praying in the Court of Priests.

As wise and scholarly as Joseph was, he still had no idea what to do or what would happen concerning Rome. Joseph's mind raced uncontrollably with thoughts of the Roman reprisal sure to come.

For over an hour Joseph stayed on his knees talking to God.

He was a high priest as was his father. From a very young age Matthias had educated his son for a life of scholarship and the priesthood. Joseph was employed as one of the preeminent scholars in Jerusalem, expertly trained in languages. He could read, write, and speak Aramaic, Hebrew, Latin, Greek, and Arabic. Joseph also possessed a working knowledge of a half-dozen lesser-known tongues.

He was also a student of Judean theology. He was so respected for his scholarly prowess older priests would approach him with intricate questions of the Torah. Much more often he was asked to translate the different languages of Judea, Arabia, and the Roman Empire.

Despite his youth, other high priests, ministers of Jerusalem, and judges of the Sanhedrin regularly consulted him on matters relating to city and religious politics—Joseph's insight was nearly always accurate.

He was known to his peers and friends as wise, educated, competent, trustworthy, and kind. Joseph had no leadership credits other than being a high priest, but he was an important member of the Pharisees, a moderate sect of Hebrews that championed living by traditional Hebrew, non-Hellenistic values. This was uncommon as Joseph was born into a family of Sadducees as most priests were, but he had chosen to become a Pharisee at age nineteen. Joseph had been influenced by the growing Pharisee movement, in no small part because of his knowledge of Jesus Christ. Living a humble and honest life in dedication to God had a great appeal to his young mind.

Joseph physically was not a large man but not a small man either—he stood a few inches under six feet with an average frame. At almost thirty years of age now, he was in his peak physical condition with muscle on his bones.

Most people first noticed his facial hair, which he kept at a medium length, though well-trimmed. At this time, many priests wore their beards well-kept, arguing the true meaning of God's prohibition on cutting the ends of one's beard did not intend to take away from the beauty of properly cared-for facial hair.

On top of his head, Joseph's hair showed no signs of thinning or turning grey—it was medium-length, down to his shoulders, and of a golden brown, slightly curly nature. His hands were soft, free from a lifetime of toiling on the soil, erecting buildings, or herding beasts.

His most striking feature was his eyes, which were the rarest of colors: bright gold. In the Levant, however, golden eyes are somewhat common. His bold eyes were always receiving attention from women, even those who knew he was married. For in that time, men of wealth and prestige often had several wives, and many a woman wanted to be the next addition to his house.

When he was walking down the street one could tell by his

gait that Joseph was a man of importance, and his apparel showed it. His street clothes were free of wrinkles, stains, and wear. But he did not dress himself with gold lace or ornaments the way many other men of similar wealth did. He wore the sandals of a commoner and a simple braided-leather necklace carrying a golden amulet under his robe.

With regards to his ideology concerning the Romans, Joseph believed that Judeans should never instigate war but instead seek a non-violent compromise. He did not participate in the uprising at the Roman barracks, but like much of Jerusalem, he was a witness. The sight of the little Roman girl engulfed in oily flames and her head exploding was burnt forever into his memory.

The thought of what Rome would do in retaliation was even more horrible. The Romans took great pleasure and pride in executing their enemies and in employing the most brutal and painful ways invented.

Joseph pledged to God that he would do everything in his power to avert the destruction of the city, the Temple, and the people, whether it be through a truce or a military defense.

He changed out of his priestly gown, ephod, turban, and Oracle, and left the Temple. Though worth more than a man's lifetime wages, there was no need to put the Oracle under lock and key at the Temple—a non-priest found with the gold and bejeweled Plate of Decision would be stoned on sight as a high traitor to God.

On his way home the afternoon before the Sabbath began, he would first visit the marketplace. As Joseph walked the small, twisting streets of Jerusalem, he saw children playing with wooden figurines. He smiled, but his smile quickly fled—the sight of joyous youngsters reminded him of his lack thereof.

Continuing along the familiar streets, Joseph could tell he was close to the marketplace as its smells traveled far beyond its physical boundaries.

Every Friday afternoon his routine was the same: he would walk through the Upper Marketplace collecting the needed items for his family's Shabbat feast.

Joseph walked up to a local butcher to purchase a small goat's liver that his father had requested. Neither Joseph nor his wife Mariamne enjoyed liver, but respect for one's elders was of paramount importance in the Hebrew faith.

"Blessings, Joseph!" The butcher greeted Joseph with enthusiasm as he did each week. "How is your family? Healthy, I hope," he asked cheerfully.

"My family *is* healthy. I thank you for your well wishes," Joseph answered.

"I will say a prayer for you this Shabbat," the butcher said. "You are the best of us, Joseph. You inspire our people to learn, love, and evolve. I pray my children's children will rise to your level one day," the butcher said.

"You are too generous with your words, Asher. I too will say a prayer for you this Shabbat."

"You remember Asher's name! I think sometimes you forget?" The butcher laughed merrily.

"I may be a priest, but I can remember the names of my Israelite friends as well," Joseph said fraternally.

"Ah. How nice. Today you make Asher a happy, happy man," Asher said to Joseph.

Then in a fit of joyous excitement, Asher yelled out to the marketplace—"I am the friend of a high priest!"

The marketplace kept about its business, though one commoner did holler back sarcastically: "And I'm a friend of the king!"

Turning their attention to commerce, the butcher asked, "What is your fancy, Joseph? I have a delicious brisket cut. For you a special price, of course. Or perhaps some sheep's legs?"

"I would enjoy those, but my father requested goat's liver," Joseph replied.

"Tell me something, Joseph. The priests receive meat of all kinds for free by working at the Temple. Why then do you pay me for meat?"

"Because I choose to spend my time in scholarly pursuits and do not perform animal sacrifices with enough regularity to deserve the blessed meat. Therefore, I pay you," Joseph answered.

"I understand." The butcher nodded with great respect. "Goat liver, you got it!"

The butcher turned around to look through his assorted meats on the table behind him which housed various innards. "Sheep liver, cow liver, goat kidney—*goat* liver!" The butcher turned around again and slammed down the liver in front of Joseph with pride. "How about this beauty?"

"It's perfect," Joseph said.

"Can I interest you in anything else? A few birds perhaps?" the butcher asked.

"Not today, my friend," Joseph answered.

The butcher wrapped the liver in brown paper, tying it with string.

As the butcher handed over the liver, Joseph spied an emaciated orphan with a pale white face sitting across the street, cloaked in a black robe. The orphan eyeballed Joseph and the meat, now in his hand.

"What do I owe you?" Joseph asked the butcher while still staring at the orphan.

"Two shekels."

"Here are three shekels. You see that orphan across the way without an ounce of fat on his body?"

The butcher looked over at the boy and acknowledged to Joseph he saw the child.

"Give him something to eat. It can be your cheapest cut, just make sure it will fill him."

"You are as wise as you are kind, good priest. Shabbat shalom!" the butcher said.

"Shabbat shalom," Joseph said back.

Continuing through the busy streets of Jerusalem, Joseph next walked to the wine merchant. He kept looking over his shoulder at the orphan, now following him, concerned the youth might be a Sicarii meaning to do him harm.

"Greetings, Joseph, and Good Shabbos!" the wine merchant said as Joseph approached.

"Good Shabbos, Ezra," replied Joseph. "What can you recommend for me today?" he asked.

"I have a delightful red wine from the hills of Galilee. It is flavorful, with a taste of berries and cinnamon, perfect for the fruit-of-the-vine blessing. I promise you will enjoy it," Ezra guaranteed.

"May I have a sample?" Joseph asked.

"But of course, my priest." The merchant obliged and quickly poured a small tasting chalice for Joseph.

Joseph raised the wine cup to his nose to sniff it first. Then he took a small sip. He swirled the wine around in his mouth for a moment and then spit it out on the ground.

"What is wrong, my lord? Do you not like it?" the merchant queried frantically at Joseph's apparent dissatisfaction.

"It's a bit too sweet for my taste," Joseph replied. "Perhaps something with a full body. And please don't call me 'lord,' for I am but a man such as yourself," he continued.

"Of course, my lord. I mean, my priest!" the merchant said.

"Please, call me Joseph."

"Are you sure? I do not feel comfortable calling you by your given name," the wine merchant said, uncertain of his place.

"Friend, I call you Ezra, as it is your name. Please call me Joseph, as it is mine," he insisted.

"Of course, my lord—Joseph! Forgive me, force of habit," the merchant, embarrassed, responded.

"There's nothing to apologize for," Joseph said.

"Good," the merchant replied, and the two looked at each other silently for an extended moment.

"Oh yes, the wine. Here, try this one. It is soft, but full-bodied," Ezra continued.

Joseph raised the wine cup to his nose and took in a swallow. Satisfaction came over his face. "I will take a carafe," said Joseph.

"Are you sure you do not want a cask?" the merchant offered, trying to push more of his wine as any good businessman would.

"A carafe will be fine," Joseph assured.

"That will be six shekels, Joseph," the wine merchant requested.

"I seem to remember paying four shekels in the past," Joseph said as he dispensed the money.

"In the past, Rome ruled Jerusalem with an iron fist. Now Jerusalem may be on the brink of destruction. Prices reflect this," the merchant explained.

Joseph nodded, feeling the pinch of Rome on his pocketbook, and took the wine.

"Good Shabbos," he said and then left, continuing his trek through the marketplace.

He needed only one more item—bread. The baker was his last stop on the way home from the Temple.

Upon seeing him approach, the baker, Jebbidiah, greeted Joseph from a distance.

"Joseph! You carry wine and meat—it can mean only two things. That today is the Sabbath and you need bread!" the baker said jovially.

"You say that every week, Jebbidiah," Joseph replied, reminding the baker the two had been casual acquaintances for many years now, religious routine bringing them together on a regular basis.

"And every week it is true!" the baker said with a hearty chuckle. "It is always good to see you, Joseph, for it means the feast is near!"

"I can say the same," Joseph said as he placed his foodstuffs onto Jebbidiah's table, and the two fully embraced each other.

"The Lord is good to us, is he not?" Jebbidiah exclaimed.

"He is the best," Joseph agreed.

"I have made a special challah today. I put a spiced oil in the dough mix—you must take a try," the baker implored.

The baker handed a piece over for Joseph to taste. At the exact moment Joseph placed the bread in his mouth, the young orphan that he had seen and anonymously patronized at the butcher's shop mysteriously appeared again. The orphan stared down Joseph, this time looking keenly at the bread Joseph placed into his mouth.

"Tell me it is not the most delicious bread you have ever tasted in your whole life!" Jebbidiah said boisterously to a distracted Joseph, who was wondering about the strange orphan who seemed to be following him.

"You like, yes?" The baker again sought Joseph's approval.

Joseph could not shake the unsettling feeling of the orphan's overpowering eyes looking directly into the back of his head.

Hearing no answer, the baker thought Joseph did not care for his creation, and the excitement on Jebbidiah's face disappeared.

"Do you not like it?" the baker asked.

Joseph turned to stare at the orphan boy, who returned the attention. He was rendered motionless by the orphan's eyes stabbing his soul.

"Joseph, are you alright?" Jebbidiah asked, becoming concerned.

"Yes," Joseph said, turning back to the baker.

"Have you ever seen that boy over there before?" Joseph asked, tilting his head in the boy's direction.

"No, never," the baker answered.

"I think he has been following me," Joseph said. "Here is a two-piece for the bread, and give the boy a selection of your leftovers, will you?" he asked Jebbidiah.

"Of course I will," the baker replied, handing Joseph the loaf.

"Thank you, friend. Good Shabbos," Joseph said, his mind still occupied with the orphan.

"Good Shabbos," Jebbidiah said back.

Joseph continued his walk home, occasionally peeking behind himself to see if the orphan was trailing—he was not.

Joseph reached the gate of his dwelling. Entering his very comfortable familial abode, he greeted his father, mother, and wife.

"Father. Mother. Mariamne. I've come!" he said in a way that invited his family to present themselves.

"My handsome son, give your mother a kiss," his elderly mother begged lovingly at the sight of her most impressive work.

Joseph leaned in and gave his mother a big kiss on her cheek and a hug as well. "I love you, Mother. Good Shabbos."

Joseph, turning to give his father a hug, said, "The Lord is good, is he not, Father? Shabbat shalom."

"The Lord is the greatest. Peace be unto you on this Shabbat as well, my son," Matthias replied.

"Hello, Joseph. What have you brought?" Mariamne asked coldly.

"Good Shabbos, Mariamne," Joseph said. "I have a delightful wine, an interesting spice bread, and a good-looking cut of goat's liver. Here, please start preparing it—I'm famished."

Mariamne took the liver and walked briskly into the kitchen. The crackling of meat touching a hot pan could soon be heard.

Joseph's wife was an enigma. She had been betrothed to him as a child, and though Joseph was by all accounts a handsome man, intelligent, providing, and kind—she did not love him.

However, Mariamne was obedient and a faithful wife, even though she did not satisfy Joseph's heart or loins. They only slept together in the same bed occasionally now and seldom had marital relations. Mariamne had not given Joseph any children. Rumors began to surface that she was barren. Others speculated Joseph was a homosexual and more interested in boys than his wife. Joseph wanted children, but he was not a man that would force himself on any woman, even his own wife.

Despite all this, Joseph was still true to Mariamne, praying that God would reveal his reasoning behind their union at some point in time.

As the beginning of the Shabbat feast neared, Joseph filled each chalice on his dinner table with only enough wine to accommodate a blessing.

"Fill up my cup, son. I want to enjoy a full belly of wine with my food as I did in years past," Matthias said.

"Father, I don't think that's a good idea," Joseph replied.

Joseph's father Matthias was elderly, and his strength had left him. His beard was long, white, and unkempt. He had no teeth left and his eyesight was failing.

"Am I not the elder of this house!" Matthias replied authoritatively. "Then do not treat me as an infant," Matthias said, still capable in his advanced years of putting Joseph in his place.

"As you wish, Father," Joseph said and filled his father's cup to the top.

Mariamne lit the two Shabbat candles on their table.

Then Joseph led his family in a blessing for Shabbat: "Baruch atah Adonai, Eloheinu Melech haolam, asher kidishanu bemitzvotav, vitsivanu, lehadlik ner, shel Shabbat."

"Amen," all said together.

Next came the blessing for the wine: "Baruch atah Adonai, Eloheinu Melech haolam, boray parie hagaffin."

"Amen."

And finally Joseph led the blessing for the bread: "Baruch atah, Adonai Eloheinu, Melech haolam, haMotzi lechem min haaretz."

"Amen."

Finally the small family began to eat. Matthias was unusually cheerful, drinking his wine the way he had when he was a younger man.

The liver made Matthias smile at the taste of it. "You have done it again, my dear!" he complimented Joseph's wife.

Mariamne did have a great talent for cooking food, and the sweet way she cooked the goat's liver made even Joseph forget for a moment that he was eating goat's liver.

"It's delicious, Mariamne," Joseph said to his wife, trying to start a pleasant conversation, though Mariamne and Joseph both knew that he abhorred the cut of meat.

"You say that, dear, but your face disagrees with your words," Mariamne openly chided passive-aggressively.

Joseph, scathed again, as he had been so many times by Mariamne since their marriage began, closed his eyes, and prayed God would see him with a new wife in the morning.

"Nothing to say back, husband? Has the great scholar lost his tongue?"

Now fully infuriated at his wife's insolence, Joseph joined in her base game and returned an insult. "You have never known my face to be anything but disagreeable, my love."

"The two of you stop now," Joseph's mother chimed in meekly, trying to halt the feud.

The quarrel of words escalated, and Joseph asked his father for support.

"Father, am I in the wrong here?"

Matthias did not respond.

"Father?" Joseph asked.

Mathias sat at the table motionless, his eyes closed.

"Father, I told you the wine was a bad idea. You've fallen asleep," Joseph said. "Father, Father."

Joseph shook Matthias on the shoulder, trying to wake him. Finally Matthias awoke violently, in a fright.

"I'm not dead yet, son," Matthias said as he woke.

"You could've fooled me," Joseph said, laughing in a crescendo, only to see stern and disgusted looks on the faces of his entire family.

Joseph ceased his laughter immediately.

"There is something else that needs to be spoken of," Matthias began. "I will not be around this world much longer. Maybe a hundred days, maybe ten, maybe a thousand, only God knows for sure, but the time is coming. And then I will be gone. Joseph, you are nearing thirty years. Not long from this moment will you be an old man as I am now. And yet you have no heirs."

Like a shockwave of galactic proportions, the word 'heirs,' made Joseph feel like a nest of venomous snakes was slithering up and down his back.

"Are you saying I am to blame, Matthias?" Mariamne interjected, preparing to defend herself.

"Yes. Equally at fault is your husband. It is Shabbat. I suggest the two of you use this holy time to…"

"Thank you, Father. I think Mariamne and I both understand what you are trying to say," Joseph interrupted, not wanting to hear his father command him to perform amorous acts with his own wife.

"Copulate! Copulate! Copulate tonight! God blesses children conceived on the Sabbath," Matthias urged.

"Thank you for the reminder, Father." Joseph placated him, trying to direct the dinner conversation to anything else.

So much as broaching the subject of children was enough to set such a foul mood in the air as to ruin the Shabbat feast. However, Joseph and Mariamne's testy exchange had already done that.

The four continued sitting at the dinner table, silently and stoically, barely eating—all thoughts were on the children Joseph and Mariamne did not have.

Matthias broke the silence. "Joseph, I want a private moment with you—now."

"Excuse us," Joseph said to Mariamne and his mother.

Joseph and Matthias stood up from the table and walked into the study, closing the doors behind them.

"There are some things I need to tell you, Joseph. And do not interrupt me as you will want to do countless times. First, stay the course. You will be victorious in life by facing your greatest fears, not by running or hiding from them. God has chosen a path for you, and in that you can never fail Him. And secondly, always have faith in God. He will be with you every moment of every day until you die. And then for all time."

"I will remember," Joseph replied.

"Finally, Joseph, see your way to having children. Take another wife if Mariamne is barren."

"We don't love each other. I don't even understand why I married her, Father."

"She comes from a royal line and was saved for you from the time of her birth. She was a virgin, was she not?"

"She was," Joseph affirmed.

"It's called marriage, son, not love, and it is primarily for children and a lifetime of stability. Love is a luxury we must pray for God to deliver."

Matthias swayed, and but for Joseph's quick hands, he would have fallen to the floor.

"Let's get you in a chair," Joseph said, still holding up Matthias.

"I've drunk too much wine, son, and I thirst. Fetch me some water, will you, my boy?" Matthias asked and Joseph complied.

When Joseph returned to his study, Matthias was again motionless, sitting on his recliner with his eyes closed.

"Father, I brought the water," Joseph said as he tapped on Matthias' shoulder.

Matthias stayed motionless.

"Too much wine for sure," Joseph muttered to his father. "Come on, Papa, let's get you into bed."

Joseph picked Matthias up from his chair. Like he was holding a Torah during a procession, Joseph carried his father to his chambers and carefully tucked him in for the night. As Joseph exited Matthias' bedroom, he turned back his head in adoration of his father, already fast asleep.

Joseph returned to the dinner table, but his wife and mother had long finished eating and had also turned in for the night.

Alone, Joseph sat at his table. His thoughts continued to race over Matthias' wish for grandchildren—a wish Joseph did not know how to satisfy. He also thought of his farcical marriage and the pain which being forced to marry an unloving betrothed had caused him.

Unable to sleep or find solitary peace, he continued sitting. His mind causing his eyes to wander, they came to rest on a jug of spirits sitting on a stand against the wall. Joseph and his father used to enjoy drinking harder spirits together years ago. A fond memory of Matthias giving Joseph his first small cup of liquor as he turned thirteen crossed his mind with great nostalgia.

He stood up and walked over to the liquor jug.

Joseph at first poured himself a cupful of the stuff then kept drinking until the entire container was empty. He fell on the ground asleep next to his dinner table.

Joseph was dreaming but not like on any other night. These dreams took a peculiar twist. Everything was white now—bright white. Joseph did not know where he was—he could barely see his hands in front of him due to the intensity of the light.

Suddenly Joseph found himself standing a thousand feet outside the city walls of Jotapata. The city seemed peaceful, and then the Roman army arrived. They built a great fortress staring the city walls squarely in the face. Joseph saw the Romans move about in a time-lapse fashion, watching day quickly turn to night and back again. He saw forty-seven of these cycles.

Next, Joseph found himself walking through the Jotapatan streets while the city was under Roman attack.

"Can any of you hear me?" he yelled to the people on the streets passing him. Attempting to touch them, Joseph found his hands moved right through the figures as if they were apparitions.

Everything Joseph saw in his dream reminded him of the number מז, Hebrew for the number forty-seven.

He saw an old goat herder, oblivious to the Roman firestones that rained down on the city—he herded forty-seven goats. A baker had forty-seven loaves of bread for sale. A wine merchant had forty-seven small casks of wine and forty-seven wine chalices on his cart.

מז was painted on the walls of the homes and buildings in this dream.

Then a voice that emanated a chilling breath began whispering into Joseph's ear.

"Do you see, Joseph?" the voice asked slowly, calmly, and soothingly.

"Who is that? Where are you? Show yourself!" Joseph yelled

back, scared at not being able to place the voice with a body.

"It is the Prophet of Yahweh, Elijah. I come to you now to guide you about your path."

The next moment, Joseph had soared a thousand feet into the air and was looking down on Jotapata from the sky. The city walls began crumbling, leaving nothing but a cloud of dust where the walls formerly stood. The homes and buildings collapsed and went up in flames. A flow of Roman soldiers could be seen streaming into the city from two directions, slaying every Jotapatan in their path.

"On the forty-seventh day it falls," Elijah's voice said, sending a shiver down Joseph's spine.

Joseph awoke, violently shaking for a moment until he realized he had been dreaming. His vision focused on a young boy playing with a ball inside the courtyard of Joseph's home. But the gates to the yard were locked closed, and no one else in the home was in sight. The boy began singing a common Hebrew song of the Shabbat:

> *Hinei ma tov umanaim, shevet aheem gam yachad.*
> *Hinei ma tov umanaim, shevet aheem gam yachad.*
> *Hinei ma tov, shevet aheem gam yachad.*
> *Hinei ma tov, shevet aheem gam yachad.*
> *Hinei ma tov umanaim, shevet aheem gam yachad.*
> *Hinei ma tov umanaim, shevet aheem gam yachad!*

Joseph joined the boy in the last verse, and they finished the Shabbat song, looking towards one another with a strange curiosity. As Joseph focused on the boy's face, he realized it was the orphan that had followed him the other day in the marketplace.

"Who are you, my child? How did you get in here? You'd need a key to the gate. Did you climb over the wall?" Joseph asked.

"I am Elijah the Prophet! Do you not know of me?" the boy questioned.

Joseph was taken aback, unsure of what type of prank was being played on him.

"Everyone has heard of Elijah," replied Joseph.

"That's right, everyone! I am the prophet of Yahweh. I am here to help guide you!"

"Look, child, I'm in no mood for foolishness. I'm not feeling well this morning, not to mention that Jerusalem is in greater peril than at any time before in our lives," Joseph said, becoming annoyed. "Tell me your business or leave me in peace."

"I was summoned to you by God. He has commanded me to serve you in every way until you are dead," Elijah explained, completely confident in his mission.

Joseph looked at the child and could not believe that such language came from the mouth of a youngster. Perhaps he was a messenger from God, Joseph thought for a moment.

Then, coming to his senses, he asked, "Serve me in every way? How would you serve me in *one* way? Can you bear a sword and cut down my enemies? Can you even pick up a sword with one hand? Can you read and write? Can you even do a woman's work of cooking and washing? No, I venture! You are nothing but another poor mouth from the orphanage, are you not? Respect my bidding and return from whence you came," Joseph cruelly chastised the boy.

With Joseph's denigrating monologue, Elijah began to cry. Joseph, not intending to demean the child to the extent he had, took a deep breath and began to console him.

"Elijah, forgive my tongue. You are a child and you are not supposed to know the cruelty of the world—no child is," Joseph said. "You must be hungry," he continued as he walked towards his table to provide Elijah with a half-loaf of bread left over from the Shabbat feast. "I bought this delicious spicy bread..." Joseph turned around to give the bread to Elijah, but he was gone.

Joseph looked through his still-locked gate in each direction, but there was no sign of where the child had gone.

He sat down with his face in his hands. A white dove flew down from the sky and landed on his head. Joseph looked up to see what was resting upon him when the dove released excrement onto Joseph's forehead.

"Damn you!" he yelled in a burst of frustration. At that very moment, Simon bar Giora appeared outside of Joseph's courtyard gate.

"I haven't even said anything yet," Simon said playfully.

"Oh, Simon, forgive me," Joseph said, jumping up to greet his longtime friend.

"You have something dripping down your forehead. What is that?" Simon inquired.

"Oh, damn bird," Joseph replied and used a cloth to wipe the excrement from his face.

"Ah. It happens. Be happy your mouth was closed," Simon joked.

"Very comical," Joseph said. "Say, did you happen to see a boy about ten, twelve years of age when you walked up just now?" he asked, still wondering what had become of young Elijah.

"I haven't seen a soul," Simon answered, causing a confused look to come over Joseph's face. "Well, are you going to let me in? Or should we talk through the iron bars?" Simon continued jovially.

"Yes, of course, my friend. I'm not myself today. I had a bit too much of the holy spirits last night," Joseph explained.

He reached into his pocket for the key and opened the gate.

"I see." Simon chuckled lightly. "I never took you for a drinker. In fact I don't think I've ever seen you intoxicated."

"I'm not, but last night, it was—necessary. Please join me for some food. Perhaps you would like some wine or bread?" Joseph asked Simon.

"No, thank you, Joseph, I'm not here to feast. I come on official business."

"That's about the last thing I wanted to hear you say."

"I need you, Joseph. Israel needs you. Galilee in particular needs you," Simon said.

"Well, you don't beat around the burning bush," Joseph flippantly replied.

"This is serious, Joseph," Simon said solemnly.

"Yes, it is. Do you have any idea what you are asking me?" Joseph questioned.

"Why do you think I came to you?" Simon asked. "This is not a permanent position. It is only until the fortifications of the Galilean cities are complete and a sufficient military force is raised. You will be the most powerful Judean outside of Jerusalem."

"I have no interest in power. I am a priest, not a governor, and certainly not a warrior," Joseph declared.

"I am a merchant by trade, not a judge or minister. We all must rise to the call of duty when it comes, regardless of our past," Simon argued.

"The fight to come will be like no other Judea has seen in over six hundred years. You are asking me to hang myself on a Roman scaffolding—you realize that?" Joseph asked.

"Oh, Joseph, they won't hang you, they'll crucify you," Simon joked sardonically, though the joke was completely truthful.

"Better still," Joseph replied sarcastically. He took a long moment to think through all the ramifications of Simon's request. "How long do you think I'll be gone? A year? A decade? Until I'm dead?"

"All I am asking is for you to oversee Galilee as it prepares for the return of Rome. My spies all tell me Galilee will be hit first," said Simon. "I understand you do not want to be in the center of the fighting. You can delegate the governorship as soon as the basic preparations are made. If you find a man worthy of leading the troops in Galilee, fine. If you require a commander from Jerusalem, that is fine too. But no one is better suited to lay the groundwork for a defense than you. Do you want me to beg you on my hands and knees?"

Joseph thought seriously for a moment of answering affirmatively.

"When do I leave?" Joseph acquiesced.

"I will have a wagon train prepared to leave in two days."

Joseph nodded his head and then reached across the table for two cups and the carafe of wine he had purchased the day before.

"Baruch atah Adonai, Elocheinu Melech haolam, boray parie hagaffin," Joseph blessed.

"Amen," Simon added.

The two men sat silently drinking their wine together.

# Chapter 7:

# Joseph, Governor of Galilee

**THE RUMORS** of a Roman attack on Galilee were now too loud to ignore. This area of land, known as the 'breadbasket,' was the most fertile in all of Judea and produced vast olive, grape, and grain harvests as well as a limitless supply of fish from the Sea of Galilee. Protecting this immense source of food and wealth was of paramount importance during the resistance.

Simon had called upon Joseph to serve and tasked him with the Galilee governorship. Joseph set out for the city of Jotapata in Galilee. Word of Joseph's character had preceded him. Crowds numbering in the thousands welcomed his arrival with rose petals as they saw Joseph's coming as their only means of salvation from the Romans.

After a day of welcoming festivities, Joseph put the citizens of Jotapata to work. All able-bodied men, women, and children were now employed with the defense of the city.

Blacksmiths were employed to fashion an armory of new weapons. Spears, gladii, bows and arrows, mace balls, daggers, halberds, caltrops, batons, and scimitars were forged and distributed to the military men. Joseph quickly built up a fighting force of twenty thousand soldiers.

Day and night he made his soldiers drill, exercise, and study the art of war. He organized his troops to mimic the Roman model by appointing commanders and sub-commanders. Joseph taught them how to pass along signals to direct troops to flank and encircle the enemy. His soldiers learned to hear and obey the shofar calls for advancing and retreating.

There was also the training of the soul. Most of his troops were novices in war and had to be instructed how to mentally prepare for a Roman assault to prevent the lines from breaking, leading to inevitable doom. Joseph had his men practice in simulated battles.

Beyond the raising and training of an army, fortifications of Jotapata were underway. Strong walls were essential in this effort, and Joseph oversaw the building of them. The materials necessary for such preparations were seemingly infinite, and Joseph was constantly concerned with his meager budget for this massive effort. But the townspeople in Jotapata were understanding and provided their labor free of charge, knowing that it was their own preservation for which they were truly working. Most even gave a portion of their valuables to further assist the defense effort.

Joseph ordered a dry moat—it was dug around the Jotapatan city walls. The Jotapatans worked all day long—even into the evening hours. They all went home drenched in sweat and dirty.

The Jotapatans began to believe there would be no end to their work when Joseph ordered the height of the walls around Jotapata raised. They were increased from a mere ten feet to thirty feet. The width of these same walls was doubled. Lookout towers were constructed, creating positions of great strength, able to rain down hellfire on all would-be invaders. Armaments, including mini-catapults and spear-throwers, were erected on top of the wall walk.

All orders were dispensed by Joseph. And for the most part, the inhabitants obeyed, seeing him as their unofficial messiah.

- - -

**AT THE** same time Joseph was busy with his new position as governor of Galilee, John of Gischala was growing mad with envy at Joseph's increasing power.

John shifted his efforts towards gaining control of the entire Galilean territory. He escalated his raids in severity and frequency and expanded them against the wagon trains of noblemen, commoners, and anyone else in Galilee that crossed his path except the Romans—his one feared enemy.

John hijacked merchant vessels on the Mediterranean, becoming a pirate of the high seas. He took the women he captured as slaves and auctioned them off as fast as he could, but not before first enjoying the females that caught his eye.

He was always coming into possession of gold and silver trinkets from his raids—he kept metal workers with him all the time so that he might smelt his stolen gold and silver down into adulterated coins on the spot.

Never did he spend a moment contemplating the evil of his actions. John had normalized raiding and was completely desensitized to it. Killing men, women, and children was nothing more than a day's work and quickly forgotten as such.

John enlisted men for their fighting physique, military experience, steadfastness, and nastiness. He preferred young men as their minds were 'completely malleable.' The number of John's followers swelled as he continued to bring treasure to his men, raid after raid. Many of these rogues were mentally-deranged murderers who enjoyed pillaging more than plundering. Other men looked to satisfy their lust upon the helpless women in their path. John obliged them all.

His devious mind worked up lies and plots against Joseph. If Joseph would not or could not stop his raids, John would slander Joseph as a weak leader, seeking to turn public opinion against him.

The first slander John circulated was that Joseph was collaborating with the Romans. The rumor spread quickly and violently throughout Galilee. Though not many believed it at first, that was about to change once Joseph came into possession of Agrippa's gold.

King Agrippa was the *de jure* ruler of Judea. Operating out of Caesarea, his power was derived from Rome as he was essentially a puppet. He commanded only a small military force of about a hundred loyal men. While he was welcomed throughout the land and paid respects by most of his subjects, he rarely made any command decisions—those were left to the ministers in Jerusalem and of course Rome. However, Agrippa did genuinely care about his Judean subjects and wanted to do right by them to the extent he was able—he was simply too weak to do much of anything.

Agrippa as a specimen was rather unimpressive. He was no taller than five feet and a few inches. His skin was tan but not dark. His eyes were brown as was his hair. He was not frail but not muscular either. Only his crown, ring, and clothes identified him as anyone of importance.

John had not even previously considered tangling with Agrippa. A strike against Agrippa was effectively a strike against Rome— John could not afford to be endlessly pursued by the Roman army.

It was by mere coincidence that John's young raiders happened upon Agrippa's caravan outside the city of Dabarittha, close to Nazareth. John had ordered raids in the area while personally commanding his pilfering forces in other parts of Galilee. He was busy raiding what he believed were 'more lucrative opportunities.'

Agrippa's men hauling the cargo pleaded with John's young raiders for mercy and even warned them that they were plundering the king's property. John's men, not believing it or not caring, pillaged and plundered anyway, leaving no man on the wagon train alive.

The caravan contained silks and woolen garments of the finest quality. A large collection of silver goblets was also seized. But the greatest prize was a cache of six thousand gold talents—a fortune for a nation.

The young raiders became terrified at the sight of their overwhelming score as they knew they were dead men for such a violation, should they ever be discovered. Knowing Agrippa was a Roman puppet, they feared that they had pinched Rome's gold—all the talents were embossed with Caesar's face. These men knew how Roman justice was inflicted on thieves, and this heist was too large to be forgiven or forgotten.

The raiders furiously tried to trade the gold for other items of value. No merchants or bankers would do business with them as they also feared Rome's reprisal. Additionally, the quantity of gold was too great to trade with even the wealthiest of private citizens in Galilee willing to do black-market business. Not knowing what to do, the young raiders turned over nearly the entire haul of gold to Joseph, content with their silver chalices and regal civvies.

John was furious. So enraged was he that, upon hearing the news, he cut the tongue out of his own messenger. He knew the gold could have been used to help him gain control of Galilee. Gold meant weapons, men, food, armaments, beasts, and everything else an army needed to be effective and victorious.

Of course, John had not wanted to personally meddle with the Romans, but the deed being done, he thought the gold should have been his.

John convinced himself he would have found a way of implicating other raiders to the Romans, escaping personal culpability.

Mostly he raged.

This was the greatest setback John had faced yet, and he was going to dispense his own form of justice.

The young raiders were summoned by John under the pretense of celebration. Though presented with gifts of silver goblets and silk clothes, John could not be dissuaded from his unabated treachery.

"Greetings, brothers. Peace be unto you," John said to the four young raiders of Agrippa's gold who came before him.

"Peace be unto you," the four men replied. "My lord, we have brought gifts of silver goblets and silk wares," the lead bandit Josiah said.

"What a generous offering. I am so happy that you are all here. Rest assured there is no ill will between us concerning King Agrippa's gold. I'm sure I would have been frightened too at the sight of such great wealth. Rome would have surely come for you and your families had you been discovered. Come. Let us eat and drink together and put the past aside while exploring the future," John said cheerfully.

John's chief rogue, Sadius, unknown to the raiders and masquerading as a servant, took five silver chalices from the raiders' tribute and distributed them among John and the four young men. From a stand by the side of John's tent, he picked up and carried over a golden wine carafe beautifully decorated with topaz, sapphire, and peridot stones that together made a mosaic of the Ark of the Covenant. Sadius moved to fill John's chalice first.

"Fill mine to the top! For tonight I get drunk!" John said joyously to a relaxing troop.

"Yes, my lord." Sadius obliged.

Sadius continued to pour wine for the young raiders, starting with Josiah, the shortest member of the four. Five filled wine cups sat on a center table between John and his men.

"Bring us some food too!" John commanded Sadius.

"Yes, my lord. Right away, my lord," said Sadius, and he hurried off, carafe still in hand, to retrieve a food plate.

"Let us pray," John said.

All the men raised their cups in salutation to God.

"Blessed art Thou, Lord our God, King of the World, Creator of the fruit of the vine," John blessed.

"Amen," the group said in unison.

With their cups raised to their lips, the young raiders began to slowly sip the wine. But before John could take a sip of his, Sadius feigned an accident while presenting John food from a platter, causing John's wine cup to fall to the floor, with the cold meats from the food plate landing across his chest.

"Fool!" John exclaimed, smacking Sadius across the face backhandedly—the raiders laughed at Sadius' misfortune.

"Fill me another cupful!" John yelled.

Unbeknownst to the raiders, Sadius had switched the first carafe of wine for an identical one sitting by the far side of the stand's pedestal—out of sight of the young raiders. The covertly-exchanged carafe brought no suspicion from the young raiders as it was so opulent and seemingly so unique as to rise above scrutiny.

The young raiders paused in drinking from their chalices, not having taken more than a sip apiece. They waited for John's chalice to be refilled and they could drink together so they could be assured they were not being poisoned.

"Good lads you are to wait for me. Let's try this again," and he repeated the blessing for the wine.

Then they all drank together.

John, seeing the men swallow their wine, let out a slightly maniacal grin. This troubled the shortest raider, Josiah. Noticing a curious look on the raiders' faces at the sight of his furtive smile, John quickly chugged his drink, slamming the empty chalice on the center of the table. At the sight of John's speedy drinking, the short raider's puzzled face disappeared and returned to one reveling in a joyous occasion.

"Servant, refill me!" John ordered Sadius.

"Yes, my lord," Sadius replied sycophantically.

"That is good wine, is it not, friends?" John asked in a jolly tone to his raiders.

"Oh yes, my lord, very good!" the fattest raider said.

Sadius refilled John's goblet from the untainted wine carafe and then returned to his serving station.

The raiders continued drinking and soon emptied their cups.

By the time the raiders' cups needed a refilling, Sadius had replaced the untainted wine carafe from which he poured John's wine by the side of the stand pedestal. He then retook the carafe with the poison to replenish the cups of the young men.

Before long, three raiders had drunk two full cups worth, and Josiah had drunk three. Their speech slowed and their eyesight turned cloudy. The raiders felt as if they were spinning while sitting still. Their bodies began to freeze up into complete paralysis. Immobilized, they were still conscious, though their perception was askew under the influence.

"This is very special wine, my friends." John began to speak with a tone that was the polar opposite of his merry disposition from just a few moments past.

"Do any of you know what hemlock is?" he continued. "Don't answer; I'll explain. Hemlock is a lovely little plant that when distilled into a powder creates a fatal poison. There is no known cure, and death is slow. First, the victim becomes paralyzed. Then the lungs stop working. Finally death comes by asphyxiation. The entire duration of this death is experienced in a waking state, allowing the victim to enjoy the poison's full effects."

"Unfortunately, you have all drunk multiple doses of a super-concentrated hemlock formula. I purchased it from a witch, no less. How many men did she say it could kill, Sadius?" John yelled out to his man.

"One hundred, my lord," Sadius replied.

"You may be asking yourself, why am I dying of poison and yet John lives unscathed? The answer to that lies with the chicanery of my second-in-command. Sadius, come over here and take a bow," John demonically ordered.

"Thank you all. This night could never have been possible without your stupidity," Sadius said sardonically with a dead-pan delivery while mockingly bowing before the four young raiders.

"Originally I poured everyone poisoned wine, but you remember I spilled Master John's cup. I did that intentionally and refilled his cup with untainted wine from this identical carafe!" Sadius said, presenting both identical golden carafes, one in each hand.

A wheezing chuckle transformed itself into booming maniacal laughter. Sadius got so carried away, he fell to his knees uncontrollably. John joined in—his laughter exploded like crackling thunder.

Now the four poisoned men were beginning to foam at their mouths. Terror from the knowledge of their impending deaths emanated from their bright, bloodshot eyes. Each man, unimaginably frightened, fought for every breath as his lungs froze from the toxic hemlock.

The smallest raider, Josiah, who had had an extra serving of wine beyond everyone else, was in particularly bad shape—his entire body was convulsing, with blood pouring out of his nose.

The toxic stratagem revealed, John began to vent his anger about losing Agrippa's gold.

"Call the men in here. I want them all to see this," John commanded.

Sadius brought forth all of John's followers in the camp at the time—about fifty men.

John began to speak. "I lead our raids whether I am present or not!" he screamed at the young raiders at the top of his lungs. "You continue to live because I permit it! All treasure comes to me, and you should thank God I give you a piece of it! Do you see what happens when you disobey my orders?"

John's men stood with their heads sunk low, averting their eyes from the desperate gasps of breath coming from the dying raiders.

John could have let the raiders die from asphyxiation, but he enjoyed participating in acts of extreme cruelty and genuinely believed it was the only way to keep the rest of his followers in line. John reached for the short filet knife on the platter of food he had been using to cut the cold meats.

"Sadius, disrobe them," John ordered.

Sadius began taking the clothing off all the young men. Four naked and paralyzed men now sat before John.

"This is what happens to those who steal from me!" he yelled in a terrifying rage.

Then John took the filet knife and scored cuts on the chests of the young men in the shape of a box, the top line cutting from breast to breast, one across the belly, and two connecting cuts on both sides of the ribs.

John pulled the skin from the top horizontal score and began to filet the chest off each man. Horrid dying screams struck terror into the hearts of each of John's followers made to watch.

"This one has bosoms!" John laughed out loud as he continued flaying.

This cutting did not injure any major organs; the chest shave did not kill them. Instead it created a rush of adrenaline in the victims, causing them to remain conscious and endure the full agony.

John piled the chest skins four layers high.

"Sadius, I want to keep my trophies. Make me sandals or a satchel from the skins," John said.

"Perhaps a fine belt, my lord?" Sadius queried in a sadistic monotone.

"I've always liked your style, Sadius," John replied.

The young raiders sat completely paralyzed, their intestines spilled onto their laps. Their breathing slowed to inaudible levels. Their faces turned blue. And then they were with God.

"Now that the festivities are completed, send in the whores! Whenever I flay someone, my staff grows long!" John said.

"Of course, my lord," Sadius replied and walked out of the main tent.

All of John's men who had witnessed the horror quickly followed behind Sadius. Several of the men fell to their hands and knees and vomited uncontrollably.

Sadius walked over to the red tent that housed John's women. They were considered unclean at the sight of the new moon. But John was not a religious man and would use them whether they were bleeding or not.

"Take off your gowns—Lord John demands your company," Sadius ordered.

Ten beautiful young women walked naked into John's tent. They stood before him, and he took several moments to gaze upon their young, milky breasts and blooming loins. John disrobed himself and was fully erect.

"You there!" he barked out to one of the youngest slaves. "Sit on my lap," he ordered.

The young girl mounted John.

"Don't look at me, you whore. Look at all your whore sisters," John yelled, smacking her in the face. She turned around, still on top of him. Tears rolled down her face from both eyes, showing her fear and humiliation simultaneously.

Using his dagger to point, he threatened the rest of his women: "Don't forget what happens to those people who disobey me," and John pointed to the layers of hides he had just harvested.

John, again pressing the dagger against his concubine's throat causing mild razor cuts, continued thrusting and then grotesquely climaxed—throwing the girl off him like refuse the moment he was finished with her.

That night, all the men of John's order and all the women owned by him remembered why they needed to fear him. He would not only brutally kill those who crossed him—he enjoyed it.

*  *  *

**JOSEPH, UPON** receiving the lot of six thousand gold pieces, initially sought to return the money to King Agrippa, if possible, or use it in the construction of Galilee's defenses.

John's false allegations of conspiracy grew overbearing once the people heard that Joseph was in possession of such a great treasure—the news of which John was also responsible for spreading. The public soon all knew about Agrippa's gold and began accusing Joseph of pocketing it for himself.

The false allegations against Joseph whipped Galilee up into such a fury that ten thousand Jotapatan residents gathered in front of Joseph's residence. Calls of 'traitor' and 'thief' rang out. Joseph's bodyguards formed a human wall around the governor's mansion to protect him as he slept at night and while he worked in the day.

The next night, when the mob became particularly riotous, four of Joseph's personal guards woke him to the harrowing sight of the massing murderous mob bearing torches.

His guards beseeched Joseph to escape through the underground tunnel connecting the mansion to an exit outside of the city walls. But Joseph would not cower in the face of a crowd that had been misinformed—he was convinced that he could appease even a rowdy mob with his words of reason.

He walked out the doorway entrance of his mansion to his front steps. Behind him were two bodyguards carrying the opposite ends of a large wooden chest. The guards put the chest down next to Joseph's feet. Joseph appealed to the Jotapatans' intellect, using his words as his best tool.

"Jotapatans!" Joseph yelled out while raising his arms to quiet the crowd. "I know you are angry. But before you cut me to pieces, hear my words."

"We tire of your words!" one Jotapatan exclaimed.

"You make us work for nothing and pocket the king's money behind our backs!" another accused.

The mob continued to stir themselves into a frenzy. Joseph signaled the guards holding the chest—they opened its lid and turned the box upside down. Six thousand talents spilled in a waterfall of sparkling gold coins onto the ground, illuminating the night's darkness with flickering golden light. At the sight of this great and unexpected treasure, the Jotapatans' jaws dropped, and total silence broke out.

Joseph continued, "Do you now believe me that I do not steal? I toil as you do—day in and day out, and my thanks is a greeting party of would-be murderers—drawn from the very people I work so hard to protect!"

Joseph looked out at the people—all eyes drooped, solemn and guilty-looking. The Jotapatans knew in their hearts that Joseph was their protector, not their swindler, and that they were wrong to have ever doubted him.

"I have no intention of lining my pockets or returning this money to Agrippa," Joseph continued. "I sought to use this money to erect the fortifications you now see standing through-out Jotapata and the rest of Galilee. Would you rather have Agrippa's gold or protection from the Romans? Any fool can see that without fortifications, as costly as they may be, the Romans will storm in and take the gold and your lives. Well, here is the gold! Take it if you wish, but if you do, look to me no further for salvation!"

After Joseph spoke, the mob dissolved into pacifists and mostly dispersed. However, a thousand men, still unconvinced, began to move in towards Joseph with their weapons raised. Upon seeing these men rushing at him, Joseph ran back into his mansion. His guards followed directly behind him, locking all the doors. Again his men implored Joseph to take the underground tunnel, and again Joseph refused. He would try once again to placate the Judeans, but this time, in addition to his words, he would use his guile.

Joseph raced to the top floor of the mansion and opened the center windows so he could speak to the remaining mob from the overhanging portico. The crowd began to yell all sorts of obscenities and curses towards Joseph. A thousand voices called out simultaneously. Hundreds of Jotapatans attempted to breach the locked doors.

"Friends! I know not what you want! I cannot understand a one of you when all of you speak at the same time. I will cater to every last demand upon me. I only ask that you send your leaders to me so that we may formalize a comprehensive agreement, even if it means my resignation as governor," Joseph requested loudly for all to hear.

The crowd was appeased by Joseph's reasonable proposal, satisfied that their leaders would depose Joseph and resolve all their grievances. The mob rested for the night and sent their self-chosen leaders to Joseph the next morning to conclude the saga of Agrippa's gold.

But Joseph fooled these leaders as he had no intention of making any concessions nor resigning. He needed to put his constituents in line or face a greater revolt throughout Galilee. When the Jotapatan leaders entered his governor's mansion, Joseph brought them into the most secure room in the complex, feigning friendship.

Then, without warning, he had the doors sealed shut. His loyal bodyguards, fifty fit youths, began flogging the ten elderly leaders until their flesh hung from their bodies like ribbons on a wrapped gift.

Joseph then opened the front doors of his house and dumped the dying and dead bodies into the street for all to gaze upon. The horrific sight struck such fear into his enemies' hearts that they all dropped their swords and spears and ran.

Joseph had restored order.

■ ■ ■

**JOHN QUICKLY** heard about the mob scene at Joseph's residence. He became enraged at the news that Joseph still lived and, worse yet, still ruled. John soon cooked up a plot to depose Joseph himself. He wrote to Joseph that he was ill and required treatment at the hot baths of the city. Joseph, not wanting a violent confrontation with John, acquiesced to this request, believing it could be an olive branch in furtherance of peace across Galilee.

John and a band of men entered Jotapata after receiving an assurance of safe passage from Joseph.

"Shalom Aleichem. Greetings, John," Joseph said upon meeting John at the entrance to the city.

"Aleichem Shalom. Greetings, brother," John replied. "I am happy to finally meet you face to face. Our acquaintance is long past due."

"I agree," Joseph said. "Tell me, what is the nature of your illness?"

"I burn, my lord. I am in need of the spa and hearty sleep," John responded.

"You burn from sickness?" Joseph asked, unsure if John had a serious illness or was just seeking a romp.

"Yes, my lord. I have the disease of the loins," John duplicitously replied, covering his mouth with his hand to not broadcast his 'illness' to the entire city.

"You and your men are welcome to enter Jotapata. The spa in Jotapata is the best in Galilee. You shall be well looked after at all times during your stay," Joseph said. "I pray to God that we can negotiate a peace so that I may call you my brother and not my enemy."

"I too seek peace, my Hebrew brother," John said. "But first I must tend to my belly, my men, and my illness," John said coyly.

"I am pleased to hear that, and I will pray to God for His blessings. Very good. We will talk again soon," Joseph said.

John walked with his men into the city.

"What do you make of him, Aaron?" Joseph asked his second-in-command.

"I'm not yet sure, my lord. Perhaps he does seek peace. Maybe his forces and pockets are not as deep as we thought?" Aaron wondered curiously. "Let's see what he does next."

"I agree. But keep eyes on him and his men at all hours. His mischief is as well-known as women of the night," Joseph commanded.

"Of course, my lord," Aaron replied.

John and his men spent the night in Jotapata free from incident. The next morning he went to the bathhouse, continuing to feign illness to further his ruse to kill Joseph.

"I want to invite Joseph to bathe with me," John said to Sadius. "I want to make him feel comfortable so he puts his guard down. What better way to do that than by standing naked next to another man in a delightful bath?" John asked rhetorically.

"I will go to Joseph myself, my lord," Sadius stated and set off for the governor's mansion to invite Joseph to join John in the bathhouse.

John smiled while he enjoyed the hot spring water, giddy with the thought that Joseph would finally be murdered, allowing himself a clear path to control of all Galilee and perhaps, with Agrippa's gold, even Jerusalem.

However, a Jotapatan soldier, Jeremiah, keeping the peace in the street adjacent to the bathhouse overheard one of John's raiders plotting.

"He'll be dead before my master dries," John's man said.

Being a scholar that had been conscripted to the soldiery, Jeremiah immediately knew the context of the statement—John was intending to assassinate Joseph.

Jeremiah calmly but quickly moved from his post outside the bathhouse and began to run directly for the governor's mansion.

"I have news of the utmost importance and urgency for our Lord Governor," Jeremiah said to the guards protecting the entrance to the mansion.

"Tell us what you think you know, and we'll determine if the governor needs to be disturbed," one heavyset and unkempt guard said smugly.

"John intends to assassinate Joseph. I have heard of his plot with my own ears," Jeremiah explained. "He will murder the governor in the bathhouse."

"Joseph is protected by hundreds of the best men Jotapata can muster. He will be fine," the guards at the entrance assured Jeremiah.

"Fools! Damn you!" Jeremiah shouted.

"Get ye lost, or you'll be the one that ends up murdered" was the snarky reply from the guard.

Jeremiah grabbed the heavyset guard by his tunic and brought their faces close to one another. "I'm telling you as your fellow soldier, the governor is in trouble!"

The heavyset guard kneed Jeremiah in the crotch.

Jeremiah squirmed and fell to the ground.

"Touch me again and it's off to the stockade with you!" the guard shouted back.

Standing up slowly, Jeremiah limped back as fast as he could to his post by the bathhouse, eagerly hoping to uncover more of John's scheming in an effort to save Joseph from any harm.

A short while later, Sadius arrived at the mansion and was immediately admitted by the same guards that had denied Jeremiah. Sadius requested Joseph join John in the bathhouse to settle all and any further disputes between them. Joseph consented and walked side by side with Sadius to the bathhouse surrounded by all of his personal guards. Joseph was mildly concerned for his safety, but his security was the best it could be. He arrived at the bathhouse to see John relaxing in a tranquil state, waist-deep in water.

The bath John was in was essentially a circular pool with underwater terraced levels to accommodate sitting and standing. The bath was large enough to serve upwards of fifty people at the same time. There were a dozen men in the bath with John, mostly elderly men of wealth.

But before Joseph arrived, Axius, an ambitious young follower of John's looking to advance himself in the clan, stood at the far end of the pool, busying himself unsuspectingly as an average bath-goer. Tucked in his rear cheeks was a curled-up cheese-cutting wire. To keep the thin metal wire light, it was without conventional wooden end handles—each end of the wire cable was designed into five finger holes. The wire was virtually invisible as the light green water, mostly translucent, obscured the view of all things below the waterline.

John and Joseph began to talk. John insincerely apologized profusely for all the trouble that had occurred while Joseph was governor of Galilee. They came to an understanding—Joseph would deliver a third of Agrippa's gold to John, and John agreed to leave Galilee permanently for the northerly lands in eastern Syria.

Axius, the assassin lying in wait, watched John and Joseph from a modest distance. Then he began to move about the pool slowly and calmly, in a random manner, inevitably moving closer to Joseph, yet drawing no suspicion from the guards. He was now within ten feet of Joseph when he reached for the hidden wire.

Slowly Axius began unwinding the cheese wire under the waterline—the wire was as sharp as a blade's edge when pulled taut.

Jeremiah looked outside the bathhouse and saw no sign of trouble. He walked back inside the bathhouse to see countless bodyguards keeping watch over Joseph and John. Then Jeremiah happened to glance into the pool and saw a flicker of light reflected from the metal wire in Axius' hands under the waterline.

"Assassin!" Jeremiah yelled out for all to hear. Five bodyguards leapt from the deck of the pool into the water to protect Joseph. Axius had already wrapped the wire around Joseph's neck.

But before Axius could pull the wire taut, a bodyguard threw his spear into Axius' back—the spear partially exited through his chest. He collapsed into the pool, turning it red with blood.

Ten spears turned now to John, sitting on the ledge of the bath.

Joseph emerged from the bath with nothing more than a minor cut to his neck.

"Why won't you die?" John grumbled while he was rendered motionless by Joseph's bodyguards.

"Take this lawless filth to a cell. No one is to give him food—he's fat enough to do without," Joseph commanded and then turned to dry and cover himself with a towel.

"I do not know you," Joseph addressed Jeremiah, "but if not for your keen sight, I'd be the dead body floating in the bath. I could use a man with your eyes and sense as my hundreds of bodyguards all seem to have been ineffective."

"My lord," said Jeremiah, "I only warned of the danger. Your man speared the assassin."

"Humble as well. What is your name?" Joseph asked.

"Jeremiah, my lord."

"Jeremiah, you are hereby promoted to captain. You are to be by my side always unless I say otherwise," Joseph proclaimed.

"I will serve you to the death, my lord," Jeremiah pledged with great excitement.

"If today is a harbinger of what is to come, you may well meet that fate," Joseph said.

Jeremiah's excitement quickly diffused.

"I want every last one of John's men arrested. Go now!" Joseph yelled out to his personal bodyguards and left the bathhouse, returning to his residence.

John's men were all arrested without major incident and placed in cells in the Jotapatan jail.

*  *  *

"A HUNDRED gold talents. Have you ever seen such a fortune?" John stood talking to the jailor on duty outside his cell.

"John, shut it, you're wasting your breath. I'd never betray Governor Joseph," the jailor retorted.

"What do you think is going to happen when the Romans come hither? Do you think they will not slay you where you stand? The Romans will slaughter every living thing in all of Galilee before their thirst is quenched. With a hundred gold talents you can set off to distant lands, assured you will be met with welcoming arms."

The jailor was tempted by John's offer as he knew of John's reputation for paying his men great bounties, especially when he was in duress. But honor and duty kept the jailor from falling prey to the venomous bite of John's manipulative tongue.

"For the last time, shut your yapper or I'll give you something to yap about!" was the jailor's reply while shaking his baton threateningly.

John sat back in his jail cell, frustrated he was not able to penetrate the soul of his captor.

"What are we to do?" Sadius murmured into John's ears.

"I'm working on it, Sadius," John answered.

For several months John and his men were imprisoned, being fed only scraps for sustenance and muddy water to drink.

Convinced John had had enough time to calm down, Joseph went to pay him a visit. John's hair seemed to have turned from grey to white in captivity almost overnight. He lost nearly fifty pounds in the course of a three-month period, but he was still fat. However, his eyes now lacked the intensity Joseph had seen when John revealed himself as the brains behind the assassination attempt at the bathhouse.

"What am I supposed to do with you?" Joseph asked.

"Execute me, of course," John answered, laughing.

"If I could execute you, I would have already done it," Joseph said back. "We both know you have untold followers who would like nothing more than to use your martyrdom as cause to start a rebellion in Galilee. I can't set you free or you'd return to raiding the countryside, slaughtering more innocents for their small pockets—not to mention that you'd probably try to kill me again."

"Probably. You could always deliver me to the Romans," John suggested.

It was not the worst idea Joseph had heard. If the Romans executed him, Joseph would not bear the same level of blame as if he oversaw John's execution himself. But handing John over to the Romans meant acknowledging Roman authority and whatever judgement that brought henceforth. The Romans might decide to set John free, and then Joseph would be again burdened with the task of stopping him once more. The best place for John, in Joseph's mind, was right where John sat; however, Joseph knew it was not a permanent solution.

"You and your men will stay jailed until I can find a better place for you," Joseph answered John's speculation.

"I will get out of here sometime soon, you know," John threatened. "And when I do, I will not rest until I see you delivered into the hands of destruction. Set me free now—I will ride for Syria, never to be heard from again."

Joseph was tempted but unconvinced. John would stay put where he was, and Joseph would first worry about more pressing adversaries, such as the Roman army.

# Chapter 8:

# Nero Summons Vespasian

**NERO, THE** sitting Roman Emperor, upon hearing of the Judean revolt, immediately recalled Gessius from his post as governor. Failure was not tolerated by the young Caesar. A new presence was required to crush the insurrection, and there was no greater commander of men than General Flavius Vespasian.

Vespasian was a lifelong soldier. At fifty-five years of age, his body was still in the shape of a gladiator champion's. Standing a tall six feet, he looked down at most of his men. He was clean-shaven from head to face—he believed in obscuring his greying hair to present himself as full of virility. He had a large scar under his right eye and another one on his left cheek for he was a general that joined his men in the fiercest of battles. His eyes were sky blue and pierced all those that looked upon them. Vespasian did not wear all the regalia of most Roman generals for he knew it would distance him from his men. He was mostly indistinguishable from the lowest foot soldier from only a few dozen yards away.

Vespasian had routed the Germanic tribes and beaten Britannia into submission. He was well liked and respected by his men as he brought them victories and great treasures, plundered from those conquered.

He was the father of Titus, the newly-promoted tribune who had served under Gessius Florus. Titus had barely escaped Jerusalem the night of the uprising and made his way back to Rome.

From his son Vespasian knew of the latest and most detailed accounts of the uprising in Judea.

Now Nero summoned Vespasian to his palace to task him with crushing the Judean uprising and restoring Roman peace throughout the Holy Land.

"Caesar will see you now, general," said Ulysses, Nero's chief of staff.

Vespasian rose from his seat and began to follow Ulysses through the palace's corridors to Nero's private working office.

"Vespasian, come! Join us in a drink," Nero said upon Vespasian's entrance.

Pompey, a fawn Chinese pug named after the great Roman general, a gift from Emperor Han of China, ran directly at Vespasian with his tail wagging uncontrollably. Pompey began jumping up and down on his leg and spinning around, trying to give Vespasian his full affection. Vespasian bent down to pet Pompey, and the pug purred from the attention.

Standing up straight to address the emperor properly, Vespasian said, "I thank Caesar for his generosity, but I do not drink on duty, Your Majesty."

"A fine general you are indeed. A time not so long ago, your predecessor, Gessius Florus, stood on that same great seal of Rome you now tread upon. But he did not think twice to pass over a goblet of wine. In fact, we believe he drank an entire cask. We should have known then his quality was not up to the task."

"If Caesar wishes me to join him in a drink, I will of course submit, but I respectfully ask for tea," Vespasian countered.

"Boy!" Nero turned to his young cupbearer. "Bring the General some *tea*."

The boy servant quickly hurried off at the emperor's demand.

Pompey began jumping on Vespasian's leg again, begging for the petting to resume.

"Pompey, enough!" Nero shouted, pointing to the dog's fluffy pillow. "Bed!"

The dog cowered and slowly walked to his plush bed with his normally curly pug tail hanging straight down between his legs.

"Great Caesar, I love dogs—he does not annoy me," Vespasian said.

"Perhaps—but he does annoy us," Nero said and then pivoted the conversation. "Tell us, Vespasian, what know you of Judea?"

"I know the Hebrews are engaged in active rebellion all across the land, Jerusalem being the heart of their insurrection. I know they are fractured by multiple sects. The Sadducees, Pharisees, Zealots, and a new murderous rogue group that call themselves the Sicarii all vie for control of Jerusalem and its great treasures."

"They rose up against us, unwilling to bend the knee to our standards nor pay our just taxes," Nero said. "They have slain the entire garrison stationed in Jerusalem. They now openly rebel in almost every town across Judea. In the last year, they have been busy fortifying city walls, raising armies, and forging weapons of all kinds. Tell me, Vespasian, how would you quash this uprising?"

"The great strength of the Hebrews is their complete faith in their God," Vespasian stated. "They believe they fight Rome for eternal salvation, that their God hath commanded it. We must show them that they worship a false god by destroying Him!" Vespasian said forcefully, slamming his fist into his hand.

"How would you accomplish this goal?" Nero continued his questioning.

"We must burn their most holy Temple of David to the ground—that will show the Hebrews that their God is false. Then we force all to abandon Him for the true gods of Rome. Those that resist will be crucified for all to see," Vespasian answered.

Nero evaluated the proposal in his mind and was impressed.

The boy cupbearer returned and gave Vespasian a Chinese porcelain teacup on a plate.

Vespasian began to sip his tea. Nero attempted to join Vespasian in drinking, but his goblet was empty. He turned his head to look directly at his cupbearer and made an annoyed face because it had not been refilled properly. The boy nervously raced to retrieve more wine.

The young cupbearer returned in a hurry with a full carafe. But his hands were trembling with fear for already dissatisfying Nero. His fingers shaking, the young cupbearer poured wine into the cup in Nero's hand, spilling a few drops of wine on Nero's fingers.

"Damn it! You have one job, boy! And an easy one at that. Would you prefer to be food for our pets?"

Sporus, Nero's eunuch husband, until now unseen under a pile of pillows on the oversize sofa, began laughing hysterically. It was at such a high pitch and intensity, all were startled.

"Forgive me, Your Greatness," the boy mumbled, terrified his error might mean his execution.

"Sporus, shut it!" Nero yelled and then turned back to the terrified cupbearer. "Fill it to the top, boy!"

After Nero's goblet was replenished, the emperor continued speaking to Vespasian. "Would you kill every last one of our Hebrew subjects?"

"Without hesitation," Vespasian replied.

At this immediate response, Nero was taken aback for a moment—he knew the great wealth the Judeans produced in taxes every year for the empire.

"Judea brings us ten thousand gold talents a year. You would see our taxes from Judea dry up as well?" Nero retorted curiously.

"With all respect, Caesar, if the Hebrews can escape Roman justice, would not the whole of your dominion soon revolt, drying up the entirety of Rome's treasury?" Vespasian responded.

Nero paused for a moment to take a drink of wine. Vespasian drank his tea. Then a grand smile appeared on Nero's face.

"You are as wise as you are victorious in combat. A greater man for this position we could not ask for."

Nero began to walk in slow circles around Vespasian and continued, "You will have five legions, divisions of our finest cavalry. Slaves to build countless war machines and coin to pay for all other necessities needed in your campaign."

Vespasian kept a straight face, but he knew he had pleased Caesar.

The emperor began to smile strangely. "Vespasian, we'll need you to step off the seal for a moment."

Nero turned to Ulysses. "Bring in the prisoner!"

Ulysses moved swiftly and opened the double doors to Nero's office. A man chained with his arms secured around a wooden beam was dragged in by two Roman soldiers who held the beam by its ends. The soldiers stood him before the great seal of Rome. It was a grandiose circumscribed solid-gold circle, centered with a magnificent eagle. The Latin phrases inscribed in the seal read: 'Semper Caesar. Semper Rome.'

The prisoner's face was black, bloodied, and torn from the savage beatings he had endured. His left ear was missing as was his right hand—a tourniquet was clasped around his wrist keeping him from bleeding out.

The man was Gessius Florus.

Pompey rose from his bed and ran at full speed towards Gessius. He growled his meanest growl and barked his most vicious bark, which for a pug was rather adorable.

Upon realizing who the prisoner was, Vespasian's heart sank in his chest and his eyes dilated.

"Hello, Governor," Nero said to Gessius with a sardonic tone.

Gessius did not even have the strength to beg for his life. He could only be heard pathetically sobbing.

The pug continued barking viciously at Gessius.

"Pompey, enough!" Nero yelled and picked up his dog.

Pompey began to lick Nero's face. After a few licks, Pompey turned his head around only to continue growling at Gessius.

Gessius muttered inaudibly.

"What's that? We can't hear you," Caesar mocked. "Because of your foolishness with the damn Hebrews, we are forced to expend untold men and treasure to reconquer our subjects. Now we have one last assignment for you. You are going to teach General Vespasian a lesson that will inspire him for his upcoming campaign."

Nero turned to Ulysses. "Open it up."

Ulysses walked to the wall and pulled down a mechanical lever. On the floor, the great seal began to open—it was a trap door. The seal's gold doors turned down and in from both sides.

"We have some friends we'd like you to meet—goodbye, Governor," Nero said and then nodded to the soldiers.

The Roman guards tossed Gessius down into the pit of death.

"Do you care to watch, Vespasian? We get a good show from up here."

"No, thank you, Your Majesty." Vespasian declined.

Growls and screams could be heard. Tearing noises rose up through the floor opening. A pack of rabid hyenas were viciously mauling Gessius to death. He wailed and screamed until there were no more cries—only the sounds of beasts ripping flesh and feeding remained.

Caesar motioned to Ulysses to close up the floor, and then he continued his conversation with Vespasian as if nothing had happened.

"General, do not fail us, do not embarrass us, or you will find yourself the one that disappears through Rome's seal next time."

"My emperor, I will not fail you nor Rome, and if by some means I do fail, I will take my own life." With Vespasian's reply, Nero was satisfied and assured of success in the conflict concerning the Judeans.

"Go now. May all our gods see you victorious in exacting Roman justice," Nero blessed Vespasian.

"Hail, Caesar!" Vespasian shouted, his right arm fully extended in salute.

And with that, Vespasian left the emperor's palace.

# Nero About to Execute Gessius

# Chapter 9:

# The Siege of Jotapata

**JOSEPH CONTINUED** his work as governor of Galilee, building fortifications in and around the cities. The central Galilean town of Jotapata was Joseph's stronghold, and he spent most of his time there readying the place for a Roman siege.

General Vespasian and the Fifth, Ninth, Tenth, and Fifteenth Legions arrived by sea at the port town of Caesarea directly from Rome. Titus and the Third Legion rendezvoused with Vespasian in the city. The Roman cavalry totaled six thousand men. There were five thousand more unmounted bowmen, part of the larger infantry force totaling nearly fifty thousand. Local lords from Syria, aiming to stay in Rome's good graces, sent a legion's worth of mercenaries. There were also ten thousand non-combatant servant and slave types responsible for the multitude of tasks required to maintain such a large military force.

The general understood that his goal was not just the recapture of Jerusalem but the submission of the entire Holy Land. There were several advantages in attacking Galilee first. He believed it possible that Jerusalem might surrender after hearing of the destruction and savagery he would inflict on Galilee.

Vespasian also received reports that the Jotapatan city walls were lower and less reinforced than those of Jerusalem and therefore easier to breach and destroy. Additionally, he thought from intelligence reports that the Jotapatan arsenal was old and poorly stocked compared to the Romans'. Vespasian would discover he had been misinformed on both counts.

A master general by trade, Vespasian understood the vast number of details that went into preparing a victorious campaign. There was little idle time spent in their fortified basecamp or castrum. Training was incessant. Battle drills were conducted in the same fashion as if they were in active combat with the enemy.

Vespasian taught his soldiers to avoid panicking while fighting by always following their commander's orders on the field of battle. Discipline was paramount to Roman victories. Few disobeyed as those insubordinate to their commanders would receive severe corporal punishment at a minimum. Even fewer deserted as those caught would be crucified in front of the entire army.

First on Vespasian's list was the small Galilean city of Gabara. When his forces descended upon the city, they were somewhat surprised to find it mostly deserted with only inconsequential Hebrew commoners about. Gabara was not a serious military proposition.

The Romans could tell from the withered apparel and general lackluster presentation that the residents of Gabara were in no way responsible for the uprising nor dangerous. They were simply common people getting about the business of staying alive in a desert climate. That did not stop the Roman blade. Soldiers took revenge for the slaughter at Antonia Fortress—they blamed every Hebrew for it.

First, the Romans attacked the male residents of the town, gutting them with daggers and putting others on the cross. Some Hebrews were tied to trees and burnt at the stake. Then the Romans turned their attention to the few hundred women and slew them just the same. Most females were given a lighter sentence: death by slicing of the throat. The Romans murdered everyone, even young babies by snapping their necks or launching them as high into the air as their biceps allowed, shattering the babies' bodies when they returned to the firm earth.

After the slaughter, the entire city was set on fire and totally destroyed. Every small hut or home within sight of Gabara was also razed.

The Romans suffered no losses.

Within a half-day's time, Joseph heard from a scout that Vespasian's army had destroyed Gabara.

"They have come," Joseph said to his top officers.

The very next morning at dawn, the Romans appeared on the Jotapatan horizon. Some two miles lay between the Roman army and the city walls.

A volley of shofar blows wailed, alerting the city to the Roman presence. Joseph raced up the stairs of the tallest watchtower to survey the Roman force himself. He could not believe its size. There were countless men. The metalwork of the Roman arms and armor gleamed in a hundred thousand directions. Joseph's first thought was that the fight to defend the city was unwinnable. He thought of suing for peace and asking for terms. But he knew if he surrendered the city, he would most likely be executed.

Though Jotapata was in sight, the last two miles proved rather difficult for the Roman army to navigate. The city lies essentially on the side of a mountain, accessible only by the narrowest of curvy roads from the northern side. Vespasian sent his entire division of engineers ahead of his foot soldiers—it took four days before a makeshift road sufficient to transport his army was finished.

The Roman army had come to the precipice of war. But Vespasian, always the master tactician and disciplinarian, dug in first.

Before the general would initiate a siege on Jotapata, he first started construction of a fortified castrum, no more than five hundred yards from the city wall. It took four more days to complete the Roman fortress.

The castrum was designed in the shape of a rectangle, but before its construction began, the entire area of the camp was graded flat to avoid problems inherent with operating on uneven terrain. Then came the building of a perimeter wall. Towers were spaced out along the fort, capable of supporting a battery of spear-launchers and mini-catapults. Allowing egress were four great gates, one in the middle of each side of every fort wall. The gates rose to the top of the walls some thirty feet. Vespasian also constructed a dry moat six feet deep and six feet wide around the walls.

Inside the castrum, streets were clearly delineated. Sitting in the middle of the camp was Vespasian's headquarters. There was also a marketplace, servant quarters, and even tents designated for official business such as resolving disputes and prosecuting those men who were insubordinate.

Throughout the day, Roman horns blasted out different melodies. In the camp, there was a musical code for everything. There was the shift-change tune: quick, nervous, annoying. There was the call-to-arms alarm: a single blaring high note, whining back and forth.

When a fort needed to be struck, horns would sound the grand-exit melody: the tents would be quickly dismantled and Roman soldiers would then gather all their personal and soldierly belongings, putting them into their cargo bags and securing them on their beasts. The soldiers would wait for the 'stand to march' tune which commenced the exodus of camels, mules, and horses hauling Roman parcels of all sorts.

Once the Romans exited the fort, a clarion would play the 'burn the whole thing down' chant. The fort was then set ablaze to prevent enemy forces from using the installation to their advantage.

Vespasian's men were required to move in perfect synchronicity with one another—keeping his men moving in unison facilitated maintaining soldiers ever ready for war.

They ate breakfast and dinner together. They washed together. They awoke at the same time together by horns playing reveille— loud, proud, Roman. Ten minutes after reveille, the tirones and legionaries assembled in their units and saluted their centurions. The centurions in turn assembled before their tribunes and saluted them. Then the generals proceeded to Vespasian's tent to receive the daily orders, discuss strategy, and provide progress reports on all matters related to the army.

On the other side of the city wall, Joseph was still feverishly arranging every detail for the city's defense. He had significantly heightened the walls, strengthened the defenses, and forged new weapons. Joseph had a four-foot dry moat dug around the city, some twenty yards out from the walls to defend against the Roman wall-breachers sure to come. His soldiers were outfitted with all sorts of hand weapons including hatchets, maces, hammers, and, of course, swords, spears, and daggers. The Galileans were as ready as they could be.

Vespasian's infantry was well prepared for every possibility. To protect their bodies, all troops wore thick breastplates of bronze metal as well as steel helmets. The soldiers carried two blades, one on each side. On the left side they carried their gladius; on the right they carried a dagger. Many carried eight-foot-long spears as well. Across their backs were wooden batons secured by leather straps. The soldiers also lugged their bronze shields, steel pickaxes, and three days' rations. A fully outfitted soldier on the march looked much like a camel or horse hauling luggage, nearly bent half over at the waist to counter their cargo weight.

Several days passed and no attack came. The siege had been on effectively two weeks now without so much as one Roman arrow being fired.

The Jotapatans became so terrified at the sight of the Roman army and its massive castrum that a few took their own lives. An older man of no significance and without family jumped from one of the city watchtowers to his death. More than several parents gave hemlock tea to their children and themselves, preferring to die a slow death by asphyxiation rather than endure the Roman slaughter.

◢ ◢ ◢

**ON THE** fifteenth day after Vespasian's army had arrived at Jotapata, the assault finally began.

Towering Roman war machines, nearly one hundred of them, stood assembled a quarter-mile out from the city walls.

"Ready the payloads," Vespasian ordered.

"Ready the payloads!" Cestius relayed the order to his batteries of stone-throwing catapults. "Apply oil and ignite!"

At his command, Roman bombardiers added ladles of black oil to the tops of their boulders and ignited the petrol with their hand torches. Over a hundred small dots of fire appeared from the Roman catapults.

"Blow the damn shofar!" a Galilean sentry cried out.

The blaring sound of the shofar indicating incoming projectiles woke the entire city. The frightened people started running around in a chaotic panic.

Joseph rose from his bed and raced to the watchtower to see for himself about the situation.

"Fire," Vespasian commanded.

"Fire!" Cestius yelled out to his men.

A hundred catapults began their mechanical motion and cast their fiery stones into the air.

Joseph looked out towards the Roman camp. Flaming rocks illuminated the early morning sky as they soared hundreds of yards through the air towards the Jotapatan walls, leaving smoke trails behind their flight paths.

"Take cover! Everyone take cover!" Joseph yelled out.

Some of the flying stones exploded against the city walls; others soared over the walls, blasting into homes, buildings, animals, and residents.

Joseph, while giving orders from one of the watchtowers, was nearly hit by a stone shooting by just a few feet over his head.

"Joseph, get down from there! If you die, we're all lost!" Captain Jeremiah yelled out.

Seeing the onslaught of the catapults was not going to diminish anytime soon, Joseph took heed of Jeremiah's advice. He descended the watchtower, sliding down a wooden pole, using his garb to protect his hands from splinters, finally landing flat on his feet.

"Aaron!" Joseph called out to his second-in-command. "Get all these people up to the mountain landing. They'll be safe on high ground. Sitting still in the path of the Roman firestones is asking for death!"

Aaron led the evacuating city residents from their homes and made haste up to the mountain landing. Women picked up their children and covered their eyes and ears to prevent their young from hearing or seeing the horror that now befell Jotapata. The residents raced behind Aaron. It was a thousand-yard winding climb up Mt. Jotapata to the plateaued landing where the Galileans would be safe from the incoming firestones.

A fast-moving snake of people could be seen slithering up the mountain trail in the twilight of the new day.

Joseph and a company of ten thousand men stayed in the city to defend in case of a Roman infantry advance.

Boulder after flaming boulder, the Roman catapult onslaught continued for hours. It was now midday, and the engines showed no signs of letting up.

Several fires had broken out in the city, spawned from the flaming projectiles. Half the men on the ground—five thousand—could be seen racing from building to building, dowsing flames with buckets of water. The Jotapatans worked speedily at the cistern and passed filled buckets down a sprawling line of soldiers turned into firemen.

Joseph raced out to coordinate the fire brigade.

"Forget those houses! They are already gone! Get to the city center!" he shouted to men futilely trying to extinguish small hut fires.

In the city center, a large ministerial building made of cut marble was bombed by one of the firestones. Fire began to spread from the drapes of the building to the walls. Joseph had his men expeditiously fight the flames—it was working. Due to Joseph's fast response, no major buildings were destroyed by fire.

After a feverish day of watering, half the city was wet, but it was still standing. However, Jotapata depended on its cistern to provide the residents with drinking water. The water supply had been greatly diminished from the firefighting efforts. The cistern could only be replenished by rainfall—it was summer, with no steady rain expected for months.

The constant bombardment of projectiles ceased in the late-night hours. At first light, a mass of ten thousand residents who had waited on the high plateau of Mt. Jotapata came back down into the city, frantically assessing the damage done to their homes and property.

A thin layer of smoke still hovered over the city. Animals were wandering the streets, having escaped their pens. Youths stood in an endless line by the cistern to refill their familial drinking-water supply. The water level was running below thirty percent.

The city walls held. The Romans had depleted their stockpile of stones. Dissatisfied that the catapults failed to penetrate the

Jotapatan walls, Vespasian ordered the wall-breachers to advance.

The breachers, or siege towers, were essentially mobile watch-towers three floors high. They would be hauled up as close to the walls of the city as possible. Inside each tower was space for a company of men to lie in wait. Their bows, shields, and swords at the ready, a retractable bridge would then be lowered from the top level of the tower until the end of the bridge came to rest on top of the wall parapet, allowing the soldiers to breach the city.

The breachers moved forward, pulled by men with attached ropes. They were quadrupeds, moving on four wheels. But the breachers became stuck. Engineers needed to first build bridges across the small Jotapatan moat, which was temporarily effective in preventing the wall-breachers from advancing.

Vespasian, seeing that the wall-breachers had come to a halt, personally went out to see about the trouble. He had a dozen of his bodyguards, all with shields raised in a half-tortoise, protecting him from the Galilean arrows and spear-throwing engines. But one of the soldiers protecting Vespasian tripped over a rock he did not see as it blended into the dirt. The guard's fall exposed Vespasian's entire body to the Jotapatan archers.

Upon the soldier falling over and dropping his shield, Aaron caught sight of the general. "My god, that's Vespasian!" Aaron yelled out from his eagle-eye view atop one of the watchtowers. "All archers, fire!"

A bevy of a hundred arrows went soaring directly into the gap in the tortoise. Vespasian was struck in the foot with an arrow before his bodyguards were able to reform his wall of shielding.

"The general has been hit! Get him the hell out of here!" one of Vespasian's bodyguards yelled out.

Four men in the back of the tortoise dropped their shields and began carrying Vespasian back towards the castrum. Arrows continued to fly into the Roman formation, but the wall of shields protected the Romans from the incoming arrows.

After Vespasian had been escorted out of range from the Judean arrows, he cursed at his own bodyguards. "Get the hell off of me! I can walk!" Vespasian stood up slowly, inspected the arrow still sticking out of his foot, and ripped it out in one swift motion.

"Damn the gods!" Vespasian screamed at the pain caused by the arrow's removal.

Luckily for Vespasian, the arrow had not hit any major arteries, and though he was bloody, he was not in any danger of bleeding out.

"Where is he?" he said in a hot fury.

"Where is whom, my lord?" one of his bodyguards asked.

"The little shit that tripped over his own feet!"

When Vespasian used such foul language, it was time to back away from him as he would only be able to quench his wrath with blood.

"I am here, my lord," the guilty bodyguard said, presenting himself.

Vespasian reached for the hilt of his sword and walked up to the bodyguard as fast as his injured foot allowed. He drew his blade from his sheath and pierced the soldier's gut. A strike to a man's stomach was a cruel way to inflict death as the victim would not die immediately. First bile would spread throughout his abdomen, causing excruciating pain. Vespasian and all his men watching knew this.

The soldier fell down to his knees. Vespasian spit in his face and then kicked him in his testicles, knocking him on his rear. The bodyguard lay bleeding to death in the dirt, only his groans breaking the deafening silence of Vespasian's watching men.

*■ ■ ■*

## Vespasian is Shot!

**IT TOOK** two full days to complete several dozen bridges to cross the Jotapatan moat. On the twentieth day of the siege, the Roman wall-breachers began advancing again. At the sight of the breachers closing in, Joseph ordered the town's oil supply to be boiled immediately. Before the Roman breachers could reach the wall, large soup pots and buckets were filled with hot oil and distributed among the Jotapatan soldiers defending on the wall walk.

The breachers crossed the moat some twenty yards out from the city walls—they were almost within striking distance. When the wall-breachers were within ten yards of the wall, the Galilean defenders plastered them with a thick coat of scalding black oil, hitting both men and wooden structures. Then hand torches were tossed upon the greasy war engines—each tower erupted into an inferno of flames.

At the sight of the breachers burning and Vespasian's men retreating back into their fortress, a great cheer of victory rose among the Galileans. Joseph urged caution, knowing Vespasian was far from finished.

The Romans had been stymied. Their wall-breachers were all destroyed. The catapults had failed to break through the stone walls of the city. Despondent, Vespasian's army retreated into their castrum, and all hostilities stopped.

To lift his men's spirits, Vespasian ordered a taunting. He knew the Galileans were low on water, so he had his soldiers mock their situation by tossing countless barrels full of water into the dirt some couple of hundred yards out from the city walls at midday in full sight of every Jotapatan on the wall walk and in the watchtowers.

The Galileans, on Joseph's order, performed a retaliatory slight—they decided to do laundry. They washed their clothes and then hung the wet garments over the city walls in full sight of Vespasian and his army. It was effective, causing the Romans to become dejected. They now believed the Jotapatans had such a vast supply of water, it would outlast even their own, though that was hardly the case.

◾ ◾ ◾

**THE CELEBRATION** over halting the Romans' advance continued through the next day, though looking at Joseph, one would have thought the city had already fallen.

Joseph sat alone in the governor's mansion unable to think of much else besides his prophecy of the fall of the city on the forty-seventh day. He shut his eyes. A relentless voice in his head kept seducing him with thoughts of flight. His breathing relaxed. Finally he decided to make his case to the city residents—if and only if they would sanction his departure, he would flee Jotapata.

He gathered the residents to his governor's mansion to preach—"Jotapatans! Hear me. I believe it is in your best interest if I leave Jotapata for some undisclosed location. If I leave, Rome will show you less animosity for surely it is *me* they now seek. If I leave, their forces will be occupied with my capture and not your destruction."

Upon hearing this, the residents of Jotapata became furious, mad, depressed, and scared. They begged Joseph to stay and maintain their defense.

"We are doomed!" one resident cried.

"You will abandon us and run for your own hide?" another asked.

"Jotapatans, I have experienced a prophecy that this city will fall on the forty-seventh day. I have been told by God's prophet, Elijah. What would you have me do, knowing this city will be razed as surely as the sun rises?"

"It is true! We are doomed!" another citizen cried out.

"You would leave us here to die, Joseph?" another Jotapatan questioned furiously.

"You will not die if I leave right now. Surely the Romans care more about capturing and executing me than they do about commoners caught in a war," Joseph responded.

The people were not impressed, convinced Joseph wanted to save his own skin at their expense. Joseph began to see that he was destined to defend Jotapata to its ultimate end—total destruction.

"If you wish me to stay, I will fight with you until the last man standing. I am loyal to you above all things but God Almighty Himself!" Joseph yelled out across the city.

The residents were quiet, unsure what to make of the entire situation.

"Even if we cannot defeat these Roman bastards, we will surely kill so many it will be remembered for generations," Joseph exclaimed, full of passion.

Seeing the firm constitution of Joseph's resolve, the men of Jotapata began to fall into line, preparing themselves for the long fight to come.

"Then we will fight even if we all perish. All able-bodied men, gather before me!"

Joseph suddenly awoke.

"Ahh!" he screamed.

He had asked the city residents for permission to flee in his dreams. And even in Joseph's own dreams he was denied.

He sat up on his bed, his hands in his face, crying in ignorance of how to face the Roman force that appeared invincible.

As he sobbed quietly, he looked out his window. A shooting star came into his view and then hovered. It then slowly moved itself above the Roman-built fortress. As the star hovered, the Roman fort appeared to turn fiery red.

"I know what I have to do," Joseph said to himself and then alerted his officers.

"Assemble the men," Joseph said to Aaron. "We have work to do."

"Immediately, my lord," Aaron replied. "Companies, assemble. Governor Joseph demands your presence!"

Joseph nodded his appreciation to Aaron as the Jotapatans readied to hear him speak.

"We are going into the lion's den, and if you cannot stomach being brutally killed, go over and help the elders reinforce the city."

Joseph looked out and not even one man deserted his warrior camp.

"Excellent," Joseph said proudly at the full retention rate of his comrades. "This is our aim. By cover of darkness we will set fire to all munitions, food stocks, fortress works, and anything else in the Roman camp that burns. Gather all weapons, hand torches, lighting stones, and iron-striking blocks, and meet me here two hours before the dawn. Dismissed," Joseph yelled out.

The mass of men sought a good night's rest, but few could sleep. Adrenaline was pumping through every Jotapatan's veins who had volunteered to attack the Roman castrum.

The warriors began to assemble around Joseph a couple of hours before dawn. At approximately 4 a.m., Joseph gave the signal to the company commanders. Twenty-five hundred men, divided into five groups of five hundred, began to move covertly, in dark-colored garments that obscured them in the thick of night. The companies of Galileans hustled silently into the no man's land between the Jotapatan walls and the Roman fortress. They began to close in on the Roman fort. The Galileans looked like a mass of black snakes slowly slithering around an unsuspecting prey.

The Roman guards atop their fortress watchtowers were inattentive at this early hour. Some were sitting in chairs tilted back on the pegs with their feet up. Others were ensconced in petty conversations about unfaithful wives, desired lovers, and military gripes. Some were even asleep. The Romans, who were usually always prepared and alert, strangely did not suspect any Galilean plot. They believed if the Galileans were to attack, their movement would be easily seen, giving them enough time to alert their sleeping superiors and prepare a defense—at least, that was the Roman mindset. The Hebrews had not launched any assault on the Roman fortress during the siege, and a sneak attack on the fortress was not considered a threat, especially at four in the morning.

A few Roman patrols walked around the outside of the fort every fifteen minutes or so, but these guards were mostly looking for Roman deserters, and like the men in the watchtowers, they were not keenly alert.

The Jotapatans waited for the patrol's shift change, providing a window within which to attack. All the other patrols on duty were taken by surprise from behind—the Jotapatans slit their throats, preventing the patrols from crying out and informing the entire Roman force that they were under attack.

Those Jotapatans carrying oil began to dowse the wooden fort walls on all sides except the rear one. It took no more than a minute to toss hundreds of buckets and pots of oil on the front and side walls—the Jotapatans moved in unison. After they had covered the walls with oil, Companies One, Two, and Three pulled out their unlit hand torches and waited.

Aaron, leading the forward wall company, took a piece of flint and an iron striking block out of his burlap sack.

"Here we go," he thought to himself.

He struck the flint against the steel block, producing sparks, but the oil did not ignite. Again he struck the flint and again got only sparks, no fire. "Damn it!" he whispered to himself. Zachariah, a comrade Jotapatan, saw Aaron was having trouble. Being a blacksmith, he knew he could help.

Zachariah ran up to Aaron in a sprint.

"Here, strike the flint against my sawdust. I brought some just in case, knowing flint can be difficult," Zachariah said and reached into his sack, then held out a handful of dust in his hands for Aaron to light.

Aaron again struck the flint on the steel block, and the sawdust dust ignited. Zachariah allowed his hands to burn some, letting the fire build, and then pressed the burning dust against the oil. Fire raced across the oil slick on the fort wall. The other companies on the left and right sides of the fortress immediately followed Aaron's lead, having better luck igniting the oil than Aaron had had. Within moments, walls of flames ran across the entirety of the three oiled-up wooden fort walls.

"Fire! Fire!" a forward watchtower guard screamed out as loud as he could.

Next, the Roman trumpets were sounding the call-to-arms alarm. Men chaotically rose from their slumber to see three sides of their fortress on fire. There was no orderly assembly of the Roman soldiers—it was a mass panic.

Hundreds of Romans, seeing and feeling the flames from the fire, charged out the rear fort gate right into a thick wall of twenty-five hundred Jotapatans, all standing at the ready, swords in hand. The Romans had no chance, and every last one of them trying to flee was slain.

Five hundred Jotapatans, all bearing lit torches, breached the rear gate and spread their fire to all items capable of burning. Entire stocks of wheat and barley were set ablaze. The hay feed of the horses was lit. Tents were burned to the ground. The wooden staffs of spears and arrows were incinerated. Even wooden carts and chariots were torched.

The Jotapatans knocked over water barrels, preventing the Romans from having the opportunity to douse the fires spreading throughout the castrum. They even slew horses and oxen to deprive the Romans of their beasts.

Finally, the Roman army began to come together and forced the Jotapatans out the back of the fort through the same gate from which they came. But by the time the Romans had regained control, the Jotapatans had slipped through the blackness of night back to safety behind the Jotapatan walls.

The damage was done.

Two thousand Romans were dead. The entire Roman fort caught fire and was crumbling around many men that were still inside. The Jotapatans had also destroyed a month of provisions and military supplies of all sorts.

Returning to Jotapata, the Hebrews were in a grand cheer. They had accomplished their mission of burning the Roman fort to the ground. Their losses were fewer than a hundred men killed, another hundred captured, and two hundred wounded.

The sun began to light the morning sky, and the Jotapatans were still celebrating like it was a Shabbat feast. Wine was flowing everywhere. The last bites of good food like bread and cheese were passed around. Sheep and goats were slaughtered and put on the spit. Drunken Jotapatans mounted the wall walk, bending their bare asses between the merlons to taunt the Romans.

For the first time in a month there was no longer the dread of imminent death. There was actually an upbeat sense of victory close at hand. The Romans would now surely retreat; at least that was the prevailing thought. They were no longer protected by their fortress, and they were short on provisions, beasts, and even water.

Joseph stood tall on the wall walk, watching the flames consume the Roman castrum.

"Today is surely a great day," Aaron said to a stoic Joseph.

"Yes, but how long will it last?" Joseph countered.

"You could depress a man during his wedding night *and* his divorce party," Aaron replied.

"What of my prophecy? The city will fall on the forty-seventh day. This much I am sure of, my friend. You see why it is difficult for me to join in the celebration?" Joseph asked.

"I understand. But even if what you say comes to pass, there is no harm in enjoying tonight surely?" Aaron questioned back.

"I suppose I could be tempted to have a cup of wine."

"Here, my lord, have a bag!" Aaron cheerfully said, passing Joseph the hide filled with wine.

＊ ＊ ＊

**THERE WAS** no deterring Vespasian. After executing the sleeping and derelict guards before the entire army, he crucified the Jotapatans captured in the raid. Then Vespasian had his fortress rebuilt from the ground up—even importing wood from Damascus and armaments from Caesarea.

By the time the Romans had regrouped and reassembled in their remade castrum, forty-five days had passed since the start of the siege.

# Chapter 10:

# The 47ᵗʰ Day

**A JOTAPATAN** youth, starving and fearing the Roman onslaught that now appeared all but unstoppable, decided to flee the city. Caleb's father and mother had both been killed less than a month prior by the hellfire of Roman projectiles. His small hut had burned halfway to the ground, and the few animals that he owned had escaped his care during the chaos to be slaughtered and eaten by other starving Jotapatans.

Caleb now had almost nothing. No home, no family, and little sustenance. Shell shocked by the death of his family, he sought to flee Jotapata for the undesirable lands to the northeast which the Romans had shown little interest in attacking.

He lay in his cot awake all night long. He would make a run for it in the early hours of the morning while both the Jotapatans and the Romans mostly slept. There was no roof left to cover his burnt dwelling—he watched the stars moving overhead.

Learning the position of the stars was one of the commonly-taught skills—he knew that when Orion rose in the late summer sky, morning was near.

Caleb stood up from his cot. He packed the few items of any value he owned in a makeshift cloth sack: thirty feet of rope, a half-loaf of bread, a small piece of smoked goat jerky, and a half-full water bag.

Carrying the burlap sack on his back secured by a piece of

rope, Caleb looked around, searching for guards patrolling the silent streets. He moved towards the southeastern part of the city wall that was accessible due to the lack of Jotapatan guards stationed there. Caleb needed to climb up the wall first, and then he could scale some twenty-five feet down its outside.

Jotapatan guards stood at all the gates all the hours of the day with orders to kill all deserters on sight, and Caleb had no money to bribe them.

Caleb worked his feet to make as little noise as possible as he moved under the cover of darkness. He hid alongside buildings to shield himself from being seen as he moved towards his escape point.

A guard walked out of a side street just in front of Caleb—he was sure he would be caught. The guard was swaying back and forth noticeably, and he began singing a drinking song because he was drunk. Caleb had not been seen. Once the guard had passed, Caleb continued covertly through the streets.

The Jotapatan walls had been reinforced under Joseph's command, but the southeast section had been somewhat overlooked as it was semi-protected by the foot of Mount Jotapata. The inside wall, or city-facing side, was made in haste and not smoothed like the outside face had been. It was important to create an unclimbable barrier, thus the outside wall which faced the Romans was smoothed to stop the opposing force from being able to scale it freely—the inside portion of the wall was bumpy, not having been given the same care.

Caleb began to climb. There were plenty of natural hand and footholds. It took him no more than two minutes to climb to the wall walk. He took the rope out of his sack. He tied one end around a stone merlon on top of the parapet and then dropped the rope down over the outside section of the wall. The rope did not reach the ground but was only about four feet short—an acceptable distance for a jump down to the dirt. He rappeled much slower than he had climbed for he had no hand or foot supports, only the smooth outer wall surface to bounce his feet upon as he descended.

Caleb made it to the bottom of the rope and leaped. He rolled as he hit the ground to prevent breaking his bones.

Still on his hands and knees, he looked out towards the Roman camp. All was still and silent. Caleb began to move to the southeast around the left flank of the Roman fortress.

He was jogging with his head lowered. There was no moon and even the bright desert stars did not illuminate the ground. He would not be able to make out a figure even if it was only a few dozen yards in front of him.

Caleb reached the first dune, beyond which he would almost assuredly be safe from discovery. He rose over the dune, tripping on a rock he could not see in the darkness. He fell face down into the sand. He looked up, his face covered in silicon granules.

Four Romans stood over him. The patrols were looking for Roman deserters and Hebrew spies. All four drew their swords.

Caleb slowly raised his hands and gave himself up.

Vespasian had let it be known that he wanted to personally interrogate all Jotapatan spies captured—the four Roman soldiers led Caleb, his arms now chained, directly to Vespasian's tent.

"General. We caught this Hebrew," one of the soldiers said, presenting Caleb to Vespasian. "He was found by the southeast side of the city wall—we only find spies there, my lord."

"Excellent. Bind him to the post," Vespasian ordered, and the soldiers obliged.

"Raise up your hands, Jotapatan!" one of the Romans said as he tied Caleb to the wooden beam securely so he was in a completely helpless position.

Vespasian began his inquiry with "Do you know who I am, son?"

Caleb nodded his head affirmatively, petrified of what was to become of him.

"Good," Vespasian continued. "You are in a unique position. If you tell me what I need to know, I will permit you to walk out of this tent unscathed. I will even put food in your belly. Do you understand me?" Vespasian asked.

Again, Caleb nodded his head.

"Good. I need to know the condition of the city. How many men remain able to fight? Are the water supplies exhausted? What are the residents and soldiers doing for food? How is their spirit? Does Joseph fight with determination or does he defend with despair?"

"Water, please, my lord," Caleb quietly asked.

"Get the boy some water," Vespasian ordered.

A Roman soldier handed Caleb a cup, and he chugged the entire contents in one motion.

"Now that your tongue is quenched, put it to good use," Vespasian demanded.

"Yes, my lord. The city has all but fallen from the inside. The men do not see a way to prevail in the contest. Water supplies are very low, nearly exhausted, and men are only allowed to drink from the cistern twice a day—in small quantities at that. The food supplies are also almost spent. All the livestock has been butchered. Women and children spend their time catching rats for meat. The men still able to bear arms would all desert, but Joseph has guards posted at every gate with orders to slay all deserters on sight. I was able to escape by scaling the lowest and least-guarded part of the wall," Caleb explained.

"You fled by the southeast wall?" Vespasian curiously asked.

"Yes, my lord," Caleb answered.

"How does the strength of the wall fare?"

"The southeast wall is full of fissures and has all but collapsed," Caleb replied.

Vespasian, hearing this news, looked over to his engineers, inquiring to the veracity of Caleb's statement merely by raising his eyebrows. The engineers meekly shook their heads and shoulders in ignorance.

"What hour do the soldiers rise?" Vespasian queried.

"The men begin to rise an hour before first light," Caleb answered. Vespasian's mind was in deep contemplation with every detail of Jotapatan intelligence Caleb provided.

"I am certain that if you attempt to breach the wall in the early morning, you will capture the city," Caleb said, unsolicited.

Vespasian had heard everything he needed to know.

"Well done, boy," Vespasian said. "Tribune—take good care of this Galilean," Vespasian commanded, slightly nodding his head.

"Hail, Caesar!" The tribune saluted with a fiendish smile.

A soldier cut the rope securing Caleb to the wooden beam and also removed the chains around his wrists. Two other Romans escorted Caleb out of Vespasian's tent. Following behind was the tribune.

"Feed him first," the tribune said to the soldiers guarding Caleb.

Caleb followed the two Roman guards to the mess tent. He stood in the serving line and was encouraged to eat as much as his stomach could keep down.

He sat in the middle of a long dining table, overjoyed to see beef, bread, and even a jug of wine before him. Caleb looked as though he had been delivered. He assured himself that the Romans were decent people and not interested in anything more than their rightfully renewed dominion over the Holy Land.

He moaned with pleasure as he stuffed the best food he had eaten in months down his throat at a breakneck pace. A Roman soldier was even thoughtful enough to fix Caleb a second serving, seeing how he had finished his first helping so quickly.

"General Vespasian truly appreciated the information you provided him," one of the Roman guards complimented Caleb, a big, unmissable grin on the guard's face.

"It was my pleasure." Caleb smiled back at the guard as he continued to plow through his food.

He was soon finished with his second plate.

"Feel better?" the other Roman guard inquired.

"I feel fantastic," Caleb sincerely admitted.

"We're so happy to hear that."

Then the Roman guard sitting to Caleb's left side swiftly pulled out his dagger and slammed it down into Caleb's left hand, pinning him to the wood table.

The Roman on the right side of Caleb grabbed Caleb's right hand, forcing it out flat onto the table, and also impaled Caleb through his hand into the wood.

Caleb sat wailing, crying, screaming, and convulsing. Both his hands were bleeding, a dagger sticking into each—the Romans divulged their true intent to Caleb's face.

"All spies are executed. We're sorry, Hebrew—general's orders, you understand," one of the guards explained. "Go get the cross," he ordered the other guard.

"I'm not a spy!" Caleb shouted.

The Roman struck him in the face with a baton.

"Speak again, and I'll shove this stick up your ass!" the Roman soldier threatened Caleb.

The other soldier began speaking. "We need you to scream and cry for as long as possible, but only once on the cross. It should have the proper effect on your fellow Jotapatan Hebrews—you understand. And after the meal you just ate, you'll last a good four, maybe five days on the cross before you give up the ghost. I think it harsh, but when you consider the lives that might be saved should your suffering cause the rest of the Hebrews to surrender, well, I'd say it'd all be worth it. Wouldn't you?"

"What the hell are you talking about? Let me go, you pagan bastards! I did my duty! Get General Vespasian!" Caleb yelled.

His voice was heard but only responded to with hearty laughter and punches to his gut and back via iron baton.

"Shut your mouth until you're on the cross, you Galilean garbage!" the Roman that had hit Caleb shouted, threatening to extend Caleb another beating by waving his baton.

Caleb was affixed to a wooden cross, and four other captured Jotapatan deserters were made to carry and erect it with him facing the walls of Jotapata as a message to the residents. "Surrender or Join Me" was painted on a large plank of wood in Aramaic and nailed on the cross above Caleb's head.

Symmetrical lines of hundreds of vertical wood beams littered the road. The view from the highway into Jotapata had become a graveyard with all the crosses standing straight up and thoughtfully arranged with mathematical precision, courtesy of the Romans.

Caleb was now just another Hebrew victim on a cross in a sea of many. Of those still alive, some cried, some begged God for forgiveness, some were silent, but everyone bled.

*  *  *

**"SUMMON TITUS,"** Vespasian ordered one of his junior staff officers.

Titus, newly promoted to general, soon appeared at the entrance to Vespasian's tent. "You called for me, my lord," Titus said to his father.

"Yes, I did. Everyone out!" Vespasian shouted to the assorted officers and servants in his tent.

"I just finished interrogating a spy. He told me of a situation in the city much more dire than any of us were led to believe. The boy said the Jotapatans are almost out of water and are rationing the men to two small cups a day. Dehydration will have set in by now if this is true. No man can fight on two cups of water a day. They are also starving. All the animals have long been slaughtered, and they now are reduced to eating rats."

"Gods," Titus said. "I would desert too if the best meal I could find was a rat."

"There is more," Vespasian continued. "The boy claimed the southeasternmost part of the wall is close to failing."

Vespasian pointed to the location on a crude map of the city set up on his main war table.

"This spot, where the wall ends and the mountain begins, is supposedly close to breaking. I want you to send an engineer under cover of darkness to assess its integrity. Can it be razed by projectiles? Or must it be scaled?"

"I understand, Father. I will commission a scout for this coming night," Titus replied.

"There are still two hours of darkness. Send the engineer now," Vespasian commanded.

"I will see to it this moment," Titus stated.

"Son," Vespasian continued, "if the engineer reports the wall is indeed susceptible, we will ready the men for a full attack early tomorrow morning. Now off with you."

Titus gave a Roman salute and left. He enlisted the chief engineer to scout the southeast wall.

The report came back in.

"What say you?" Titus asked the engineer.

"It is in a perilous condition. There are cracks on the wall face indicative of weakened stones. I would surmise it would take no more than a few direct hits to break through. It looks as though the wall was almost torn down by the initial catapult assault and now stands despite itself."

"Good. Very good," Titus replied.

The sun was beginning to rise, and the Romans began moving about the day's duties. Titus marched to Vespasian's tent. Vespasian sat on a chair by his war table, engrossed in thought.

"Father, the report has come back. The wall is weak. It seems to have been greatly damaged by the catapults and is ready to crumble with another assault."

"That is good news, son. Today is the forty-sixth day since the siege began and I tire of this desert. I wish to finish our business here post-haste and retire temporarily to Caesarea for some fresh and cool sea air," Vespasian responded.

"I echo your sentiments, Father. The men need rest. Good food, wine, and women always help morale," Titus said.

"Don't I know it. Alas, there is still hard work to be done. Ready the men. Today will be spent collecting every last stone we can find. Move all the catapults back to the front of the fort. This will fool the Jotapatans into thinking we are retreating. Later in the night, we will move the catapults into position to strike the southeast wall. Two hours before dawn and before we send hellfire from the catapults, I want the Third, Fifth, and Tenth Legions stationed at the ready here," Vespasian said, pointing at the map, moving the legion figurines around the southeastern section of the Jotapatan wall.

"The catapults will fire over the heads of the men waiting a hundred yards out from the wall. With every last catapult aimed at this section, the wall should crumble within minutes if what your engineer says is true. If we are fortunate, we will be able to breach the city before the Hebrews are able to assemble into effective defensive positions," Vespasian explained.

"I recommend an additional tactic," Titus interjected. "Place the Ninth Legion at the opposite side of the city, here," he said, moving the Ninth Legion's figurine in front of northwest gate on the map. "When the wall is breached, the fastest Roman company will fight towards the northwestern gate and open it from the city side, allowing the Ninth to flank the Hebrews defending in the southeast."

"You have mastered the art of war, my son. One day soon you will lead Rome's armies in my place. Of this much I am sure—brief all the tribunes."

Titus gave a salute and moved towards the morning briefing of tribunes to begin the preparations for the frontal assault.

Twenty thousand men were soon off in all parts of the desert, miles away from the Roman fortress, collecting all the hurling stones they could find.

Carts drawn by oxen and horses could be seen hauling boulders from every direction. A pile of stones soon became a field. Most of the projectiles were between fifty and seventy-five pounds, but some were as heavy as one hundred or slightly more.

At four in the afternoon a company of clarions blasted out, summoning the Romans to return to the fort. They had amassed a thousand projectiles, covertly placing them behind their fortress—out of sight of the Jotapatan watchtower guards.

The clarions blasted again an hour later, this time in a strange, somber beat that the Jotapatans had never before heard. Then the catapults began moving. The one hundred catapults that once surrounded the entirety of the city walls all now slowly retreated from their positions.

The Jotapatan guards on the wall walks could see the catapults withdrawing back to the Roman fort, but they had no idea what to make of it.

"What in God's name are they doing?" one guard on the wall said.

"They're retreating!" another Jotapatan soldier cried out.

A few cheers of "Victory" rang out.

Joseph urged caution.

He had observed the activity and was convinced that Rome was readying for a final assault, but he could not glean from when or where it might come.

The poor morale of the residents was only outdone by that of the soldiers. There was little left of the city. Some officers beseeched Joseph to burn what remained of it, denying the Romans anything of value. Others advised Joseph to fill the moat with the city's remaining oil, and then flee behind a wall of flames.

Joseph climbed up a ladder to the wall walk to address the apprehensive soldiers looking for leadership.

"My Hebrew brothers!" he began. "I ask you—would you stand and fight or would you run, only to be hunted down by the Roman cavalry and slain like cowardly dogs?"

"We fight to the last man!" one young soldier yelled out. A muted cheer rang out from the mass of soldiers.

Joseph could sense the exhaustion, but he still believed the majority of the Jotapatan men preferred to die fighting rather than be slaughtered running.

"I will stay here and defend the city until the Romans desist or I am killed," Joseph said. "The Romans look to firebomb the city once more and launch a frontal assault with their infantry. We are Hebrews, we are the chosen people! Whether this city falls today or a thousand years from now, you will see the Kingdom of Heaven, for our covenant with the Lord of Hosts can never be broken by Roman swords or stones! Get to the defenses!"

The morale of the soldiers was lifted, but the scales of tiredness, thirst, and hunger still weighed heavier. The men began to move about in preparation for a Roman frontal assault. The remainder of the oil stocks were poured into the moat, forming a black semicircle around the city from the northwest gate to the southeast gate. Men were busy sharpening their swords and daggers. Caltrops, those nasty multi-spiked metal barbs, were dropped all around the outside of the city walls to impede both foot soldiers and cavalry advances.

The constant business of the city preparations kept the fear of the Romans at bay mostly, but every now and then a Jotapatan resident could be heard shrieking with uncontrollable terror. Hearing someone become hysterical caused the soldiers' hearts to sink as they were instantly reminded of the direness of their situation.

The sun had begun to set. Joseph, standing on the wall walk, saw the stillness of the Roman force.

"All we can do is wait," he thought.

It was now dark, in the first hours of the night. Joseph's eyes stayed alert, watching the Romans, anticipating a strike.

Hours passed and nothing happened.

"Joseph," Aaron said, "get some rest. They are not up to anything, I tell you. The entire camp looks asleep. There has been no movement or sound for many hours now."

"There is nothing I would like to do more than rest for a while, but I can feel the Romans are up to something. Also, we are now entering the forty-seventh day," Joseph explained.

"Do you really believe that prophecy?" Aaron asked.

"A prophet came to me in Jerusalem, showing me the outcome of this fight," Joseph answered with conviction.

"How did you know he was a prophet?" Aaron further inquired.

"For one, he told me he was a prophet, and after he showed me what is to be, he disappeared into thin air and was replaced by a white dove. It was a sign from God. I know it in my bones," Joseph said adamantly.

"Well, I for one would prefer the prophecy to fail. I rather like being alive, and if we can stymie the Romans a few more weeks, they may halt their attack," Aaron opined.

"The Romans are like a great rogue ocean wave: once it is in motion, it cannot be stopped until it brings destruction, deluging down upon its desired destination," Joseph responded. "How many hours to daylight, Aaron?"

"About two, maybe a bit more," Aaron replied.

"Maybe they aren't looking to attack," Joseph said. "I think I will close my eyes for a bit."

Joseph's eyes wandered out to the Roman fortress—he saw movement.

The Romans, under cover of darkness, were busy moving the full fleet of their catapults into position for an overwhelming strike on the southeast wall.

"There! Do you see?" Joseph said as he pointed to the motion. "The catapults are on the move. Do you see it, Aaron?" he asked again.

"Yes, I see it. They are moving all the catapults to the southeast side of the city wall," Aaron responded. "What is your order, my lord?"

"Wake the men and send the women and children up to the mountain landing," Joseph ordered.

"I'm on it this moment!" Aaron said, climbing down from the wall walk.

A stone exploded above the southeast gate. The gate held, but large cracks formed in the already-fissured stone wall.

It was still dark, but the beginnings of morning light began to creep onward. The Third, Fifth, and Tenth Legions were on their stomachs a hundred yards out from the city wall, covered from view behind a five-foot dune.

A fury of spectacular explosions shook the city. All one hundred catapults were now raining down stones simultaneously. The stones were not lit aflame so as to keep the light to a minimum—the Romans used every advantage to conceal their frontal assault, protecting the soldiers lying in wait from being discovered.

The catapults continued their onslaught. The Romans had divided the projectile stones into three groups by weight class. The largest stones were assigned to the catapults closest to the wall, about two hundred yards out. The medium-size stones were hurled from some fifty yards behind the largest stones. The smallest stones were hurled from yet another fifty yards behind the medium stones. In this staggered alignment, all the projectiles seemed to meet their target destination.

The largest stones hit the southeast wall at a rate of almost ten a minute—large fissures began to form. The smaller stones furthered the damage done by the larger ones in an almost choreographed fashion.

Within five minutes of the beginning of the assault, the top of the southeastern parapet had been blown off. A crater emerged at the top of the wall and grew with each impacting projectile.

As the residents awoke due to the terrifying early morning bombing, word spread as fast as sound waves that the southeast wall was failing. Men, women, and children, running about in a total panic through the streets, looked like rats racing around on a burning and sinking ship.

The Jotapatan soldiers sprinted to the southeast section of the wall to reinforce it. There were too few soldiers, and the wall was crumbling too fast—not to mention that the sky was still pitch black.

It was no use.

Another set of large stones came flying into the southeast wall. They hit the wall precisely in its weak spot, one after another. Then the sound of a great rumble arose for every Roman and Jotapatan to hear.

A ten-foot-wide section of the wall came crashing down to the ground.

"The wall has collapsed! We are surely dead!" one Jotapatan soldier yelled out. The sound of the wall crumbling was replaced by a clamor of harrowing screams.

A single arrow with its head on fire flew into the early-morning sky. It was the sign for the Roman legions to begin their foot assault. Eighteen thousand men rose to their feet and began a full sprint towards the gap in the wall. As the Romans ran towards the breach, they bellowed out their war cry. Joseph silently trembled at the sight and sound of the Roman army advancing at full speed.

"Ignite the moat! Ignite the moat!" Joseph shouted, seeing the Roman legions quickly advancing towards the breach in the wall.

Captain Jeremiah, standing on the wall walk within earshot of Joseph, grabbed three arrows. He dipped the arrows in oil and then set them on fire with a hand torch. He took his bow from around his back and aimed the first arrow for the moat. The oil ring was no more than a few inches deep and a couple of feet wide. Jeremiah released his fiery arrow—he missed, short by less than three feet.

"Damn!" he cursed. "Help me find the oil in this blackness, Lord."

The Roman legions were less than twenty yards out. A lit moat would not do the Jotapatans a bit of good if the Romans were first able to penetrate its defensive line. The captain fired a second arrow. It overshot his target by less than a foot.

The Romans were now within five yards of the moat.

Jeremiah took a deep breath, closed his eyes, and asked God silently this time for deliverance. The vanguard of the Roman legions was now beginning to ford the moat, splashing oil about with the advance of their feet.

Captain Jeremiah released his third arrow. It hit one of the Romans leading the vanguard while he was trudging through the oil, directly in the chest. After a few seconds, he fell over dead and the flaming arrow ignited the oil-filled moat. A great wall of flames grew exponentially from where the arrow lit the oil, spreading out in all directions. Within a few seconds, the entire moat was ablaze, illuminating the night sky.

The advance of the Romans had once again been halted. But this time Vespasian was prepared. He had seen the black trail of oil lining the moat a day earlier. Seeing the oil lit on fire, he ordered the advance of a company of a thousand engineers, all standing by with bucket upon bucket of sand. The engineers stood at the edge of the moat tossing thousands of buckets' worth of sand over the oil. Within fifteen minutes, enough of the moat had been filled to put out a section of the fire large enough to accommodate ground passage by the Roman legions.

"Get your ass through the flames! Move, move!" Titus could be heard yelling at his foot soldiers.

Less than half an hour had passed since the start of the bombardment. Three Roman legions could be seen moving through the accessible bottleneck bridge of sand across the moat, bordered by a wall of flames on both sides.

Five thousand Jotapatan soldiers assembled behind the ten-foot-wide break in the wall. The Jotapatans had a slightly preferable fighting position—the very bottom few feet of the wall still stood, giving them a small height advantage against the Roman frontal assault.

# The Siege of Jotapata

The Jotapatans waited behind the collapsed wall as Romans roared forth with their swords and spears raised high.

A hint of daybreak began to peek out from the horizon while Joseph stood in the middle of his soldiers.

"Fight, men! Fight! God is watching!" Joseph yelled out as the first wave of Roman soldiers came crashing into the Jotapatan line.

The Galileans threw heavy pieces of the crumbled stone wall down on the Romans. Countless Romans died from blunt-force trauma injuries to the head and internal organs. This caused the fighting to elevate—the bodies of the dead lined the entirety of the ground. Roman soldiers trying to get at the Hebrews now stood upon two or three layers of their own comrades' corpses, crushed on top of each other.

The Romans used the bodies as a ramp and climbed and trod upon their dead brothers-in-arms to get within a sword's strike of the Galileans' throats—the fight continued like this for five hours. Three times as many Romans fell as Jotapatans.

In the end, almost all the Jotapatan soldiers lay slain. Fewer than two hundred soldiers were still capable of bearing arms against the Romans. The battle momentarily paused as the Romans regrouped for yet another forward assault.

▪ ▪ ▪

JOHN OF Gischala and his band of men were still rotting in the Jotapatan city jail. They heard the Roman bombardment and fighting in the distance. John and his men were all standing up against the jail cell bars, screaming at the jailor to set them free.

"We are Hebrews!" John shouted. "Would you leave us here to be slaughtered like sheep?"

"My lord Joseph wouldn't shed a tear at that," the jailor answered.

"Set us free and we will defend the city to the death!" John pleaded.

"I'm sure you would, you fat bastard. You'd probably kill me for my sandals the moment I let you out," the jailor replied flippantly.

"You are a fit young man. Come join my following and I will make you richer than you've ever imagined possible in your grandest dreams," John said, now trying to bribe the guard.

"Will you shut your trap?" the jailor retorted. "There is no way you are getting out of that cage until my lord Joseph comes and lets you out personally."

John was frustrated, unable to present a convincing enough argument to secure his release—then he thought of something even more wicked, as was his nature.

"My friend, here. Take my pendant," John said, presenting his gold pendant of the Ark of the Covenant to the jailor. "I have no more use for it. Would you see it returned to my family once I am slain by the Romans, if you manage to survive of course?"

The jailor did not think much of it, and it seemed an honorable request, so he walked over to the jail cell bars and put his hand out. John stretched out his hand, holding the pendant. But before he placed the piece in the jailor's hand, John dropped it to the floor.

"Apologies," John said.

The jailor bent down to pick it up, and John grabbed hold of his head through the cell bars. Two of John's men also quickly grabbed the guard's arms, each man standing on opposite sides of John. Then all three began violently pounding the jailor's head into the iron jail cell bars, again and again, until he fell to the floor unconscious.

John grabbed the jailor's limp arms and pulled his body close to the bars so he could reach the jail-cell key on the jailor's waist.

He stretched out his arm, grabbed the key, and pulled it off the jailor. He inserted the key into the lock and twisted it.

John and his bandits were sprung.

They quickly filed out of the jail cell, but not before Sadius said goodbye to the jailor.

"Goodbye, jailor," Sadius said and stomped on the unconscious jailor's head, crushing it like an eggshell.

John joined in the fun by spitting on the now-dead jailor and retrieving his pendant. John also took the jailor's sandals, putting them on his own bare feet.

"Nice fit," John said to himself at his new foot apparel. "You deserve worse, jailor," John taunted the corpse. "Come, men, we ride to Jerusalem! Take every weapon and anything else of value you can carry on your backs—follow me!"

John's men took swords, daggers, and even the dead jailor's coin purse before sneakily leaving the Jotapatan jail. They stole horses and camels, did a bit of opportune raiding, and then fled the city from the northwest gate, unnoticed by the Jotapatans during the great panic of the Roman assault. They left mere minutes before the Ninth Legion descended on the city at the very gate John had escaped from.

*␣␣*␣␣*

**THE SUMMER** sun rose high in the sky, beating down on everyone. Hundreds of Roman slaves rushed to distribute water among the regrouping troops.

The Jotapatans were now without water—the city cistern was empty. Many soldiers had passed out from dehydration and exhaustion.

"Joseph. You must flee now!" Aaron argued frantically.

"I told the men I would fight with them to the death," Joseph responded.

"Damn you, Joseph! You are no good to anyone dead. Now get away from here or I will slay you where you stand!" Aaron shouted. "Leave from the northwest gate and don't stop until your steed is dead!"

Joseph, in a moment of weakness he would come to regret the rest of his life, ran to his horse, mounted it, and raced to the northwest gate. It was the last time he would ever see Aaron alive.

He safely reached the northwest gate. The Galilean soldiers posted there had deserted, and the gate stood locked, closed from the inside.

Joseph jumped down from his horse to open the gate doors. He heaved the securing beam up from its resting position and tossed it to the ground. The doors were incredibly heavy—Joseph groaned as he swung one of them open, using the full strength of his back. He hopped back up on his horse and furiously kicked it in the side, exiting the city as fast as his beast would take him.

Only a few dozen yards outside the gate, Joseph's horse came to a halt as he lowered the reins.

The entire Ninth Legion stood before him, advancing over a dune they had been cloaked behind. There could not have been more than fifty yards separating Joseph from the front column of Romans.

An archer fired an arrow at Joseph. It hit his horse in the eye, dropping it dead and sending Joseph tumbling into the sand. His sword flew off his side, towards the Romans advancing.

The front line of Romans began to move at an increasing pace towards Joseph, now lying face down on the ground by his dead beast. Joseph started to go after his sword but quickly realized it would mean his capture, so he turned around for the city gate and retreated in a full sprint. Reaching the still-open gate only a dozen seconds before Roman soldiers behind him, Joseph used his back again to shut the heavy gate door.

Then Joseph went for the securing wood beam. It took all his strength, and for a moment he thought he would not be able to lift the beam high enough, but somehow he was able to secure the gate. Joseph fell on his bottom from the great exertion of lifting the locking beam. The Romans came crashing into the closed gate just an instant after the beam fell locked into place.

Joseph sat for a moment, his back against the gate door, knowing he was safe.

# Chapter 11:

# The Cave

**JOSEPH CAUGHT** his breath and, after hearing many curses and threats of death from the Romans outside the gate, rose to his feet.

Directly in his line of sight was a young woman standing in the doorway of a hut, wearing a plain white gown. She was motioning her hand for him to come to her. Joseph made haste to see about the woman's call.

"My dear, I fear the end has come—there is no one left to fight and nowhere left to run," he said.

"My lord, follow me up the mountain path. I know of a cave invisible to the eye and unfindable to those that do not know it exists. My family and many others are hiding there now," she said.

"The Romans will go up the mountain to find me. It is no use," Joseph replied.

"Yes, the Romans will go up the mountain, no doubt, but they will only find those on the mountain landing. The cave can conceal you for years if need be. There is even a trickle of mountain water that runs through the rock cracks, providing enough sustenance for forty people daily," she said convincingly.

Joseph looked back towards the northwestern gate—the Romans had set it on fire. With no one and no water to extinguish the flames, it was a matter of minutes before the gate would turn to ash and become passable. Joseph grabbed the young woman's hand and said: "Lead me."

The two began the journey up the mountain path. They disappeared behind wild brush—no Romans were in pursuit of them.

"Tell me your name," Joseph said.

"I'm Rachel," she replied.

"I'm surprised we haven't met," Joseph said. "I couldn't forget someone with such youthful beauty as yourself."

"You are too kind, my lord," Rachel stated, a slight blush coming over her face. "Alas, this is no time or place for platitudes surely."

"Yes, of course," Joseph agreed. "Tell me, what were you doing all alone in the city?"

"I had to go back for something very special to my father," Rachel said.

Joseph expected Rachel to disclose whatever was so special, but she remained silent.

They continued walking up the mountainside for nearly an hour—Joseph became impatient.

"Where is this cave?" Joseph asked, stopping to rest.

"As I said, it is hidden. When we reach the foot of the mountain it is a fifty-foot climb up a rock wall. Then we spiral to the left of the rock face. When we climb up to the left side of the rock, the fifty-foot drop quickly becomes a three-hundred-foot fall. So, you know, be careful."

"Sound advice," Joseph concurred.

After a few more minutes of moving through the brush, Rachel said, "We're almost there."

They came across a set of natural mountain rocks that formed a skull-like face.

"You see the skull face?" Rachel said, then placed her feet in the face's eyes and began to scale the rock. "Now stick your feet into its eyes and start climbing up. I'll lead you all the way. Take your time and be careful; there are but few places to put your hands and feet. If you fall, well—don't fall."

"More good advice," Joseph said as he began to climb the rock face behind Rachel.

"You are doing well at this," Rachel encouraged him.

Just as she spoke, Joseph's left foot slipped, and he fell down vertically two full feet before luckily catching a ledge with his hands. Joseph closed his eyes, took a deep breath, and thanked God for keeping him from falling to his death.

"I said be *careful*," Rachel reminded him, her eyes wide and incredulous.

"I'm trying."

"Try harder," Rachel chided.

Joseph continued his upward ascent.

"We're not far now," Rachel said.

"Good," Joseph replied.

Rachel shifted her climb to the left side of the rock wall. Joseph followed, with his eyes keenly planted on the rock ledge to avoid falling again.

Joseph saw Rachel's confidence and was inspired. He returned his focus to climbing. He took a few more steps up.

"This isn't so bad, Rachel," he said.

There was no response.

When Joseph looked back up for Rachel, she had vanished.

Joseph looked down, fearing she might have fallen, but he did not see her body below. His next thought was that she must have climbed out of sight. Joseph took another few steps up the rock face and suddenly two hands grabbed him and pulled him into the cave.

"Ahh!" Joseph screamed at the unexpected snatching, and he fell to the ground as he was pulled inside.

"Welcome to the cave, Governor Joseph," Rachel said, standing over him.

Thirty-nine other Jotapatans stood behind Rachel—all looking at Joseph.

They were mostly women, children, and elders—people incapable of defending themselves.

"Lord Governor!" Rachel's father, an elder Jotapatan, exclaimed. "You live! Surely this is good news!"

"The city is overrun and burning to the ground!" Joseph said scornfully, rising to his feet. "Helpless women and children are being slain. All my soldiers are dead or captured. There is surely no good news!"

"Forgive me, my lord. We have been here for several days and knew not the severity of the situation," the elder stated.

"Now you know," Joseph said curtly. "I starve and I thirst. It has been two days since my last meal and half a day since my last drink. Is there food and water?"

A young child no more than half his height walked up to Joseph with bread and water. Joseph ate unashamedly like a rabid animal and gulped the entire cool drink in one motion. "Thank you, child," he said and patted the young boy on the head.

"Old man, do you lead these people?" Joseph asked.

"I did—now you lead them," he replied.

"What is your name?" Joseph questioned.

"Saul."

"Saul, tell me what the conditions are here? Do you have water? Do you have food?" Joseph inquired.

"We have as much water as you can drink. Follow me," Saul said and led Joseph to the sound of droplets hitting the cave floor.

"Water trapped in the mountain flows out here," Saul explained. "It may not look like much, but you only need to hold up a saucer for a minute to collect a refreshing swallow."

"This is good," Joseph said. "And your food stock?"

"You just ate the last crumb we had," Saul responded.

Joseph knew sooner rather than later someone would need to leave the cave and find food—that meant trouble.

"Well, I suppose we don't have to worry about rationing," Joseph said sardonically. "And arms? Does anyone have a sword? I lost mine in the chaos when my horse fell."

"There are no swords, my lord, but we do have a spear," Saul replied and motioned to one of the other elders to produce the weapon.

"This spear is broken in half, with no more than four feet of shaft remaining," Joseph griped.

"It was all anyone was able to bring, Lord Governor," said Saul, ashamed.

"It will have to do," Joseph responded. "I suppose it could defend against those trying to climb their way into the cave."

Suddenly a wave of exhaustion washed over Joseph, and he would have collapsed but for Saul steadying him upright.

"You need sleep, my lord. Here—take my cot. I do not need it for I am wide awake and rested. It is nothing more than a few sheets atop some dried weeds, but it beats lying on the rock floor," Saul offered.

"I thank you, Saul," Joseph said, and then he lay down on the cot—he drifted off into a deep sleep in less than five minutes.

Joseph slept sixteen hours straight, arising the morning of the following day.

"How long have I been asleep?" he asked the young boy sitting next to him who had been watching him sleep—it was the same boy that had given up the last piece of bread.

"Over half a day, my lord. It is now morning," the boy answered.

Joseph unconsciously leapt to his feet at the news but then realized there was little more he could do awake than asleep in his present situation.

"Here," the boy said and gave Joseph a cup of water.

Joseph gave the boy a nod of recognition and drank.

Saul, seeing that Joseph had awoken, came walking over to him.

"I trust you are well rested, Lord Governor," Saul said.

"That I am," Joseph replied. "Is there any news I should know of?" he asked.

"One of my scouts climbed down and around the mountain to look over the city. Smoke fills the air from the destruction. Bodies can be seen everywhere. The only motion seen was from the Romans. They have already sent a large force up the mountain trail to the landing in pursuit of those taking refuge there. Of course, they want you most. We are cut off from the world now, without food and without hope. Please give us hope, my lord." Saul beckoned.

"Hope? There is no hope! You yourself said it. We are cut off and starving. If we leave the cave in search of food, we are sure to be seen, captured, and slaughtered. If we stay hidden, we slowly starve to death. God foretold through his prophet the destruction of this city, and it is so. We are meant to die!" Joseph said angrily to Saul.

Hearing this, the young boy that had given Joseph food and water began to cry hysterically.

"Doesn't this child have a mother to suckle?" Joseph asked cruelly.

"Both his parents were killed in the firebombing," Saul responded.

Joseph took a deep breath, realizing how much he had hurt the child with his words. He leaned down to the boy and whispered into his ear, "I will do whatever I can to see us out of this situation."

The boy locked onto Joseph with his arms and legs, and the two stood holding each other tight for a long moment before parting.

"There seems no way around it. We must find food," Joseph said to the mass of survivors. "We will draw lots. Ten of us will go out daily to gather spring onions, berries, and anything else that can be consumed. This will be a dangerous mission as there is only so much mountain you can forage without being discovered by the Romans. There are forty able adults present and one child who is incapable of performing the task."

"Adults, split into pairs. Those to the left side, gather a small stone. Place it in one of your palms behind your back. Those to the right side, pick the hand of your partner that you believe contains the stone. If your selection is correct, move to the back of the cave. If your selection is false, move forward."

"What about you, Joseph?" a commoner asked. "Won't you risk getting food, or are you better than the rest of us?"

"I will pick a stone and take my chances like the rest of you," Joseph declared, quickly quashing all dissension among the forty.

The forty Jotapatans did as Joseph bid, and twenty were now standing towards the front of the cave and twenty in the back. Joseph had the Jotapatans repeat this process again—ten people were chosen to gather food for the rest. Mostly women were selected to scavenge. Rachel was one of them—Joseph was not.

"Now listen here. If you are captured by the Romans, they will execute you. They may torture you for information on my position. If you give me up, you will be giving up everyone in the cave. If you are caught, you must trust in God and not open your mouth, or we will all be killed and this entire effort will have been in vain," Joseph explained.

All of the Jotapatans nodded their heads in understanding.

"Those chosen—you will wait until dawn to further conceal yourselves. At that hour there is just enough light to see the vegetation. Fabricate a satchel from whatever clothes you can spare without causing indecency. Drink your fill of water before you go. And most importantly, say a silent prayer to God for salvation," Joseph exhorted.

"Father, I will only be gone a few hours," Rachel said to Saul, who was terrified at the thought of his only remaining daughter being taken by the Romans.

Rachel handed something to her father while whispering in his ear. Joseph could not see exactly what it was, only catching sight of a flash of gold light from the object. Saul smiled at the receipt of the item and kissed Rachel dearly.

"I fear for you. Let me go in your place," Saul stated.

"You are too old, Papa. You barely made it into the cave with my help. Do not worry for me. I promise I will return."

The ten selected began to exit the cave, climbing down and around the vertical rock to prowl for anything capable of being eaten.

Rachel moved towards the cave's exit. "My lord, I will not fail you. Wait for me," she said, taking Joseph's hand into hers. She had heard of his tottering relationship with Mariamne—it was well-known he had no offspring, and in that moment, she conveyed her desire to join Joseph's house as his second wife.

"Be careful, Rachel. I will expect you back with or without a cache of food," Joseph cautioned.

Rachel gave Joseph a deep, acknowledging stare and climbed down the rock face. Joseph remained in the cave, sick to his stomach that he let Rachel risk her life for his.

Saul approached Joseph.

"Lord Governor," Saul began, "if we are discovered, what shall we do?"

"I do not know, Saul," Joseph said back. "What say the rest of you?"

The young boy said, "I would rather die from my own blade than let the Romans take me alive."

"Son, do not speak of such things. It is against God's law to kill oneself," Joseph said.

"The Romans will skin and rape me. Here I will die a quick death by a cut to my neck," the boy argued.

Joseph, upon hearing words that should not be known to children, was silenced and stupefied—he nearly shed a tear.

"Come here, child," a choked-up Joseph said. "If it comes to that, I promise you will feel as little pain as possible."

The boy again embraced Joseph, and the two of them stood holding each other, water dripping from the boy's eyes down his face.

Several hours later, a pair of female hands reached onto the opening ledge of the cave. Joseph, seeing a woman entering, possibly Rachel, ran to help her into the cave.

"Rach—" Joseph stopped himself before he could finish saying her name.

It was not Rachel but a homely, middle-aged woman who had momentarily fooled Joseph's eyes and mind.

"We're glad you're back safe, umm…" Joseph impliedly asked the woman for her name.

"Ruth."

"We're glad you're safe, Ruth—good work collecting food," he said, taking her sack full of greens.

But all Joseph could think about was Rachel.

Every hour, a couple more of the Jotapatans sent out for food returned. Some had wild berries, some had spring onions, others filled their bags with blades of grass and plant leaves.

The sun was going down now, and nine of the ten Jotapatans sent out had returned. Only Rachel remained unaccounted for.

"We must eat," Joseph said to the people in the cave.

Saul divided the berries, onions, leaves, and grass. There was little more than a couple of bites of solid food for each person. Joseph saved a portion for Rachel, believing that she would soon return, and hopefully with more food.

The hours continued to pass. The sun had fallen below the horizon—Rachel was still missing.

"She may have fallen. I should go check to see if she is wounded—I nearly fell myself on the trek up here," Joseph suggested to Saul.

"No need, my lord. She knows the rocks better than anyone," Saul said dismissively. "If she slipped—she's dead, and we can't help her. My greater fear is that she has been captured by the Romans."

Once again Joseph's heart sank into his chest as he knew Saul was probably right.

"We shall know soon enough," Joseph replied.

"Aye," Saul said despondently.

▬ ▬ ▬

RACHEL SAT bound in a chair by chains and gagged by cloth, under the guard of four Roman soldiers.

"Send in the prisoner," Vespasian barked from inside his tent.

The four soldiers lifted the chair up with Rachel sitting on it and carried her into Vespasian's tent, setting her down before the general.

"My soldiers tell me you were found on the mountain," Vespasian began. "If you do not tell me what I need to know, I will hurt you worse than you have ever been hurt in your entire life. So think very carefully before answering. Do you understand?"

Rachel tried to make a noise, but her gag obscured her tongue.

"Take the damn gag out of her mouth," Vespasian ordered his soldiers.

"Of, course, my lord." The soldiers obliged, removing the cloth from Rachel's mouth.

"Let's try this again," Vespasian said. "Do you understand the torturous consequences of not telling me what I want to hear?"

"Yes," Rachel answered.

"Where is Joseph?"

"I do not know, my lord," Rachel said after a moment, deliberating on whether to suffer Roman torture or give Joseph up.

Vespasian signaled to the soldier holding Rachel in her seat. The soldier took out a baton and smashed her left hand against her seat's armrest, breaking her fingers. She screamed out in writhing pain.

"Perhaps you have remembered *now?*" Vespasian asked.

"I know nothing, my lord," Rachel answered, beginning to tear up.

Again Vespasian nodded to his soldier. This time he beat her in the face with the baton, breaking her nose. A rush of blood ran down the bottom of Rachel's face.

"Now do you remember?" Vespasian questioned, becoming angered at her intransigence.

"My lord, please believe me. I know nothing," Rachel cried, moaning in pain and spitting blood.

"Perhaps a beating is too good for you. Skin her," Vespasian ordered.

A Roman soldier removed a filet knife from his belt and moved towards Rachel.

"No, no!" she screamed as the Roman took off the skin from her left arm. Another soldier took a bowl of salt and covered her flayed wound.

"Aaaahh! Aaaahh! Please, no more, no more!" Rachel pleaded as she screamed, sobbed, and gasped for each breath of air.

"Now do you remember?" Vespasian asked, fully enraged.

"Yes! Yes, my lord. He's in the cave," she wept.

"Where is this cave?" Vespasian queried.

"It is high on the mountain, invisible to those that know not of it."

"Is he alone or does he have soldiers with him?" Vespasian asked.

"There are forty civilians with Joseph, women, children, and the elderly mostly," Rachel replied.

"Lift her up," Vespasian ordered. "You will guide us to Joseph, or you will be skinned until you die."

Rachel nodded, sadly broken.

Vespasian threw a small towel on Rachel's lap. "Clean yourself."

Rachel wiped her face with her good hand and then wrapped the towel around her flayed arm for pressure support, screaming loudly in pain at the slightest touch on her wound.

"Summon Titus and have the girl lead him to Joseph," Vespasian commanded an officer.

Titus quickly came to Vespasian's tent and collected Rachel—the journey from the Roman fortress up the mountain began.

Rachel was followed by Titus and five hundred Roman soldiers. They marched halfway up to the mountain landing when Rachel directed Titus to veer off the path towards the rock with the skull face.

"We are almost there, my lord. The cave is fifty feet up and twists to the left," Rachel said, trying to hide her humiliation.

"Polinus, Galicanus. Go fetch the Hebrew," Titus ordered his best tribunes. "Stay here, Hebrew woman. I wouldn't want you to disappear into the cave too."

The two Romans began their climb, looking down to Rachel for guidance. She obliged them, pointing to the left as they had not spiraled around the rock far enough to reach the cave—they adjusted their climb.

Then Polinus' foot slipped on the same rock that Joseph's had the prior day. "Aaah!" he shouted, but he was also able to catch himself by the same handholds that Joseph had.

Joseph and the thirty-nine other Hebrews in the cave heard the Roman scream and moved towards the opening to see about the noise. Joseph hoped the sound was from Rachel, but when he peeked out the cave, he only saw the glimmering of Roman armor reflecting sunlight. Joseph withdrew back inside the cave.

"The Romans have come," Joseph said to the rest of the Galileans in the cave.

Panic set in—Joseph put his finger over his lips to silence everyone.

Then Joseph softly and deliberately said, "Give me the spear."

Saul quickly passed Joseph the spear.

Polinus was closing in on the cave. Galicanus was no more than a few feet behind him.

Joseph kept his head and back against the rock wall of the cave to avoid being spotted by the Romans. He took a deep breath and began to count to ten slowly and silently. He thought of the ten plagues God smote down upon the Egyptians in ancient times. "Was God smiting the Hebrews in this hour?" he asked himself, but then quickly dismissed the idea, being reassured with the thought of God's sacred covenant with the Israelites.

Joseph heard a rustling right outside the cave. He spun his body around from the rock wall to the cave's opening with the short spear in his right hand. Polinus looked up and saw Joseph emerge from the cave opening. They stared at each other in the eye for a long second.

"He's here!" Polinus yelled out to Galicanus.

Joseph jabbed the spear into Polinus' neck, right through his jugular. Polinus kept his hold on the rock while choking from the impaling blade. Joseph twisted the spear. Blood gushed out from Polinus' throat. He lost his grip and fell some three hundred feet to his death.

Galicanus, upon seeing his comrade fall, reached for his sword and slid it halfway out of its sheath. Now unable to climb with one hand occupied, Galicanus realized he would not be able to defend himself if he followed in Polinus' footsteps, so he climbed back down the rock to inform Titus of the impenetrable nature of the cave.

"What the hell happened up there?" Titus furiously asked Galicanus before he had fully descended the rock face.

Galicanus jumped down a good five feet, landing on his hands and knees. "My lord, Joseph is in the cave. He stuck Polinus with a spear, sending him to his death. There is no way to penetrate the cave as it is only accessible by climbing—one is defenseless until entering it. If I hadn't turned back when I did, I would now lie dead next to Polinus."

Titus was frustrated—very frustrated. "Now that we know where he is, we don't need this bitch any longer," Titus said angrily.

In a rage, he drew his dagger and sliced Rachel's throat open —she quickly dropped to the ground and bled to death.

There was little that came to Titus' mind on how to expedite the capture of Joseph in the current situation. No arrows or catapults could reach him. No oil could be poured on him. And even if there was a way to kill Joseph, Vespasian had been very clear that he was to be taken alive.

"You will wait," Titus said to Galicanus. "They surely want for food. If there are indeed forty Jotapatans trapped, it is only a matter of time before they are all weak from starvation. I expect to be briefed immediately on all developments."

Titus turned to the assembly of regular soldiers. "Make yourselves comfortable, men. You may be here for days. I want all companies stationed at this point until we have Joseph in chains," Titus shouted to his assembly of Roman troops. He turned around and headed down the mountain to deliver his report to Vespasian.

"We have him trapped, Father," Titus said, "but reaching him is nearly impossible. I have ordered the men to lie in wait until he is forced to leave his safe position to gather food."

"I give the Hebrew much credit," Vespasian began. "The German barbarians did not put up such a fight as this ragtag bunch. You will wait for him, but I am returning to Caesarea. I expect Joseph to be delivered to me before the moon is full."

"He will be, I swear by the gods."

***

**"WHAT ARE** we to do, Joseph?" Saul asked. "The Romans have found us. We are starving and trapped. Are we to die from the Roman blade or our growling stomachs?

"I don't know." Joseph answered like a man defeated.

The young boy stepped forward. "Take my life. I will not be taken by the Romans, but I will be comforted by a quick death at your hands," he said.

Joseph knew that it was probably the smartest, easiest, and only honorable way out of their situation. He stood silenced, not knowing how to respond. Then others rose up and echoed the same sentiments.

"Let me die with honor and dignity. Take my life too!" an older woman yelled.

Thirty-nine voices began crying out, "Take my life!"

"It is for the best," Saul concurred.

Joseph nodded to Saul, resigned to a homicidal end.

"When I was in Rome many years ago," Joseph began, "while seeking the freedom of some wrongly-imprisoned Hebrews, I overheard a group of Romans talk of a time when a small company, not much larger than all of us, chose to end their own lives together rather than be certainly burned alive by the Gauls' overwhelming force of ten thousand. They all sat in a large circle and gave each other peace. If you wish this and you trust me, sit with me in a circle now."

All the people in the cave followed Joseph's instructions, arranging themselves in a close circle.

"Now," Joseph continued, "we will take the spear and spin it in the middle of the circle. The person to whom it points will be the first to slay the person to their left. The person to the left of the departed will take the spear and slay the person to their left, and so on and so on until there is a single person remaining. That last person will be cursed with the choice of breaking God's law by taking their own life painlessly or surrendering to the Romans—most certainly to be crucified or worse. But in this situation, I don't think God will fail to forgive the last soul standing, should that person choose to take their own life. Are we all agreed?"

The thirty-nine other Jotapatans in the cave all nodded solemnly in agreement.

"First, I will lead us in prayer. On your knees—all of you," Joseph said.

All of the Hebrews in the cave knelt down and joined hands together in solace while they prayed.

"Baruch atah Adonai Eloheinu Melech haolam. Be with us Lord now as we are about to enter your kingdom. We are your faithful children. We thank you for our time on this Earth, and we praise you for giving us the choice in how we leave it. Amen," Joseph prayed.

As the prayer ended, hardly a soul had dry eyes.

"Saul, give me the spear," Joseph commanded.

Joseph took the spear and moved to the center of the circle. He placed the spear down on the flat cave floor. Twisting his wrist with all his strength, he spun the broken spear like a top with a strong force, creating a palpable anticipation of where it might stop.

While the spear spun, Joseph said, "Remember, whomever the spear points to, you will take the spear and slay the person to your left."

Ten revolutions later, the spear tip pointed directly at Saul— to the left of Saul sat the young boy that had formed an emotional bond with Joseph.

"Give me the spear, my lord," Saul said to Joseph.

Joseph was unable to move, seeing his young friend would be the first to perish.

"Governor, give me the spear. It's best he doesn't see anything happen to the rest of us," Saul declared.

Joseph began to stand up, the spear in his hand. He walked over to Saul. Saul reached out his arm to take the spear from Joseph.

The young boy, being aware of the situation, voluntarily raised his neck.

Joseph handed the spear to Saul. Saul tried to take the spear, but Joseph could not let go.

"No—I must do this, Saul," Joseph stated.

Saul released his grip on the spear and nodded to Joseph.

"You're going home, son. God loves you," Joseph said, whispering into the little boy's ear.

Joseph kissed him on the forehead, then he swiftly stuck the spear into the child's neck, severing his carotid artery instantly. The boy bled out and was dead within seconds.

Joseph handed the spear to the person to his left, an older woman. She took the spear and slew her daughter to her left.

The spear moved around the circle, slaying every other person, creating a killer out of everyone left living. After the first round of the spear traveling about the circle, twenty of the forty Jotapatans lay dead. After the second round, thirty of the forty were dead. After the third round only five men remained alive. After the fourth round, only three were left—Joseph was one of them. Ebenezer was the third last to be killed, by Abraham. Now Joseph had the blade, and it was his turn to slay Abraham.

Abraham was ten years younger but about the same size as Joseph. His face cowered with fear, tears, and mucus. Seeing no one left to mock his cowardliness, he pleaded for deliverance.

"Lord Governor! Please spare me! I will take my chances with the Romans!" Abraham cried, begging on his knees.

Joseph hesitated. He could not slay one of his people if they were not consenting or he would break the arguably most sacred commandment. Then Joseph raised the spear to his own neck, but he could not bring himself to take his life either. An unbearable weight rested on his shoulders from the sight of almost forty dead bodies lying in the cave. Joseph thought of asking Abraham to use the spear on himself, but then the idea of prolonging his own life became too strong to ignore. Joseph threw the spear out of the cave opening, where it fell hundreds of feet to the ground below.

"There will be no more death by our hands today," Joseph said.

## Joseph in the Cave

Abraham burst out crying in shame, terror, sadness, and relief. He wrapped his arms around Joseph's legs, kneeling before him.

"Thank you, my great lord! Bless you! Bless you! Bless you!" Abraham tearfully wailed, kissing Joseph's feet.

"Enough of that. Come, we will surrender to the Romans. Perhaps they will feed us one last time before they execute us," Joseph said cynically.

As Joseph looked over the nearly forty dead Hebrews his eye caught a flicker of gold light coming from Saul's motionless hand.

Joseph went over to investigate. Saul was holding a large coin of pure gold with a menorah and Hebrew writing on one side—on the other side of the coin was an image of the Temple as built originally by King Solomon. The coin commemorated the establishment of the first Temple a thousand years earlier.

"I have a feeling I'm supposed to take this," Joseph said to himself and put the coin into his most secure pocket.

"Are you coming?" he asked Abraham.

"Yes, my lord."

Joseph and Abraham, both weak but not completely feeble, began to descend the rock face to surrender themselves.

# Chapter 12:

# The Trek in the Desert

**"LOOK! THE** Hebrew is coming down!" a soldier on the lookout yelled out to the company of Roman troops waiting for Joseph.

"I am Joseph, governor of Galilee, and I am your prisoner," Joseph said to the Romans once he had fully descended the rock wall.

"Who is the man next to you?" Galicanus asked Joseph.

"He is Abraham, a citizen of Jotapata," Joseph replied.

Hearing this, Galicanus pulled his gladius and ran Abraham through.

"We don't take common prisoners," he said to Joseph. "Chain the Hebrew and take him to Titus."

Roman soldiers took Joseph into custody.

Joseph, now a prisoner of Rome, expected to be executed for his rebellion—he even prepared his soul for the torture he was sure would precede his death. His notoriety had reached Nero, who was curious about the Judean who had thwarted his greatest general for over a month and a half, costing thousands of gold talents and men.

Nero ordered Joseph delivered to Rome for a public execution—he wanted Joseph alive.

The Romans set Joseph on a journey from Galilee through the desert towards Caesarea, some forty miles away on the Mediterranean coast. From there he would be sailed to Rome.

Joseph was marched from a still burning Jotapata in chains, led by Titus and a force of a thousand Romans dedicated completely to Joseph's transportation. The Romans regularly beat Joseph in his stomach, back, and chest. He was provided with just enough water and food to keep him alive. His clothes quickly tattered. His face turned tan with the hardship of his scorching journey.

He had now endured two days of this torture.

"Hurry up, Judean!" a Roman soldier barked while beating Joseph on the lower back with a wooden baton.

Joseph fell down into the hot, grainy sand. The granules stuck to his sweaty face, making it look like he had been caked with flour. He was dead tired. He could not bring himself to his feet. The rope tied to his chains drew taut. The horse pulling the rope continued walking and began to pull Joseph's motionless body through the sand.

"Damn it!" Titus yelled out at the Roman soldier by Joseph's side. "He is to be presented to Caesar *alive!* If he dies, so do *you!* Now put him in my carriage until he regains his strength—and bring him water!"

"Yes, my lord, right away, my lord," the Roman soldier responded sycophantically.

Joseph was quickly lifted from the ground by two Romans and laid on his back in Titus' carriage. A Roman soldier handed Titus a canvas water bag, and he personally poured it through Joseph's lips. He was so weak he was not even able to sit up to drink. Joseph partially gagged from the water, his throat being completely dry.

"Bring me spirits and a dry cloth. And don't make me wait!" Titus ordered an underling soldier.

Titus grabbed the cloth and the bottle of grain alcohol from the soldier. He doused the cloth with the alcohol and laid it upon Joseph's forehead.

"This will cool you," he said to Joseph.

Joseph tried to thank Titus, but he could not move his tongue. He was dizzy from dehydration, the inferno of the desert sun, and the hot sand that had burned his skin.

As he rested, Joseph was not asleep, but he was not awake either. He was in that strange place one travels between a dream and consciousness. Thoughts of his wife cooking the goat's liver on his last Shabbat in Jerusalem flashed through his head. He was transported back to his youth and remembered studying the Torah next to his father. Anon, the dreaded memory of nearly forty slain Judeans in the hidden cave entered his mind.

A flash of light, a hundred times the brightness of the Sun, came over him. Everything was white and overpowered his eyes. Then he heard a soothing and soft voice speaking slowly, but he could not see anyone.

"Joseph, I am Elijah, the prophet of your ancestors. I come to you again so that you may better serve the Lord."

"Where am I? What is this?" Joseph replied.

"Do not ask questions. Just observe. All will be revealed in time," Elijah said.

Suddenly Joseph was standing in the emperor's palace in Rome. He looked around and saw Nero dead on the floor, his sword sticking through his chest and out his back.

"The emperor is dead! He has slain himself! Long live Caesar, long live Rome!" Ulysses, Nero's chief of staff, cried out.

The blinding white light returned for a moment. Then Joseph found himself at a coronation ceremony. Vespasian was sitting on Caesar's throne, wearing a golden laurel wreath.

Another blast of white light came upon Joseph, and he was transported to Vespasian's crypt. Titus stood over his father's dead body, a solitary tear slowing rolling down his cheek. Titus had aged at least ten years.

White light shined down on Joseph once more, and then he was standing in the Roman Senate hall. A hundred Roman senators sat before Titus, all applauding. Titus now wore the golden laurel wreath upon his head.

The next moment, Joseph was back in the desert with Titus standing over him. Joseph instinctively sat up in the carriage, shaken from his ordeal and unsure of what had just happened to him.

Out of nowhere, a white dove landed on Joseph's head, sending a watery white turd down his face.

"Get, damn bird!" Titus yelled, swatting at the dove.

The bird flew away. The dove was completely out of place, for there was desert ten miles in every direction.

The memory of Joseph's bizarre encounter with young Elijah in the courtyard of his home in Jerusalem flashed through his mind, when another white dove had also relieved itself on his forehead. He wondered what became of the young boy. Was God trying to send him a message through the dove? If so, he did not understand it.

Joseph's physical weakness overcame his mental power. He lay back down and quickly returned to a deep sleep.

Several hours later, a Roman soldier tossed a bucketful of water on Joseph's face, waking him in a sudden fright.

"Wake up, Joseph," Titus said, leaning over him. "Drink." He offered a water bag.

Joseph's strength had been greatly restored by his rest in Titus' carriage. He took the bag from Titus' hand and began guzzling the water.

"I'm glad that you are still alive. If you had died on me, Nero might have had my head instead of yours," Titus opined. "We're stopping in Caesarea, and from there we sail to Rome. Nero ordered you to suffer as punishment for Jotapata. I believe you have suffered quite enough from my hands, especially since you're not looking at a very pleasant end."

"I owe my life to you, for your care this past day," Joseph said.

"Considering it was under my command that you almost lost your life, I'll count us even," Titus replied. "Rest more in my carriage—we are not far from Caesarea now."

\#\#\#

**"FATHER!" TITUS** exclaimed. "We have him!"

"Good work, son—but then again, I expected no less," Vespasian replied. "I am eager to speak with this Hebrew. Send him to me at once."

"I will have him sent up this moment," Titus said and moved to go retrieve Joseph.

"Wait!" Vespasian stood up from his desk and walked up close to Titus, putting his arm around his shoulders. "You'll want to hear this piece first—tonight we celebrate! The soldiers have been waiting a long time for a grand diversion. You will be the man of honor at tonight's feast. There will be women, dancing, and an unending flow of wine. Surely we are all deserving. Rest, wash, and change into some livery that doesn't weigh fifty pounds—I will see you at sunset."

Titus embraced his father and then made his way to his quarters, but first he ordered Captain Frachas to deliver Joseph to Vespasian.

After entering his chamber, Titus disrobed, leaving a trail of armor, weapons, and clothes from the threshold of his door to his bed. Titus' face hit the pillow—he quickly fell asleep with a smile of tired satisfaction on his face from a job well done.

\#\#\#

**"MY LORD** Vespasian. I present Joseph, governor of Galilee," Captain Frachas said as he delivered Joseph into Vespasian's custody.

"Good—you may go." Vespasian quickly waved away the captain.

"Hail, Caesar!" Frachas said, saluting, and then left.

Vespasian stood some ten feet from Joseph. They both evaluated the other with their eyes.

In rags, unclean, and unkempt, Joseph was not much to look at.

"Was this really the man that defied me for over a month and a half?" Vespasian thought to himself.

Joseph looked down and saw a bandage over Vespasian's left foot, and a modest smile came over his face.

"Is something funny, Hebrew?" Vespasian asked furiously, sensing that Joseph was mocking his injury from the Jotapatan archers.

"No, my lord. It is just strange to meet a battlefield enemy, now that you wear a toga and I wear chains," Joseph countered.

"Yes, perhaps it is strange." Vespasian was brought back to memories of similar previous encounters with foes throughout his career. "Once in Germania, I met the leader of the barbarians off the battlefield. His name was Hansel, or Hans—who can remember those barbarian names? He had snuck behind the lines in the middle of the night while I lay in bed with a barbarian woman. My gods, the tits and ass those Germanic people give their daughters. Hans was keen on assassinating me in my sleep, you see. But when he came upon me in my tent, I was in the *act* with a barbarianess, very much awake. Still, he was able to place his dagger on my throat here." Vespasian pointed to a very small scar on his neck. "But before he sliced me through, he saw I was inside his very wife!"

Vespasian could not help but laugh nostalgically.

"Instead of assassinating me as he had intended, he became so enraged at the sight of his woman's infidelity that he threw me out of the way and savagely stabbed his wife countless times, to death. In his murderous rage, Hans seemed to forget about me entirely, allowing me time to return with my own blade, which I placed against his neck, but I did not fail to slice him. Alas, that is the mentality of the barbarians: act first, plan later. That is why they now submit to Rome, just as you, Joseph, now submit to me."

"A great tale, my lord. But surely you did not summon me to recount fond times past, nor state the obviousness of our current stations?" Joseph asked.

"I like a man that gets down to business. Good. I summoned you here because I wanted to know how a priest was able to ward off my army for as long as you did. Is it true that your God fights on your behalf as described by the Hebrews in ancient times? Do you have a mystical weapon that we do not know of?"

"My God does fight for me, every moment of every day," Joseph said firmly.

"Does He? Then why are you in chains instead of a toga?" Vespasian asked wryly.

"My God works in mysterious ways, my lord," Joseph answered.

"You don't say? Please tell me of the mysterious works of your Hebrew God," Vespasian said facetiously.

"I have been blessed with the power of prophecy. I was informed you would take Jotapata on the forty-seventh day, and on the forty-seventh day you took it. You may ask my men. They will attest to my telling of this prophecy," Joseph explained.

"Suppose I believe you, Hebrew. But that is in the past. What use have I for it now?"

"None," Joseph said tersely.

"You play games with me?" Vespasian shouted, showing rage in his voice and face.

"Far from it, my lord. What I mean to say is that I explained my prior prophecy so that you would hear the latest word of what will come, told to me by a prophet of my God," Joseph elucidated.

Vespasian instantly became attentive.

"You are to be Emperor of Rome one day soon, Lord Vespasian," Joseph continued. "A white dove comes to me from time to time, and when it comes, I am given knowledge of what will be. On my trek from Jotapata, the dove came to me again, in a part of the land where no dove could survive nor travel. I saw a vision of Nero falling on his sword. A great chaos consumed Rome. In the end, you rose up and were crowned Caesar."

Vespasian paused for a moment, deep in curious thought and unsure how to respond.

Joseph stood humbly with a mild grin.

"Is Joseph telling me what I want to hear to try and save his own skin?" Vespasian asked himself. "Is he a true recipient of prophecies?"

"I do not quite believe you, Hebrew. But what I believe is hardly important at the moment. Emperor Nero has heard of your defiance, of the great cost in men and treasure needed to bring Jotapata back under his control. You have been summoned to Rome. I know not what the emperor's intentions are, but I doubt you will live to see me crowned Caesar even if your prophecy comes true. Captain!" Vespasian shouted.

Captain Frachas pushed through the doors to Vespasian's office. "Yes, my lord?" he said obediently.

"Frachas, take this Hebrew back to his holding cell. He is to be escorted to Rome via warship the morning after next. See that he arrives alive and still able to speak. The emperor demands his presence."

"Hail, Caesar!" Frachas said, saluting Vespasian, and he then led Joseph back to the stockade.

# Chapter 13:

# A Roman Party

**GOLDEN RAYS** of the setting sun ushered in the beginning of the late summer evening. Titus awoke fully refreshed from his nap. Excitement was running through his veins as he knew he would be celebrated almost as much as his father at the evening's grand feast.

After bathing himself in exotic oils, Titus put on his finest linen toga with his newest leather sandals. He donned his shiniest rings, crested with his largest jewels. Around his neck hung a gold pendant, minted in Caesar's image.

He studied his figure and face in a silver mirror and smiled. Titus was handsome, important, and young—and he knew it.

Three successive knocks sounded from his chamber door. "Titus!" Captain Frachas called out. "You don't want to be late to your own feast, do you?"

Titus and Frachas had been childhood friends. They had served together in Germania and now Judea, creating a bond that reached far beyond Rome. They were essentially brothers.

"The feast is in honor of my father, but I thank you for the sentiment," Titus replied as he opened the door for his friend.

"You have the honor of capturing the Hebrew," Frachas countered.

"True, but my father has the honor for capturing Jotapata," Titus countered.

"You really don't know how to take a compliment," Frachas griped.

"I didn't ask for a compliment, Frachas," Titus retorted.

"My gods, man! This is a party! Cheer up! No woman will want to lie with you if you act like a crabby grandfather all night long," Frachas chastised him.

"They are paid for, Frachas. What they want is irrelevant."

"Ugh! You need to relax. Here, take my goblet. Not only is it the sweetest wine in all of Caesarea, it has a little additive to fully awaken the Roman senses."

"Of course it does. You know I'm allergic to opium," Titus reminded him.

"Worry not, my friend. It is something special, from the Far East. Don't ask what it is, but if you don't care for it, you'll be the first man in a hundred I've seen balk," Frachas assured him. Putting his hand on Titus' shoulder affectionately, he continued, "They say it makes your male spear extra stiff and strong." Frachas burst into laughter.

"You're incorrigible, Frachas. Give me the damn cup," Titus ordered, and he began sipping the laced wine. "Well, the wine is good," Titus confirmed.

"Take it slow. Its effects engage as fast as the alcohol," Frachas explained.

"Well, any Roman party worth having is worth having right!" Titus concluded and gulped down the goblet's full contents.

"Did you not hear me say, *Take it slow?*" Frachas asked incredulously.

"WHAT?" Titus answered sarcastically loud as if he was deaf.

The two began laughing together.

"Come, the celebration awaits," Frachas said, and the two left Titus' chamber, walking down to the first floor of the Roman barracks.

The smells of roasted mutton and pig were intoxicating. Titus and Frachas began to salivate unknowingly as the effects of the drug in their wine quickly began to take hold.

The servants were in the final stages of assembling the dishes on the buffet table. The eating tables were in a U-shape. The buffet table was set in the middle of the U. Upon it sat platters of every food Caesarea had to offer. There was baked snapper, raw oysters, steamed crabs, and tilapia for the seafood fare. Loaves of bread were piled three layers high. No Roman feast would be complete without both black and green olives—there were large bowls filled to the brim with each. Quarter wheels of assorted cheeses were laid flat on the table, covered with fresh grapes, figs, and cherries.

And then there was the *pièce de résistance:* a huge, fat roasted wild boar with a red apple in its mouth. Carving knives and two-pronged forks were stuck in the animal's rump. Alongside the hog were trays of mutton legs and rotisserie-cooked chickens. Cabbage, radishes, and spring onions garnished the meat plates.

On the dining tables, a small piece of spiced toast sat on the dinner plates before each guest. Only a knife for a utensil accompanied each table setting.

And then there was the wine and ale. Each guest had two cups, a chalice for the wine and a mug for the beer. A carafe of each beverage was distributed for every two guests—they would both have to be refilled at least once. The Romans did not understand the word "excess," hence their delight in frequenting vomitoriums.

Some of the younger officers had already been ingesting alcohol well before the start of the feast. The elder officers mostly sipped on their beverages, learning many years prior that a drunk Roman soldier often leads to a dead Roman soldier.

But before the feeding frenzy commenced, all the attendees were required to be seated—then, and only then, would Vespasian grace his subordinates with his presence. The assembly of generals, tribunes, centurions, captains, honored legionnaires, and local dignitaries finished their pre-meal reception yammering and made their way to their assigned seating areas.

Two clarions burst forth, signaling Vespasian's entrance. At the sight of the general, all the partygoers stood to attention.

"All hail Caesar! All hail Vespasian!" Vespasian's squire bellowed out.

The guests then repeated the allegiance.

"Friends, Romans, countrymen!" Vespasian began, to a great cry of laughter for everyone knew of Mark Antony's famous speech. "First, a toast." Vespasian took the small piece of spiced toast from his dinner plate and placed it in his wine goblet.

The assembly followed suit and then everyone raised up their goblets, held out towards Vespasian.

"To the best damn army ever assembled in the history of Rome!" A riotous cheer rang out as did continuous rapping on the wooden tabletops, coupled with thunderous stomping. "To my son and your great general, for his successful capture of the Hebrew!" Another cheer roared forth from the congregation. "I am proud of you, Titus," Vespasian said affectionately, with a smile of paternal pride.

Vespasian moved his goblet in salute to Titus. The Romans clanked their vessels of wine together, and all took a drink in unison.

"Well—what the hell are you all looking at? EAT!" Vespasian ordered jovially.

The feast commenced. A mass of men began moving about the dining hall, selecting their desired foods. The Roman military feast was served buffet-style. The horde of men trying to get at the roasted pig resembled pigs at a feeding trough, ironically. Within minutes the buffet table went from bursting with fare to a tabletop of meager morsels. The sounds of Romans loading up their plates turned into slurps, crunches, belches, and cracking noises.

Titus sat next to Vespasian at the head table. Titus was doubly intoxicated and was devouring his food like the wild beast he was feasting upon. Vespasian noticed his son was acting a bit peculiarly.

"Titus, I don't know what you have taken, but remember, a general of Rome *never* runs around like a fool in front of his men," Vespasian reminded his son.

Titus wanted to shell out a litany of guilt-shifting explanations—blaming Frachas came to mind, but knowing how Vespasian responded to excuses, he simply said, "Yes, Father."

As the meal came to an end, Vespasian rose and clapped his hands firmly twice.

It was time for the entertainment to begin.

Judean-slaves lifted up the buffet table and removed it to another room. They returned just as quickly and rushed to sweep the floor clean of the feast's debris.

Then a troupe of musicians entered, playing their instruments. The sweet sounds of the lyre, tambourine, and wooden Pan flute began to soothe the spirits of all in attendance.

Next came ten of the fairest women in Caesarea, dressed in exotic gowns with their bellies exposed, their nipples nearly visible through their costumes, and their faces veiled below the eyes.

They began to move in a stylized dance, first forming a circle in the center of the hall.

The dinner guests remained seated at their tables eagerly watching.

The dance was simple but erotically performed. The girls took a few slow steps forward, a few slow steps back, crouched down low, jumped up high, and then twirled around—all while gyrating their hips and bosoms. Then the circle rotated halfway

The Feast Celebrating the Capture of Jotapata

around clockwise, and the dance repeated, ensuring each guest would have a good look at both sides of every dancer.

One hundred sets of eyes examined these women over every inch of their ripe bodies. Any man that had not finished his meal by the time the dancers began now sat with his mouth open, not because he was still eating, but because he was staring covetously.

Titus caught one of the most voluptuous dancers looking into his glazed-over eyes. Desire flowed over him like a rolling tidal wave. He took the wine carafe and refilled his goblet to the top to help calm his lusting nerves.

The company of musicians and female dancers performed a total of three dances, to roaring applause after each. After the final dance, the men rose in ovation and cheered.

The musical entertainment had ended, but the dancers were far from finished. As the females moved to exit, each one took the hand of a preferred male guest and led him into the parlor room. The girl that had caught Titus' eye took Titus' hand.

Another gorgeous dancer tried to take the hand of Vespasian, but always the savvy leader, he did not partake in public scenes of debauchery. He moved to exit the celebration at this time, leaving his men to play amongst themselves.

Inside the parlor room sat partially-clothed women, young boys, and girls. Each was busy sipping or guzzling wine to dull their senses. The Roman soldiers were notorious for violent sexual acts, and it could be hours before they were done with their paid-for playthings.

"Titus! Join me with this boy!" Frachas shouted across the room. "He can service us both at the same time!"

But Titus was infatuated with his busty dancer. "I'm occupied, Frachas," Titus said back.

He slowly undressed his courtesan dancer, exposing her supple pink bosom. She was even more lovely than he could have imagined. She could not have been more than twenty years of age, and her breasts, though enormous, lay firm on her chest. Titus began to kiss one, caressing the other with his hand.

On the other side of the parlor, a few Romans that had been drinking heavily soon expelled their entire feast. Frachas was hit by a regurgitation while he was busy with his young boy. It did not faze the drunk and drugged Frachas a bit; in fact, he chuckled.

There were only two rules at a Roman sex party. First, no infighting—the Romans were well aware how a petty quarrel ruined even a state-sponsored orgy. And second, cup-bearers were off limits, not because cup-bearers had any prestige of position, but they were essential in ensuring that the goblets of everyone drinking stayed full. A boy or girl cannot well pour and refill carafes while being buggered by the party guests. Two Roman guards stood in full uniform at the entrance of the parlor to ensure obedience to the rules and keep the peace should a fight break out.

Before long, the parlor room stank of sex, spilt wine and ale, sweat, vomit, and a hint of blood. The moans, growls, screams, and rocking noises could be heard across the entire barracks.

Vespasian sat working at his desk, reading a scroll, when the sounds of lechery overcame him.

"Guard!" he blurted out.

"Yes, my lord," the guard said as he entered Vespasian's office.

"Go and have a young girl brought to my chambers—and don't tell anyone who she's for," Vespasian commanded.

"This minute, my lord," the guard replied, then struck his chest and hurried off.

"Papa is going to have some fun tonight," Vespasian said quietly to himself and walked to his bedchamber sporting a licentious grin.

# PART II

"For I know the plans I have for you, plans to prosper you and not to harm you, plans to give you hope and a future."—*Jeremiah 29:11*

# Chapter 14:

# The Voyage to Rome

**A PRISON** guard tossed a bucket of water onto Joseph's face as he slept, waking him instantly.

"Rise and shine, Judean!" the Roman jailer belched out. "I hear you are for Rome today. I'm sure Caesar will find a special way of dealing with you." He grinned maniacally.

"Lend me a towel, or am I expecting too much of Roman hospitality?" Joseph queried.

"What do I look like? A governess?" the jailor barked back.

"No. I would never imply a that man who watches over captives all day long is a governess," Joseph replied slyly.

"Are you looking for a head-smashing? You're lucky you're on the way out or we'd have a rumble. Now up with you! Your escort is here," the jailor ordered.

He walked Joseph out of his cell. Four Roman soldiers approached, all armed to the teeth. Joseph sulked momentarily at the sight. Then Titus stepped forth from between the four Romans, presenting himself.

"Hello, Joseph."

"My lord Titus! It is good to see you," Joseph answered.

"Come, I'm sure you're eager to leave this place," Titus said.

Joseph and his Roman entourage began walking towards the jail's exit.

"I trust you have been treated well?" Titus questioned Joseph, still wet from his awakening bath.

"As well as could be expected from Roman jailors, my lord," Joseph said.

Titus nodded his head, all too well familiar with Roman methods used on those incarcerated in their custody.

"We make way for Rome by vessel. Nero has heard of your rebellion and personally ordered you to be brought to the capital. Come with me," Titus directed.

The two walked side by side. Captain Frachas led the way to the dock while four of Titus' bodyguards followed directly behind Joseph and Titus.

"The journey across the sea is fraught with danger. Many a ship leaves harbor never to be seen again. The winds have been especially malevolent this season," Titus explained.

"My God will see us through. I cannot believe I have endured what has so far come to pass only to find a watery grave," Joseph asserted.

"Your fanaticism in your God is something I will never understand, Hebrew," Titus replied.

Caesarea was not a large city, and most of it could be traversed by foot in less than fifteen minutes.

They were soon coming up on the harbor.

"There she is. The *Temptress*. Isn't she beautiful?" Frachas asked. "She is newly built, featuring all the latest designs to increase her speed and strength."

"Forgive me, my lord, if I do not share your enthusiasm," Joseph replied.

"Understandable, in your present position, Hebrew."

Frachas, Titus, Joseph, and the Roman guards boarded the ship.

"Let me show you to your sleeping quarters," Titus said, leading Joseph below the quarterdeck to the main cabin. "Here you are."

Joseph stood queerly, looking at a hammock attached to the ceiling with rope.

"Have you never been at sea?" Titus asked. "We all sleep on hammocks. Believe me, when we get to choppy waters, you'll be thankful. There's nothing fun about being tossed from your cot into the ship's bulkheads while you sleep."

"Nothing fun," Frachas reiterated.

"I've been at sea. And I'm really not tired, I'm hungry—the jailor fed me but once in two days," Joseph complained.

"Of course. Follow me to the mess deck," Titus directed, and the three men walked out of the main cabin into the adjoining eating area.

"Say hello to Perseus," Titus commanded.

"Hello, Perseus," Joseph said.

Perseus took one look at Joseph and scoffed audibly.

"Perseus is our resident cook. Treat him well, and he will treat your stomach well," Titus professed.

"Treat him poorly, and well—don't treat him poorly," Frachas added.

"Always the wise one you are, captain," Perseus added with a snicker under his breath.

Perseus was an old seaman, approaching seventy. His life at sea was harsh—he had become surlier with each passing year. White whiskers bulged from his lip, nose, and ears. He had no hair on the top of his head. But he did have the largest belly on the ship. Perseus was predictably peg-legged (on his left side) and detested being forced to walk, which always reminded him of his deficiency.

"What would you care for, my lord?" Perseus asked Joseph sassily.

"I would love some mutton or chicken, or perhaps some beef," Joseph answered.

"We have fish," Perseus said snappily.

"Why then did you ask?" a slightly irritated Joseph questioned.

"Because I have a dry sense of humor and few people to exercise it on," Perseus sardonically admitted.

"Ah. Fish it is," Joseph replied.

"Excellent, my lord," Perseus said and then disappeared below his cooking counter.

The sounds of splashing water and Perseus grunting emanated from under the galley counter.

"Come here—ye lil' basterd!" Joseph, Titus, and Frachas heard Perseus yell out.

The splashing and grunting continued for an awkward moment.

"Gotcha, ye devil!" Perseus said, lifting his head back up above the counter, proudly presenting the fish he had caught by its tail.

"Looks great," Joseph said.

"Glad you approve, my lord," Perseus said facetiously and then violently slammed the fish's head on his cooking counter, killing it instantly.

Titus and Frachas jumped at this startling noise. Joseph, not succumbing to Perseus' intimidation, stared him back in the eyes for an awkward moment—Perseus grumbled a bit but desisted and returned to cooking.

"May I have some bread to tide me over while you cook?" Joseph petitioned him.

Perseus, already in the process of gutting Joseph's fish, took an exasperated breath and banged his cutlery down on his workstation.

"We have hardtack," he said, slamming a brittle piece down on the counter.

"I suppose you don't have wine either?" Joseph asked.

"We have wine, my lord, but only for officers. Are you an officer, my lord?" Perseus asked, already knowing the answer.

"No."

"Then you get water," Perseus said flippantly, banging down a wooden cup on the counter and sloppily filling it with a brownish liquid.

"Lovely. I can already tell I'm going to enjoy my time here," Joseph responded sarcastically.

"Perseus, Joseph is our guest. Give him a cup of wine for the sake of the gods," Titus interjected, trying to ease the tension.

"Right away, my lord," Perseus said obsequiously, and he hurriedly poured Joseph a goblet full.

"I'll take a cup too," Titus added.

"Make that three," Frachas additionally requested.

Perseus obliged them all and then returned to cook Joseph's fish.

Joseph, Titus, and Frachas sat down at the long mess hall dining table, each sipping his wine, and Joseph nibbling on the less-than-appetizing desiccated bread.

Titus began to talk. "When we get to Rome you will be transferred to the Ward of Prisons to await whatever Nero has in store for you. You'll most likely be tortured and executed in some kind of spectacle."

"I thought as much," Joseph replied.

"But while you are on my ship, you are my guest and will be treated well," Titus continued.

"For that I thank you, my lord," Joseph responded.

"It's *my* ship," Frachas clarified.

"While I—a general—am on it, it is *my* ship!" Titus retorted to Frachas and then returned his attention to Joseph. "Tell me something, Hebrew. My father says you prophesied his rise to Caesar."

"This is true, my lord," Joseph answered.

Titus moved his head forward to look Joseph in the eyes more clearly. "Was that just a ruse to try and impress my father in an attempt to evade your own death?" he questioned.

"No, my lord, it was told to me by a prophet of my God," Joseph explained. "There is more I did not mention to General Vespasian. He will reign for ten years, and then you will emerge as Caesar."

"Now you're pulling my leg," Titus said dismissively.

Overhearing Titus' comment, Perseus growled a bit, unhappily reminded of his peg.

"Before you and the Roman army laid siege to Jotapata, I divulged to my own comrades that the city would fall on the forty-seventh day. What day did the city fall, my lord?" Joseph questioned.

"The forty-seventh," Titus answered. "How can I believe that you made this prophecy? Will the entire population of Jotapata testify on your behalf? Oh, that's right, everyone in the city is dead—everyone except you, that is. And even if you were to convince me you did prophesize the fall of Jotapata, prophesizing the future Caesars of Rome is another business entirely, is it not?" Titus inquired, becoming a bit incensed.

"My lord, I understand that you have no reason to believe me, but hear my words and decide for yourself. You have already said my fate is entirely in Nero's hands, thus there is nothing that could benefit me to motivate duplicity. I am telling you the truth, for the truth's sake alone."

Titus was silenced, convinced by Joseph's argument but still uncertain of his prophecy.

Breaking the silence was Perseus, banging his peg leg about the deck, making a great deal of noise. He tossed the fish plate down in front of Joseph.

"Enjoy, my lord," Perseus said, knowing the presentation was less than appetizing.

"Do you have any spice, Perseus? Or perhaps some salt?" Joseph asked hopefully.

"Of course, my lord," Perseus said, grumpily picking up Joseph's plate, stomping his peg, and taking the fish back to the galley for seasoning.

Perseus disappeared into the kitchen.

"A Judean slave demands spice. I'll spice it up for him," Perseus quietly muttered to himself. Then he took the fish and tossed it into the front of his trousers, jiggling it about his loins for a few moments. Perseus removed the fish from his pants, spat on it, and then slathered it in a thick coat of paprika.

"Here we are, my lord. I hope it's to your liking now—I spiced it up good for ya," Perseus said sycophantically, placing the fish back in front of Joseph.

"Wonderful. Thank you, Perseus," Joseph said ingratiatingly while Perseus donned a fiendish smile. "Could I also trouble you for a knife, Perseus?" Joseph requested.

"You've troubled me for everything else. Why not for a knife as well?" Perseus asked sarcastically, this time shaking the floor with the violent banging of his wooden leg as he went back into the galley once more, this time to retrieve a utensil. "Here we are *again*, my lord. Is there anything else I can do for you? Does your arse need a wiping? Or perhaps your cock needs a tug?"

"That's enough, Perseus," Titus interrupted.

"Very good, my lord," Perseus replied humbly to Titus. He slowly waddled back into the kitchen muttering under his breath. "Not sure I'd trust a Hebrew slave with a knife."

Joseph began eating his fish. The expression on his face was lukewarm at best, but he was starving and it was the first protein he had consumed in over a day. While Joseph ate the fish, he coughed repeatedly from the overwhelming paprika, never knowing that Perseus had also added his own personal seasoning.

"You'd love Perseus if you got to know him better," Titus lauded.

"I'm sure I would," Joseph coughed out.

"We sail in less than an hour. I have duties to see to. You may sleep or walk about the quarterdeck so long as you do not get in anyone's way. Please do not make me chain you," Titus implored.

"I will give neither you nor your men any trouble," Joseph said.

"You'd best not, Hebrew," Frachas added with as much menace as he could muster, which was not very much.

Titus gazed over to Frachas with disbelief at his non-threatening stupidity.

"Good," Titus said to Joseph before standing up and leaving the mess hall for the quarterdeck.

Frachas trailed behind Titus but not before first making a menacing face at Joseph.

Joseph nodded back to Frachas, feigning respect.

Now sitting alone, Joseph took his cup and had the last swig of wine.

"Perseus," Joseph called out towards the galley. "Would you refill my wine?"

The only reply Joseph received was Perseus' unabated laughter.

Joseph stood up and left the mess hall for the main cabin and jumped into his hammock. His eyes closed and before long he was asleep.

*  *  *

**THE *TEMPTRESS*** cast off into the Mediterranean. A new vessel, the *Temptress* was specifically designed for sailing the high seas. It had no oars like most Roman ships, allowing it to travel much faster. It was a true sailboat, sporting double the number of sails as a regular Roman Man of War.

The voyage to Rome would take about three weeks if they encountered no serious storms. However, the skies, which were mostly clear in Caesarea, began to turn cloudier and darker with each passing day—it was not a good omen.

The sailors of the ship, nearly one hundred strong, spent their idle time playing games of strategy and chance. The officers preferred Roman chess, a variation on the game which allowed the pieces to move and jump with a special set of rules. It was played on a modified four by eight checkerboard. Additionally, all the identically-shaped pieces were either light or dark, each player using a different solitary color.

Captain Frachas was the reigning champion, and men would hover over him while he played, examining his every move and waiting for their turn to upset the champ.

"Will you move already?" Frachas yelled out, annoyed at his competitor, who was paralyzed with uncertainty.

"Shut it, captain" was the reply. "I'll move when I move."

Frachas rolled his eyes and sat back on his stool. "We'll arrive in Rome before the game is finished at this rate," Frachas taunted. "What does it matter? You're going to lose anyway."

"Fine!" the sailor said and took one of Frachas' pieces. "Ha! Didn't expect that one, did you, captain?"

"No, I didn't, because that ends the game. Mate!" Frachas yelled triumphantly, moving his piece into the winning position while laughing.

"I hate this bloody game," the sailor replied.

**Perseus Seasoning Joseph's Fish**

"Next!" Frachas boasted while he took the prize pot and counted his winnings.

"Frachas, I need you on the quarterdeck," Titus interrupted.

"Yes, my lord," Frachas said, standing up. "The rest of you—hold onto your money until I come back."

Frachas walked up the stairs behind Titus to the quarterdeck.

The boat had been at sea two weeks without incident. It was now clear they were headed for a monster storm.

"What do you think, Frachas?" Titus asked his captain.

"Not good, my lord. Perhaps we should return to port before we have no other options?"

"If it was just you and me, I'd say yes. But Caesar is expecting Joseph, and you know how impatient he is. If we turn back now, we'll lose a month, plus however long we have to wait out the weather, which may not pass until the end of the season. No—we keep going. I'd rather die at sea than face Nero's unbridled wrath," Titus confessed.

"Very good, sir," Frachas replied.

In the distance, Titus and Frachas saw a flash of light in the clouds. Small intermittent rain droplets began to gently fall.

"Do we veer due south and try to avoid the storm?" Frachas asked.

Titus took a good look towards the horizon and said, "There is no avoiding this one, my friend."

The day turned to night as the rain droplets developed into a heavier and more forceful downpour. Crackling and booming thunder in the distance could now be heard and steadily increased in volume.

An hour later, exploding thunder descended down from the heavens, deafening all other noises. The precipitation was so intense that the rain felt like stinging needles as the sailors' faces were deluged.

The sea waves crashed harder and higher against the ship's hull. The waves became so powerful they began washing over the quarterdeck, slapping men off their feet.

The *Temptress* swayed from port to starboard, each pitch inching closer to capsizing the vessel. Men on the quarterdeck held onto ropes and wooden beams for dear life to prevent being cast out to sea.

A three-hundred-and-sixty-degree view of the horizon was all the same: pitch-blackness, intermittently illuminated with lightning bolts, momentarily showing the behemoth waves in the sea.

The majority of the men on the ship were below deck to avoid being washed overboard. Only a handful of officers responsible for navigating the boat stayed on the quarterdeck.

In the main cabin, sailors were thrown from their hammocks and sent tumbling into the wooden bulkhead—several unfortunates had their heads split open. Others broke arms, legs, and ribs, unable to adequately secure themselves—completely at the mercy of the storm.

Joseph fastened himself in a crook of the ship where the bulkhead met the floor planks. Rocking back and forth with the vessel, he shut his eyes tightly while reciting a prayer for times of need:

## PSALM 23

*The Lord is my shepherd; I shall not want. He maketh me to lie down in green pastures: he leadeth me beside the still waters. He restoreth my soul: he leadeth me in the paths of righteousness for his name's sake. Yea, though I walk through the valley of the shadow of death, I will fear no evil: for thou art with me; thy rod and thy staff they comfort me. Thou preparest a table before me in the presence of mine enemies: thou anointest my head with oil; my cup runneth over. Surely goodness and mercy shall follow me all the days of my life: and I will dwell in the House of the Lord for ever and ever. Amen.*

Above deck, Frachas and Titus were at the helm, holding onto the wheel, using all their might to keep the ship's rudder steady.

"We're not going to make it, captain!" Titus yelled out as loud as he could.

Frachas was right alongside Titus, but the overwhelming roar of the storm made it seem like Titus was calling from a hundred yards away.

"You think I don't know that?" Frachas responded in a full shout.

Another huge bolt of lightning came blasting down from the sky, illuminating a small patch of land in the distance—Titus caught sight of it.

"There! I saw land—three points off the starboard bow!" Titus screamed out to Frachas.

"Are you sure?" Frachas asked.

"Positive! On my mark, turn the wheel, captain!" Titus ordered.

Both men hooked their legs around the ropes by their feet for added support.

"Mark!" Titus yelled out, and the men began turning the wheel clockwise with all their might, holding on so tight that the muscles throughout their entire bodies flexed.

The ship began to come about. Another flash of lightning came pounding down into the sea.

"I saw land too! Less than two miles out!" Frachas yelled. "Pray to the gods we can hold on that long. I'm going to run us aground!"

The *Temptress* was closing in on the island. It was now no more than a mile in the distance. The severity of the storm continued to increase. The ship had pitched so far onto its side that the quarterdeck touched the water line when a bolt of lightning came down right on top of the *Temptress*, hitting the mainsail mast. The bolt split the vessel in two, right down the middle.

Titus and Frachas were cast out to sea by the explosion. Many men in the main cabin took a direct hit and were killed or knocked unconscious. Joseph, bracing below deck, went flying across the cabin, his body smashing into the other side of the hull—he cracked a couple of ribs but was not immobilized.

The two ends of the ship, the bow and stern, began to take on water. Men fell through the gap in the split ship, disappearing down into the sea's abyss.

Joseph was able to race to the quarterdeck, up the ship's stairs, before his section of the boat sank. From his vantage he could see the stern, fully broken off at the ship's midsection. Joseph moved to the deck railing and was thinking about jumping out to sea rather than sink with the ship when another bolt of lightning hit the forward mast. He was propelled a hundred feet through the air into the sea.

# Chapter 15:

# The Greek Island of Zakynthos

**THE SKIES** completely cleared, and the morning sun shined down upon Joseph, lying unconscious on the beach.

"Joseph! Joseph! Are you alive, Hebrew?" Titus asked while slapping Joseph's face, trying to wake him.

"He looks dead to me," Frachas said.

Joseph was back in the white space. He heard echoing voices coming at him from all directions. He felt as though he was spinning around while standing still. There was nothing to see except bright white light.

"Who's there?" Joseph yelled out. This experience was different from his prior ones in the white space. No one replied; just snippets of incomprehensible voices continued peppering him from all sides.

"Elijah. Are you there? What is this?" Joseph asked—still no reply came forth.

Now he felt his body begin to float upwards, though he could not be certain of it as he was still only able to see white light. He turned his head around, and suddenly he was hovering a thousand feet in the air outside the walls of Jerusalem, looking towards the city center below.

Joseph raised his head to see a pillar of fire come down from the sky. The pillar landed directly on top of the Temple of David. For a moment the Temple, engulfed in a spiraling flame, appeared

Joseph's Prophecy of the Temple

unscathed from the fire raining down upon it. A burning mush-room cloud rose up, spreading over the entire city, though not so much as one brick was destroyed.

Then a great explosion consumed the Temple Mount, send-ing its stones flying out in all directions. Joseph clasped his ears unconsciously against the deafening explosion.

Looking down to the ground, Joseph could see the bodies of men, women, and children quickly turn to lifeless black ash. The silhouettes of the people flew away into nothingness. No one was left living, and everyone had disappeared.

Next, the earth began to shake. The sound of the quake was so intense Joseph closed his eyes, trying to distance himself from the horror he was witnessing. Increasing in volume and strength, the shaking came to a sudden halt.

Joseph opened his eyes. Then the walls of the city, the houses, the ministerial buildings, and every other part built by man came crashing down to the ground, leaving an immense cloud of dust where the city once stood. Jerusalem looked like a barren hilltop as in the days of Abraham.

Joseph continued hovering in the air, looking at the pillar of fire still churning down on the Temple Mount. In a flash, the pillar was gone, and the city was covered in darkness.

Joseph violently gasped for breath as he sat up on the beach. "Aaaahh! Aaaahh!" He screamed uncontrollably until Frachas punched him in the face, knocking his head back to the beach sand.

"I believe he is alive, my lord," Frachas said to Titus.

Titus turned his head to look Frachas in the eyes, silently telling him he was not amused by his humor. "Did you have to punch him in the face, Frachas?"

"No, my lord. But I *wanted* to punch him in the face. I don't much care for incessant screaming—why do you think I left my wife?"

"You left your wife because you found a man," Titus replied.

"I also left her because I found a man," Frachas added. "You remember the mouth that bitch had on her?"

"She could talk, that I clearly remember."

"Am I dead?" Joseph queried, sitting up slowly. "Last I remember, we were in the midst of a biblical storm. Now we are set upon a beach paradise."

"Good, you're awake! And I assure you, we're not dead," Titus confirmed. "Look down the beach." Titus pointed to a string of Roman bodies lying still. "They are dead. We were somehow more fortunate. Come, Joseph, the sun will not wait for us and we must prepare a camp for our present situation.

"Help him up, Frachas. We need to get moving," Titus ordered.

Frachas took both of Joseph's arms in his hands and helped Joseph to his feet.

"Ahh!" Joseph screamed at the pain from his broken bones.

"What wrong?" Titus asked.

"I think I cracked a rib or two in the shipwreck."

"Let me take a look," Frachas said. "I'm a trained medic."

Joseph submitted.

"Ouch. Looks like you broke one, two," Frachas said as he touched and probed each of Joseph's broken bones individually. "Two ribs. Avoid heavy lifting for the next two weeks if you can," Frachas recommended.

Joseph, Titus, and Frachas were the only survivors of the *Temptress'* great wreck. After examining the bodies of those washed ashore looking for signs of life, they walked along the beach scouring the washed-up debris for any items of use.

"Frachas. Pull that log up to the tree line. We can use every piece of functional wood, either to build a tent or burn in a campfire," Titus ordered.

Wandering off a quarter-mile down the beach from where Frachas and Joseph were gathering wood, Titus scavenged through the *Temptress'* debris. Though he did not want to look at his dead men again as he had done earlier in the day, he had no choice—the items of most use were undoubtedly in the pockets of the deceased and attached to their waists. Titus went from body to body, not looking for life this time, but for daggers, canteens, flasks, lighting stones, and anything else worth salvaging. He carried his found items across his back in a burlap sack which he had also saved from the wreck.

Titus walked by a young legionnaire, no more than sixteen years of age. He was going to say a Roman prayer for the young man, but before he could utter his first word, he noticed a silver pendant in the shape of the two tablet stones of the Ten Commandments.

"The boy was a Hebrew?" Titus thought to himself and instinctively removed the pendant from the dead soldier for safekeeping.

"Titus!" Frachas called out from far down the beach, waving a jug in his hand. "We have wine!"

*＊＊*

**THE THREE** men salvaged items for the good part of the morning. Their finds included: a pound of sheep jerky, a jug of wine, a lambskin canteen mostly full of water, three burlap sacks, three steel daggers, one of which was rusted, a half portion of a linen sail, one hundred feet of thick rope, several bundles of clothes from the deceased, and one flintstone. They had also hauled several dozen logs and wooden beams to the beach's tree line for miscellaneous uses.

Satisfied with their pickings, their attention shifted to constructing a simple ridge tent. Titus and Frachas heaved wooden beams together to form the skeleton of the tent, securing the beams with the salvaged rope. Part of the ship's sail was repurposed as a roof, lashed across the top of the beams. Joseph collected a mass of shrubs and weeds, and lined the roof of the tent for added protection and camouflaged privacy.

"We need to eat, Frachas," Titus said as they finished working on the small tent.

"We have jerky," Frachas said.

"We need more than a pound of meat split between the three of us, captain," Titus responded.

"We still have a half-day of sun. Let's go on a hunt," Frachas suggested.

"I can make a fish trap," Joseph offered, "but we need to find a lake or a river for that to work. Maybe we should search the island, see what wildlife, plants, and perhaps fish it has to offer."

"That actually sounds like a good plan, Hebrew," Frachas said. "Titus, what say you?"

"I agree. Let's split up the jerky, and we'll go on an exploratory hike," Titus decided.

Frachas broke out the small bag of sheep jerky, and the three men ate like savages, having had no food since before the storm.

Frachas moved to pick up the wine bottle but was denied by Titus smacking his hand.

"Captain, there will be no wine drinking until we have finished the day's business," Titus commanded a disappointed Frachas. "I need you sober and able to pounce on a fox."

"Surely one drink never hurt anyone," Frachas begged.

"Take a drink then," Titus responded, throwing him the lambskin canteen of *water*. "You can drink wine to your heart's content *after* we catch our dinner," Titus continued.

Titus, Frachas, and Joseph set out for the island's wilderness, completely unsure of what to expect. The journey led them under trees, over rocks, and through prickly bushes before they came to a twenty-foot waterfall dropping into a calm basin pool. Joseph saw the splashing of life in the water; it was the perfect place to lay a fish trap.

"My lords, this is the spot to fish," Joseph declared. "I need only make a trap, and this basin should feed us indefinitely.

"Good, make it happen," Titus ordered. "But we need food now. Frachas and I are going on a hunt. Can you make the trap on your own?"

"I suppose I need nothing more than a dagger," Joseph answered.

"Here," Titus said, handing the rusty salvaged dagger to Joseph. "We're off—meet us back at the beach campsite at sunset, agreed?"

"Agreed."

*　　*　　*

**JOSEPH BUSIED** himself searching for weed stalks for a fish trap. He was in the middle of a lush, water-rich land overflowing with plants and trees. But to be successful making a trap, he needed the right weeds that were as strong as a tree branch, and long, straight, and flexible—like bamboo.

Looking around the brush for no more than ten minutes, Joseph came upon an endless supply of long mallows. He cut the plants with his rusted blade just above their roots. He must have picked fifty of them. He put the lot on his shoulder and carried them back to the edge of the water basin to his fishing spot—it looked like he was carrying bundles of green rods laced with flowers.

Next, Joseph needed something durable to use as twine. Directly in front of him, he spied a set of pink flowers in the distance.

"Ask and ye shall receive," Joseph said to himself.

He had come across a patch of fireweed. He could not have asked for a better natural rope material. Fireweed is thin like twine, somewhat straight and very durable. But most importantly it is able to withstand being tied into knots and holds firm.

Joseph labored to pull all the fireweed he could carry on his shoulder and hauled the load back to the water basin, dropping it next to the pile of mallows.

First he trimmed all the mallows of their leaves and branches, putting the bare mallow stalks in a pile. Then he cut a third of the stalks into smaller half-size pieces, making equal piles of even-length short stalks and even-length long stalks.

Joseph next turned to the fireweed and repeated the brush-removal process. He took the ends of the fireweed plants and tied them together in a double-fisherman's knot. After some time, he had over a hundred feet of weed rope.

He returned to the pile of short mallow stalks. He took one end of each stalk, and one end only, and sharpened it with his rusty dagger. He now had two dozen short stalks, each about two feet in length, with one sharp point.

He next curved one long stalk into a hoop about a foot in diameter, securing it in this position with weed rope. Then he took a short, sharpened stalk and wove a figure-eight loop with the fireweed, connecting the unsharpened end of the mallow stalk to the outside of the hoop with the sharpened end pointing away.

Joseph spaced out an inch on the hoop and then tied another short mallow stalk's unsharpened end on the hoop. He repeated the process until the hoop was ringed with short stalks, their sharpened ends all coming together to create a spiked round opening.

Next, he interwove the fireweed rope around the midpoint of the short stalks, connecting them to one another, giving the creation a cone-like shape. This formed a narrow opening at the end of the sharpened stalks—it was the mouth of the trap. Here the fish would swim in but would be unable to swim back out without being pricked by the sharp points.

Now Joseph needed to make a cage to hold the fish once they passed through the mouth he had just constructed. This was easily accomplished by attaching the long mallow stalks to the very same hoop and tying their ends together closed.

Joseph took a long stalk, about four feet in length, and placed one end on the hoop in one of the one-inch spaces he had apportioned while rimming the small mallow stalks around the hoop. He secured the long stalk to the hoop with fireweed rope and continued the process until he had once again ringed the entire hoop.

Then Joseph made another hoop and interwove the rope weed between this hoop and the midpoints of the long stalks for added support. He gathered the ends of the long stalks and tied them together solidly with the fireweed.

The entire creation looked like a striped green cone inside of a larger striped green cone.

Joseph took some of the remaining rope and attached it to the midsection hoop of the trap. He secured the other end of the rope to an exposed tree root. He put a five-pound stone through the mouth and into the belly of the trap to weigh it down in the water. Then he set the trap in the calm area of the waterfall basin. No bait was even needed. It was just a matter of time before fish would cruise through the mouth of the trap and get stuck.

Having finished and set the fish trap, Joseph walked back to the beach campsite to meet up with Titus and Frachas.

Once back, he busied himself setting up a firepit in anticipation of Titus and Frachas returning with something to cook. He laid stones in a ring and collected twigs for kindling. He used the piece of flint that he had taken from the salvage and began to strike it on the rusty dagger. Everything was still damp from the storm. Joseph stayed at it, striking the flintstone furiously against the rusted dagger for at least fifteen straight minutes—nothing was catching fire.

Titus and Frachas walked up to the firepit from deep inside the island's wilderness. They dropped a burlap sack in front of Joseph.

"Take a guess what we have," Frachas said proudly.

"A sheep or a goat?" Joseph mused facetiously.

The only reply was a 'ribbit.'

"We have all the toad legs you can eat!" Frachas exclaimed victoriously and then opened the burlap sack to show a dozen toads in captivity.

Upon seeing the toads, Joseph was less than excited.

"I can't eat those, my lord," Joseph stated. "Toads are unclean animals and forbidden to my people."

"Do you believe this bullshit?" Frachas yelled out. "We've been killing ourselves running after toads all day long in the hot sun while you haven't even so much as started a fire. Now you refuse to eat!"

"Lord Frachas," Joseph began to explain calmly, "I worked on a fish trap all day long so that we may all eat a pure creature, not the filth that you picked up."

"You thankless Hebrew bastard…" Frachas angrily said, stepping up to Joseph's face.

Titus could see this confrontation escalating and stepped in.

"Both of you shut your mouths. That is an order!" Titus yelled. "If Joseph does not want to eat toad, we'll have more for ourselves," he said directly to Frachas. "Joseph, you said you made a trap, correct?"

"Yes. I set it in the basin of the waterfall a couple of hours ago. It may already have caught a fish or two," Joseph answered.

"Well done," Titus acknowledged. "But, right now, we need to get this fire going."

"I'm working on that and have been for the last fifteen minutes. The sparks are put out by the dampness on the kindling," Joseph said while continuing to strike flint against the rusted dagger. "It's not happening," he said, exhausted from the constant striking. He threw the dagger to the ground, put the flint in his pocket, and stood up.

Then Joseph was struck with a thought, unknown in origin.

"I think I have an idea: dandelions. Or more specifically, the white puff balls that are left after the petals fall off. They are highly combustible like wool—light a bunch of puff balls on fire, and the wood, though damp, might just catch."

"That sounds crazy enough to work," Frachas interjected. "If there is a chance to cook these green critters, I'm all for it."

"Very well, go find what you need. Just don't wander off too far," Titus instructed.

"Yes, my lord."

Joseph began walking out into the wilderness of the island to search through the overgrown weeds for dandelion puffs.

"I'm not excited about the prospect of us eating raw toad," Frachas said to Titus.

"You don't have to eat if you'd prefer to wither away and die," Titus suggested.

"What a lovely set of options: raw toad or death," Frachas said back.

"Can you start a fire with sticks?" Titus asked.

"I've seen it done, but I've never been able to do it myself. With the moisture on the wood from the storm, I don't see how it is possible," Frachas stated.

"Not to mention, with no fire, sleeping in the cold won't be much fun. Maybe the Hebrew will surprise us," Titus speculated.

"Maybe." Frachas pondered. "I do have something that can warm us up though," he said with a fiendish grin.

"Like you ever needed an excuse to drink, captain," Titus replied mockingly. "Wait for the food before you open the wine. We're going to need it to swallow the toad, especially if we have to eat it raw."

Joseph returned with a sack full of dandelion puffs. He must have picked two hundred. Joseph now sat in the tent to protect the puffs from blowing away in the beach wind. Discarding the dandelion stems, he gathered a sizeable pile of puff fibers. When Joseph emerged from the tent, he had an entire handful of what looked like raw wool. He carefully placed the fibers around the base of the little twig teepee in the firepit. He took the flintstone and struck it against the rusted dagger. Sparks hit the plant fibers, and a small flame started up almost instantly.

"Fire on the first strike!" Joseph yelled out, almost not believing it himself.

"Good work, Hebrew," Frachas congratulated. "I never doubted you for a second."

The fire began to grow with Joseph carefully minding it, adding larger and larger pieces of wood until the fire was fully roaring.

Titus and Frachas impaled their toads with small roasting sticks and began to cook the poor creatures while they were still alive.

Joseph jeered at the sounds of the toads screaming.

"They're just toads, Hebrew," Frachas said. "Have you never had frog legs?"

"Never," Joseph answered resolutely.

The toads were nearly finished cooking.

"Doesn't that smell good?" Frachas asked.

"It smells different," Titus modified Frachas' declaration.

"If my stomach had food in it, I'd want to throw it up." Joseph spoke in his mind but kept his words from Titus and Frachas on this thought.

Frachas grabbed the wine jug. He took a swig. Holding the

wine in his mouth, he lowered in the legs of the roasted toad.

"It's not horrible if you pretend it's wine and cheese," Frachas joked, chewed, swallowed, and then gagged.

Titus sighed at the sight of Frachas munching on the toad.

"Let me help you," Frachas said. "Open up your mouth and put your head back."

"For the sake of the gods, Frachas—hand me the jug!" Titus yelled, not about to let Frachas pour wine into his mouth like a helpless child.

Titus took a drink and followed Frachas' way of eating. As the two continued to eat the meat of the roasted toads, blood ran down each of their faces. It was obvious they were both working hard to keep the toad from immediately coming back up their throats.

"At least the wine is good," Frachas said after finishing his first toad. "This must have been a bottle from poor old Perseus' private stock. May the gods rest his soul." Frachas poured out a little wine into the dirt for Perseus.

"Gods rest his soul." Titus joined in the benediction.

"God rest his soul," Joseph said, taking the wine from Titus.

Titus and Frachas both looked curiously at Joseph, noticing the singular nature of his blessing.

"That reminds me, Joseph," Titus said as Joseph began to drink from the bottle. "Here, this is for you."

Titus handed Joseph the silver pendant of the Ten Commandments. Joseph took one look at it and froze in deep thought. A million memories seemed to race through his mind.

Not knowing how to thank Titus, he merely said, "Thank you, my lord."

Titus nodded, acknowledging Joseph's gracious acceptance.

"Are you going to pass that jug, Hebrew?" an annoyed Frachas said, waiting for Joseph, who was still holding the wine but now occupied with his pendant.

"Forgive me." Joseph apologized and passed the jug on to Frachas.

"Well, I'm starting to feel good!" Frachas exclaimed as he finished his next set of swigs. "How about the rest of you?"

Whenever Frachas drank, he invariably became excited. Titus could see where this was going. Either a tale of yore, an exhibition of strength, or some type of sexual deviance was sure to follow.

"Frachas, I know when you drink, you like to play—given the circumstances of our situation, perhaps going straight to sleep might be a better idea?" Titus asked, attempting to avert another 'classic Frachas' drunken episode.

"If anything, my great Lord General Flavius Titus Vespasianus…" Frachas began, starting to slur his words and speak in hyperbole. "If anything, we should celebrate! We are three souls out of a hundred that have been blessed with an extended life, foiling the gods of the sea! We were even given sacred vino to consecrate this divine providence!" And with that Frachas ripped off his tunic and began dancing around the campsite bare-naked, singing merrily:

*I am the champion of the sea!*
*There is no better captain than me!*
*My mates is dead and I gots no bread,*
*As long as I've wine, I'm more than fine,*
*For it's just Titus, the Hebrew, and me!*

"Is this usual behavior, my lord?" Joseph asked Titus.

"More usual than you know," Titus confessed back.

"You should be a poet, captain!" Joseph said, amused at Frachas' naked song-and-dance number.

"Don't encourage him, Joseph. He'll only strive to impress us further," Titus said, pleasantly annoyed with Frachas' spectacle.

*Today I've cheated the gods of the sea!*
*My sailors have all taken their last pee,*
*I sing out loud, jolly and proud,*
*Flopping my cock, naked as a rock,*
*For it's just Titus, the Hebrew, and me!*

"That's quite enough. Put your clothes back on, man. Surely the cold night air is embarrassing," Titus teased playfully.

*The great General Titus is jealous of me!*
*Every time he sees me pee!*
*His cock's so small, it mustn't please women at all,*
*That's why he can't land a wife, to save his life,*
*For it's just Titus, the Hebrew, and me!*

"Lovely performance," Titus said, clapping his hands facetiously. "Now will you shut up? I'm for bed."

"Titus, the night is young. We haven't even, you know?" Frachas said, laughing uncontrollably while gyrating his pelvis back and forth.

"Shut your drunken mouth this moment!" Titus ordered, showing true anger boiling up.

"Who cares? In Rome it's all the same. Man, woman; man, man; man, boy; *boy, boy*—it's all the same," Frachas said, reminding Titus of a secret time in their childhood.

Titus had had enough. He walked up to the naked Frachas and kicked him in his testicles. Frachas fell to his knees moaning, and then Titus connected a right hook to Frachas' jaw, knocking him out instantly.

"I thought that asshole would never stop moving his mouth," Titus explained to Joseph. "If you would like to punch him back for that hit he gave you this morning, now's your chance."

"Perhaps next time," Joseph said, not wanting to participate in Roman violence.

"Suit yourself—then sleep it is. But first, help me drag Frachas into the tent."

Joseph complied, using his left hand to avoid putting pressure on the right side of his chest where his fractures were.

Joseph and Titus lay down with the unconscious Frachas between them. Joseph put a burlap sack over Frachas' manhood. Soon all three were asleep.

*  *  *

**MORNING CAME** and Joseph was starving, so much so that he could feel his body becoming weaker, not wanting to do much of anything but rest and of course eat.

"Lord Titus, my body is weak, my cracked ribs ache, and my mind is becoming delirious with hunger. You or Frachas need to go fetch the fish from the trap," Joseph explained. "I think I'd collapse if I tried."

Titus nodded in agreement. "Frachas," he called out. "You've been promoted to 'chief fisherman.' Now go get the fish."

Frachas gave Titus a look to let him know just how delighted he was with being tasked as a bag man, but he put up no argument. After grabbing his burlap sack, Frachas began making his way to the waterfall basin.

Joseph had the strength to clear the ashes out of the firepit, readying it for Frachas' return. He still had a small handful of dandelion puffs—again Joseph arranged a teepee of kindling wood and lined the base with the dandelion fibers. Striking the flintstone against the rusted dagger, he was able to recreate his fire-starting magic from the night before.

The next moment, a small flame emerged and began to grow onto the kindling wood. Joseph worked the fire with a stick and blew on it. Within a couple of minutes, the fire was going strong.

A short time later Frachas came walking out of the island wilderness with his burlap sack on his shoulder—it was moving from the inside.

"Two big ones!" Frachas said, putting the sack down on the ground and opening it to show off the catch.

Joseph smiled, knowing he had done well making the fish trap.

"I'll cut these fat bastards up," Frachas said.

First he removed the heads and tails, then he gutted the fish. Next, he chopped the meat up into two dozen one-inch squares. He took a few roasting sticks and shoved them through the fish squares, making three full kabobs.

Frachas placed the kabobs over the fire, turning them every other minute, careful not to burn or overcook the fish. All three men's mouths watered as the smell of fresh cooked fish was divine to the olfactory senses.

As soon as the meat was barely cooked well enough, Frachas handed out the kabobs. All three moaned with pleasure, Joseph regained part of his strength with every bite.

"Oh, gods, this fish is good," Frachas lauded. "Beats the hell out of toad guts."

The three sat around the fire, each holding a kabob, satisfying their stomachs and their souls.

Now that they had a proven fish trap, neither Titus nor Frachas wanted any more toad—they released the remaining uncooked animals back into the wild, more than content to eat only fish.

It was still morning time, but the three men were in an after-meal state of relaxation, nearly asleep besides the waning fire.

Frachas got up and walked a small way down the beach and behind a thick patch of shrubs. He pulled his tunic up and squatted down.

"There's not much better in this world than a good shit," he thought while busy in the process.

From his vantage, he could see the white sandy beach and the horizon line of the sea. Something was not quite right. But for a long moment while Frachas excreted his waste, he could not glean what was out of place. Then, with a sensation of a hammer smashing into his stomach, Frachas saw it.

Every last corpse had vanished.

"The bodies of the dead Romans should be lying on the beach," Frachas thought to himself.

Then he noticed hundreds of footprints in the sand, many more than they had left the other day while searching for live sailors and salvaging debris. A deep panic hit Frachas and coursed through his entire body.

Then he heard a 'snap.'

Frachas looked up. The sound did not emanate from the campsite; it was from farther back in the wilderness. He finished defecating and slowly stood up from his squat, looking for whatever made the noise. He only saw shrubs and trees.

Another 'snap,' closer than the first, made Frachas' heart skip a beat. He scanned left and saw movement. Two Greek savages were walking slowly towards the campsite. They had white paint covering their faces and spears at their sides.

The rogues had not seen him.

"They must have smelled the fire," Frachas thought to himself and pulled his dagger from his waist.

The rogues were close, less than fifty yards away from Titus and Joseph, who were relaxing around the firepit, oblivious to any danger. Frachas saw the two rogues whisper something to each other, and then they raised their spears forward into a striking position.

One Greek began charging at Titus and the other one at Joseph. Titus sat facing the two men and was quick to react, rolling over on the ground to avoid impalement. Joseph had his back turned to his would-be spearman. But before the other Greek could spear Joseph through, Frachas jumped on him from the side, knocking the savage down to the beach sand. After a quick struggle, Frachas slit the savage's throat with his dagger.

The savage who had tried to impale Titus was now wrestling with him on the ground. Titus head-butted the Greek—the rogue head-butted back. Titus pulled his dagger and slashed the savage across the chest, scoring a deep cut but not a mortal or incapacitating wound. The Greek connected an uppercut, knocking Titus to the ground and causing his dagger to fall from his hand.

"Frachas, I could use some help!" Titus called.

But before Frachas could get himself up and off the dead savage, Joseph grabbed an egg-sized stone and flung it into the back of the Greek's head, cracking the back of his skull and killing him instantly. He fell limp to the ground, right next to Titus.

"Nice shot," Frachas congratulated Joseph's stone-throwing skills.

"Thank you, Joseph," Titus said as he slowly stood up.

"We have a situation here," Frachas said to Titus.

"Don't I know it—there might be more Greek barbarians out there right beyond the tree line," Titus said.

"Yes, but I was referring to our dead Romans. They've taken the bodies," Frachas told him.

"What are you talking about?" Titus asked.

"Look. They're all gone!" Frachas said.

The three men rushed to inspect the beach.

"The sea might have washed them out," Titus speculated.

"The rest of the debris is still there, general. And there are ruts all over the beach. They dragged the bodies, and their feet made those marks in the sand."

"What would they want with dead bodies?" Titus asked before thinking about it more clearly. "Did they bury them?"

Then Joseph tapped Titus on the shoulder. Titus turned around and looked at a huge plume of black smoke in the sky.

"They're burning the bodies," Frachas said.

"Perhaps, but they have certainly made our signal flare," Titus added.

The three men stood watching the tall plume of smoke when Titus was struck in the head from behind with a wooden baton, knocking him out. Frachas and Joseph turned around—a dozen spears were pointed at their midsections and heads.

# Chapter 16:

# The Feast

**ALL THREE** men's hands were bound with rope. Joseph and Frachas were marched by a tribe of Greek savages down the beach towards the plume of smoke. One of the savages carried the unconscious Titus on his back.

"Grigter! Grigter!" A Greek yelled at Joseph and Frachas to move more quickly.

A couple of other men carried the bodies of the two dead rogues who had been killed by Joseph and Frachas.

"This is bad. This is very, very bad," Frachas said.

"Think of a way to escape, captain," Joseph urged.

"I am thinking!" a frustrated Frachas shouted back. "But I can't come up with anything—that's why I said this is bad!"

"Shazee Shazee!" a rogue Greek said and then violently slapped Frachas in the face, advising him to be quiet.

Joseph thought the savage rogue might be saying 'shut up' in Greek, but it sounded funny. Joseph had learned the King's Greek—whatever these natives were speaking was definitely not that.

As they moved closer towards the smoke, the smell of flesh burning became more obvious. Joseph had learned what human meat set ablaze smelled like during the uprising in Jerusalem and again during the siege of Jotapata—Frachas had learned this many years ago from the beginning of his service in the Roman military.

Joseph, thinking of any possible escape, first attempted to use his guile and spoke some words in Greek.

"Eimaste filoi. Psachnoume gia to Romaiko skafos mas—einai konta."

This translated to: 'We are friends. We are searching for our Roman vessel—it is close.'

Joseph received a hard slap on the face from the same brute who had also chastised Frachas.

"I should have learned from Frachas," Joseph thought to himself. "Perhaps they speak some kind of Greek dialect so thick they can't understand formal Greek." His thoughts continued racing through his mind.

They were approaching the source of the great smoke plume. As they moved further down the beach, the voices of a clan of Greek barbarians chanting could now be heard as well as the beating of drums.

They continued walking across the beach a good five minutes longer—passing over a dune when the great fire finally came into sight. Joseph could see walls of flames nearly twenty feet high. The firepit looked like a funeral pyre of a Nordic king.

"They're burning all the bodies to prevent disease from spreading," Joseph speculated internally.

An entire community of Greek rogue savages came into view. They were sitting around the firepit like it was a theater in the round. All of them had their faces painted white. Little babies rested by their mothers' bosoms. Small children were running around knocking each other down. And the adult males were laid out on the ground, seemingly resting. Every last one of their bellies was bulging almost like they were pregnant. Joseph did not know what to make of it.

The natives, male and female alike, wore only loincloths for modesty and makeshift sandals—though they did have the most exotic forms of piercings throughout their faces and ears. Some of their ears had been stretched so far, they hung all the way down to their shoulders. Others had gold and silver barbs protruding from both sides of their noses. All of them had tattoos from ink—many more had markings by mutilation.

The band of Greeks marched their captives towards a small wooden hut. It stood outside the ring of savages frolicking and resting around the great fire. There, the chief sat in his dais.

As they walked to the chief, they saw dozens of severed heads all lined up in a row around the bottom of the firepit. There were also at least a dozen naked corpses lying next to each other, all Romans, all decapitated and disemboweled. Another pile of unmutilated Roman bodies lay on the other side of the fire.

Savage Greek women were busy stripping every last thread from the dead to sell or to use in a garment. It was a symbiotic relationship where the body would be delivered naked by the females after scavenging the clothes off the dead Roman before being dissected by the males.

Then Joseph and Frachas saw a small mountain of stacked bones and skulls.

"My God, Frachas, they're cannibals," Joseph said as his heart sank.

A savage with a golden headdress, the apparent shaman of this strange community, with red and yellow paint covering his body in addition to his white face paint, kneeled over one of the Roman corpses. He took a large hatchet with an obsidian blade from his side and decapitated the corpse. A great scream from the natives arose, and chanting followed. The chant sounded like mostly vowels, and Joseph could not understand its meaning: "Addaa uttaa! Addaa uttaa!"

The shaman raised the decapitated head high while shaking his body in a violent dance. Then he passed the head along to savages standing in a line until all had taken their turn caressing it.

The shaman then took a dagger and began carving up the corpse. He pulled out the intestines and handed them to a dancing female native who extended the small intestine twenty feet out for all to see.

Then he severed the intestines from the remaining guts.

Another female took the severed end. The two holding the opposite ends of the intestine began swinging it around together. Two more women jumped into the swinging intestine, and the clan of Greeks began counting with each successful jump.

"Alpaa, Besta, Gamme, Detta, Epis!"

Then one of the jumping savages got tripped up, tangling the small intestine between the jumpers. The watching clan of rogues started laughing hysterically.

Finished jumping guts, the women tossed the entire intestine into the fire.

"They speak a form of Greek, Frachas. Did you hear them chanting? They were counting out numbers!" Joseph said, excited at the renewed prospects of communicating with them.

"Hebrew—I thought of something. Look over there. These savages have a ship in the bay. If we can get loose, I can sail us home," Frachas proposed.

"That sounds workable," Joseph replied optimistically.

The shaman was still at it with the Roman corpse. Next, the stomach was removed, shown to all, and thrown into the fire. The liver was taken next, but this they put in a black pan which they rested on the edge of the fire. The kidneys soon followed the liver in the pan. The lungs and all the vestigial organs were cut out and tossed into the fire. Then came the heart. At the sight of the shaman holding the severed heart high in the air, the entire tribe became quiet, bending over in submission towards the red muscle.

"Addaa uttaa!" the shaman yelled.

And with that, the heart was launched high into the air from the hands of the shaman.

Dozens of men rose up and followed the heart's trajectory, running in a full sprint. The heart came falling back to the earth, and the natives began fighting over it as Romans would fight over gold. Kicking, punching, and biting—they were trying to lay their claim to the talisman, which was now covered in sand from rolling around on the beach as each savage fought for possession of it. The only thing the Greek savages did not do was stab each other for it.

Finally, one man emerged with the heart after fending off countless adversaries. He took the heart back to his resting area, washed it off, and placed it next to him, showing adoration for his prize, treating it more like a baby than a lucky charm.

Joseph and Frachas approached the chief. Titus was tossed beside the two men, unconscious.

The band of rogues that had captured Joseph, Frachas, and Titus also delivered the two dead bodies of their fallen comrades on the ground, next to Titus.

An old man wearing a crown of bird feathers came forward. He looked the foreigners up and down.

"Skitoni. Eisi kris!" which translated roughly to: "You kill. You are meat!"

The chief pointed to the two dead rogues Frachas and Joseph had killed.

Joseph was unable to speak. He could not quite understand the dialect of Greek. Communication had always been his strongest weapon, and now it failed him.

"For the sake of the gods, Joseph—say something!" Frachas cried out.

"We were only defending ourselves," Joseph said in formal Greek. "They snuck up on us and tried to spear us," he continued.

The chief replied in perfect Greek, "And why shouldn't they spear you? You are Roman, are you not?"

"I am a Hebrew, but my friends are Romans," Joseph replied in Greek.

The chief nodded his head, comprehending Joseph's response. He uttered a command in the tribe's native dialect that Joseph could not make out. Then the chief informed Joseph of his directive. "We do not take prisoners. Your friends will be cooked and fill our bellies. You, Hebrew, are free to leave this island, but make no mistake, you are not welcome here. If you do not leave, you will end up like your Roman friends."

Joseph was horrified at the idea of Titus and Frachas ending up as food. Quickly he called upon his mind, and brilliant words came out of his mouth: "Chief, would you eat meat that has been sullied?"

The chief did not understand. "What are you speaking of?" was his reply.

"These men are possessed by a devil. Their meat will drive whoever eats it into a murdering madman before falling over dead," Joseph explained.

The chief was totally taken off guard by Joseph's words. He looked deep into Joseph's eyes and then began to laugh uncontrollably. He made a signal with his hands to his clan, and Frachas and the still-unconscious Titus had their clothes torn off—they were being prepped to be cooked.

"What the hell is going on, Hebrew?" Frachas screamed at the top of his lungs.

"They are going to kill you, cook you, and then eat you," Joseph replied.

"You treacherous Hebrew bastard!" Frachas shouted. "I knew you'd betray us at the first opportunity!"

Joseph had an idea and he began addressing the chief. "My great chief, before you cook these men, allow me to perform my sacred ritual to remove the devil I speak of from them. I am a Hebrew priest and trained in such matters. If I do not free their souls, they will rest in the bodies of the men that eat them, causing them to go mad. You are all already fat from the bodies of the dead Romans your tribe has already gorged upon. Let me protect you and your clan."

The chief thought seriously on the matter as mystical beliefs were rife among his tribe—he approved Joseph's exorcism.

"Frachas, I have convinced them to let me perform a ritual to remove the devil from both you and Titus," Joseph explained.

"What the hell are you talking about?" Frachas replied, completely bewildered by Joseph's statement.

"I am trying to buy time until I can figure a way out of this situation that includes you and Titus remaining alive," Joseph said. "Follow my lead, and we'll figure out an escape together."

First Joseph demanded that a four-foot scaffolding be erected, a necessity for the exorcism, or so he insisted to the chief. After an hour, the savages finished the scaffolding. Frachas and Titus, now awake, were laid on top of it, bound by ropes around their hands and feet.

"What is going on?" A dazed Titus lifted up his head.

"We've been caught by Greek savages, and we're soon to be killed, cooked, and then eaten," Frachas informed Titus.

"Oh, joy. Too bad I couldn't have remained unconscious," Titus said, laying his head back down on the scaffolding.

"Joseph is working on a ruse, or so he says. I hate to say this, my friend, but I think we are done for," Frachas confessed.

"Have faith in the Hebrew. He's not betrayed us yet. And we're not yet dead," Titus replied.

Joseph approached the scaffolding to conduct his séance. All the members of the rogue clan were keenly watching. He began chanting in Hebrew, confident that chanting in a foreign tongue would seem and sound appropriate to the uncomprehending natives.

*Sh'ma Yisrael, Adonai Eloheinu, Adonai Echad! Echad Eloheinu gadol Adoneinu, kadosh sh'mo. Gadlu l'Adonai iti, un'rom'mah sh'mo yachdav!*

Joseph finished the blessing, not knowing what to do next to prolong Titus and Frachas' lives. Then it came to him. He was a priest by trade—he would recite the entire Shabbat prayer service.

*Lecha Adonai hagadulah, vehagavurah, vehatiferet, vehanetzach vehahod. Ki chol bashamyim uva'aretz, ki chol bashamyim uva'aretz. Lecha Adonai hamamlacha, v'hamitnaseh, lechol lerosh.*

Joseph continued chanting:

*Romemu, romemu, Adonai Eloheinu, vehishtachavu, vehishtachavu, la'adom raglav kadosh hu. Romemu, romemu, Adonai Eloheinu, vehishtachavu, vehishtachavu, lehar kodsho lehar kodsho. Ki kadosh, Adonai Eloheinu.*

Joseph could see that his prayer service was being well received by the tribe members. The Greeks were dancing in a great circle around the firepit. Even the chief could be seen swaying to Joseph's incantations.

He continued his service, singing with extra pizzazz and enthusiasm. The savages seemed to love it. They all lifted their arms high toward the sky, reaching for their gods. The shaman began moving man to man, giving them some kind of divine blessing through the powerful shaking of his hands over each head.

"How long can I keep this up?" Joseph silently asked himself. Not knowing the answer, he continued his charade.

Joseph next began chanting Psalm 150.

He was not running out of prayers to sing, but he was very cognizant of the chief's disposition, specifically how long he could keep chanting before he was stopped.

After singing Psalm 150, Joseph could sense from the chief's body language that he was becoming restless with the growing length of the exorcism and beginning to question the effectiveness of Joseph's powers as nothing seemed to be happening to indicate the exorcism was making any difference. Even so, the tribe seemed to genuinely enjoy Joseph's singing. He kept it up, next reciting Psalm 23.

In the middle of the psalm, Joseph saw the chief call the shaman over to him with his hand. Though Joseph could not hear them speak, it appeared the chief was asking the shaman his opinions of the exorcism. Then the shaman noticeably disparaged Joseph to the chief with his hand and body gestures.

Joseph thought fast on his feet and muttered to Titus and Frachas covertly. "The chief is losing faith in my service. I need the two of you to help convince him that the devil is being drawn out of you," he said.

Then Joseph felt a hand on his shoulder. It was the chief telling him he was finished, and it was time to put Titus and Frachas to the knife and then the fire.

"The devil has almost been exorcised," Joseph argued in Greek to the chief.

The chief was not hearing his words. He motioned to the shaman to approach the scaffolding with his decapitation axe.

## Joseph Leads a Charade Exorcism

Joseph yelled out, "Submit to the power of Yahweh!" while moving his hands mystically as if wielding magical powers.

Titus and Frachas began a high-pitched screaming. Their bodies began convulsing, twisting, and twitching like a mighty spirit was stirring within them.

The chief, upon seeing the evil spirits manifest themselves in Titus and Frachas, instinctively pedaled backwards with his feet, so overwhelmed he fell to the ground in his retreat. Gathering himself quickly to his knees, he held his arms out crossed, attempting to shield himself from the evil spirits. All the tribesmen dropped to their knees and followed the chief's lead.

Joseph, seeing the reaction to Titus' and Frachas' performance, continued his act for maximum effect.

He continued yelling out words in Hebrew, using his inflection as a cue for Titus and Frachas to respond with the appropriate screams and undulations. Quickly they fell into a united rhythm, and at each prayer sent forth from Joseph's mouth, an appropriate response in the form of shouts and violent body movements came back from Titus and Frachas.

Joseph engaged in a shouting match with the 'devilish spirits' inside Titus and Frachas. Each time the iteration of screams was longer lasting than the time before.

"Scream if you are the devil!" Joseph yelled out in Greek, making sure the chief could hear him.

Though Joseph's Greek could only be understood by the chief, he was the only person that mattered. Titus and Frachas' fate was directly tied to his perception of reality.

Joseph built the exorcism to a climax. After intense shouting and a sorcerer's conjuring, Titus and Frachas fell completely silent and still.

The chief, shaman, and the rest of the tribe looked up.

"The Hebrew has done it!" the chief lauded him in his native tongue.

Joseph moved over Titus, lifted his arm, and dropped it, showing it to be limp. He did the same to Frachas. He nodded proudly to the chief that the deed was done. But before the shaman could make his way to the scaffolding, Joseph flung a line in Hebrew while pointing at Titus as one points to accuse a murderer—Titus began contorting violently again.

The 'devil' had not completely been expunged, requiring Joseph to go back into the more laborious parts of his exorcism—yet again.

For two whole hours now, the clan of Greek savages had been expertly played by Joseph accompanied by Titus and Frachas.

After hours of performing, Joseph, Titus, and Frachas were exhausted. Joseph finally collapsed from his great exertion. Frachas and Titus were nearly motionless now as well. It appeared the exorcism had concluded successfully to the natives.

"The Hebrew truly did it!" the chief yelled out to the tribe.

Motioning to the shaman, who was busy sharpening his knives, he stood up and began walking to the scaffolding with his great axe, ready to perform the ritual killing.

The chief called for a couple of men to help Joseph up and deliver him some water.

Joseph was splashed in the face with a gourdful of water. Two men lifted him up by his arms, straining his cracked ribs.

"Ahh!" He awoke screaming in pain.

He saw the back of the shaman wielding his axe over Titus and Frachas.

Seeing the shaman about to strike, Joseph summoned his last ounce of strength and rushed at him. The impact of their two bodies colliding sent the axe flying away from the platform.

The shaman hit Joseph in the face with a headbutt. Joseph struck him back with a knee to the groin.

Finally, a half dozen rogues pounced on Joseph and held him in a kneeling submission. The shaman punched Joseph in the face.

"Let's finish the ceremony!" the chief yelled out in his Greek dialect. "Addaa uttaa!"

The native drums began beating. They were struck at an increasing pace. A communal, tongue-rolling scream blasted from all the Greeks.

A savage retrieved the shaman's axe and ran it back to its owner, who resumed his executionary position.

"It looks like we're done for," Frachas said to Titus.

"Travel well, brother," Titus said back.

The shaman raised his sharper-than-steel obsidian axe over Frachas' neck. The entire tribe changed their chant as the blade hung in the air. "Addaa uttaa! Addaa uttaa! Addaa uttaa!"

Then an arrow flew into the head of the shaman, dropping him dead, down by the side of the scaffold.

"Kill every last Greek savage!" Captain Romulus yelled out, leading the charge.

Titus, Frachas, and Joseph looked up. It was an entire Roman centuria descending on the tribe.

The hundred Romans screamed as they raced forward towards the Greek rogues, their blades and spears raised high.

The savages did not have a chance. Those that resisted the Romans were slain easily. Many others fled into the island's wilderness. Within five minutes of fighting, the Romans were victorious, losing less than a handful of men.

A beastly Roman legionnaire, wielding two swords, decapitated the shaman with a scissor-like slicing of both his gladii simultaneously.

Joseph, freed in the melee, grabbed the axe out of the sha-man's dead hands, ran over to the scaffold, and cut Titus and Frachas' rope restraints.

"You're free, my lords," Joseph said.

"Gods, Hebrew! What took you so long?" Frachas roared.

Joseph's head shook with disbelief at Frachas' ingratitude.

"Thank you, Joseph," Titus said, looking backwards at Fra-chas and mouthing, "What is wrong with you?"

"Follow me, mates!" Captain Romulus yelled out, with the joy of a glorious victory. "To the *Enchanted!*"

# Chapter 17:

# A Ride on the *Enchanted*

**"PERMISSION TO** come aboard, captain?" Titus requested as a formality.

"Permission granted, general," said Captain Romulus. "We're pleased to have you aboard—even more pleased that you are still alive."

"I'm still alive too!" Frachas interjected as he boarded the ship.

"Ah yes, and you are?" Romulus asked.

"Frachas, Captain Frachas," he replied.

"Well, it's good to have you too," Romulus said indifferently. "And who do we have here?

"Joseph, son of Matthias, prisoner of Rome."

"He may be a prisoner, but make no mistake, captain, he's more like a brother," Titus added.

"Interesting. Perhaps I can hear more about this strange brotherly captive over food. I'm sure you are hungry. Please follow me to the mess deck."

Titus, Frachas, and Joseph followed Romulus below deck to the mess hall. Surprisingly, Perseus was working behind the cooking counter.

"Perseus!" Titus and Frachas cheered at the same time.

"General Titus!" Perseus excitedly answered. "And Captain Frachas," he said less than enthusiastically.

"It is so good to see you," Titus said, joining Perseus' arm in a Roman handshake.

"We thought you were dead," Frachas added.

"I should be so lucky, captain," Perseus said back. "I found myself washed up ashore a few miles down from where you were found. The *Enchanted* came by, seeing the black plume of smoke, and saw me hailing them from the beach."

"I see," Frachas replied.

"*I see* the Hebrew has also survived," Perseus stated, noticing Joseph.

"He's saved Frachas' and my skin more than once now," Titus said. "Treat him with top Roman honors."

Perseus' demeanor towards Joseph changed instantly.

"The Hebrew slave saved his Roman captors? What honor, what rarely-seen honor," Perseus said. "How about some wine and some meat for all—especially the Hebrew savior!"

"That would be perfect," Titus declared.

Perseus served up four wine-filled wooden goblets at the counter.

"Perhaps a loaf of fresh bread to nibble on while I cook the steaks? You're in luck. The *Enchanted* just restocked before rescuing us."

"You always know best," Titus said jovially.

"Now please sit, my lords. You all look starved, especially the Hebrew," Perseus suggested.

"A grand piece of advice," Frachas interjected.

All four men took their wine and bread and sat at an open mess table that common tirones had cleared for their high-ranking Roman officers.

"General, please recount your adventure in full detail. I'm anxious to hear how two Romans bound by ropes were aided by a Hebrew against those Greek savages," Romulus requested.

"Ah, how Romans soldiers love a good tale of battle and survival," Titus said. "Very well, captain, I'll indulge you, but only with the short version. If you want more details, provide my man Frachas with a bottle of wine, and he'll tell you everything you want to know—until it's empty.

"Alright, here it is. We were tasked with bringing Master Joseph here, the Defender of Jotapata, to Rome for justice, as commanded by Emperor Nero. We captured Joseph after a siege of a month and a half and put him on a ship with Frachas and myself commanding. Then the storm of storms approached us around the Greek islands. Our mast took a direct hit from Jupiter's bolt, sending me and Frachas out into the sea. We woke up, and Master Joseph was the only other living man on the beach besides me and Frachas.

"We had ourselves a camping party. Then the Greek savages emerged and tried to kill us. Master Joseph killed one with a throw of a rock to the head, and Frachas killed another with his blade. Then we were ambushed and abducted by a larger party of the Greeks. They wanted to cook and eat me and Frachas. Interestingly enough, the bastards sympathized with Joseph because he is a Hebrew. But Joseph did not betray us. He worked, using all his efforts for our salvation."

"I think I had something to do with your salvation as well, general, if I do say so myself," Romulus griped.

"As I was saying, Joseph kept us alive until Captain Romulus here saved the day! Happy with that ending, Romulus?" Titus asked.

"Very happy, general, sir," Romulus concurred.

Perseus' eavesdropping ears overheard the story, and he burst alive with sentiment.

"Master Joseph," Perseus said cheerfully, "well done on the island! You have proven yourself!"

"Three cheers for the Hebrew!" Titus declared.

The regular soldiers in the mess hall all joined in with a "Hip, hip, huzzah! Hip, hip, huzzah! Hip, hip, huzzah!"

Everyone took a drink in unison.

"Tell me something, Joseph. Why did you save us? It means your own death, you surely know," Titus inquired.

"I have faith in my God, that He will see me through all my trials, including the one yet to come in Rome," Joseph answered. "Plus my prophecy of your rise to Caesar would not be possible if you had died by the hands of those Greek savages," he said, winking.

Joseph took a bite of the fresh loaf of bread. "This sure beats hardtack," he said, smiling.

"Perseus," Romulus cried out. "Where the hell are those steaks? We starve!"

"Ask again and you won't be getting them!" Perseus yelled back from the galley.

All four men at the table chuckled at Perseus' crabby response.

"Joseph, is there some way I can show you thanks for saving me and Frachas?" Titus questioned.

"Sure, my lord—don't deliver me into Nero's hands," Joseph said, fully knowing the request was ludicrous.

"That is the one thing beyond my power," Titus replied. "Perhaps you want a woman? Or a boy?"

"I am married, my lord," Joseph responded.

"Ah. How many children do you have?" Frachas questioned.

"I have yet to be blessed with children," Joseph answered.

"Surely a marriage is not consummated until children are produced," Frachas mused.

"I fear we do things a bit differently in Jerusalem than Rome, Lord Frachas," Joseph said.

"Obviously," Frachas said back.

Perseus, pounding his peg leg, came out of the galley carrying four twenty-ounce steaks.

"I hear a peg banging into the floor. That can only mean one thing: dinner is served!" Frachas said jovially.

"Here, Captain Frachas," Perseus said, presenting him his steak. "I gave it an extra special seasoning, just for ya."

Frachas' face went limp, knowing Perseus' disposition in the kitchen.

After placing a plate down in front of each man with knives, Perseus refilled the goblets on the table.

"Enjoy!"

He then stomped off just as loud as he stomped in.

"What the hell did he mean by special seasoning?" Frachas asked the table quietly so that Perseus would not hear.

"He was just joking with you, I'm sure. Eat, man," Titus encouraged him.

Frachas complied as he was hungry and the steak looked delicious, but he would never find out if or how Perseus had tainted his food.

*  *  *

"**ANCHORS UP** and set sail!" Captain Romulus bellowed out.

The Roman sailors rushed about the quarterdeck. Four men were needed for cranking both the forward and aft capstans to raise up the anchors. Another dozen men busied themselves, letting down the ship's sails.

The *Enchanted* began its short journey to Rome—a week at most.

Titus, Frachas, and Romulus stood tall on the quarterdeck, a picture of Roman pride. Joseph was below deck, napping in a hammock.

Frachas turned to Titus. "What say you to a game of Roman chess, general?"

"You know you always win. How about a game of dice?" Titus replied.

"Games of chance are not my strong suit, you know, because they require absolutely no talent. Hence the name, *games of chance*," Frachas said snippily.

"Perhaps you should go below deck and hustle some sailors?" Titus suggested.

"Perhaps I will!" Frachas declared impetuously.

Titus nodded his approval, mostly happy to be free of Frachas' presence for a while.

The captain went below deck and immediately started up a game.

"Two silver talents." Frachas named the stakes.

"Make it four silver talents," a young officer said back.

"Cocky fella, are you? I like that. I've been known to have some cock myself," Frachas replied.

The two men began an intense game of Roman chess. Soon there were twenty sailors and soldiers hovering about them, watching, betting, and mostly cheering the young officer.

Frachas did not bring his best game. He struggled to make decisive moves and was on the defensive most of the match.

"Good move," Frachas admitted, losing a couple of pieces.

"I've been the champion on this vessel for a year," the young officer bragged.

"The game's not over yet," Frachas countered.

Frachas made a solid move, to the amusement of the viewing gallery, scoring two pieces.

"Good one, captain. But it won't change the game's outcome," the officer said fiendishly and then slammed a piece about the board victoriously. "Mate!"

Frachas was deflated; it had been years since he lost a game of Roman chess.

"Good match," Frachas said, holding out his right hand.

"Good match" was the officer's reply, shaking Frachas' hand. "Now how about those four silver pieces?"

Frachas had no money on him, having lost everything during the shipwreck of the *Temptress*. Plus he never even considered the notion that he might lose a game—and to a young officer that looked more like a boy.

"Ah, yes," Frachas said, working hard to extricate himself from his debt.

The young officer was perceptive and could sense that Frachas was trying to welsh.

"You know what the law says about those that fail to pay their gambling debts, don't you, captain?" the officer asked.

"Yes, I know."

"This isn't your ship, and I ain't your sailor. No one in Rome will give two shits about a captain that lost his new vessel and his men, and then reneged on a bet. So I ask you one more time, where's the coin?"

Frachas was rendered speechless.

"I think I'll take your left hand," the officer said.

Three men jumped Frachas from all sides, one holding his left arm down on the table, the two others holding Frachas' waist and legs. The young officer took a hatchet from his waist.

"Wait, wait! We can talk about this." Frachas opened his mouth—it was not what the officer wanted to hear.

"The time for talk is over, captain."

The officer raised the hatchet into the air and then a silver pendant in the shape of the Ten Commandment tablets came clanking down on the table.

**Frachas Unable to Pay His Gambling Debt**

"That's worth at least ten silver pieces," Joseph said. "Now let him go!"

Frachas was immediately released.

"No hard feelings, captain. A debt is a debt is all. You understand," the officer said and left the mess hall with his lackeys, contented by his winnings.

"Thank you, Hebrew," Frachas said.

"Don't mention it, captain," Joseph responded.

Frachas grabbed a jug of wine and began gulping from it, too distraught from almost losing his hand to be bothered to fill the empty goblet sitting in front of him.

"Perhaps we keep this event between the two of us? No point in telling Titus. He'd probably just punch me in the stomach," Frachas said between swallows.

"Of course, my lord," Joseph agreed.

*  *  *

**THE SHIP** continued its way past the Port of Messina and up the Italian coast, untouched by storms. The port of Rome, by the mouth of the river Tiber, was now in sight.

The boat docked. Titus put chains around Joseph's wrists. He now had the unpleasant business of transferring Joseph to the Ward of Prisons.

Titus, Frachas, and Joseph emerged from the *Enchanted* the same way they had entered the *Temptress*: Romans leading a prisoner.

"I will never forget your bravery or your cunning, Master Joseph," Titus said as he transferred Joseph into the care of a company of soldiers that would oversee his transit to a jail cell.

Frachas stood behind Titus and was also solemn, knowing the fate that awaited his savior.

"Thank you, Hebrew," Frachas said. "I shall remember you until the day I die."

"Nor will I forget either of you, my lords. Fear not, for my God will see us all brought together again," Joseph said and winked, full of certainty.

"I wish I knew your God and had your faith," Titus declared, emotion overcoming him. "Take him!"

# Chapter 18:

# The Jail of the Colosseum

**JOSEPH WAS** escorted from holding cell to jail cell, and from bureaucrat to magistrate. Each transfer brought him closer to the center of Rome until he finally ended up jailed in the bowels of the great Colosseum itself.

His fate, as per Nero's order, was to receive death by spectacle execution. The particulars he was not yet aware of, but he knew the methods employed in the Colosseum, as did half the known world. There was the simple, but always popular, gladiator-versus-challenger match. Or he might find himself surrounded by exotic beasts and made to run until caught and torn limb from limb. There was always the chance he would be beheaded, crucified, disemboweled, or burnt at the stake, which was the one death Joseph feared above all else. Rome's creativity truly shined when it came to inflicting death on its condemned.

As Joseph sat in jail underneath the stadium, he looked at the other unfortunates that shared a similar fate.

There was a long-haired Asian man. He looked insane, arguing with seemingly no one in Chinese.

There was an old Arab, sitting cross-legged in a state of meditation.

There was a big and brutish blond German. He kept screaming at the jailors to get any attention they would pay him. When a Roman guard got too close, the German would try to grab him through the jail bars in an attempt to injure the guard and break whatever Roman bone he could—a team of Romans always responded with batons to his head and stomach.

Then there were two very tall and thin Africans. They stood quietly next to each other, observing everything but not participating in anything.

And there also was an able-bodied Spaniard, expertly trained in sailing and maneuvering sea vessels. He slept and snored, unaffected by the raucousness in the jailhouse.

Most strange of all prisoners was a young Indian boy wearing a turban. He looked lost more than anything else, and Joseph could not imagine what this boy had done to capitally offend the Roman government.

And then there was an old Roman sage in the cell next to Joseph's. He looked resigned to his death sentence, and nothing seemed to bother him. He did, however, find enough interest in Joseph to start a conversation.

"Are you the Hebrew they speak of all throughout the empire?" the old Roman asked.

"I can confirm I am a Hebrew, but spoken about throughout the Roman Empire? I know nothing of that," Joseph replied.

"They speak of a great leader, warrior, and mind. His name is Joseph. What is your name?"

"I too bear the name you speak of, but a great leader, warrior, and mind, I know nothing of those things," Joseph answered.

"I knew it! My name is Felix," the old man exclaimed and moved closer to Joseph, speaking with his face between the cell bars. "You have been all the talk across Rome this moon past. They say you held out against Vespasian for two months and even shot an arrow into his foot. They say you burned his fortress to the ground while he slept. All told, they say you slayed tens of thousands of Roman soldiers before you were captured."

"Don't believe everything they say, Felix," Joseph replied humbly.

"I do not, but when the stories are so vibrant, so similar, and from so many different sources, they are sure to contain many truths."

"I fought against Rome and lost. That is the truth," Joseph responded.

"Ahh, but your fight is not yet over, is it? Can you hear the water flowing above us? That is the sound of every aqueduct line being directed into the pool of the Colosseum. Look at the water droplets falling from the ceiling," the old Roman said while pointing to leaking water above them. "They are flooding the Colosseum. This means only one thing: a great naval battle!"

"I don't understand what you are talking about."

"The Colosseum is a stadium like many others, though much grander. The arena floor is surrounded by twenty-foot-high walls, the entirety of which can be flooded and made into a pool which can float ships. The Romans enjoy putting their condemned in the most farcical of deadly situations. But fear not—you can win this fight."

"My fight is over. I will go out there and I will die!" Joseph yelled in a burst of anger, not understanding what the old man was driving at.

"Yes, you will go out there, but you have a chance at life. Look around. You would all be slaughtered like baby lambs in a hand-to-hand contest with the gladiators. But a Roman vessel to fight with gives you a chance at victory!" Felix shouted enthusiastically.

"I know nothing of sailing nor naval warfare," Joseph said.

"You will have help," Felix said back. "Look over there. That is Gregor, the German. He fought against the Nordics and the Romans, on ships both times—he is said to have the strength of ten men. The Spaniard is the best navigator in all of Hispañia. Over there is Mohammed, the archer—he is rumored never to have missed a target. The Africans are the tallest and fastest people on Earth. The crazy Asian there, Chiang Chao, he's a warrior monk, skilled at killing men with his bare hands. And now there is you, the Judean commander who nearly brought Vespasian to his knees. You will all be comrades in the battle to come."

"Have you wagered your freedom on my victory, Felix? What care you about my welfare?" Joseph asked.

"I have my reasons. All you need to know is that Rome took everything from me: my family, my wealth, my freedom, and soon enough my life. I wish to see Nero cower to the Hebrew that almost rained down destruction upon his great army. Beyond that, I'll be on the condemned vessel with you, and if I can prolong my life at the expense of Rome's prestige, then my mission is clear."

"Perhaps these other condemned souls possess the talents and experiences you have described. I still do not see how this translates into a victory over Rome," Joseph said, unconvinced by the old Roman's argument.

The old man began laughing hysterically. Joseph looked at him like he was insane.

"Of course not. I haven't told you how to be victorious yet!" the old Roman said. "You will face Captain Remus, no doubt. He is a great naval champion of Rome and undefeated in the Colosseum. But he is easy to beat. He employs the same tactic on each enemy, and each time it works as he has never faced a challenger that had prior knowledge of his battle tactics. Now I want you to listen very carefully to me…"

Felix began speaking in whispers to Joseph through the jail cell bars. Joseph's face noticeably showed intrigue at the words he heard.

"Thank you. Perhaps it has a chance at success; only God knows," Joseph said.

Then a great rapping of a wooden baton on the steel jail bars broke up their conversation.

"Condemned men!" a voice roared out—it was the warden of the Colosseum's prisoners. "Today you will go out into the Colosseum and die! Have no doubts about it. In all my years, I have never seen a Roman vessel lose in a Colosseum battle. Make your peace with your gods, whoever they may be. You board the challenger ship in five minutes. Die fighting and you will die with honor. Hail, Caesar! Those who are about to die, I salute you!" and the warden finished with an enthusiastic Roman salute.

Joseph stood tall, his faith in God renewed by his conversation with old Felix. He thought of his father's last words to him before he left Jerusalem for Galilee.

"God will see you through on your journey, my son." Joseph heard Matthias' voice of months past in his mind.

He wondered if God had sent Felix to guide him, just as it seemed God had sent Elijah.

"Show me the path, Lord, and I will follow, no matter how hard the road may be," Joseph prayed.

"It's time!" the warden yelled out.

# Chapter 19:

# Battle in the Colosseum

**THE GREAT** Colosseum in Rome was used to host a bevy of important events, not the least of which were gladiator matches. But as with any grand entertainment in Rome, variety was the spice of death. The most popular events in addition to gladiator fights were musical concerts, wild beast slaughters, and free-for-all rumbles to the last man.

From time to time, Caesar would address Rome from the center rostrum of the stadium. He would proclaim edicts, play his lyre—of which he was fond and well trained, award Rome's greatest gladiator champions, and distribute prizes to the masses in the form of food, coin, and slaves.

While admission to the Colosseum was free of charge, there was much a person could purchase once inside the arena. Wine was by far the most popular item for sale, and slave boys vending the drink would rush up and down the stadium steps, endlessly refilling goblets.

A Colosseum merchant and wealthy old Chinese man known as Uncle Ming boasted that he had a hundred items for sale. He carried his goods and other various curiosities within row upon row of pockets sewn into the shawls of his garb. He jingled while he walked as the glass bottles of the different products he peddled gently clanked against one another, creating a beautiful disharmony.

He offered mercury and the strongest grain alcohol. Opium was his most popular item. He sold very small bottles of the stuff which were just enough to last for the day's festivities. Medium-sized bottles sufficed for a very large man or a regular-sized pair. Then there were large bottles of opium for familial parties. If ordered in advance, Uncle Ming advertised he could deliver as much as 'his back could carry.'

Concerning transactions, he was fair, reliable, accurate, and fast. But one never expected Uncle Ming to opine about the state of the weather or to inquire about one's family. As soon as the product was dispensed and the coin collected, he would tap the small golden bell hanging across his chest and say in a low and respectful voice: "Beneficia." Then in the next instant, he was ringing the bell again, proclaiming 'blessings' in Latin to his next customer.

Over the years he had become exponentially crabbier—if someone got on his wrong side, he would let them know it in explicit Chinese and then banish them from his one-man marketplace for life.

He usually banned those who tried to endlessly haggle with him. Occasionally, a drunk attendee would say something racially offensive, and Uncle Ming, knowing more than he let on, would burst into a foreign diatribe.

Once he had finished skewering a customer in Chinese, Uncle Ming would end his sermon with a ding, ding, ding of his bell and then loudly proclaim: "Expulso!"

This announcement always caught the attention of the crowd. And then a moment later, invariably, a great cheer of laughter would break out—Uncle Ming enjoyed shaming poor customers now cast into the eternal club of his *personae non gratae*.

Ming was one of hundreds of merchants all peddling their goods and paying Caesar a nice tax for the opportunity.

Beyond opium and wine, nearly everything else imaginable was for sale inside the Colosseum. Some sold new togas, anticipating the vomit and wine stains a Colosseum event regularly brought. Other merchants offered souvenirs, gambling stubs, and female necessities—but most vended food.

Figs, grapes, pheasant, and shellfish were popular fare. Candies of chocolate and sugar were some of the bestsellers as the Roman lust for sweets was never satisfied. It was not uncommon to see an entire row of onlookers with large mutton legs in one hand and ale in the other.

In addition to feasting on good edibles and drink, spectators were encouraged to participate in the wrangling. Spoiled apples and eggs were sold by the bushel—pelting gladiator challengers in the midst of combat was a pastime that few could resist.

The great quantity of food and drink served and *refused* in the Colosseum necessitated onsite sanitation facilities. Roman ingenuity provided flowing sewage lines that dispatched the waste from both the male and female rest areas with rushing running water to keep the facilities clean. However, there was still a mild stench of excrement and urine apparent to the senses in most of the arena.

Maintaining the sanitation inside the stadium was a small army of slaves. After each event, the Colosseum grounds were cleaned—hundreds of buckets were employed to carry away the empty clam shells, fruit pits, and bones discarded on the floor during every event. Slaves sometimes worked sixteen-hour days selling and delivering food, and then later picking up the thrown-away scraps. Men of importance would be happy to create a grand mess and pay handsomely for it, but the same gluttons would refuse to reenter the facility if it was not first properly cleaned.

There were three main seating areas. The field boxes which were on the ground floor, the mezzanine which required stairs to access it, and the upper deck. The classes of Romans were divided accordingly. Spectators would present their tickets, issued beforehand through various channels. The Roman government oversaw the distribution of the field boxes. The mezzanine tickets were distributed through a chain of merchants and bankers. The upper deck seats were passed out to the masses at public houses and in the streets at regular times.

The seating arrangements among the patrons were anything but unexpected. In the preferred seats close to the field sat Caesar, senators, generals, tribunes, and families of great wealth and influence. These men dressed in their finest togas, keenly aware all of Rome would be watching to see who adorned themselves with the greatest symbols of wealth. The women of status wore countless pieces of fine jewelry—diamond and gold necklaces were standard accoutrements. Silk dresses of all colors, especially red and purple, were the most impressive and most expensive. A light rose blush was applied to the cheeks of those patrons, both male and female alike, able to afford it.

The Colosseum itself was a marvel of engineering and architecture. Fifty thousand attendees made up the average headcount, but as many as eighty-five thousand could be accommodated at the most stupendous events.

The façade of the Colosseum was just as opulent as the structural engineering. Columns of supporting stones were carved into Ionic, Doric, and Corinthian works of art. Great statues of emperors both past and present stood prominently under the arches. Artists using paint and chisels finished the details to the massive edifice, adorning the building with the names of Caesars as well as less regal information such as gate and seat numbers.

The arena was also beautifully decorated with a crimson awning that covered the entire ellipse of the Colosseum. Only a hole in the center of the cloth allowed sunlight in. The awning was retractable and opened and closed depending on the time of day.

# The Colosseum in Rome

It was morning still—the awning was open. The sun had not yet risen high enough to bother the spectators.

The floor of the Colosseum was also innovatively designed with built-in elevators. These elevators would raise condemned souls and devices of death to the stadium floor. A system of ropes, pulleys, and counterweights was employed to function the elevators. Lions and tigers were staples in most gladiator events and were regularly placed on elevator platforms, surprising the challengers with their beastly entrance. Colosseum animals were always starved for three days before their match to ensure their voracious brutality.

Trumpets blared—the entire audience of the Colosseum rose. Nero came walking up the stadium steps to his field box. He wore a golden laurel wreath upon his head so all knew he was Caesar. His toga cloth was of the finest white wool lined with gold lace. A gold silk cape accentuated his every movement. On his fingers were multiple gold rings set with large red rubies, emeralds, and diamonds. The necklaces around Nero's neck were gold. Even his sandals were gold.

With one arm Nero waved joyously to his subjects; with the other arm he carried his quadruped—the fat Chinese pug, Pompey. Pompey loved his owner genuinely but also because Nero provided him with every indulgence—sausage bites were Pompey's favorite and always on hand.

The dog loved to lick his master's face. When Nero had tired of a weak performance, he would turn his attention to his pug. Seeing Pompey lick his master for more than a few seconds was considered a death sentence for all defeated warriors still breathing as they were always duly given the thumbs-down—Pompey was to be feared as much as the gladiators.

However, sometimes Pompey would bark with jovial excitement, and Nero would pardon the condemned. Caesar enjoyed his role as arbitrator of the gladiators and challengers, and used the power to his advantage. His main concern was with pleasing his subjects. Though only in his late twenties, Nero understood that a great Caesar was both loved *and* feared.

On this day, the games were of a very special nature. Though beyond expensive, the Colosseum had been outfitted so that the field could be flooded nearly twenty feet high with water flowing in from Rome's aqueducts. Small warships already in the arena would then slowly float with the rising of the water level.

Water from a dozen different aqueduct lines was diverted into the Colosseum, drying up fountains across the entire city. It took a full day to fill the arena with the amount of water sufficient for a naval battle. Thirty million cubic feet of water now floated both the *Cross* and the *Victorius* from their underbellies.

Designed to create the maximum damage for the optimal spectacle, the ships were equipped with special pointed bronze rams on their bows. A direct hit from the ram could easily breach an enemy's hull, causing it to capsize. The ships also bore catapults from which the combatants would rain down heavy stones upon one another. These stones were covered with burning oil in the effort to set enemy ships ablaze as well as sink them.

Joseph was now facing his most deadly trial. Nero wanted to make an example of the Judean who had rebelled against the empire. He knew well of Joseph from Vespasian's dispatches. Nero was eager to annihilate the Defender of Jotapata and the Hebrew responsible for thousands of Roman deaths.

Delighted at the news of Joseph's capture, Nero ordered that Joseph be placed in the middle of the greatly-anticipated naval battle.

As Joseph was a proven military leader who had halted Vespasian for over a month and a half at Jotapata, he was given effective command of the challenger vessel. Prisoners from all across the empire were bundled together on the ship bearing flags with a cross. The story of Jesus was well-known throughout Rome, and the crucifix was the symbol of those condemned by the state. Romans, Germans, Spaniards, Africans, Indians, Judeans, Arabs, and even some Asians were assembled as Joseph's comrades.

The ship, known colloquially by the Romans as the 'Cross,' contained such a variety of men that the different languages spoken at times on the vessel resembled the Tower of Babel. Roman fanatics watching from the Colosseum stands laughed uncontrollably at the sight and sound of men unable to communicate with each other in the heat of battle.

Joseph stood on the quarterdeck of the *Cross,* readying himself and his company of thirty other damned men. As the battle was nearing its beginning, Joseph thought about his battles against the Romans in Galilee. He could not believe God would see him perish in a senseless display of gore when he had survived Vespasian's siege, a shipwreck, and escaped Greek cannibals!

Joseph was uniquely qualified to be commander of this particular vessel as he could speak half a dozen languages and thus was able to communicate with just about every man aboard his ship. He said a silent prayer and then spoke to his crew.

"Condemned men, hear me! We do not have to perish today. Yes, we fight Rome. Yes, they want to see us die spectacularly. Give these Romans something else to cheer about. Give them the show they want, and we will live to see tomorrow. That I promise you!" Joseph said.

Anger radiating through the condemned men's eyes, hate building in their hearts, every member of the *Cross* wanted to exact revenge on those they blamed for their predicament. There was an indescribable craving to beat the Romans at their own game.

"Follow me into this fight! Follow me to victory! We will not go quietly. We will win, and tonight you will drink wine and bed Rome's whores!" Joseph yelled to a boat-wide cheer.

"Spaniard, you have the helm. Much will depend on your navigational skills and speed," Joseph ordered.

"Sic!" the Spaniard replied.

"Gregor, I want you by the bow of the quarterdeck, ready to board the *Victorius* and slay every Roman soul."

"Jawohl!" Gregor acknowledged.

"Mohammed, you will lead the archers."

"Nem sayidi!" Mohammed said.

"Chang Chao, stand by my side, I don't yet know what I will need from you, but when I need it, you'll know."

"Shi duizhang!" said Chang Chao, even though it was obvious he had no idea what Joseph had said.

"Africans, I want you ready with buckets of oil. Your great reach and athleticism will be needed to slather the Roman ship when I command it," Joseph said.

"Awoni getaye newi!" was their reply.

Joseph's men were ready.

Commanding the *Victorius* stood Captain Remus. He was the undefeated naval tribune of seven previous Colosseum mock battles. Standing six feet tall, muscles bulging from his arms, chest, and legs, Remus was only twenty-three years old but already expertly skilled in naval warfare. The wagering odds were not unusual at seven to one in Captain Remus' favor.

Remus understood that once a ship's hull was breached, it was only a matter of time before the top deck submerged. His *modus operandi* was to ram his enemy's vessel, breaching the hull. Then Remus would retreat, firing burning catapult stones while waiting for his enemy's ship to sink or burn. Effectuating this attack pattern, Remus would press his men from the drop of Caesar's handkerchief to a rowing sprint. Ramming speed was the only speed Remus understood. He had been supremely successful with this lightning method of attack.

Horns blasted the call to attention. The audience quieted. Nero rose from his throne and began to address the crowd.

"Our Roman brothers and sisters, we present Joseph, governor of Galilee, Defender of Jotapata, and condemned captain of the *Cross!*"

A great cheering roar broke out across the entire Colosseum.

"Let today be a message to all of Judea," Nero continued. "When you become a traitor to the Roman government, you become a captain in the Roman Colosseum!"

Again the crowd erupted with laughter and cheers.

Drums began to beat at a slow but increasing pace. A customary ceremonial cheering chant from the crowd broke out: "Jugulo, obtrunco, mortifico!" which translated to 'Kill, slay, murder!' The cheer started as a whisper and grew and grew in volume with each repetition. The beat of the drums continued to speed up while getting louder. The chant accelerated until the volume became deafening.

Caesar grabbed a red handkerchief from atop a golden silk pillow held by one of his manservants. Nero raised the handkerchief high into the air. The Roman drums beat to their fastest speed and then suddenly the drums beat to a halt.

All cheers stopped.

For a moment the stadium was as quiet as when empty. Looking left towards the *Cross* and right towards the *Victorius*, Nero dropped the handkerchief.

"Rowers! Battle speed! Now!" Remus yelled upon the commencement of the contest.

The two boats started at opposite sides of the elliptical Colosseum pool facing each other. The *Victorius* began to move slowly at first, gaining speed with every row of the slave galley.

"Hold! All men hold!" Joseph shouted out in Latin and then repeating himself in Arabic and Greek.

He sought to use Remus' favored method of attack to his advantage, allowing Remus to initiate a ramming course, with the *Cross* appearing frozen and vulnerable. Once Remus' speed committed the *Victorius* to a ram, Joseph would turn his boat just in time. Remus' ship would then hopefully beach itself along the Colosseum pool walls, providing the *Cross* with an easy slaughter from behind.

Joseph's boat stood still in the water, looking at Remus' head on. The *Victorius* began to gain forward momentum.

"Helm, full to starboard! Rowers, cruising speed!" Joseph ordered, again repeating every command in multiple languages.

The Spaniard began furiously swinging the helm into a pinwheel, turning the ship to starboard.

The boat began to turn, exposing its port hull to the *Victorius'* ram.

Upon seeing the opportunity to crush the *Cross* in its midsection, Remus yelled out, "Maximum ramming speed!"

The *Victorius* was making a beeline directly for the *Cross'* port hull.

The *Cross* was now turning towards a ninety-degree angle in relation to the bow of the *Victorius*.

"Fire all catapults!" Joseph ordered.

Within a moment, rocks burning with black oil were cast toward the enemy ship. Only one of the projectiles hit its target, smacking a Roman warrior unconscious who then fell from the deck of the ship to a watery grave. The rest of the stones overshot the *Victorius*.

"Reload and reduce attitude," Joseph directed. "Rowers, hold steady. Prepare to increase speed on my command."

"The *Victorius* is returning fire!" Felix yelled out. "All hands, down!"

Upon hearing this warning, most of the men on the *Cross* hit the deck. Chang Chao, not understanding the Latin that Felix was speaking, was hit in the sternum by a projectile and lifted off his feet into the arena pool to a drowning demise which delighted the Colosseum spectators.

"Damn!" Joseph lamented. "Hold steady, men!"

The *Victorius* had sailed halfway through the pool. Its ram was closing in on the *Cross'* port hull. Joseph was now attempting to lure the *Victorius* in and then tactically encircle her.

This play was very dangerous, for if the *Cross* was rammed before it could turn clear of the *Victorius*, Joseph and his motley crew would all assuredly die. It was a feat of timing to turn the ship at the exact moment necessary to avoid being crushed.

"Helm, full to port! Battle speed!" Joseph screamed out with a booming call.

The *Cross* was beginning to turn back to the left slowly. The *Victorius* continued on a true course. Fifty yards away… forty-five yards away and closing.

"Catapults fire at will!" Joseph ordered. The adjusted trajectory of the projectiles met with success. The burning rocks hit the *Victorius* in the center of its port hull. Holes were blown into the side of the *Victorius*, but they were above the water level, incapable of sinking the ship.

"Archers ignite!" Remus ordered. "Fire!"

A dozen archers on the *Victorius'* deck unleashed a shower of flaming arrows upon the *Cross*. Joseph was struck in his left shoulder. The arrow had torn through his flesh and the arrowhead exited though Joseph's back. The arrow's tail stuck out of his front side. The head of the arrow was still on fire.

"Damn it to hell!" Joseph cursed at the intense pain.

Looking at his wound and realizing it was not fatal, he snapped the end of the arrow off that was protruding from his front torso and pulled the arrow out of his body from behind. Screaming in agony, he threw the bloodied, burning, and broken arrow off the side of the ship.

"Rowers! Ramming speed!" Joseph ordered.

The slaves rowed harder and faster, sensing their lives depended on it.

Then one of the slave rowers looked through a porthole. He saw the breakneck speed of the *Victorius'* true course.

"We are doomed! Their ram is aimed for our hull!" the slave yelled.

"We are almost clear!" Joseph answered. "Keep rowing, damn you!" Joseph shouted below deck to the chained galley slaves.

The *Victorius* was now within twenty yards of ramming the *Cross*. Joseph's ship was finally turning about, but the bow of the *Victorius* was closing in fast.

"Spaniard! Swing our stern out of the way of their ram!" Joseph ordered.

"I've turned the wheel as far as it will go, Capitán!" the Spaniard yelled to Joseph.

The hull was now clear, but the stern of the *Cross* still lay in the *Victorius'* path—the two boats remained on a collision course.

Ten yards away... five yards. The *Cross* was not swinging its tail back fast enough.

"We're not going to make it," Joseph declared. "Brace for impact!" he shouted out to his men.

The stern of the *Cross* and the bow of the *Victorius* met one another. Wooden shrapnel exploded through the air—the *Cross'* rudder was blown off.

"Capitán! We have no more helm control! The rudder has been destroyed," the Spaniard cried out.

Essentially dead in the water, Joseph did not know what to do next. The only silver lining was that with the *Cross'* turn and collision, momentum was on their side. The *Cross* was now in a rudderless roundabout maneuver, coming up on the *Victorius* from behind.

The *Victorius* continued its momentum towards the edge of the Colosseum wall. Its speed had been partially diminished by the collision with the *Cross*, but it was still moving quickly to the edge of the arena wall.

"Full reverse!" Remus yelled out.

The *Victorius* slowed as its bow went over the side of the arena wall. A man on the quarterdeck flew over the side of the ship into the viewing gallery. Galley slaves were tossed upside down on one another. The bow of the *Victorius* was now stuck on the top of the pool wall!

"Up, all of you! Full reverse! Grind us off the top of the wall!" Remus ordered.

Joseph was frantically trying to make sense of his predicament on the *Cross*. There was no steering left, only forward or backwards motions available, but the *Cross* was drifting up behind the *Victorius*, beached and paralyzed.

After a moment of deep contemplation, Joseph saw a grappling hook attached to a coil of rope lying on the deck by the bow of the ship. He ran towards the hook in a full sprint, sliding down to the deck to grab the grapple in one swift motion. He jumped to a stand, and with a magnificent windup, he launched the hook high in the air over towards the *Victorius*. The grappling hook caught the stern of the enemy ship on his first throw.

"Men!" he cried out. "Form a line! Pull us into the rear of the *Victorius!*"

The archers dropped their bows, several bombardiers left their catapults, and even Felix raced to the rope line. A dozen men took hold of the rope hooked onto the back of the *Victorius*.

Gregor the German took the lead. "Zieh dir bastardes!" he yelled out.

The men began pulling the rope with all their strength.

"Heave! Ho! Heave! Ho!" was the cry heard from the men in the line as they pulled in unison.

The muscles of the men pulling the rope bulged to the max. They pulled so hard that some lost their footing and fell down. But the effort was working. The *Cross* had the *Victorius* by the ass despite not being able to steer.

Closing in on the *Victorius* from behind, the distance between the boats diminished with each pull of the rope. Thirty yards... twenty-nine... twenty-eight.

"Catapults fire!" Joseph ordered.

A volley of five fiery stones came flying directly into the *Victorius'* quarterdeck, blowing off one man's head and another man's leg.

Remus saw the grappling hook holding onto his ship's stern and yelled out, "Cut that damn rope!"

A young Roman archer seeing the situation, dropped his bow, grabbed the hatchet next to him, and raced to cut the line.

"Archers!" Joseph bellowed. "Fire at their stern!"

With that command, Mohammed led the archers, sending flying death towards the *Victorius*. Arrows pierced the flesh of several of the crew, including the young Roman who had grabbed the hatchet in an effort to sever the grappling hook from the rear of the vessel.

The *Cross* moved to within twenty yards of the stern of *Victorius*, nineteen, eighteen, seventeen yards and closing.

Remus knew if he could not release his ship from the grapple, the *Cross* would almost certainly prevail in the contest. Upon seeing the hatchet fall to the deck next to the dead young Roman, Remus raced toward it.

"If you want something done, you have to do it yourself," Remus thought to himself. He picked up the hatchet and then ran to the stern.

The *Cross* closed to within ten yards of the *Victorius'* stern.

"Oil now!" Joseph ordered.

The two tall Africans standing at the bow of the ship, tossed buckets of oil onto the stern of the *Victorius*, covering it with a thick black coat. Remus, holding on to the hatchet, was hit with a heavy spattering.

Mohammed lit an arrowhead, and Remus saw it was over. He looked up towards the heavens and asked his Roman gods for deliverance.

"Flame!" Joseph shouted.

Mohammed released the burning arrow.

The Arab's dart flew straight by Remus and before it could even hit a target, the flammable vapors of the oil ignited, setting the stern of the *Victorius* ablaze. The rear of the vessel exploded in a great fireball. Remus disappeared into an inferno of billowing flames.

A half-dozen other crewmen were also engulfed in the fire. Some of the men alight dove off the ship into the water to extinguish themselves, but none of the men knew how to swim. Those drowning could be seen grasping for help with only their hands and the tops of their heads protruding from the waterline before sinking to the Colosseum floor.

The fire from the *Victorius* spread from the stern to its midsection. Joseph ordered the grappling rope severed to prevent the *Cross* from catching fire from the towering flames of the *Victorius*.

"Full reverse!" Joseph ordered, looking to increase his distance from the burning enemy ship.

Joseph and crew now watched the *Victorius*, completely engulfed in flames, disintegrate. Joseph walked up close to the bow of the ship to gain a greater view of the vessel's destruction. The *Cross'* men stared at the horror they had inflicted on their Roman counterparts. The screams of Romans burning alive filled the stadium.

The crowd was dumbstruck and completely silenced by the total destruction of the *Victorius*. Only Pompey could be heard, barking in his little high-pitched voice.

As the *Victorius'* hull sunk, horns from Caesar's side began to blare once again. Four small rowboats were lowered into the Colosseum pool from a mechanical platform. The boats were the deliverance vehicles for the crew of the victorious vessel—in this case, it was not the *Victorius*.

The boats aligned themselves next to the *Cross*, and the condemned men climbed down the ship's rope ladder and into the rowboats. The small boats began to ferry the survivors to the edge of the Colosseum pool.

Joseph and his crew of misfits had defied the Roman Empire. Though he had not yet won his freedom, and his future was still uncertain, Joseph looked up to the sky and thanked God for his safe passage from the Roman pool of death.

The Praetorian guards seized Joseph and his men as soon as they were able to climb over the pool walls of the Colosseum. Joseph accepted that he was going to be executed. Obviously Nero wanted him dead, and despite his grand performance, Joseph still expected to die.

Drums began to beat at an execution rhythm. Roman soldiers took each condemned man by the arms and vigorously walked them before Caesar for judgement. Twenty souls now stood, heads bowed, before the Emperor of Rome. Behind every condemned man was a Roman with his sword drawn, ready to exact a death sentence.

The drums beat faster and faster. Caesar believed that his fellow Roman spectators would favor the execution of those responsible for the brave Roman men lost in battle.

Then the crowd of eighty-five thousand strong began to chant for the salvation of the *Cross'* men.

"Vivo Joseph! Vivo *Crux!*" The Colosseum cheer continued, growing louder with every repetition.

The cry reached an eardrum-piercing roar.

Nero hesitated. He saw the fervor with which his countrymen championed the naval victors. Additionally, Pompey began jumping up and down incessantly by Caesar's feet, imploring him to oblige his audience.

Nero held up his hand, and the Colosseum audience, Pompey included, was brought to a quick silence. Slowly he turned his thumb up, signaling life. A great cry blasted from the Colosseum. The men and women in attendance jumped up and down as if they themselves had been delivered by the gods.

Roman guards pushed Joseph and his crewmen from the Colosseum landing back to the bowels of the stadium, into the same jail cells where they had begun the day.

"Congratulations, condemned men!" the Roman jailor said to Joseph and the rest of his crew as he locked the barred cell door.

Then the jailor put his hand on one of the bars of the door and pulled it firmly to make sure it was securely locked.

"You almost died from arrows, burning oil, flying rocks, and rams of bronze. And you end up in the same shithole you started the day in!" The Roman laughed with a hint of malicious enjoyment. "Don't you get it, Judean? They'll only let you out of the Colosseum when you're dead."

"I think otherwise," Joseph countered.

"Oh, do you?" the jailor asked.

Joseph, not wanting to argue, made a 'come closer' gesture with his hand.

"Look, I promised my men wine and whores if they were victorious," Joseph said quietly into the Roman's ear.

The jailor looked at Joseph sternly in the eyes and began to laugh so hard he nearly collapsed.

"You have spirit, Judean; I'll give you that! Give me one reason why I should waste my lovely wine, and it is lovely, on a bunch of condemned men?"

Joseph took out from his trousers the impressive gold coin he had taken from Saul in the cave and held it in clear view between his thumb and index finger for all to see. The jailer's eyes dilated slightly at the oversize pure gold coin—it was worth triple his entire month's pay.

"Do you want it or not?" Joseph asked, breaking the silence. The guard reached his hand through the jail bars, motioning for Joseph to give him the gold coin. "Bring me the wine first— enough wine for all my men," Joseph demanded.

"It really is your lucky day, Judean. A small barrel just arrived," the Roman responded. "But I'll be damned before I carry it for you. You there, and you." The jailer pointed to two of the older and weaker-looking men, one of whom was Felix. "Get up and help carry the wine!" the jailor shouted.

The jailor grasped for the cell door key and placed it into the lock. The two elderly men scurried out of the jail cell, wide-eyed at the prospect of an alcoholic beverage. They walked behind the Roman jailor to the underground Colosseum mess hall.

"Here is the wine, and here are the mugs," the Roman said.

One of the men picked up the little barrel of wine and carried it upon his shoulder. Felix carried a tray of mugs. They returned to the jail cell in less than ten minutes. Upon seeing the barrel of wine and wooden mugs, a cheer broke out from the men.

"Joseph! Joseph! Joseph!" was the mantra, and it grew louder and louder until the cheering morphed into celebratory, sonorous screams of jubilation.

The Roman put his hand out through the jail bars. Joseph placed the gold coin into the jailor's hand. The jailor reached for his cell key and opened the gate.

The wine barrel, the cups, and the two elderly carriers entered. The spigot on the barrel was immediately turned open, and red wine started flowing. The men lined up and tasted instant satisfaction.

"But where are the whores?" the large German yelled in a thick accent.

Another great cheer of laughter broke out among the men.

Joseph, partially celebrating but mostly medicating his wounded shoulder, drank all night long with his men until the wine was gone.

Everyone passed out drunk.

# Chapter 20:

# Nero Summons Joseph

**NEWS OF** Joseph's great victory over the *Victorius* was all the talk throughout Rome. Nero, eager to meet the champion, summoned Joseph to his palace. Three Roman guards escorted Joseph, his arm in a sling due to his arrow wound, to the waiting room outside Nero's office.

Sitting on a marble bench waiting for Caesar, Joseph stared at the fresco on the wall facing him. It was a depiction of Caligula sleeping with his sister while simultaneously slaying his sister's husband. Underneath the painting stood a table; upon it rested busts of Julius Caesar, Augustus, Tiberius, Caligula, Claudius, and Nero. Below Nero's bust a small pug figurine stood—it was Pompey, his dog.

The gross idolatry made Joseph think of the golden calf and how his people once dabbled with idols. Satisfaction rolled over him with the knowledge that the Hebrews had elevated themselves spiritually above where even great Rome was today and had done so hundreds of years before Rome even existed.

Ulysses, Nero's chief of staff, appeared from the grand golden double office doors, which were promptly closed behind him by two Praetorian guards stationed in front of Nero's office.

"The emperor will now see the prisoner," Ulysses informed Joseph's party.

The Praetorian guards opened both doors in unison.

"Come!" Nero said sternly but not menacingly from his desk at the back of his long office.

The emperor sat busy in paperwork. Sporus, always half naked or more, lounged across a chair drinking wine and eating biscuits. He only laughed inappropriately loud on occasion, not speaking any words.

The Roman guards escorted Joseph onto the great golden seal of Rome on the floor.

Joseph stood, head bowed and his legs chained in submission. He looked most pathetic in his dirty prison rags and makeshift sling.

More than that, he was hungover from the previous night's wine party. But mostly Joseph was thirsty.

Nero walked slowly around Joseph as if to examine his every aspect. Pompey ran to Joseph and smelled him, then he began jumping up and down while wiggling his curly pug tail. The dog made little yelping sounds signifying he liked Joseph.

"Pompey! Bed!" Nero yelled, pointing at the dog and then at its bed. Pompey whimpered, his tail went down, and he sadly walked to his plush bed and lay down.

"Take off all your clothes," Nero commanded.

Joseph was taken off guard by this order and froze for a moment.

"Don't worry, Hebrew. We did not summon you here for a buggering," Nero said, reassuring Joseph with a laugh.

Sporus cackled uncontrollably.

All of Jerusalem knew of the Roman normalization of man-on--man sex acts.

Joseph complied, slowly removing his shirt and loincloth. He stood completely naked on the great seal of Rome.

Nero stood inspecting Joseph's manhood as if it was a matter of scientific discovery.

"I will never understand why you Hebrews cut your own pricks. Explain this to me," Caesar commanded.

"It is our covenant with God to give him a piece of our flesh," Joseph replied.

"As I said, I'll never understand the custom. I could understand a toe or an ear. But the male member? Roman gods are not half so cruel," Nero declared.

He turned to Wagnus, his manservant. "Bring this man something to wear that is respectable and doesn't smell of shit. And burn those rags," he commanded.

"Yes, great Caesar," the manservant said and rushed to deliver Joseph a fresh toga.

Wagnus handed Joseph clean clothes—he put them on, his body aching with every motion. He was even presented a fresh sling.

"That's better," Nero said.

Nero moved to take a sip from his goblet—it was empty. "Wine!" Nero shouted, and his cupbearer quickly scuttled to refill the emperor's cup from a large and opulent royal carafe. "Bring a cup for Captain Joseph, too."

"My Caesar, I thank you for your hospitality, but I thirst for water," Joseph said respectfully.

Nero nodded.

"Change that. Bring the captain some *water*," Nero amended his order then continued, "All of Rome speaks of your great victory. Such cheers in the Colosseum we have not heard in all our years. Even our dog wanted to see you victorious. You must be very impressed with yourself, are you not?"

"Your Majesty, I fought to save the lives of myself and my crew, not to impress a soul," Joseph answered humbly.

"We see," Nero said. "You are the Defender of Jotapata, are you not?"

"I am."

"Then you are responsible for thousands of our Roman soldiers' deaths, are you not?" Nero asked sharply.

"Yes, Your Majesty. But I pray you hear my reasoning. I did not fight you—I did not fight Rome. I only fought for my God who hath promised me and my people a great land of milk and honey for all time," Joseph explained.

"It would seem our gods have a great disagreement." Nero continued, "Today your god is Rome. It is because we say it is, and you and the rest of the Hebrews are helpless to resist us. Your people have cowered to our empire for over a hundred years. More importantly, your people produce ten thousand gold talents a year for Rome—we cannot allow that to change while we are Caesar."

"The God of my people is the true God. I also say that there is no way to defeat my God," Joseph added without being asked.

"You speak impertinently," Nero said aggressively. "We have executed men for much less."

"Do you intend to execute me, great Caesar?" Joseph asked.

"We haven't yet decided. Tell us, Joseph. If we were to set you free, what would you do? Where would you go?" Nero inquired.

"I would go to Jerusalem to tell the Judeans to come to terms with Rome," Joseph answered.

"We see an absurd irony in a man that defends to the death with armies yet desires to preach peace to others," Nero retorted.

"Perhaps, Caesar, but hear me. I say that you and your empire will be better served by my being alive than dead. Do you not intend to retake Judea? Of course you do, for excusing a rebellion would be the beginning of the end of the Roman Empire. So this is what I have to offer: I will join your great army, and I will negotiate the surrender of Jerusalem."

"You are rather confident. Tell us why we should put any faith in a man who defends his country with deadly force and then turns to assist his enemy?" Nero countered.

"Your Majesty, I offer myself for this mission because I believe I will save countless lives. Roman lives and Judean lives. Is there a more meaningful purpose than the preservation of those we hold most dear?" Joseph queried.

"We cannot deny that you are most impressive, Hebrew. We cannot much disagree with your grasp of the Judean situation either. In fact, we believe you have a part yet to play," Nero said.

The emperor grasped for his chalice and sipped his wine while in great contemplation.

"You will be assigned to one of our finest officers. He will observe you for a period of time, and if he believes you are of value in the campaign in Judea, so be it," Nero proclaimed.

Joseph bowed his head in submission. Nero motioned his hand to take Joseph away, returning to play with Pompey.

Roman soldiers moved quickly in response to Nero's commanding gesture; they grabbed Joseph by each arm and rushed him back to his prison cell.

*  *  *

**THE NEXT** morning a Roman general came calling for Joseph.

A jailor burst through the main door separating the corridors from the holding cells. Four Roman bodyguards trailed him, all walking with militaristic conviction. Titus stood out from the group as the red Roman faux mohawk on his helmet made him look a foot taller. His armor was decorated with a golden eagle on the chest. Frachas tried to poke his head through the wall of bodyguards with lukewarm success.

"Here he is, my lord," the jailor said to Titus.

"Get him out of there," Titus snapped.

"Yes, my lord," the jailor responded. "Get up off your Judean ass!"

Joseph rose from the floor and walked to the gate of his cell. The jailor feverishly searched his keyring for the appropriate key.

"I don't have all day," Titus griped.

"Yes, my lord," the jailor said, hurriedly turning the key in the lock—the gate opened.

Joseph was freed. And this time he was not being whisked off to an execution.

"Follow me, Joseph," Titus said, leading the way out of the Colosseum jail. "You must be hungry."

"Starving."

"We'll get some food directly," Titus stated.

"Thank you, my lord," Joseph said.

"Ah, good fresh Roman air," Titus mused as they exited the jail, now walking through the downtown streets of Rome. "It smelled like death in that jail, but I suppose with good reason."

"I still can't believe you're alive, Hebrew," Frachas interjected incredulously. "I seriously can't believe it."

"My God saw me through," Joseph said back.

"I'd enjoy meeting your God," Frachas replied.

"Perhaps one day you will, but I sincerely doubt it," Joseph quipped.

The men continued walking through the capital's streets looking for a place to eat a hearty meal.

"What becomes of us, my lord?" Joseph inquired of Titus, getting down to business.

"You're free. Well, almost. You are no longer a condemned man. In fact, you are to be my ward until I determine exactly what to do with you. But in the interim, you will serve me and enjoy all the hospitality afforded to those in a general's service," Titus explained proudly.

"What will my duties include, my lord?" Joseph asked.

"Well, I haven't completely worked that out yet, but don't fret over it. In fact, put it out of your mind for the time being. It's your first day of freedom since you were captured in Jotapata. I haven't forgotten that you saved my life in Greece, and I owe you a life debt," Titus declared.

"I assure you, my lord, I hold no debt over you," Joseph replied.

"When you saved my life, I was indebted and *will be* until I can repay that debt—whether you acknowledge it or not. Also, take this—you will receive a monthly stipend whilst in my service," Titus said as he placed a coin purse in Joseph's hand. "Don't squander it all in one place."

"Thank you, my lord," Joseph said, tickled beyond belief at the idea that Titus was paying *him*.

"Damn—don't look now, but Jupiter just walked out of that shop behind you," Titus said covertly to Frachas.

Frachas immediately turned around to look.

"Is that 'Frachas the Flaccid'?" a deep voice boomed out, laughing.

Publicly insulted, Frachas flew into an instant rage, charging at Jupiter—Titus grabbed Frachas before he could throw a punch.

"Let's finish this here and now!" Frachas yelled, held back by Titus' overpowering strength.

"Good to see you, General Titus, sire!" Jupiter said, overzealously standing up crisply to attention while saluting, voicing his sarcasm through physical overcompensation.

"How are you, Jupiter?" Titus asked, merely to make an obligatory acknowledgement.

"Good as ever, sire. I can't wait for the next war your father sends me to. Warring the Germanic girls, that warring was my favorite!"

"I thank the gods I don't have a daughter that can be violated by a monster like you," Frachas said to Jupiter.

Titus turned around and grabbed Frachas by the neck ring of his tunic.

"Shut up, Frachas!" Titus ordered.

"Hahaha!" Jupiter cackled. "That's right, tell your mutt to stay silent if he knows what's good for him."

"What do you want, Jupiter? Are you looking for a fight?" Titus asked.

"Lord General, I have no quarrel with you. Your little prancing captain here, well, that's another story. He still owes me—" but before Jupiter could finish, Titus had already taken over his sentence.

"Yes, he still owes you for cheating at Roman chess—we've all heard this one before," Titus said, annoyed at rehashing this ongoing conflict.

"He swindled six months' wages out of me—that's something I'll not quickly forget!" Jupiter growled.

"Do you want a rematch?" Frachas offered.

"I thought I told you to shut up," Titus said sternly, looking Frachas in the eye.

"What's the matter, Frachas? Can't defend yourself? You need to hide behind the great General Flavius Titus!" Jupiter taunted. "Without him, you'd be food in my belly by now!"

"Let me at him," Frachas barked, again trying and failing to free himself from Titus' grip.

"There will be no bloodshed today, captain," Titus commanded.

"That dumb bastard brute doesn't deserve to call himself a Roman!" Frachas yelled.

Jupiter's smile disappeared and he pulled his dagger out of its sheath. He came quickly at Frachas. Titus' back was turned. But Joseph saw Jupiter lift his dagger. Unconsciously, Joseph took the gold coins from his purse and one by one began chucking them at Jupiter in the head with all his might. One coin connected into Jupiter's temple and, weighing a full ounce, collapsed the human giant to the ground.

Across the market, a man in a silk purple cape and white linen toga, surrounded by a dozen Roman military bodyguards, stood clapping slowly and firmly.

It was Vespasian.

"This Hebrew can fight, saves the lives of those I hold most dear, and even resolves petty squabbles among my officers. Titus, you must bring him for dinner at my estate in the country. I am holding a party with many notable guests—it's on the morrow," Vespasian requested.

"Of course, Father," Titus replied.

"Thank you, my lord," Joseph said, bowing his head slightly.

"What brings you round these parts, Father?" Titus queried.

"It's the eatery, son—I think you can figure it out."

# Chapter 21:

# Vespasian's Party

**TITUS, FRACHAS,** and Joseph moved about in Titus' apartment residence in Rome. They were preparing for the evening festivities at Vespasian's mansion, some ten miles outside the capital or about a half-hour ride by horse-drawn chariot. Each man was dressed in an elegant white toga. Titus and Frachas were adorned with beautiful bejeweled gold rings as well as necklaces of the yellow metal, carrying pendants embossed on one side with Caesar's profile.

Titus even loaned Joseph a gold ring and necklace for the occasion.

"You almost look Roman," Frachas said to Joseph.

"Is that a compliment or an insult, my lord?" Joseph asked.

"I should think it a high compliment, Hebrew. Romans rule the Earth," Frachas proclaimed.

"Are the two of you ready?" Titus interrupted. "We need to get going. Joseph, you will be the guest of honor. My father is beyond impressed with you, and he wishes to introduce you to the finest men in Rome. Do *not* squander this opportunity."

"I have every intention of satisfying your and your father's expectations," Joseph acknowledged.

"Excellent," Titus conferred. "Shall we?"

The three men mounted a chariot drawn by four beautiful white Arabian steeds. Titus drove the horses at a fast gallop all the way to the countryside.

"Gods, what a beautiful night," Titus said, holding the reins.

"It will be even more beautiful after a few goblets of wine," Frachas added, amused with himself.

Joseph just rolled his eyes slightly, now fully aware of Frachas' *modus operandi*.

The sun continued to fade as the sky became darker and finally black. The sounds of crickets chirping and bullfrogs ribbiting were ever-present. The crisp night air warmed the blood and kept the spirit fully awake.

Vespasian's white mansion, illuminated by torches and candlelight, could be seen over a mile down the road.

"There she is," Titus said. "Emperor Tiberius' old mansion—now it belongs to my father."

The house was impressive. It looked more like a city edifice than a dwelling. Great Ionic columns lined the front of the façade. Majestic white marble steps led to the mansion's entrance. Statues of Caesars present and past stood between each pair of columns.

Vespasian's landscape matched the beauty of his Hellenistic house. The grass, the hedges, and the flower beds were all neatly kept. There was even a reflecting pool in front of the mansion, complete with a fountain at its center, sculpted in the likeness of Mars, the Roman god of war.

Dozens of chariots and horses lined the circular driveway of the estate. The elite of Rome descended in full force to Vespasian's party.

Titus drove the chariot directly up to the front steps of his father's estate.

A chauffeur approached and began to speak. "Excuse me, my lord, chariot parking is over in the adjacent..." But before he could finish, the chauffeur recognized Titus' face and humbly said, "I'd be honored to park your chariot, my lord."

"How good of you," Titus said somewhat arrogantly, amused with the power being a Flavius provided him. "See that my beasts are watered and fed carrots as well."

"Of course, my lord Titus," the chauffeur replied.

"There are a few perks being the son of Rome's greatest general," Titus bragged to Joseph and Frachas as they all walked up the steps to the mansion.

"If you're going to be a cocky bastard all night, I'll disappear into the fields with a carafe and a schoolboy," Frachas said, jealous of Titus' inherited stature.

"You'll end up with a boy regardless of how modest or pompous you find me," Titus declared. "Just remember, I'm leaving by two hours before first light—I prefer to sleep in my own bed. If I can't find you, enjoy begging my father for a cot."

"Your father's house is so large I could fall asleep on a sofa and he wouldn't find me for weeks, maybe longer," Frachas replied.

"I'm starving—I do hope the food is good," Joseph said, attempting to join the conversation.

"You'll never have better the rest of your days," Titus said.

The three men walked through Vespasian's grand double-door entrance. The smells of Roman decadence were paralyzing to the senses. Incense mixed with opium smoke, steaming foods, and the perfumes of the guests all combined, forming the unique scent of Roman aristocracy.

There were mostly older men in attendance with their wives or concubines or both. All were dressed in their finest livery and overly gaudy jewelry.

The women wore colored togas, while the men preferred white accentuated with flares of rich colors. The guests were short and fat, and tall and thin. Gone were the days of their youth. Joseph, Titus, and Frachas were studs by comparison.

Vespasian saw Titus and made a beeline to greet his son.

"Ah, Titus!" Vespasian rejoiced, embracing his son. "And my former enemy, the Defender of Jotapata, Joseph the Hebrew! Welcome!" Vespasian continued his jolliness, which was rather rare for the top general.

Frachas stood behind Titus, knowing he was too unimportant to receive Vespasian's praise.

"I see you brought Captain Frachas as well. Good to see you too, Frachas," Vespasian said. "Now make yourself useful and bring us all a round of drinks and some food."

Frachas nodded in submission and went about obeying Vespasian's order.

Vespasian sidled alongside Joseph, putting his arm around Joseph's shoulders and said, "You know I have not forgotten of the prophecy you made. In fact, I think of it more often than I should."

"The time is coming near for your rise, my lord," Joseph said.

"Yes, I remember the entirety of your prophecy," Vespasian replied. "I soon return to Judea, specifically to crush Jerusalem."

"There must be a way to force the Judeans back to submission without their extinction and the destruction of the entire city, my lord," Joseph asserted.

"Before I campaigned in Judea, I would have agreed with you. But then I came to Jotapata," Vespasian retorted with a smile of admiration.

Frachas made his way back to Titus, Joseph, and Vespasian, carrying four goblets of wine in his two hands, a plate of food resting on the top of the goblets.

"Ah, thank you, captain," Vespasian said as Frachas distributed the wine.

"It's very good," Joseph complimented the wine.

"I didn't know exactly what everyone wanted to eat, so I brought a little of everything," Frachas said, chewing food like a juvenile with his mouth open.

Frachas presented an array of cheese squares, crackers, olives, and thin slices of mutton. He stood holding his goblet in one hand and the food tray in another, part servant and part guest.

Vespasian took a couple of pieces of cheese and an olive. He ate the cheese first, then popped the olive in his mouth. Joseph took a few crackers and lined them with mutton, as did Titus.

Then a young boy, a child of one of the party guests, came running through the room. He was playing tag with the other children. The boy accidentally ran into Vespasian from behind. The impact did not hurt Vespasian, but it startled him, causing the olive in his mouth to become lodged in the back of his throat. He grasped for his neck while gasping for air, asphyxiating sounds emanating from his mouth. The sticky cheese was blocking the olive in his throat!

Joseph, seeing the general choking, maneuvered himself behind Vespasian and positioned his hands and arms around his stomach. After two lifting pulls, the olive came flying out of Vespasian's mouth and hit Frachas in the forehead.

Vespasian took a few moments to compose himself, and then he turned to Joseph. "Thank you, truly. If I had died from an olive, I would have been remembered only for the farcical nature of my death."

"Do not mention it, my lord," Joseph replied.

"And modest too," Vespasian said. "Come, I want you to meet some of the most important people in the world. Titus, Frachas, go enjoy yourselves. I want Joseph to myself."

Vespasian took Joseph around to every notable guest. He met the treasurer of the entire Roman Empire—he was concerned with the Judean war only because it had such an adverse effect on tax receipts and military appropriations.

With every encounter, another silver goblet of wine was put into Joseph's hand.

Joseph met the governor of Alexandria, who was visit-
ing Rome for unknown reasons, but Vespasian whispered into
Joseph's ear that the true purpose of the governor's visit was to size
up the contenders for the crown once the heirless Nero was either
dispatched or dead from natural causes.

A beautiful older woman—the "Madam of Rome," they called
her—was the richest woman in Roman history. She retained
power over the ministers and senators by ensuring they all had
sizable debts payable to her. All knew being publicly called out
for defaulting on a debt meant impugning one's entire reputation.

There were several military men Joseph was introduced to,
all of whom wanted a full recounting of the battle of Jotapata
from Joseph's perspective. He obliged them as best he could without stepping on Vespasian's toes. Others wanted a play-by-play
recounting of his Colosseum victory.

After his fifth cup of wine Joseph was noticeably tipsy.

Joseph, while making his rounds by Vespasian's side, also
caught sight of a beautiful young woman. She was near Joseph's
age, in her mid-twenties. Her long brown hair flowed perfectly
down to the small of her back. Her green eyes were penetrating.
And her bosom was so lovely Joseph caught himself staring for a
long enough moment to alert the woman to his keenness.

"Who is that beautiful young woman in the purple silk?"
Joseph inquired of Vespasian.

"Ah, yes, let me introduce you. Her name is Violet, and she
is a Hebrew like you, and the fairest of skin, though she is from
Alexandria originally. Come, let's get the two of you acquainted."

Seeing Vespasian and Joseph approach, the young woman
stood still, lowered her head a little and took an everlasting look
directly into Joseph's eyes.

"My dear Violet," Vespasian began. "Let me introduce you
to the Defender of Jotapata, the Captain of the Colosseum, and

as of tonight, my personal savior: the Hebrew, Joseph, son of Matthias."

Joseph took Violet's hand and softly kissed it. "I am honored to meet you, my lady."

"The honor is all mine, my lord," Violet replied.

"I'll let the two of you familiarize yourselves. My wine goblet is empty and needs refilling," Vespasian said, leaving Joseph and Violet to silently look over the other's body.

"They say you have no children, my lord," Violet inquired. "Do you also have no wife?"

"My reputation precedes me. I do not have children, but I am married," Joseph responded.

"How many wives do you have?" Violet asked.

"Only one."

"Maybe that's your problem," Violet said and pinched Joseph's rear.

This excited Joseph, and it began to show through his toga. Violet noticed and started giggling.

"Is that for me?" Violet asked coquettishly.

"Please forgive me, my lady. I wasn't expecting you to grab my backside," Joseph apologized while trying to cover his growing excitement with his goblet and hands.

"I think you were erecting a tall Roman column long before I grabbed you," Violet said, giving Joseph another deep look into his eyes.

"Now tell me, why do you not have any children?" Violet questioned.

"That is a sensitive matter." Joseph deflected the question.

"Do you not want children?" Violet asked.

"I do want children, but it is not God's will at the current time."

"Not God's will? A young, handsome man like yourself that beats Rome at its own games—in the Colosseum no less? You do like women, don't you?" Violet asked.

"My male excitement already answered that question as I noticed you taking an extended look," Joseph answered with a grin on his face.

Violet began laughing. "You're funny too," she said, clutching Joseph's arm. "One thing I love about Hebrew men is that their serpents are cut to look pretty, not loose and ugly like the Romans."

"Do you want to look at my serpent?" Joseph joked, but after the words came out of his mouth, he realized there was true desire within him.

"I thought you'd never ask," Violet answered. She took his hand and led Joseph through the hundreds of guests to a door under Vespasian's floating staircase. "I'll go in. Follow me a minute later—bring a candle if you want to see what I look like," she said and kissed Joseph on the cheek, leaving a rouge mark on his face.

Violet entered a small servant's workroom and closed the door behind her. Joseph quickly searched for a candle. He took a candelabra from one of the buffet tables and returned to the closet door, looking over his shoulder to see if anyone was watching.

Of course, Frachas caught Joseph's eye and made a pelvic thrusting motion while smiling and nodding in approval. Joseph was somewhat embarrassed and tried to ignore him.

He opened the closet door, entered, and quickly closed it behind him. Raising the candelabra, he saw Violet standing before him as naked as the day she was born.

"Kiss me," she whispered and then turned around and bent over, exposing her loins.

Joseph placed the candelabra on a shelf besides him. Then he kneeled down and grabbed Violet by her thighs. He leaned in to smell Violet's essence. She was intoxicating. He began kissing her. With each kiss she let out a light moan.

After a few minutes of this, Violet blurted out: "I can't take it anymore. I need to feel you inside me."

Joseph stood up and parted his toga, exposing his erect manhood.

"Very nice. Like I said, they're a lot prettier than the Roman ones." Violet snickered.

Joseph grabbed Violet firmly by the waist and thrust deep inside her. His eyes rolled back into his head as he breathed heavily, overcome with pleasure.

"You... are... a... perfect... fit," Violet said in between moans.

Frachas had walked up to the closet door and surreptitiously placed his ear upon it—he did not have to as the cries of their ecstasy were easily heard. Frachas continued drinking his wine, enjoying the spectacle, all with a big stupid smile on his face.

Violet started screaming. She became so loud that other partygoers started looking around wondering where the noise was coming from. Then after a good little while, she climaxed and quieted, sweat pouring down her naked body.

Joseph now began making the loud noises as he began to orgasm. He clawed into Violet's skin with his fingers and released himself. "Aaahhhrrrhhh!" he moaned and clasped his arms around Violet's waist as he caught his breath.

Violet smiled at his big finish.

"My God, you gave me enough cream for a hundred children," she joked.

"I'd be happy with just one," Joseph replied genuinely.

"I need a towel to clean up," Violet said.

Joseph picked up the candelabra and searched around the closet. There were no towels in sight.

"I'll go fetch one," he said.

"Don't leave me here alone, naked and dripping," Violet countered.

"What would you suggest I do?"

"Kiss me," Violet demanded.

The two joined mouths and tongues passionately for a good few moments. Then Violet slapped Joseph gently on his butt.

"*Go*," she said.

Joseph placed the candelabra back on the shelf to not leave Violet in total darkness and opened the closet door slowly. He exited and closed the door behind him immediately. When he turned back around, none other greeted him than a smiling Frachas.

"I thought you might need this," Frachas said in a licentious tone, handing Joseph a towel.

"I'll go so far to venture you've had a closet experience in your past," Joseph said, snatching the towel from Frachas' hand.

"More than you know, but I didn't have a friend waiting outside to help me clean up," Frachas added.

"You're definitely the right friend for the right moment, Frachas," Joseph declared and began to turn back around to re-enter the closet.

"Aw, the Hebrew thinks I'm his friend," Frachas mused.

Joseph slammed the door shut in Frachas' face.

*＊＊＊*

**IT WAS** beginning to get late. The party guests had nearly all gone—the ones remaining were mostly passed out on Vespasian's floor and furniture.

"Time to head back, gentlemen," Titus declared to both Joseph and Frachas.

The three men exited Vespasian's mansion and made their way to their parked chariot, returning the same way from whence they came.

"My father was talking about you like you almost… almost…"

"Almost like you gave him a sexual desire!" Frachas obnoxiously interjected.

"Shut up, you drunk!" Titus said, though Frachas continued to laugh in a high-pitched chuckle.

"But the fact remains, I've never seen him so taken with anyone before, especially a defeated enemy. You did well, Joseph," Titus commended him.

"He did very well," Frachas added with a sly, licentious smirk.

"Though I still have my doubts, my father seems to believe your prophecy is no hoax—he fancies you as one of his ministers should he indeed rise to Caesar. This he told me in confidence, so don't go telling the whole world and making a fool out of me," Titus ordered. "If Nero hears one word of treason, we're all dead."

"I understand completely," Joseph replied.

As soon as he spoke the words, Joseph realized he had become part of the Roman Empire, which only mere months ago he had fought so hard to resist. Joseph did not even feel shame for his transformation.

In his new station as an advisor, he could even help prevent further bloodshed as opposed to what he could do serving as a military commander. In fact, he felt pride to be on the side of Rome. He reveled in the idea that his place was secure and that he was no longer responsible for the defense of a city or people.

Joseph was acting the part of a Roman even if he was still technically just a Judean.

# Chapter 22:

# Uncle Ming's Opium Den

**THE WEEKS** began to pass, and Joseph became more ingratiated with the Roman elite at every interaction. Titus was propositioned by half a dozen ministers and military leaders across the empire with requests to enlist Joseph as their own chief of staff. One general in Alexandria even offered to make Joseph a tribune. But Joseph was dedicated to Titus, and through Titus also to Vespasian. Having prophesied their future rise to Caesar, Joseph was content to remain in their service.

In the back of Joseph's mind was the Judean war in his homeland. Vespasian had taken a respite from executing the campaign, waiting for desperately-needed supplies and a fresh complement of men. Joseph had constantly lobbied to return to Jerusalem with Vespasian, hoping to negotiate a surrender, saving the city, the Temple, and its people.

While he waited in Rome for Vespasian to renew his military efforts in Judea, Joseph degenerated. Parties, feasts, and celebrations of all types were now a staple in Joseph's life.

He was becoming Romanized.

On one night, he became so drunk he completely forgot about the Sabbath, something that had never happened in his entire life.

He began to fully question everything he had come to believe about Judaism. He even became critical of the very doctrine he had preached less than a year prior.

Joseph became open to things he had previously scorned as hedonistic and sacrilegious. He visited vomitoriums and brothels. His heart and mind rejected Mariamne for failing to provide him with the children and the love he longed for—Roman women now filled the void as they gave him his long-sought-after affection.

Violet became a regular addition to Titus' entourage, and within a month Joseph was in love, but more in lust—he had never experienced the true joys of a woman's body with his wife Mariamne or anyone else.

Joseph called on Titus, who was easily able to get Nero's signature on an official divorce decree.

Titus waltzed into Nero's office with little sausage treats for Pompey and a medium-size bottle of Uncle Ming's finest opium for the emperor who was always happy to see Titus. They were the same approximate age, and Nero was not threatened by the younger Flavius but more concerned existentially with Vespasian.

After Titus presented Nero and Pompey with their respective gifts, and gave a thirty-second pitch about himself and how his loveless Judean wife had failed to provide him with offspring, Nero was pleased to sign Joseph's divorce decree directly.

"Judean bitches," Nero cackled as he affixed his official seal from the imprint of his ring, voiding Joseph's marriage across the entire empire, which included Judea even in its current state of rebellion.

Joseph was now officially a single man again. And being single, his thoughts turned towards marrying Violet. Though Judeans were allowed to have multiple wives, it was not the common practice.

Within two weeks of the issuance of his divorce decree Joseph had proposed and assembled before Vespasian who, as a sanctioned official, performed the wedding ceremony. Titus, Frachas, and a few other Roman officers and friends were in attendance. Violet looked more beautiful that day than any other time in her life.

"Kiss the bride, Joseph," Vespasian joyously commanded.

Joseph's tongue was already down Violet's throat before Vespasian could finish speaking. All smiled and were happy.

Joseph was married again, but this time it was for him and not because his family had arranged it. It was for love, something that Joseph had never known before. He wore that stupid, silly grin on his face that men carry about when they are happily coupled and carefree about the rest of the world's problems.

To celebrate the new union as well as Nero's thirteenth year in power, Frachas organized a small party of a dozen Romans including Titus, Violet, Joseph, and Domitian, Titus' younger brother who was barely sixteen years of age.

They were headed to Uncle Ming's opium den in the Chinese quarter. Joseph had never tried opium before, and he truly had no idea what to expect. But as his personality changed, his acceptance of all things Roman overcame any objections he had, religious or otherwise.

"Are you ready for the time of your life, Hebrew?" Frachas asked, giddy with anticipation.

"I suppose I'm as ready as I can be," Joseph replied, assuredly unassured.

The troop entered the Chinese quarter, demarcated by rows of hanging lanterns over the streets. They walked down a back alley to a small unmarked black door. Frachas knocked three times quickly, then two times slowly.

A tiny black metal window in the door opened horizontally, and two Asian eyeballs stared out at the company for a long moment. The window slammed shut and the door opened—the Romans had to bend down to avoid hitting their heads on the archway as they entered.

A harp was playing inside. It was slow music, mostly major chords and scales, just enough to tantalize the ears while not overwhelming the mind. Red Chinese lanterns illuminated the den with a soothing, mild light, easy on the eyes. A sweet candy-like smell, mixed with a hint of flowers, filled the room as the haze of gray opium smoke lingered in the air.

Young Chinese women walked around nude indifferently, seemingly unaware of their nakedness. They carried trays with all things opium-related upon them: pipes, candles, and an array of different opium types. Also on the tray was a small woven basket filled with gold, silver, and copper coins.

A Chinese maître d' welcomed Titus' party and escorted them to a premier sitting area—they took their seats on pillows around a low-rising table.

Then an elderly woman came, pushing a tea cart. Grandma Chia dressed in exquisite silk Chinese clothes and looked divine despite her advanced age. She slowly progressed forward, using her tea cart for support.

On her cart, she assembled enough porcelain cups and saucers for the entire party. She filled a dozen cups of tea without ever stopping her pour. An awkward silence rushed across the party as everyone was mesmerized by her performance. Of course, she did not spill a drop, and the tea was perfect.

"The service is fast here," Joseph opined. "And good."

"The service here is the best," Frachas said as he continued to watch not the impossible perfection of Grandma Chia, but the naked Chinese courtesan dealers moving about erotically. "I could go for a naked Oriental on my lap tonight."

"Man or woman?" Joseph asked mockingly.

Titus spit out his tea with hearty laughter.

"Hahaha!" Titus exclaimed, tea coming out his nose while laughing at Frachas' denigration.

"At least with men you know there is no chance at a pregnancy," Frachas said, attempting to justify his preferences. "And you're allowed to punch them in the face when they won't shut up!"

"I love you, Frachas. For now and all time. Let us toast!" Titus diverted the conversation while raising his teacup. "To Caesar! His thirteenth year! But mostly to Joseph and Violet's union!"

All took a drink in unison.

Then a naked Chinese girl approached with a tray.

"Beneficia. What type opium you want? Happy-happy? Happy-mad or sad-sad?" the girl asked.

Each variety of opium carried a corresponding mental state described by its name.

"Tonight is a happy-happy night!" Frachas declared emphatically.

"Ok, for party this size, half gold," the Chinese girl replied.

Frachas obliged with half a gold talent.

"Beneficia," she said kindly and began preparing the pipe.

The server smiled as she placed the pipe in Frachas' mouth. She took the candle and ignited Frachas' black tar. Frachas puffed.

"Oh, yes, that's the stuff," Frachas said as he exhaled a cloud of smoke.

He passed the pipe to Joseph.

The Chinese girl took the candle and lit up Joseph. He immediately coughed at his first inhalation.

"Take it slow, Hebrew. You don't need a lot of it," Frachas advised.

Joseph took another couple of puffs more successfully, then offered the pipe to Titus, who refused.

"I'm allergic to the stuff," Titus explained.

"Judean, give it here," Domitian demanded.

Joseph complied.

"Bring me some wine," Titus said to the Chinese server.

"Ok," the girl said, and then clapped twice, yelling indecipherable words in Chinese to a boy holding a wine carafe.

The boy quickly arrived at Titus' table and served the wine.

Titus was pleasantly surprised with his Chinese wine—content to drink the night away while watching his Roman friends smoke opium and turn comatose.

Joseph and Frachas were now more than mellow. Joseph began to sway slightly. Frachas began softly rocking his head back and forth. Titus slammed back wine goblet after wine goblet, attempting to keep up with the party, though only with alcohol. The rest of the group, which had been talkative earlier in the night before smoking, now had total calm on their faces.

"This… is… amazing," Joseph said between exhalations, and he started chuckling uncontrollably. "Why do we not do this in Judea? God definitely erred on this one."

The entire party burst forth with opium-diminished laughter, except for Titus, whose drunken laughs rose above the rest.

"You are a natural comedian, my dear," Violet said to Joseph.

"You know, being Roman isn't so bad," Joseph confessed.

"To Romans!" Titus cheered with his wine.

The entire party followed in Titus' cheer, though much less enthusiastically due to their drugged state. "To Romans."

The girl serving the opium continued to assist the party, cleaning and refilling the pipe. After this latest round, Frachas slipped into a semi-consciouss state, unable to move or speak much.

Titus sat staring at Violet's bosom covetously, drunk on wine.

Joseph's attention had waned from the entourage and waxed towards Violet. He kept smelling her, each sniff bringing a lifetime of pleasure.

"You smell so divine, I want nothing more than to stay in this moment for the rest of my life," Joseph whispered into Violet's ear.

"Kiss me, my wonderful husband."

The night ran away. It was late—the sun would rise in a few hours.

Titus slapped Frachas across his face with such force it made a muted thudding sound.

"Can you walk?" Titus asked.

The only response Titus received was droning sound—Frachas was drooling.

"That's what I thought," Titus said and stood up.

He made his way to the maître d' and requested cots. Two large Chinese men walked back with Titus to the seating section and tossed Joseph and Frachas over their shoulders, carrying them to the sleeping area. They returned for the remainder of Titus' drug induced partygoers, securing each a resting spot.

In the sleeping room, there were over a hundred souls unconscious, all paying for both opium and temporary beds.

Titus slept off his wine while Joseph, Frachas, Domitian, and Violet slept off their opium. But all began to have equally surreal and confusing lucid dreams.

Titus was having a most violent dream. He found himself in the Colosseum, battling thousands of wild man-beasts. Some had four hands, others had two heads, and yet more were a mix of both.

They growled like the devils they resembled, trying to eat and maul Titus with every motion.

No matter how many of them Titus slayed, they sprang up from the ground the moment after they had fallen.

They started their reincarnation in a small, glowing green egg, crushing it open as they matured back to full-size beasts in a matter of seconds, their lethal claws the first thing seen when they emerged from the eggs.

Titus became more and more swamped by the monsters closing in on all sides, re-spawning with every swing of his gladius.

Overwhelmed, Titus reached up towards the sky with his one free hand, shouting a scream of ultimate desperation—the beasts brought him back to the ground, enveloping him with their vicious pointed teeth, quadra-arms and duo-heads.

Violet was having much more of a personal dream. She lay on her bed alone, pregnant. Blood started gushing out from her womanhood. She felt herself getting dizzier and dizzier, and then her baby came out—the baby was African.

"No! No! It can't be! Joseph! Joseph!" she screamed with her full spirit to the heavens.

Joseph appeared next to Violet with a caring smile.

"What is wrong, my love?" Joseph asked.

Violet presented the black baby.

Joseph's face was overcome with confusion and anger. Then his skin began to morph into different colors. Joseph began phasing out of existence before Violet's eyes. Every moment she looked at Joseph, he became more and more transparent. He now looked less like a face and more like an outline until he vanished entirely.

"No!!!!!!!!" Violet screamed.

Frachas was having the most predictable dream. He was back aboard the quarterdeck of the *Temptress,* his wrecked ship—now without a splinter of damage to her.

He began strutting around the deck, ordering his old crew to 'look alive,' 'raise anchor,' 'drop anchor,' and his personal favorite, 'swab the deck!'

The sun began beating down heavy from its zenith—all the men began dripping thick balls of sweat. Then they began taking off their shirts and trousers to escape the heat, leaving nothing more than a company of sailors working hard in their skivvies.

Frachas stood proudly erect on the quarterdeck ogling his men.

Suddenly, without explanation, his seamen all started laughing at him—Frachas realized he was completely naked. Worse, his penis was not its actual size, but a baby's member. He ran frantically about the ship looking for a loincloth or at least a towel to cover himself, but as could be expected, he found nothing.

Frachas' sailors laughed the whole time; he finally broke down in tears.

"I'm sorry! I'm sorry! Forgive me! I never wanted to lose a soul! Titus ordered me to continue the voyage. Forgive me!"

Domitian found himself a toddler again, playing with wooden toy horses and ships on the floor of Vespasian's office.

Vespasian and Titus were readying themselves for the upcoming campaign in Germania.

Vespasian took a break from his study and kneeled down by little Domitian. "Take care, little one. I shouldn't be gone more than two years."

"No leave me, Papa. I scared." Domitian started crying.

Vespasian grabbed his son by his garment and then smacked him across the face. "There is no place for weakness in this family, son. Never forget that, you spoiled brat!"

Joseph was experiencing another prophecy. It began again with overpowering white light. He heard a growing ringing in his ears. Covering his eardrums with his index fingers, he closed his eyes tightly.

Slowly Joseph opened his eyes—he was floating thousands of feet in the air, looking fifteen hundred feet down onto the top of the great desert mountain butte, Masada. He could see a crowd of a thousand Sicarii, all wearing their terrifyingly eerie black garbs. There were even some children and women, also all dressed in black.

Spiraling around the steep mountain fortress was a ramp made of wood and stone, spanning from the bottom of the butte to the very top.

A legion of Roman soldiers mystically appeared, all racing up and around the ramp, swords and spears raised high, in a full Roman battle cry.

The Sicarii made two lines. The Sicarii in one line raised their daggers and killed the person in the line facing them. The lines collapsed on themselves, and the slaughter continued until there was only one Sicarii left standing. The last man then slew himself.

The Romans raced to the top of the mountain and found nothing but blood, black cloth, and dead bodies. Only two women and three children remained alive, as they had hidden themselves during the mass suicide.

A legion of Romans, seeing the thousand lifeless bodies, walked around inspecting the dead, jabbing spears into the corpses to ensure they truly were departed.

"Arrest the women and children!" a centurion yelled out. "It looks like the Hebrews have had all the fun themselves. Great work today, men!"

■ ■ ■

**TITUS, JOSEPH,** Frachas, Domitian, and Violet all found themselves waking at the exact same moment, unconsciously sitting up in their cots—still at Uncle Ming's.

As it was already midday, Titus' entourage began to congregate around him, hungry and hungover.

# Chapter 23:

# Paul of Tarsus

**TITUS, FRACHAS,** Joseph, Violet, Domitian, and the rest of their Roman entourage were now awake. They simply all nodded to each other for their morning greeting so they did not have to speak, or worse yet, listen to someone else speak. Only Titus said one word as he led his dazed party out of Uncle Ming's opium den.

"Food," Titus groaned as his group closely followed behind him.

They made their way through the streets of Rome in search of a simple but hearty Roman eatery when they came upon a large crowd gathering. There were hundreds of bodies blocking the entire breadth of the street's passage. Titus and company began pushing the closely-packed people aside as they made their way through the assembly.

As they navigated through the crowd, they looked up and saw a man standing on a rooftop speaking to the masses.

"Take Jesus into your heart! That is all you need to do to be blessed eternally by the Lord!" he shouted.

Titus stopped and began to listen, as did Joseph, Violet, Frachas, Domitian, and the other Romans in their company.

"He died on the cross for *you*, his brothers and sisters, and you will find everlasting paradise in his service. Do not be tempted by false Roman gods! There is only one God! The God of Jesus, the God of Moses, the God of Abraham, Isaac, and Jacob!"

"This man is a troublemaker," Titus quipped.

"Hebrews are always troublemakers," Frachas added. "Present company excepted." He directed his ancillary comment to Joseph.

"There is a new faction in Judea, completely consumed with this Jesus. His followers think of him as more of a god than a man," Joseph interjected.

"This Christ figure will cause more deaths than my father," Titus speculated.

Paul continued to speak. "Ask yourselves, what will you say to the Lord on your day of judgement? Will you excuse your lack of faith because you feared the Roman fist? Will you hide behind Saturn, Jupiter, Cupid, Luna, or countless other false Roman gods? Let yourself be cleansed, baptized with the pure water of the true Almighty. Renounce your Roman deities and pledge allegiance to Jesus—*you will be saved!*"

"This man should be executed for sedition," Titus declared.

Upon hearing his dissent, several Christ followers began screaming obscenities at Titus, who quickly extinguished the confrontation with the presentation of his dagger.

"We need to get out of here—now!" Titus said to his entire party. "Keep pushing forward."

"Who goes there?" Paul cried out, seeing the disturbance in the crowd. "Non-believers, are you?"

The horde of followers became riotous at Paul's incitement.

"Burn in hell, Christ-killers!" one follower yelled out.

"Down with Caesar!" was yelled out by another.

"Do not harm them, my brothers and sisters," Paul ordered. "They need our salvation more than all of us combined. Now let us pray our Roman friends see the light of Jesus as we have."

And with that, all the followers prostrated themselves. Paul raised his hands towards the heavens and prayed:

*Our Father, who art in heaven. Hallowed be thy name. Thy Kingdom come. Thy will be done, on earth as it is in heaven. Give us this day our daily bread, and forgive us our trespasses, as we forgive those who trespass against us. And lead us not into temptation, but deliver us from evil. For thine is the power, and the glory, and the kingdom for ever and ever, Amen.*

Titus and his party stood standing among a group of no less than a thousand Jesus worshippers, all under the control of Paul. There was that eerie feeling in the air of electricity passing through one's body.

"That man is driving a wedge into the heart of Rome," Titus said to Frachas.

"He's trying to cause an uprising," Frachas replied supportively.

"Do you want a civil war?" Titus asked Paul, loudly so all could hear.

"Rather a civil war than Rome's daily war against her own people," Paul advocated.

"You preach of a false messiah!" Joseph declared to Paul and the assembly, bringing a hush across the people.

"There is no son of God, there is only God!" Joseph continued to Paul. "Embracing a false prophet is idolatrous. It's one of the Ten Commandments, for the Lord's sake!"

Paul and his followers were so overcome with anger at Joseph attempting to debunk their beliefs, they were unable to foment an oral defense.

"Jesus is the Christ, as foretold by the prophets!" Paul rebutted passionately.

"Then why have we no Kingdom of God? And no peace among men that the prophets foretold the true messiah would usher in?" Joseph questioned, to Paul's increasing frustration.

"He will return!" Paul declared. "And when He does, only the believers will be saved. You and your lot will burn in the bowels of hell for all time!"

Joseph stood looking at Paul the way a man looks at another when one cannot believe the lunacy of another's beliefs.

"I'm surprised Nero hasn't dispatched him yet," Frachas said to Titus quietly.

"I think Nero is terrified of that man," Titus replied. "He's on house arrest, preaching treason, and if Nero didn't fear his followers, he would have disposed of Paul a long while ago."

"The whole situation is strange," Frachas admitted.

"Hebrews have come and gone, attempting to spread their gospel across the empire, but not until this Paul arrived were the Roman people so taken in," Titus added.

"Who is the ranking Roman among you? A senator or a tribune perhaps?" Paul queried.

"General Flavius Titus," Titus said proudly and firmly.

"Oh, a general, how grand!" Paul remarked.

"And who are you, sir?" Titus asked.

"I am the son of man. I am an apostle of the Lord. But I simply go by Paul," he answered. "General Titus, you may be disappointed to find that your rank and family name will grant you less than nothing in the afterlife. You will only gain entrance to heaven and everlasting paradise by asking the Lord, Jesus Christ, for salvation."

"I'll take my chances with my Roman gods, thank you—the gods that rule half the known world seem to be doing just fine."

"See, my brothers and sisters, these poor wretched souls are doomed to an eternity in hell, burning in endless flames!" Paul exclaimed.

"Save it, old man. You're about five seconds away from being taken into custody," Titus threatened.

"Oh, really? I'm a Roman citizen, and therefore you'll need cause to arrest me. What cause have you to arrest an old man talking on his rooftop to friends?"

"Disturbing the peace, inciting a rebellion, sedition. What else do you want added in there? I could have you locked up for the rest of your miserable short life," Titus replied, impressed with his saber-rattling.

"Oh! Hear the Roman general threaten me with even less freedom than I already have, and for only trying to save the souls of my fellow man. How very Roman of you, sir!"

"I want to hit this old madman in his gonads," Frachas said.

"Let's arrest him," Titus said.

"We're with you, my lord," the Roman officers in Titus' party said with full allegiance.

Frachas also nodded his approval.

"If you try and take him, we may not live to see the night—there are hundreds of these fanatics and a dozen of us," Joseph advised.

"Frankly, I don't care," Titus replied. "Something needs to be done about this man, and I'll be damned if I just stand by while he pushes Rome towards civil war."

Then Titus yelled out, "You there, citizen Paul! You are hereby arrested!"

At this proclamation, the entire gathering began to cry and scream in support of their apostle.

"Get down from there, or I will have you slain where you stand," Titus continued.

The crowd was now standing tall. They were shouting down Titus' directive with religious gospel, epithets, and pleas for mercy. Any stratagem that had a hint of winning over Titus' mind was employed—all to no avail.

Paul raised up his arms to quiet his followers. "My dear brothers and sisters, do not be alarmed. Everything that occurs is God's will. We will all be with Jesus in the afterlife. Bless you, everyone!"

Paul descended from the rooftop and surrendered himself to Titus. Roman officers were needed to hold back the frantic flailing of believers trying to secure Paul's release. In the end, no violence broke out, to Titus and his party's surprise.

Titus took Paul to the central Roman jail and issued a brief to Nero describing the entire situation concerning the arrest. Upon reading Titus' account, Nero had Paul summarily condemned to a speedy death.

◼ ◼ ◼

"**HEAR YE!** Hear ye!" a posted scroll, affixed to walls in every neighborhood in Rome, began. "The man formerly known as 'Saul of Tarsus' a.k.a. 'Paul of Tarsus' a.k.a. 'Paul the Apostle' a.k.a. 'Paul the Seeing, the formerly blind, and the formerly not blind' a.k.a. 'The Turkish Heeb'—is condemned by Caesar for his traitorous teachings and sedition against the Roman government. He is to be executed publicly in the Colosseum this Wednesday when the moon is full. All are welcome to attend! Door prizes will be awarded!"

Nero personally attended the execution. The overflowing crowd of Roman citizens in the Colosseum reassured Nero that he was acting in both his and Rome's best interest—what Nero did not understand was that half of the people watching Paul's death were actually his supporters.

"Let this be a lesson to all the enemies of Rome," Nero shouted out to the Colosseum attendees. "If you preach of false gods, false messiahs, and insurrection against the empire, you will be dispatched, to the great enjoyment of the empire!"

Paul of Tarsus Preaches
the Word of Jesus

Raucous laughter spread like a contagion throughout the stadium.

"Bring out the prisoner!" Nero ordered.

Drums began beating, slowly, at an executioner's pace. The drums increased their speed with each four-beat measure.

Paul slowly ascended on an elevator from the bowels of the Colosseum. He had been locked in the very same jail cell that had held Joseph not so long ago. A raucous sixty thousand Romans, delighted at the sight of Paul's bondage and condemnation, began chanting: "Jugulo, obtrunco, mortifico!" the same chant that accompanied every display of death in the stadium.

Paul was rushed in his chains up to the center platform where a beastly executioner, bare-chested and wearing a black mask, awaited with an axe. Paul's head was laid over a wooden table and fastened down by a leather belt.

"Do what you do best, executioner," Nero commanded.

The cheering crowd came to a maddening roar as the executioner's axe rose up to its highest position and hung in the air. Then Caesar motioned to the executioner to proceed, and the audience noise immediately ran silent. Everyone in attendance wanted to hear the crunching slice of the decapitation.

The large blade came swinging down. Paul's head popped off and fell to the floor, directly into a basket.

The Colosseum burst forth with cheers of jubilation at the execution. Though many of the onlookers were supporters of Paul, they did not scream or cry. They knew the slightest showing of support of Paul might lead to their own death. They merely watched in silent horror as Jesus' most ardent apostle lost his head.

Nero walked over to the basket, picked up Paul's head by the hair on the sides of his head, and raised the decapitated skull high to the approval of the crowd.

"Now that the heretic is purified, let's have some music!" Nero yelled out—the loyalist Romans in attendance cheered.

Quickly a band began to strike up a Roman military tune with flutes, lyres, drums, cymbals, and tambourines.

Titus, Joseph, and Frachas stood looking at the entire spectacle with a strange bewilderment. Titus knew that it was justifiable to execute a man that championed an uprising, but a tingling in his gut made him wonder if Paul's death was in fact in Rome's best interest.

Joseph asked himself why a Hebrew like Paul would leave the faith and give his life to the service of a peasant who had not proven to be the messiah. Another part of him wondered if there was any truth to his claims about the Nazarene rising from the dead.

And Frachas, well—he enjoyed gore, but even he knew this was not a normal execution and could not enjoy it with the same zeal as with executions of murderers, thieves, or foreign heads of state.

Though unseen to Titus and company, Vespasian was also in attendance for Paul's execution. His thoughts were of a much more sinister nature. Vespasian indulged himself in the thought that Paul's death might actually lead to Nero's downfall, and ultimately to his own ascension—he was more right than he knew.

Paul's head was put on a pike and marched around the streets of Rome, per Nero's orders, to dissuade any other agitators from following in his footsteps. For a short while it was successful in thwarting sedition, but the Christians were becoming organized and surging in numbers.

# PART III

"You shall not take vengeance or bear a grudge against the sons of your own people, but you shall love your neighbor as yourself: I am the Lord." —*Leviticus 19:18*

# Chapter 24:

# Nero Falls, Vespasian Rises

**THE NEWS** of Paul's execution moved like a ripple throughout the Roman Empire. Paul had thousands of followers who believed in his gospel and in Jesus as the messiah. When all of Rome heard Paul had been slain for championing Jesus, even more Romans who had been loyal to the state openly declared their support for the Christ.

Crowds of thousands started praying to their savior openly, in broad daylight, all over the streets of Rome. Whenever someone got down on the ground and prayed in the name of Jesus, the event became magnetic. Within minutes, a half-dozen worshippers turned into a thousand or more, and each day the following was growing.

Before long, the followers of Jesus were met with resistance from the Roman government—the military began using force to arrest all Christ-worshippers. Nero was livid at the idea that citizens of Rome, during a war with Judea, would abandon him for a Hebrew messiah who was nothing more than what he considered a 'seditious dead peasant magician.'

As the followers of Jesus increased, so did Nero's cruelty. Romans were being crucified throughout the capital as a deterrent against following the 'false messiah.' Nero soon decided crucifixion was too good for the Christians, and he began burning them alive in the thousands. This policy had the exact opposite of its intended effect.

The followers of Jesus became violent, meeting their Roman oppressors with the same lethal force they received. Their tactics were guerilla in nature. They struck down soldiers in the dark. They burned down Roman government buildings and the quarters of Roman soldiers.

Roman officers, seeing the conviction of the followers of Christ, began to defect to their cause. As a result, the mass of Christians began using Roman military tactics against Caesar's loyalist Romans.

Every decision Nero made seemed to lead to a greater calamity. The Praetorian Guard took notice and began to have backroom discussions at the highest levels over who to support should Nero fall.

Full civil war eventually broke out.

The rebellion littered the streets of Rome with bodies—tens of thousands were killed. So outraged were they at Nero's cruelty and disastrous mismanagement that even those who did not believe in Jesus rose to oppose him.

Finally, all of Rome had had enough of Nero. A Roman court of law tried and convicted the emperor of treason in absentia and sentenced him to death. The Senate declared him an enemy of the people—it was the last straw.

Thousands of Romans against Nero surrounded the emperor's palace. They broke through the palace's locked doors and gates—some even scaled the multi-level structure.

Nero's Praetorian Guard was put to an impossible task: cutting down the endless mass of angry Romans that had breached the palace's fortifications. The Guard demurred and defected, joining the rebelling forces rather than be slain in vain for Nero.

"What in Hades is happening?" Nero screamed to his closest advisors while looking out from his palace into the streets, teeming with angry Romans.

"A message just arrived from the Praetorian Guard, Your Excellency," Ulysses said, and handed over a sealed scroll.

*Great Caesar,*

*Forgive us, but you have put us all in this intolerable situation. You have one quarter hour to do it, or we will come up there and do it for you. Best wishes for you in the afterlife. Hail, Caesar!*

*Signed,*

*Praetorian Guard Prefect,*
*Nymphidius Sabinus*

"Fuck!" Nero screamed. "Out! Everyone out!"

Realizing the graveness of his situation, Nero picked up his dog and barricaded himself in his own bathroom.

Pompey, the Emperor's trusty pug, was yelping inconsolably, not knowing what was happening, yet full of fear, sensing his master's consternation.

Nero reached up for a gold gladius, ceremonially displayed over his matching commode, and took it down off the wall.

Pompey, held in Nero's arms, licked his master with a fury. Nero returned the affection to Pompey. Then he raised the edge of the sword's blade to Pompey's neck.

"I love you," Nero whispered to his dog.

In a quick motion, he slit the helpless dog's throat. Pompey bled out in less than five seconds.

"I will be with you directly," Nero said to his dead dog and then kissed him on the forehead while placing him carefully down on the ground.

Then Nero placed the hilt of the sword on the marble floor by the edge of the bathroom wall. He placed the tip of the blade under his ribcage.

"What an artist dies in me," Nero lamented himself.

Then he jumped up and fell upon on the sword, impaling his heart. Nero collapsed next to Pompey, dead.

News of Nero's suicide sent shockwaves throughout the country and beyond. Generals, senators, and ministers were already fast at work, contemplating their own rise to Caesar.

The Roman governor of Hispania, Galba, rose up and seized power with the assistance of Nero's former Praetorian Guard.

But Galba was old and his physical weakness transferred to mental weakness. He relied on counselors and ministers who had more personal motivations in mind than support for Galba or Rome. Thus, all his efforts were diluted at best or sabotaged at worst.

Otho, Galba's first and most ardent supporter, saw the feebleness of the new emperor and began to scheme with the same Praetorian Guard that had secured Galba's throne.

Galba became so weak that he could no longer walk or ride. Now bedridden, Otho saw his opportunity and planned an assassination.

As Galba saw Otho bearing a sword at his bedside, he spoke his final words: "Strike, if it be for the good of the Romans!"

Galba died having served as Caesar only seven months.

Otho was immediately crowned the new Caesar. But the fight for the crown of Rome was far from done. A powerful former governor of Africa and military veteran of Germania named Vitellius soon began to challenge Otho. Vitellius rallied tens of thousands of soldiers, loyal from their days serving together, and began to march on the capital.

Vitellius closed in on Rome with his overpowering force, and a great battle ensued, the Battle of Bedliacum. There were over forty thousand casualties, and in the end, Vitellius was victorious. Rather than be taken prisoner, Otho committed suicide, and Vitellius was crowned Emperor.

Vespasian, seeing the uproar in Rome over the course of the past year, had sat on the sidelines and neither openly supported nor disavowed any Caesar. He was on an excursion into the breadbasket of Egypt to secure desperately-needed stockpiles of grain for his ongoing campaign against the Judeans. He now sat in Alexandria discussing the future of Rome with his closest advisors and supporters.

"My lord, Rome is yours if you ask for it," Tiberius Alexander, the young governor of Alexandria, stated.

"You are the only one that can bring peace to the empire," another advisor said. "If you do not take power, thousands of Romans will suffer at the hands of Vitellius."

Vespasian, at the head of a long wooden table, sat considering all the arguments presented before him.

"The Senate and nearly the whole of the Roman army is loyal to you, my lord," an ardent supporter said passionately. "You will be greeted with flowers on your arrival in the capital!"

"You have such an overwhelming force that the resistance will dissipate at the sight of your army," another advisor affirmed.

"Rome deserves nothing but the best, does it not?" Tiberius Alexander asked.

Vespasian could not argue as he agreed with everything his supporters were saying. He relaxed his body back into his upright chair and took a deep breath in contemplation.

"Send word to the Senate that I will accept the crown if it is offered," Vespasian declared.

"I will dispatch a messenger this minute!" an excited advisor announced.

"It can wait," Vespasian said firmly. "Let us toast first. To Rome!"

All lifted their glasses and saluted Vespasian as they repeated the toast. The party of men all took a drink together, and they began banging on the table chanting: "Vespasian! Vespasian! Caesar! Caesar!"

Vespasian sat back in his chair with a small grin of success and contentment. He thought about Joseph and the prophecy foretold to him over a year ago while Vespasian had the Hebrew in chains in Caesarea.

Vespasian decided at that moment Joseph would become part of his family should he indeed be named Caesar.

*  *  *

**BACK IN** Rome, Titus received word from his father that he intended to attempt a rise to Caesar. Joseph, upon hearing this news, was filled with excitement, seeing his prophecy work its way towards fruition.

"Do you believe in my God now?" Joseph asked Titus.

"I don't know what to believe, except that you are the most prodigious man I have ever met in my entire life, and that includes my father," Titus replied.

"No need for compliments, my lord," Joseph assured Titus, beaming.

"Joseph, my father has decided to add you to our house when he is crowned. You will be a Flavius. You will be my brother, and as such, you shall never call me 'my lord' ever again. My name is Titus, and I order you to call me that."

Joseph was speechless. He never expected to rise to such a position as to call his father Caesar, or himself a Flavius—it now seemed like the inevitable reality.

■ ■ ■

**VESPASIAN RECEIVED** a communique back from the Senate that he was the preferred choice for Caesar and that the body's allegiance rested with him instead of Vitellius.

Upon hearing this news, Vespasian gave the order to his trusted commanders to begin a march on Rome.

Legions loyal to Vespasian from Germania, the Balkans, Africa, and of course Italy began closing in on the capital.

Vitellius' force was greatly weakened by the Battle of Bedliacum. Though Vitellius fought to the last man, his force was eventually overtaken by Vespasian's.

Attempting to flee the capital, Vitellius was captured by the Praetorian Guard who had abandoned him in favor of Vespasian.

The Guard decided to kill and make an example out of Vitellius rather than risk his return to power. They led him on a naked walk of shame to the Gemonian stairs.

The stairs were located in the center of the capital and were used for those deserving of punishment beyond crucifixion. The steep stone-cut stairs numbered in the hundreds and led directly into the Forum so that onlookers could see the horror inflicted on the body as it tumbled down to a gruesome death. Usually a fall down the stairs caused every bone in the body to break, some many times over. Often the victim's head would crack open on its way to the bottom of the stairs, the brain scattering all over the steps.

Vitellius was first racked, separating his arms from his shoulders and his legs from his hips. Then he was bound and nearly choked to death. But before he could suffocate to death, the Praetorian ceased his asphyxiation and presented Vitellius' broken body before all those watching from the forum below.

"Vespasian is your emperor!" the commander of the Praetorian Guard shouted out.

Vitellius replied hoarsely with his last words, "Yet I was once your emperor."

The Praetorian commander and his men tossed Vitellius down the flight of stairs with such force as to ensure his body would tumble to the bottom.

Once Vitellius' remaining corpse came to rest at the bottom of the stairs, the cheering crowd further abused his body. There was nothing left of him but a pool of blood, mangled flesh, and bone.

Upon word that Vitellius had been executed, the Senate convened immediately and unanimously proclaimed Vespasian as Caesar.

Vespasian was still in Alexandria when the message came from the Senate that he was the new emperor.

Now Vespasian was in a quandary. The revolt of the Judeans had not yet been settled. The civil war had greatly weakened Rome, and his new position required him to govern from the capital, which took great precedence over the subjugation of Jerusalem. Vespasian decided to focus his attention on Rome and enlisted Titus to continue prosecuting the Judean war.

Upon Vespasian's arrival in Rome, he was greeted by his son and protégé Titus.

"My Caesar, my general, my father, you have done it!" Titus said, embracing Vespasian fully.

"I have done little more than watch on the sidelines as Rome has nearly destroyed itself," Vespasian replied.

"Do not be so modest. Any rise to Caesar requires greatness, and there is hardly a man in the empire that could be called greater than you."

"Enough compliments, son," Vespasian quipped. "It is good to see you. Tell me, where is Joseph? He is to be your new brother and my newest son. His prophecy has come true, and his loyalty is about to be greatly rewarded."

Joseph was summoned before Vespasian, who now sat in the chair of Caesar in his office at the emperor's palace. Titus, Frachas, Domitian, and an assembly of Roman officers stood before Joseph in ceremonial robes.

"Joseph, son of Matthias," Vespasian began, "you are the savior of my firstborn and heir. You have been my own guardian as well. But most importantly, you have proven to be a wise and trustworthy friend to my family and to Rome. Kneel!"

Joseph, who had never knelt before anyone except God, saw the full ramifications of his situation. Realizing he was not being asked to pray to a false Roman god, Joseph followed Vespasian's order.

Vespasian stood. "I hereby proclaim you a citizen of Rome, I deed to you a grand estate outside the capital and a pension for life. With this ring of my house, I declare you my son, with entitlements to all the rights and privileges of House Flavius," he said.

Vespasian then put the gold ring with his house's seal engraved into it on Joseph's right ring finger.

"Arise, Flavius Josephus, citizen of Rome."

# Chapter 25:

# John of Gischala

**JOHN OF** Gischala had been busy following his escape from the Jotapatan jail. He and his men made their way through Galilee to Jerusalem, continuing their banditry along the journey—ever in search of gold, men, and weapons.

John also employed new methods to achieve his goals. First he let it be known that he would pay a bounty of one denarius to all new recruits and give each man a fat cut of all the spoils from every raid. John did all the accounting and never paid his men as many coins as they had actually agreed upon, but a gold coin here and there makes a poor man happy. By the time he closed in on Jerusalem, he had a following of nearly five thousand able-bodied men.

"You boys, there—look at you pathetic wretches," John said to a dozen or so very thin and meek-looking Judean youths by the side of the road as he took a break to feed and water his horse during his march to Jerusalem. "Why do you sit there like old dogs waiting to die? Do you enjoy having nothing, being nothing, and starving daily from no food in your bellies?"

John reached into his coin purse and tossed a handful of silver coins on the ground before the young Judean boys.

"Join me, and that silver is yours today, and gold it will be tomorrow!"

The young men looked at the silver wide-eyed, more money than some had ever owned personally. The boys then turned to each other, asking one another with their eyes how to respond to John's proposal.

One youth jumped up, grabbed a silver piece, and then said, "I'm also hungry."

"Get our newest brother some food!" John roared out to Sadius.

"Immediately, my lord," Sadius replied, and then clapped his hands at two lower-ranking servants, redelegating the duty.

Silver and food were too much to resist, and the rest of the youths hopped up and grabbed their silver, begging for food immediately afterwards as well.

"Yes, yes, welcome! All will be given food ample for a man," John reassured his newest recruits.

The naïve poor boys were now bought and paid for and did not yet know it. They also had no idea what they would be forced to do under threat of torture and death—John was about to explain it to them.

"I'm so happy to have young strong men like yourselves with me. In my business, which is now your business, I sometimes require my men to... how can I say—steal and kill. Now, I know what you young boys are thinking. It violates two commandments, and you'd rather not be involved with that sort of thing. So here's your chance to leave. Does anyone want to leave? Just return the silver piece."

"I want to leave," an older boy said and walked up to return the denarius.

"No ill feelings, son. Perhaps I'll see you again one day..." John said cheerfully as the boy held out the coin. But instead of taking the silver back, John grabbed the boy's wrist with his left hand and coldly whispered, "In hell!" Using his right hand, John quickly and slyly whipped his dagger into the youth's throat.

John stabbed him a dozen times with his blade, causing a fountain of blood to pump out of the young man's neck—he quickly collapsed, dead.

"Does anyone else want to leave?" John roared out like an enraged bear.

The rest of the young men who had taken John's silver quickly discovered they were now John's property—the terrified young souls fell into line directly.

■ ■ ■

**JOHN AND** his army of followers, though many were *de facto* conscripts, were now less than five miles out from Jerusalem when John decided to halt his advance and scout the city walls before potentially walking into an ambush by either the Zealots or the Sicarii.

"Looks peaceful enough, doesn't it, Sadius?" John asked, lying on his belly next to his second-in-command, both of them looking at Jerusalem from a few miles' distance.

"Looks can be deceiving, my lord," Sadius countered.

"Aye, that they can," John agreed. "Let's send a couple of men in, just to be sure."

Before John attacked the most impenetrable city in the world, he sat back and enlisted the help of his spies. They slipped into the city in the middle of the day masquerading as merchants, and immediately they came across a band of Sicarii, all dressed in black.

The Sicarii saw John's two spies and observed that they looked unfamiliar and somewhat suspicious. But the Sicarii were chasing a young girl and more interested in hurting her than confronting John's men.

Seeing the unabated Sicarii savagery, common Judean residents on the street started crying—pained that they were too weak or cowardly to help the girl being forced by the entire Sicarii gang.

"Those devils have been terrorizing us for too long," one older man watching in the street whispered, fearful of being heard by the Sicarii.

An old woman, seeing the assault, began singing psalms to cloak the sins of the street. The screams of the young girl and the song of the old woman intertwined:

*O Come, O Come, Emmanuel,*
*O Come, Thou Rod of Jesse,*
*O come, Thou Dayspring, from on High,*
*O come, Thou Key of David, come,*
*O come, Adonai, Lord of might.*

Children too young to understand the horror continued to play in the streets with their small wooden toys, unaware of any malice.

John's spies, seeing the dejection running over the populace, did further investigating.

They interviewed regular folk, young and old. But they never made their intentions known. Being trained spies, they knew how to get a man to say what was on his mind when he thought a supporter might listen sympathetically.

Sidling up to talkative complainers throughout Jerusalem, John's spies knew in less than a few hours the entire state of the city. The people had been terrorized by Eleazar and his Zealots, and the Sicarii, and wanted both factions gone. They mostly wanted Rome back as long as taxes returned to the prior reasonable rates. The lack of fresh water and food were the most common other gripes forthcoming.

Furtively exiting through the Damascus gate as covertly as they came in, the spies made their way to give their report to John.

"What say you?" John addressed the first of the two spies before him in his tent.

"There is no one in control of the city. The Sicarii and Zealots are terrorizing the people, but they are mostly tribal. There is no command structure, which leads them to fight among themselves and each other daily," the first and taller spy recounted.

"There are factions even among the Zealots. Eleazar controls the Temple Mount through his alliance with Ananus but little more of the city. The people would welcome a strong, known leader to protect all of Jerusalem. A leader such as yourself, my lord," the second spy added.

The first spy radiated silent outrage that his colleague made him look the fool by giving an unsolicited refinement on his own report.

The spies continued doing their best to present ever more poignant and sophisticated information about the state of the city. The Sicarii, on the other hand, were still mostly an unknown, but they did not appear to be a serious hurdle to John's aspirations of taking Jerusalem.

John chose to be bold. He decided he would try and walk up to the front gate with his entire force. "Let's see what happens if we walk through the front door," he said to Sadius.

Shofars from Jerusalem started blaring at the sight of the thousands of John's men coming into view on the city's horizon.

There was no coordinated enemy force to oppose him. The Sicarii all scattered at the sight of John's enormous and unified force.

The Zealots stood secure on the Temple Mount, incapable and unwilling to even try and stop John.

John and his men entered the city through the Lion's gate—it was unguarded, abandoned by the on-duty soldiers. With their hands on the hilts of their swords, John's men slowly and cautiously walked behind their master, who was leading the way through the streets of Jerusalem, examining every square inch of real estate for an enemy.

But to his great surprise, John was greeted with cheers and rose petals. The common people saw John as their savior from the Zealots, Sicarii, and every other malady which had plagued the city. Ananus, the chief high priest, upon hearing of John's arrival, even came down from the Temple Mount to personally welcome him into the city.

There was not even a hint of resistance from the commoners or other authoritatively aspiring adversarial associations.

John's main objective: becoming the ruling warlord or even King of Jerusalem. It was within reach and he could smell it.

"John, what news do you have of the Romans?" one of the city people, eager to hear of the current state of the war, asked with great consternation.

"The Romans are feeble, my friends, and almost defeated!" was John's reply.

The people were pigeons in his hands. Every question allowed him to further convince common citizens' consciences of his 'wisdom, strength, and integrity.'

"Why have you left Galilee with your entire force? Did the Romans pressure you into retreat?" another questioned.

"Only after I routed the Romans did I leave! I have come now to Jerusalem to save you, the people, the city, and of course, the Temple," John answered to a relieved crowd.

"And what of Joseph, son of Matthias? Is he dead as it has been rumored?"

John, in his raids through the Galilean countryside, had received word of Josephus' rise in station to the son of Caesar. He now used his trickery to deceive the Judeans.

"Joseph has betrayed us all!" John said convincingly. "Instead of dying in battle like the rest of the Hebrews in Jotapata, he abandoned his forces and turned for Rome. He is a traitor beyond traitors! He now calls himself Flavius Josephus, a proud citizen of the Roman Empire and son of Caesar himself!"

Hearing this news, the people of Jerusalem were devastated, furious, and more supportive of John than ever before. They shouted that Joseph should be crucified or burned at the stake for his alleged treachery.

"Fear not these bad tidings, my friends!" John exclaimed. "I have a greater force than the Romans can muster. The walls around our great city are unbreachable. The Romans could grow wings, and they would not be able to get over the top of them. And their siege engines were all destroyed by my handiwork."

With this series of cunning lies spreading across the city, John's following soon swelled nearly to twenty thousand. Foolishly naïve young men were the bulk of his new force, while older men exercised their wisdom, knowing the true fate that awaited the city when the Romans returned.

The people of Jerusalem were now split into multiple factions. John seized control of the Zealots, previously controlled by Eleazar ben Simon. Eleazar joined the ranks as John's top commander rather than fight John's overwhelming support.

The Sicarii were also still lurking unseen in Jerusalem, but they had also established a headquarters at Masada after expelling the small Roman force there. The impregnable fortress, built by Herod the Great, stood just over thirty miles southeast of the city.

John went directly to the Temple, the main repository of the city's treasure and official seat from which power emanated. There he established his headquarters in the Court of Priests.

Despite his gracious welcome, John immediately confronted Ananus, the chief high priest, demanding unwavering loyalty and complete submission. Ananas, seeing that John would seize control of the Temple whether he gave his consent or not, kowtowed, believing that John might surprise Jerusalem by being a better steward than Eleazar and his Zealots.

Now that John had legitimacy from both a mass of the citizens and Ananus, he began infiltrating the city with his cronies.

John appointed men unfit to manage a brothel to the Sanhedrin and to ministerial positions like treasurer and tax collector.

With his seized authority, he began rounding up the rich, the opposing ministers, and nearly anyone of importance who did not openly give their full support. John called those arrested "traitors of Jerusalem" and falsely alleged collaboration or treason with Rome.

With these bogus charges levied, he seized all the land, gold, food stocks, and beasts from those who had not even been granted a trial.

Nearly one thousand men of influence now languished in new jail cells built in the Court of Gentiles. The entire grounds of the Temple Mount were soon sullied with every vile substance and garbage imaginable: blood, tears, urine, feces, rank corpses, and rotting food.

John's nastiness was now in full effect as he began to inflict even greater cruelty on those he had already jailed and stolen from, merely to satisfy his own sadistic lust. The innocent prisoners were beaten with batons, scourged with spiked maces, mutilated with branding irons, swords, and boiling oil. Finally, when the arrested could no longer maintain consciousness from their brutal torture, they were executed by crucifixion around the porticos of the Temple to make them visible to the entire city.

Ananus, seeing the horrors his obedience to John had brought down upon Jerusalem, made a last-ditch effort to move the people to reject John and his rogues. Ananus stood in the amphitheater and made a plea to the masses assembled:

*Certainly it would have been good for me to die before I had seen the House of God full of so many abominations, and its sacred precincts crowded with these blood-shedding villains. What purpose is it to live among a people blind to calamities and no longer capable of tackling the troubles on their hands? You are plundered and do not protest—beaten without a murmur, witnesses to murder, without one audible groan. What unbearable tyranny! But why blame the tyrants? Do not they owe their existence to you and your lack of spirit? Was not it you who shut your eyes when the rogues slowly took over? Their growth was encouraged by your silence and by your standing idly by while they were arming and then turning those arms against yourselves.*

*The right thing would have been to nip their attacks in the bud before they were pouring abuse on your own flesh and blood. But by your indifference you encouraged these ruffians to plunder. When houses were ransacked nobody cared, so they seized their owners too and dragged them through the middle of the city without anyone raising so much as a finger to defend them. Next, they flung them into jail. Uncharged or falsely charged, and untried, they were condemned without a soul coming to the rescue. The natural consequence was that these same men were seen murdered in our Holy Temple, yet not a murmur was uttered, not a hand raised!*

*They have seized the strongest place in the whole city—from now on the Temple must be spoken of as a citadel or fortress. Tyranny is strongly entrenched there, but what do you mean to do? Have things gone so far in the city, are we so sunk in misery, that we are an object of pity even to our foes? Why do not you rise, you spiritless creatures, and turn to meet the blows as you see beasts do, and kick back at your tormentors? Why do not you remember your own per-*

*sonal miseries? Have you really lost the most honorable and deep-rooted of our instincts, the longing for freedom?*

*Are we in love with slavery and devoted to our masters as if our fathers had taught us to be doormats? Why, again and again they fought to the bitter end for independence, defying the might of both Egypt and Persia rather than take orders from anyone! But why talk about our fathers? In our present battle with Rome, what is its object? Is it not freedom? Then shall we refuse to yield to the masters of the world and put up tyrants of our own race? Subservience to the scum of our own nation would prove us willful degenerates.*

*Even if we fall into the Romans' hands—we cannot suffer any worse treatment than these men have subjected us to. Could anything be more galling than first to see offerings left in the Temple by our enemies, then spoils seized by men of our own race who have robbed and massacred the nobility of our city, murdering men whom even the Romans would have spared in their hour of triumph?*

*The Romans never went beyond the bounds set for non-believers, never trampled on one of our sacred customs but reverently gazed from a distance at the walls of the sanctuary, and men born in this country, brought up in our customs and called Judeans, stroll where they like in the inner sanctuary, their hands still reeking with the slaughter of their countrymen! In the face of that, can anyone dread a foreign war and enemies by comparison far kinder to us than our own people? What if we are to call things by their right names? We might find the Romans are the champions of our law, and its enemies are inside the city!*

*I will champion your cause with my head and hands. I will do everything I can think of to secure your safety. Every ounce of my bodily strength is at your disposal!*

Ananus' speech touched the nerves of all the many thousands of Judeans who had come to hear him speak. They knew he was telling the truth—his call to action against John's men was righteous, but they saw no visible path to victory.

Yet many young Judeans rallied behind Ananus, creating a small citizen force of about a thousand men. The people had suffered so terribly that many men who joined Ananus' force did so because they preferred to die fighting rather than continue living under the terror of John's reign.

Ananus and his small force armed themselves with all objects that could be used as weapons. From trees they made batons and spears; with stones they carried slingshots—fewer than half had swords. Then, despite overwhelming fear, they marched towards the Temple Mount in an attempt to capture John and dissolve his crew of bandits and Zealots.

Ananus led the way through the streets of the city. When they approached the Temple they saw hundreds of dead bodies from John's handiwork lying mutilated on the ground. John and his men were not going to exert the energy to properly bury those they killed, so once the bodies began to smell, they were simply tossed over the side of the Temple Mount, down some sixty yards. No citizens below bothered to give these poor souls a burial either, and most of the bodies were now black with death, having been rotting for weeks or more.

The wretched sight and smell of the dead sent such terror through Ananus' men that many deserted.

But Ananus kept going. Sadius, seeing Ananus' force approach the Temple Mount from within the Court of Gentiles, ran into the Holy of Holies to alert John. He was busy lounging on a bed with two whores, drinking wine and snacking on grapes, cheese, and crackers, when Sadius burst in.

"My lord, the high priest marches against you!" Sadius informed John.

"Bitches, get off of me," John said, rising up naked. "There's work to be done."

John put on a tunic and exited the great golden Temple doors. He looked out and down from the Temple Mount and saw Ananus, an old man barely able to exert enough energy to walk the distance, leading a company of mostly young men under twenty years of age.

John began to laugh.

"That's the best the old priest can do?" he burst out to his lackeys. "I want him taken alive if possible. Dead is fine as well—just make sure to bring his head to me."

John, unconcerned with the threat posed by Ananus' force, went back into the Temple to continue drinking wine and snacking with his concubines.

Ananus led the charge up the steps to the Temple Mount and was immediately seized, not able to slay so much as one of John's soldiers with the old and heavy sword in his hand.

The rest of Ananus' force met their deaths mostly from stones hurled down upon them. Within fifteen minutes of the charge's start, Ananus' insurrection had been completely destroyed. Every last body on the ground was inspected by John's men—the Judeans were run through with a spear to ensure they were truly departed.

A group of three monstrous bandits, their white tunics drenched red with blood, brought Ananus by his arms inside the Temple, presenting him to John.

"Well, well, well—Ananus, I see you have returned to the Temple, though we are no longer in need of a high priest!" John began laughing to his men.

Sadius walked up to Ananus and punched him in stomach and then kicked him in the testicles. Ananus heaved for breath and moaned in pain.

"Get it over with already, you rogue bastards," Ananus shot back.

"Over? Ha! We haven't even begun!" John's laughter continued. "We're going to put you on trial for being a treacherous collaborator with the Romans. We're going to show the whole city that there is law and order and justice left in Jerusalem. You are going to remind the people that I am their solitary ruler and anyone who tries to rise up against me will meet your fate. Then and only then will I crucify you."

"Let me flay him first," Sadius requested. "I want to disembowel him and gouge out his eyes too. When he meets Moses, he won't be able to see what he looks like!" He began laughing hysterically as did the rest of John's lackeys.

"I suppose you can cut his eyes out—after the trial," John said. "Put him in a cell and take him out of my sight. Remember, no torture until after the trial. He needs to look fit and healthy before all of Jerusalem, to show our enemies we do not hurt those in our custody." John continued laughing manically with his minions.

Next John selected a group of seventy land-owning ministers for jurors, representing the most powerful faction in Jerusalem that had not yet pledged their allegiance. This wasn't so much a trial as it was an obvious statement that if the wealthy did not fall into line, they too would end up in Ananus' place.

The kangaroo court assembled, and a thousand spectators crammed into the hall in the Court of Israelites. Each juror who was called appeared, fearing abstention could bring them individual ruin.

The trial began.

John sat as judge.

"Hear ye! Hear ye!" John spoke out, quieting the jurors and witnesses in attendance.

Ananus stood before John, shackled in chains.

"Today we will hear the charges levied against Ananus ben Ananus, the chief high priest. He stands accused of high treason against Jerusalem, inciting a rebellion, and collaborating with the Romans," John said. "How do you plead?"

"Not guilty, Your Majesty," Ananus facetiously teased John's illegitimate power.

"Bailiff, control the accused!" John roared, embarrassed that his authority had been openly disparaged.

A bandit standing besides Ananus removed a wooden baton from his waist belt and gave Ananus a sharp blow to the stomach. Ananus collapsed to the floor, to John's great amusement.

"I will not accept a mockery of this court!" John said sternly. "Do you understand, priest?"

"I understand perfectly," Ananus replied.

"Good." John continued, "The accused has entered a plea of not guilty. You have the right to make a statement in your own defense. Do you have anything to say?"

"I have plenty to say," Ananus replied.

Ananus mostly repeated his speech from the amphitheater, turning the trial into an indictment of John. He convinced every single juror of the injustice that John had brought down on Jerusalem and its people. John sat frustrated as Ananus mounted a powerful defense with his words. When Ananus finished, John instructed the jury to come to a verdict. There was no reason for a prosecutorial effort as John believed the jury would convict regardless of the evidence.

The jury convened privately in one of the Temple chambers for no more than fifteen minutes. Then they returned to the great hall to announce their verdict.

John sat with a fiendish grin, assured that the jury would return a verdict of guilty on all charges.

"How does this jury find the defendant?" John called out.

The foreman stood up, and unequivocally said: "We the jury in a unanimous vote find the accused, Ananus, the chief high priest of the Holy Temple, *not guilty* on all charges."

An uproar broke out through the Temple hall. Ananus, delighted with the rejection of John's entire effort, started laughing hysterically as John's face turned bright red with rage.

"Should I remove his chains?" the bailiff asked John, dumbfounded as to what a not-guilty verdict portended.

But before John could respond, Sadius took out his sword and slew Ananus in the Temple for all to see.

"Now you have our *true* verdict too, and your trials are over!" Sadius exclaimed to a jaw-dropped and horrified audience.

"Seize the jury!" John roared.

His bandits in the gallery quickly drew their swords and rounded up the jurors, who were immediately sent to jail cells to await purification and execution.

Eleazar ben Simon, the Zealot leader, was disgusted and furious by Sadius' summary execution in the Temple after Ananus had been acquitted unanimously by a jury of his peers. Torturing and executing traitors in the Court of Gentiles was one thing, but the murder of the innocent chief high priest in the Court of Israelites was quite another.

Going back to his office in the Court of Priests, John began to chide his subordinates for his own failings.

"How can I call myself master of this city if I can't even convict a man that preaches openly for the Romans and raises a force to march on the Temple Mount against me?" John screamed as he threw a side table across the room, nearly hitting a couple of his henchmen.

"John, do you realize what you have done? You have destroyed your credibility with the slaying of Ananus by your wild hound," Eleazar declared.

"Who do you work for? Are you loyal to Ananus and his traitorous followers? Or are you loyal to me?" John questioned, outraged at Eleazar's criticism.

"I'm loyal to you, my lord, but first to God" was Eleazar's reply.

"It sounds like you're not too sure. Why don't you go into the Court of Gentiles and take a good look at what happens to those that betray me?" John growled.

Eleazar's nostrils flared and his eyes bulged, then he swiftly exited.

"That bastard has gone too far, and he needs to be stopped," Eleazar thought to himself as he walked away.

He had always questioned whether or not it was prudent to ally with John. Now Eleazar realized the folly of his error. Still possessing his strength of mind and body, he decided to act.

Eleazar summoned Nathan and his other most trusted Zealot brothers who had aligned with John's tribe of bandits. They met late at night in a small hidden chamber in the tunnels under the Temple Mount to protect the meeting's secrecy.

"He offends God with every breath!" Eleazar exclaimed. "I was there when his most evil henchman, Sadius, disposed of our good Chief High Priest Ananus, may he rest in peace, Baruch Hashem—even after he was acquitted of all charges!"

"John has tortured the innocent, not in search of blasphemy or false worship, but in search of gold and power. He must be dispatched immediately!" Nathan stated.

To this call, all in Eleazar's company started chanting praises. "Hear, hear," the Zealots cried out in unison and then voiced a resolved "Amen."

"Now I want you all to approach every man you know who is likely to change allegiances and bring them to me," Eleazar entreated his comrades. "You must do this quickly. John will surely be alerted to our workings the first time someone refuses our offer. What are you all still looking at? Go, there is work to be done!"

Eleazar's men scuttled off and began recruiting. By the next week, there were two thousand Zealots under John's control that had committed to re-support Eleazar. They planned to spontaneously assemble in the Court of Israelites, and once gathered, they would seize all weapons and tactical positions on the Temple Mount, ending with John's removal from power.

At high noon the next day, the Zealots, wearing their plain clothing, began assembling in the Court of Israelites—all bearing arms. In only a few moments, a couple thousand Zealots stood at the ready.

Eleazar appeared in the center of his followers, his sword and a great wooden staff in hand. He wore a robust white cloak, a leader's garment. Nathan, Eleazar's longtime captain, stood beside his master. Sadius, seeing this unfold, turned to relay the events, running to the Court of Priests where John was busy counting his coin receipts, not wanting to be disturbed.

"Don't say a goddamned word!" John ordered as he continued his count, hearing someone approach in a great hurry. "Twenty-nine thousand nine hundred talents—thirty thousand!"

"There is a rebellion!" Sadius blurted out.

"What?" John replied.

"It's Eleazar. He's caused the Zealots to rise up against you!" Sadius explained.

"For God's sake, I knew I should have killed him when he insulted me," John railed. "What side do they attack from?"

"They are already on the Temple Mount! They are assembling in the Court of Israelites."

"Damn! Why didn't you say so?" John threw down his coins, jumped up, grabbed his sword and armor, and began making his way to see about quashing the uprising of Eleazar. "Sound the alarm! All men to their posts!"

Coming out of the Court of Priests and running into the Court of Israelites, John quickly saw the mass of Zealots that Eleazar had marshalled to move against him.

The shofar sounded out, waking everyone close enough to hear its call. John's loyal men began to scramble in response to Eleazar's assembly.

Quickly a ring of men loyal to John encircled the group of Zealots who had switched loyalty in favor of Eleazar. Two thousand men now stood surrounded by eight thousand of John's bandits and Zealots remaining loyal to their master from Gischala.

"We don't all need to die here today," Eleazar shouted out across the way to John. "Surrender—leave Jerusalem, and there will be no blood spilled on my account."

"You know I will never surrender, Eleazar!" John cried out. "Men, prove your worth and kill the traitor Eleazar ben Simon and his rebellious Zealots!"

A great war cry erupted from John's men—they began to run towards the swords and spears held by Eleazar's Zealots.

"Aaaahhh!" the men yelled as they ran at full speed to their death and dismemberment.

A ringed wall of men attacking slammed into a ringed wall of men defending. The impact sent some Zealots flying through the air into sword tips, spearheads, and metal shields. Blood spurted out from flesh wounds, causing many men to bleed to their deaths.

Spilt blood that had gathered on the slick marble floors of the Temple Mount caused men to slip and then be trampled before they could arise. The sounds of metal clashing and men screaming were deafening.

Eleazar stood in the middle of the battle, directing his men, and lending a helping swing of his staff and sword when necessary.

Sadius, his devilish mind always at work, raced to the Temple armory and fetched a crossbow. Grabbing a full quiver of steel-tipped arrows, he made his way to the roof of the Temple porticos to get a shot at the back of Eleazar.

One by one, men fell as Sadius' crossbow delivered deadly darts. He was aiming for Eleazar, but the instant before Sadius fired each arrow, Eleazar unknowingly moved out of the way. In this effort, Sadius hit men on either side of Eleazar but kept missing his main target.

Within fifteen minutes of the engagement, it became clear that Eleazar's men, though fighting courageously, did not have the strength to fend off a force four times their size.

John, sitting in a place of safety away from the ring of battle, drank wine and snacked on figs as he watched the fighting—now seeing it as a spectacle to enjoy.

"Retreat!" Eleazar called out. "Make your way to the inner sanctum!"

Quickly Eleazar's Zealots rushed to break through John's encircling ring of men. Eleazar speared a soldier of John's in the face, creating a gap in the line. Through this gap, Eleazar's surviving men dashed for the Temple's main building.

A thousand men now rushed through the golden Temple doors to the main hall. The rest of Eleazar's men lay dead, their bodies pulverized from fighting in the Court of Israelites.

Eleazar and Nathan locked the solid gold doors of the Temple shut with the securing beam. Eleazar and a thousand Zealot followers were now safe, but they were also trapped.

# Chapter 26:

# Simon bar Giora

**MEANWHILE, SIMON** bar Giora was about to degenerate from a trustworthy administrator of the city's most important business into a feared military monster.

When the Romans were expelled and slaughtered, Simon beseeched the powerful ministers of Jerusalem to grant him control of the new army. Fearing Simon would be unstoppable if given control of such a force, the decision was made to deny Simon the army.

"You will rue the day you denied Simon bar Giora command of the army!" Simon shouted at the council of ministers responsible for refusing him.

The ministers sat stoically like statues, emotionally unaffected by Simon's rage.

"Simon, listen to yourself," the head minister said slowly and calmly. "You are ever hungry for more power. Where will it stop if you control the army? You are a good judge. We need you as a *judge*."

"Power-hungry? Look at yourselves. You are the ones scared of losing power—that is the truth to the motivation behind your veto! I'm the best damn commander Judea can muster, and you all know it! I've served. Have any of you? That's what I thought," Simon said scornfully to the council.

The ministers sat silent.

"Do you old fools think you know what it takes to make an army victorious? Of course, old men think they know everything, even when they've spent their entire lives doing nothing!"

"We're done here, Simon. You know the way out, or do you need Daniel to escort you?" the minister said with a grand smirk on his face while looking over at Daniel, the six-foot-six, two-hundred-and-seventy-five-pound guard sitting in the corner of the room, who stood up and flexed his chest and arms upon being hailed.

"I formally resign my judgeship. Israel can fend for herself— she seems content to try. But mark my words—I will be back one day, and on that day you will all cower before me!" Simon threatened.

Then he walked swiftly and angrily out of the council chambers, making a great stomp with his feet.

Jaded and eager to prove his salt, Simon left his position in the Sanhedrin and became a rogue military commander. Starting with only a few dozen men who quickly grew into the hundreds, he made his way raiding rich Judean households via brutal thug force. Once he possessed a sizable coin stash, he sojourned to the land of Idumea in the southeast with his followers to expand his army from those souls so desperate they would say yes to anything if it included a meal and a drink of wine.

The Romans initially crushed the Idumeans living in Judea, not knowing, or caring about, the difference between them and the Israelites. Vespasian drove them into the Dead Sea, both dead and alive. The bodies all floated and stayed mostly preserved in the almost sticky, supersaturated salty water, now turned red.

Simon halted Vespasian's entire army at the Dead Sea. Or so it appeared to the Idumeans.

Vespasian never intended to press on beyond Judea's eastern boundary, stopping his campaign at predetermined locations. Yet the Idumeans remaining alive fully credited Simon with halting Vespasian's advance.

Simon's seemingly selfless act of bravery in holding the line against the Romans resulted in the Idumeans' salvation—thousands of them became instantly loyal to Simon until their deaths.

Simon now controlled about five thousand Idumeans from beyond the Dead Sea region. A small community of Sicarii joined his ranks as well.

As his power grew, so did his ambitions. Simon became consumed, like John of Gischala, with becoming master of Jerusalem.

Now revered throughout the land, Simon began a focused campaign through Idumea to amass more followers, knowing full well if he was serious about taking Jerusalem, he would need closer to fifty thousand men.

His methods were not too dissimilar from John's. Simon bribed, intimidated, promised, lied, murdered, and did all the other things that a man is capable of when he is fully intent on manipulating another for his own gain.

The Idumeans were so poor they would jump up and down an entire day for half a copper piece. Simon used his forces to plunder and then in turn used the plunder to grow his forces. His support from the countryside of Idumea exploded. Providing food, wine, water, and small shares of looted spoils, Simon became known by his followers as the 'Savior.' He was seen by the Idumeans as justly redistributing the wealth of the rich to those with no money, themselves specifically. Altogether, Simon now commanded almost fifteen thousand soldiers, loyal to the death and his every order.

Though his followers called him Savior, his ruthlessness towards those that did not adhere to his wishes grew with each town he sacked.

At first he only took the coin and goods of those rich merchants and traders in his path. Then he began to beat his victims even after they have given up all their wealth. Next, he started to mutilate them. Now he escalated his grotesqueness on all those souls who refused to join his forces.

Simon established a regular court in his mobile tent where he would publicly mutilate and crucify dissenters, traitors, collaborators, and anyone else that crossed him. A hundred new recruits were made to watch Simon exact his form of desert justice.

"Bring up the next bastard!" Simon shouted, sitting on a dais like a king in his great tent in the desert while stroking his Molossus hound dog beside him. "What is he accused of?" he asked, completely unconcerned with the truth of the accusation.

"He is a known Roman conspirator, my lord," Rabinus, Simon's chief of staff and sometimes assassin, said, indicting the poor soul caught in their clutches.

"And what do we do to Roman conspirators?" Simon asked.

"Eunuchize 'em!" Rabinus replied cheekily.

"A conspirator is not a man—he is less than a dog. Since you are not a man, you will no longer need your testicles," Simon declared.

"I only refused to join your army of hooligans. I never conspired with the Romans! Wait—we can work this out!" the poor man cried as two guards held him back from accosting Simon.

"Work this out? Yes, that is exactly what I'm going to do," Simon said. "Well, hold him down and get the nurse!"

"The Romans burned my house down the same as the rest of you. You're making a terrible mistake!"

"Snip his balls off already! I don't have all day to waste on garbage like this!" Simon barked.

It took four Idumean guards to hold down the 'conspirator' and one nurse to extract the man's testes.

"Noooo! Aaaahhhaaahhh!" The man screamed and cried as the deed was being done.

"I'm bored with this traitor. He rather annoys me. In fact, you know what? Crucify him! Next!" Simon shouted out.

"No, please don't kill me! Please!" the newly-minted eunuch pleaded as Simon's men carried him away to a cross.

Simon stood up from his desert throne and yelled out to a hundred men before him. "You see what happens to those that collaborate with the Romans!"

Simon continued his barbaric display until every last man accused of a form of sedition was either neutered or slain or both.

Then Simon went for his wine and wife.

In the following weeks, Simon made a move to solidify his power by joining forces with the Sicarii who had quietly taken control of Masada, making it their headquarters.

The fortress of Masada was known as the 'impregnable out-post,' built by Herod the Great for times of great instability as a haven from his enemies—particularly Cleopatra, who openly spoke of her desire to invade Judea. However, Mark Antony for-bade her from invading the Holy Land, and thus Herod never ended up needing to use his sky-high fortress to defend his own life.

With the Sicarii, Idumeans, and everyday rabble all joined together, Simon was effectively the most powerful Hebrew in Judea. His forces numbered over twenty thousand now, larger than even the force of John of Gischala.

Simon had long expected to make a move on Jerusalem with his legions in tow, but John had beaten him to it.

Steaming in fury from the reports that John was now master of Jerusalem, Simon sat in his command office at Masada exco-riating his advisors and plotting John's removal from his position of power.

"You useless idiots! I spend the last year growing my numbers into the most formidable force in Judea, and you fools allow that fat rogue to walk right into the city like he was God Almighty himself!" Simon shouted over his boardroom table, which was ringed with his closest advisors, as he walked around them in circles.

Then he surreptitiously walked behind the man he blamed the most for the breakdown in intelligence and tactics. He popped the hilt of his dagger up out of its sheath. Then in one quick motion, he pulled back the head of the advisor and sliced a cut through the man's neck from ear to ear. Simon held the man's head back to fully allow the veins and arteries to empty, sending blood rushing onto the tabletop, heavily spattering several advisors' clothes and faces.

The rest of Simon's counselors sat up straight, adrenaline coursing through their bodies at the thought that each of their throats might be next.

"My lord, we worked to increase our numbers as fast as possible. It is unfortunate that John descended down on the city before us, but we had no way of knowing his stratagem." An advisor offered excuses, though they were valid.

Eyes wide with anger, Simon took the dagger, still in his hand, and threw it across the room, hitting the advisor who had ventured to speak, in the eye with the blade, instantly dropping him over dead.

"Does anyone else have something smart to say?" Simon barked, waiting to see if he would be tasked with killing yet another advisor.

Simon waited a few long moments, looking over his remaining advisors' sunken faces.

"Good! Now let's talk about how we are going to dispatch John."

"My lord, we have a fortuitous position now that Ananus has been slain by John. The common people of Jerusalem will see us as better stewards of their care than those who execute innocent chief high priests. We may not need to shed more than a few droplets of blood if we can convince the Judeans to accept us for John," Rabinus proposed.

Simon played with the thought in his mind and nodded his head slightly in satisfied agreement.

"There are still some fifty thousand people that live within one hour's ride from us. We'll go town to town. If any able-bodied males don't want to join the following, I say we kill their entire families so the rest understand they don't have a choice," a younger Sicarii advisor said with ghoulish delight, his face cloaked by his black shawl.

"Let's crucify the families while their sons are made to watch!" another advisor added.

"Cut off their manhood and womanhood too! That always gets a good reaction," yet another advisor chimed in.

"Let's focus on getting more fighters, not torturing them. We need another ten thousand men, at least," Simon declared.

"Give us a fortnight and we'll have the men," Rabinus promised. "I'll lead the conscription effort personally, my lord."

"I'm coming with you—the new recruits need to see the face of their new leader."

■ ■ ■

**SIMON TRAVELED** across the countryside gathering followers in every small city and hut he could find. Preaching out against the Romans, John's bandits, and the Zealots, all while promising spoils to the destitute.

He raided countless towns, sometimes two or three a day. Simon took every last kernel of wheat and every last grain of barley. The gold, silver, and copper he stole, not amounting to much as the countryside was full of paupers, was barely enough to materially help his campaign.

When able-bodied men would not join his cause, he crucified all their family members: men, women, and children alike. The crosses he erected were made to face one another so the victims could enjoy seeing their friends and family members writhe in pain as they died—it was a tactic he saw the Romans employ on their campaign of destruction, pushing their enemies into the Dead Sea.

Collecting the scum of Judea along with those essentially conscripted, he amassed a total force of almost thirty thousand men who all swore allegiance to him personally. Idumeans, Sicarii, commoners, poor Judeans, conscripts, criminals, and more—all now called themselves Simon's men.

Simon now had both the men and supplies to march on Jerusalem.

John heard stories from messengers and spies about the rise of Simon. Tales abounded of Simon's expansion of his Idumean force, his growing Sicarii sect, and the common ruffians he enlisted from the desert. The reports from several independent sources all confirmed Simon traveled toward Jerusalem with a force more than double his own's size. It was the first time John was genuinely concerned in Jerusalem. But he still controlled the city, its strong walls, and the nearly impenetrable Temple Mount.

John, still the craftiest man in Judea, had a devious plan. He had heard that Simon was traveling with his beloved to Jerusalem. John sent a small horde of bandits on a special mission. In the middle of the night, John's men entered Simon's encampment and kidnapped his wife!

Instead of surrendering his campaign as John believed he would do, Simon became mad with fury, more committed to his conquest, and he also degenerated into further viciousness. Simon genuinely loved his wife for she was voluptuous, beautiful, and of childbearing age—he would do whatever was necessary to secure her release.

Simon made haste on his journey to the city and, coming up to the walls, he began shouting in a wild rage.

"John! John! John!" Simon shouted upon reaching the walls of Jerusalem.

"Give me back my wife! Give her back or the people of Jerusalem will suffer for your crime!"

John's men, standing behind the parapet on the wall walk, hearing Simon perfectly, stood silently frozen like ice, uncertain of how to respond.

"No answer? Nothing?" Simon angrily asked. "Fine, bring out the prisoner," Simon ordered Rabinus.

A twenty-year-old Judean girl, caught by Simon's army nearly immediately after their arrival at the city, was forcefully escorted by two of Simon's loyal Idumeans. The guards brought her before Simon and kicked the back of her legs in her joints, dropping her down to her knees.

"You see, John! You see what happens when you take what does not belong to you?" an incensed Simon yelled.

He removed a small serrated dagger from his waist sheath and held it high in the air so all could see its reflecting sunlight. Then Simon sawed off the left ear of the poor girl. He held it up high and then threw it towards the wall.

"Please, my lord, please stop," the girl cried out as blood ran down the side of her face.

"That all depends on John and what he does with my wife," Simon replied. "And from the looks of it, we've just begun."

Simon turned back to John's motionless bandits. "Must I harm this unfortunate soul more? Or will you release my wife?"

Nodding to his Idumeans, the girl's left arm was raised high and held in place. Simon put his dagger back in its sheath and now pulled his gladius. Aiming below the girl's elbow, Simon sliced through her flesh and bone, severing her arm. The guard that held her arm graciously offered it to Simon, who took it and raised it up high before throwing the limb towards the wall.

The young girl fainted from the horror, pain, and blood loss.

"How much more of this pitiful child must I take? I will take her breath and the breath of the hundreds more I have captured until my wife is returned!"

Again Simon looked out towards John's men, and again he received no response.

"Damn you, John! Damn your mortal soul!" Simon screamed as loud as his lungs permitted and then took another swing of his blade decapitating the girl. "Bring the next one up! This will continue day and night until I have returned to me what is mine!"

Thus began a multi-day marathon of mutilation and death. Simon personally killed over three hundred Judeans at the front gate of Jerusalem in a misguided effort to repossess his spouse.

Those he executed were mostly non-partisan commoners, caught searching for herbs, wood, and fruit. But before Simon executed those captured, he inflicted unmeasurable torture on his unfortunate victims. He cut off more than arms and ears, including male vessels, female bosoms, and even scalps—all in plain view of the bandits and Zealots under John's command, standing guard on the wall walk. Simon even made his victims swear that he was righteous and a man of God despite his violent acts. He seemed to enjoy breaking the will of the captives in addition to their bodies.

Simon's cruelty shocked the people of the city, who in turn beseeched John to return Simon's wife. John, seeing a rebellion in the making, obliged. He released Simon's wife rather than face fighting the residents of Jerusalem in addition to Simon's army.

Once Simon's wife had been returned, his butchery ceased. Now Simon began a campaign to win the hearts and minds of the people he had just terrorized. He stood before the walls of Jerusalem, lobbing propaganda towards John's men on the wall walk and to any other common resident that could hear him.

"Do you not see how John is nothing more than a tyrant? He imprisons righteous men with no trial or evidence, seizes their land, and then executes them! This is not a man that is the rightful steward of the Holy City. I have killed men too, it is true. But I *never* killed anyone that did not deserve the same punishment from God Almighty! Let me and my men into the city, through this very gate in front of me. My forces will subdue John in a day, and all will be right again in Jerusalem. You know I am just, for I am the 'Green Judge,' formerly of the Sanhedrin. Trust me and your salvation shall be given the very moment you grant me entrance," Simon said to a confused mass of John's men and common residents overhearing his speech.

Now Jerusalem was in a great quandary. So loathing John, the commoners began to listen to Simon's lies despite his own display of cruelty outside the walls regarding his wife's abduction.

Simon continued to preach salvation from John's bandits and Zealots, the Romans, and all the other destructive forces who had brought the city to the brink of destruction. He promised food, stability, and even new schools for the children and welfare for the elderly.

Soon the people cheered for Simon's entrance into the city, believing his great promises. Common residents began climbing the walls to hear and cheer on Simon's stump speeches. It was clear that the masses desired Simon to become the new master of Jerusalem.

Matthias, father of Joseph and the chief high priest now that Ananus was dead, decided it was time to give Simon entrance to the city, seeing the overwhelming majority of Jerusalem praying for his deliverance.

Under cover of darkness, Matthias marshalled a small force and overwhelmed a group of John's bandits drunkenly guarding the Damascus gate in the northwestern part of the city. Matthias opened the gates to the city, welcoming Simon much the same way Ananus had welcomed John.

Simon and his army stormed into Jerusalem.

Few of John's warriors stayed at their posts; instead, most retreated to the safety of the Temple Mount.

Thirty thousand armed men loyal to Simon now swelled through the city streets.

John's bandits and Zealots were slaughtered on sight by the all-black-clad Sicarii and Idumeans controlled by Simon.

A full battle broke out, Hebrew against Hebrew, slaying each other in the Holy City's streets.

Within a day, John's bandits and Zealots completely retreated to the Temple Mount for safety. It became their last bastion, using its great defenses to hold off Simon's forces.

Simon and his followers began an offensive to overtake John. It met with tepid success. Every man that Simon's Idumeans and Sicarii killed cost ten of their own men. Simon had overwhelming manpower, but his poor position on the ground below the Temple Mount more than negated it.

The fight continued for a week with no discernible result.

Then the great Feast of the Unleavened Bread began, and all the violence stopped.

# Chapter 27:

# Passover

**A FEW** days before Passover, Judeans throughout the countryside were arriving in the hundreds of thousands, nearly doubling the population of Jerusalem for the Festival of the Unleavened Bread, for this is considered the most sacred time to receive a blessing at the Temple other than the Day of Atonement.

Passover is also a joyous time. It commemorates the Hebrews' liberation from Pharaoh out of Egypt by God through the hand of Moses.

For a few days it seemed as if Jerusalem was renewed again, teeming with life—everything imaginable was occurring on the city streets.

From up on the Temple Mount, one could see thousands of Judeans slowly streaming into the city from all directions. With the pilgrims came cart upon cart of possessions to sell, eat, and use. Most notable were the countless live animals brought for sacrificial slaughter. Goats, pigeons, and sheep were the most common beasts used and made up the majority of the animals taken into the city.

With such a swell in foot traffic, traversing the smaller side streets became nearly impossible as they could only accommodate one-way traffic in certain tight places, creating a gridlock that was not easily cured. The main streets were little better, moving at a crawl. Crowds of people weaved in and out of the carts and the animals hauling them.

Children played outside in the streets while young men took their new brides to their beds. Unashamed screams of ecstasy pierced the raucousness of the bustling daytime business of Jerusalem.

In the middle of the chaos, solo street musicians performed for loose change. One particular performer held a six-foot-long wooden pipe. The pipe blossomed at its opening and shrank all the way to the mouthpiece.

On the musician's lap was a copper pot sitting upside down. The musician started playing the pipe. A long droning pulse morphed into a litany of high notes intermixed with low notes—the rhythm was syncopated.

Then he began tapping the copper pot with a stick that had a piece of metal attached on one end. By hitting the pot at different places, he created different bell sounds. The music reminded one of a half-dozen different-pitched church bells playing with a sonorous choir.

At least fifty people stood watching the man play. His music was unique enough to indelibly ink its sound on the mind listening for life. Many gave a donation—his cap was overflowing with copper and silver coins.

*  *  *

**ON THE** morning of the day when Passover was to begin at sundown, the Romans appeared outside the walls of Jerusalem.

Thousands of Judeans not yet inside the city walls began a mad dash for the gates. A hysteria palpable to the soul began spreading across the city as dozens of shofars began blasting the alarm together, alerting the entire city to the presence of an enemy force.

Animals began squawking, yelping, and barking. Little children burst into tears at the distress of their parents.

Then the words everyone in the city had feared since the night of the uprising spread like wildfire—"The Romans are here!"

The people instantly broke into total panic, and chaos spread out across the city. Judeans, only hours earlier in the process of preparing for Passover, now began to hoard and price-gouge their neighbors. Arguments that would have been settled with words were now settled with fists. The most unscrupulous used the madness of the Roman arrival for their own criminally-obtained pecuniary gain, stealing brazenly via home invasions and daytime muggings.

As terrifying as the word of the Romans outside the walls of Jerusalem was to some, a minority of the residents were indifferent to the news. Already butchered and brutalized at the hands of John's bandits and Zealots, and the Sicarii—many Judeans seemed to think a Roman reoccupation of Jerusalem would actually improve their lot.

Over one and a quarter million Judeans were now trapped inside the city of Jerusalem—forty years, many believe, to the very day of the arrest of Jesus by the Romans after the Last Supper.

■ ■ ■

**A FAMILY** of ten of moderate means, so far unscathed by John's bandits and Zealots and the Sicarii, sat for Passover Seder.

They said kiddush for the wine and the food. Then came the special prayer welcoming the prophet Elijah into their home. The prayer beseeches God to smite down the enemies of the Israelites and protect them as they were protected when the tenth plague passed over Hebrew households but killed all the Egyptian first-born males sleeping in their beds.

*Eliyahu haNavi,*
*Eliyahu haTishbi,*
*Eliyahu, Eliyahu, Eliyahu haGil'adi.*

*Bim'hera v'yameinu yavoh eleinu,*
*im mashiach ben David,*
*im mashiach ben David.*

*Eliyahu haNavi,*
*Eliyahu haTishbi,*
*Eliyahu, Eliyahu, Eliyahu haGil'adi.*

The Seder meal continued, and before long the ten family members all sat with their bellies bulging, matzah crumbs on their laps, and only empty wine bottles left on the table.

They began to argue.

"If we do not dispatch John now, we will all be slain sooner or later!" the eldest son exclaimed.

"And who will protect us now that the Romans have come upon us?" the father retorted.

"Simon!" the older son shouted.

"You honestly think that rogue with his savage force of Idumeans and Sicarii is the answer?" the father asked.

"Yes! He is fighting John for the city even now. He fights to free us from John's tyranny!" the son stated.

"He fights for himself! Not Jerusalem, not the Judeans, and definitely not God!" the father proclaimed.

"He fights for us all!" the son asserted. "He has said he will defend Jerusalem from the Romans. If he doesn't, he will be destroyed just like the rest of us."

"Are you so sure Simon will not take gold and land and a deal with Rome? He would sell us just as any criminal would cash a bounty," the father said.

The son was going to rebut his father once more, but before he could utter a complete word, the son's speech was shut off with the father banging his hand firmly on the table.

"That's enough!" the father said sternly.

"I say we flee for Idumea," the daughter of the family chimed in.

"And eat what? Sand?" the youngest brother asked incredulously.

"I'd rather eat sand than Roman spears!" the daughter yelled back.

"We can't leave, my dear—the Romans will surely kill us," the father declared. "If our death is God's will, we will all die as a family."

"Well, isn't this a lovely Pesach," the mother interjected.

"Dearest, we are all together and time is short—these things must be discussed, or we welcome ruin any which way it may come," the father declared.

"This is our home. This is the land promised to us by the Almighty! I am not afraid of John's bandits and Zealots, nor the Sicarii, and certainly not the Romans," the mother replied. "And I think Simon intends to fight for us. God has his messengers— He would never let the Romans destroy Jerusalem."

The entire family lowered their heads, exhausted from arguing, and frustrated they had not found a solution to their predicament.

"Ok, children, who found the afikoman?" the grandfather asked, sitting quietly for the entire meal and now trying to bring a breath of joy to what was supposed to be the happiest festival of the year.

The youngest girl, only about four years old, presented the half-piece of matzah wrapped in a cloth to her grandfather.

"Here it is, Grandpapa," the young girl said.

The tension in the dining room eased at the sight of a girl and her grandfather sharing a special moment.

"You did great, my little flower," the grandfather said, looking at the afikoman. "And here is your reward," he said, handing a thick piece of chocolate to his granddaughter.

The girl, not understanding the talk of her family, screamed with joyous excitement at the sight of the candy.

"Be sure to share with your brother and sister," the grandfather insisted.

"I will, Grandpapa," she answered.

"Don't forget," he said, tapping his index finger on his cheek.

He bent down to the girl, and she planted a big kiss on his face. The rest of the family watching were brought momentary joy at the beautiful sight—a simple act of love reunited a family worn thin by impossible politics.

*  *  *

**ALSO CELEBRATING** Passover were Eleazar ben Simon and his splinter Zealots.

As it stood, Eleazar still had control inside the enclosed Temple structure. He was camped out in front of the main sanctuary. The Holy of Holies was in the back section of the building, and Eleazar and his men did not dare think of entering that room, assured death would follow anyone who did.

As time came for the Passover blessing, Eleazar, remaining in service to God above all else, permitted worshippers entrance into the Temple. John, still holding a mortal grudge against Eleazar for his defection and betrayal, turned Passover into yet another one of his deceptive stratagems.

When Eleazar opened the gold doors of the Temple to allow in all men seeking a priestly blessing, John sent a hundred of the most pathetic-looking of his men. These men feigned a desire for a blessing inside the Temple. When Eleazar granted John's unformidable-looking rogues admittance to be blessed, the men all drew their arms out from under their cloaks and began hacking away at Eleazar's splinter Zealots.

Eleazer could not fathom that John would be so wicked as to spill blood inside the Temple on Passover.

"Get Eleazar!" one of John's men shouted while pointing out Eleazar's position.

Eleazar was horrified at using violence inside the Temple, but he had no choice. "Come get me, you heathen wretches! God will smite you down for sullying His Temple!" he cried out.

Once a full melee was underway inside the Temple, John dispatched thousands more soldiers bearing arms. In the heat of the fight, a couple of John's men, following careful instructions, opened the great gold doors to the Temple, allowing the rest of John's force to easily breach the threshold.

The splinter Zealots battled hand to hand, drawing twice as much blood in the Temple versus John's overwhelming force.

Eleazar slew nearly a dozen of his former Zealot followers who had stayed loyal to John, using his gladius, dagger, baton, and staff. He also used his forehead to headbutt, his feet to crush, and his teeth to bite.

Blood ran so freely that puddles began to form on the white marble floor of the Temple. Men slipped and broke their tailbones. Blood gathered in such quantity on the lowest-lying section of the floor that one Zealot actually tried drowning another in a pool of the human liquid.

An hour passed and five hundred corpses from each side lay on the Temple, dead.

Eleazar was severely wounded in the fighting, but he was still alive and not in danger of bleeding out. He was captured and brought before John.

"Hello again, my friend," John began, smiling in delight now that he had Eleazar in chains.

John took a noisy and obnoxious bite of an apple, taunting Eleazar's current incarcerated station.

"You gouged out my man Sadius' left eye," John said, looking at Sadius' bandaged and bloody face.

"I only regret I got but one of them," Eleazar replied obstinately.

"Leave me alone with him," Sadius beseeched John, pure rage seething through his lips.

"Ha, ha, ha." John chuckled. "He'll be yours soon enough."

"Whatever you are going to do to me, do it. Just stop the incessant yammering of your foul tongue," Eleazar quipped back.

John, instantly irate, punched Eleazar in the face and spat on him.

"How dare you show such insolence. It is by my hand that you live, suffer, or are crucified!" John said.

Reminding himself of his great power, John was calmed.

Sadius, still fuming from being violated personally by Eleazar, took out his dagger. "Hold him down."

Three Zealots tackled Eleazar and held his head still against the floor. Sadius took his blade, inserted it into Eleazar's eye, and popped out Eleazar's eyeball.

"Are you so impudent now?" John screamed out, inches away from Eleazar's face.

"Hahahahaha!" Eleazar laughed back.

John was taken aback by the laughter. After several moments of confusion, he made the motion for Sadius to continue. Eleazar's optic nerve made a distinct snapping sound as Sadius removed his other eyeball.

"How about now, Eleazar? There is sure lots we can still cut from you," John taunted.

"Thank you," Eleazar mumbled.

"What's that?" John asked, moving his ear closer to hear Eleazar better.

"Thank you for taking my other eye, my lord, for if I had to look at your repulsive face one more miserable moment, I was going to blind *myself!* Hahahaha!" Eleazar continued laughing.

"Leave me alone with him," Sadius pleaded.

"My dear Sadius, he is yours," John acquiesced.

"Beat him," Sadius ordered some goons.

Four of John's men viciously assaulted Eleazar until he was limp on the floor, unable to move himself.

"I'm going to enjoy this more than every other torture of my life, and I've had some good tortures," Sadius bragged.

Sadius cut off one of Eleazar's fingers. Eleazar continued to laugh. Sadius cut off two more fingers to more laughter and insults from Eleazar.

It was no fun torturing a man who was taunting him back and seemingly unaffected by the torture. Sadius flayed some of Eleazar's skin off next, to an even greater laughing response.

Finally, Sadius just sliced Eleazar's throat.

"Well, that was anticlimactic," Sadius said.

With Eleazer dead and his splinter force of Zealots defeated, John once again controlled the entire Temple Mount—more importantly, the Temple's impregnable inner sanctum.

# Chapter 28:

# The Siege of Jerusalem Begins

**AFTER VESPASIAN** accepted the emperorship, he sought to resume the campaign against the Judeans. Jerusalem remained rebellious, and he now sought to crush the Judeans' stronghold once and for all.

Rome was still reeling from the civil war that nearly destroyed the empire. Vespasian, now sitting as Caesar, saw Rome's predicament and understood it was best for him to remain in the capital, ensuring stability through his personal oversight. So he sent Titus in his stead to Judea with four legions to end the conflict.

Titus, Frachas, Domitian, Tiberius Alexander, Cestius, and Josephus returned to the Holy Land with a force of almost a hundred thousand Roman soldiers, servants, and slaves. They landed in Caesarea after their voyage across the Mediterranean. Ten thousand men from Arabia, Egypt, and Syria, whose lords all wanted to show their allegiance to Rome, joined the ranks as well.

"Well, Josephus, it looks like your wish is coming true," Titus ventured to say. "You will have the opportunity to save Jerusalem from destruction."

"I can present the arguments for a negotiated surrender, but the Hebrews, specifically John of Gischala and Simon bar Giora, have given the word 'stubborn' a new meaning," Josephus explained.

"When they see our assembled force, they will have to lie to themselves if they think they can prevail," Frachas, newly promoted to tribune, said.

The Romans set out on the road to Jerusalem for their final conquest. It would be two days before their arrival in the Holy City. They moved slowly for they brought war engines, wall-breachers, and beasts of all kinds.

Titus rode with the expeditionary force at the very front of the military train. Riding alongside Titus were Frachas, Tiberius Alexander, Cestius, Josephus, and a hundred other men on horseback. Domitian, Titus' youngest brother, also joined as he was sent by Vespasian personally to ensure his son learned the art of Roman warfare.

Three miles out from the city walls, Titus and his top commanders used a convex-curved glass to refract the light and see closer to the walls of Jerusalem than the naked eye alone permitted.

"No armies on the lookout," Titus reported. "Few men on the walls."

Titus passed the field glass to Cestius.

"What do you think, Cestius?" Titus asked his top artillery general.

"I can see them fighting each other. This is rather incredible. Titus, have a look," Cestius said, passing the glass back to Titus. "At the Temple wall, there—they are throwing flaming rocks over the side!" Cestius declared.

"I say we attack at dawn, before the city wakes." Domitian spoke without being asked.

"There are sojourners from every small village in Judea in the city for the holy time of Pesach," Josephus rebutted. "They are innocents."

"They are warring with themselves even as they celebrate. Let us not unite wolves killing each other. Attacking during this holy festival might have that effect," Titus determined. "Still, I want a closer look. Josephus, Domitian—go back to the army and wait for my return."

"But, brother!" Domitian protested.

"That was an order, soldier!" Titus spoke harshly to his brother in front of his entire staff of officers.

Domitian and Josephus returned to the Roman army.

Titus and his remaining entourage rode with a cavalry force of a hundred men towards the walls of the city.

All the gates had been barricaded shut.

It was far too quiet for a great city such as Jerusalem.

A couple of Idumean guards standing behind the wall's parapet saw Titus' small party of a hundred cavaliers approach the section of the wall they were responsible for watching.

"Oh, gonads! The bloody Romans are here!" Reuben, a lookout guard, blurted in a rushed surprise.

"There's a hundred Romans, all on horses," Issachar, his cohort, replied.

"Blow the bloody shofar, you dunce!" Reuben ordered.

A loud, low-pitched escalating moan was heard on the western side of the city.

"I smell a Judean rat," Tiberius Alexander declared with pompous certainty at the sound of the alarm. He was a Hebrew by birth, but he disavowed the faith, despising all those who did worship the Lord of Hosts.

"I smell death," Frachas stated the obvious.

"There must be hundreds or thousands of dead bodies lining the ground," Titus said. "Don't get near them. They might be plagued with some black affliction."

Titus and his company, just over a hundred strong, continued for a short time surveying outer sections of the city wall in hopes of finding a good military entrance point for the army.

Titus approached the Psephinus Tower on the western side of the city wall.

Suddenly the previously deserted part of the outside wall sprang to life with hundreds of Sicarii, all clothed in their signature black robes, carrying swords, daggers, bows, and arrows.

Before Titus and his horsemen could react, the Judeans had them completely encircled against the wall.

The Roman horses whinnied and jumped vertically, knowing they were in danger. Curses came from the Roman cavaliers, who knew a hard fight was coming. The sounds of metal armaments being readied rippled through the Roman ranks.

"Steady, men!" Titus yelled out.

The Judeans had not come to talk. All in unison, they charged. Titus' company of a hundred cavalrymen was overwhelmed. The Judeans hacked and stabbed with such fury that the Romans' advantage on horseback was nullified. The Judeans spared the beasts no mercy, cutting the throats of the horses just the same as their Roman foes'.

Titus, surrounded by Judeans brandishing swords and firing arrows, made a quick and calculated move.

"Romans! Follow me!" he yelled out.

Titus kicked his horse into a gallop and headed right into a force of fifty Judeans. Every arrow missed Titus as if a halo protected him, while every swing of Titus' gladius met Judean flesh.

Seeing Titus' heroism and success in charging through the Judeans, the entire cavalry force frantically followed. A dozen men were lost in the escape effort. If not for Titus, all of the Romans on horseback would have perished.

Upon returning to the main wagon train with the surviving expeditionary force, Titus immediately instructed his army to surround Jerusalem. He ordered three tremendous fortresses constructed, one on each side of the city: west, north, and east.

The southern side of the city was so rocky and hilly Titus did not even consider it a point of attack and thus left it without an accompanying Roman fortress.

To build these massive Roman forts, cedar had to be imported from Lebanon as the Romans made quick work of the Mount of Olives. Not a single olive tree was left standing.

It took nearly a month, but Titus erected three barracks around the walls of Jerusalem.

Since the Romans had arrived at the gates of the Holy City, the supplies into and out of Jerusalem diminished by almost one hundred percent. Merchants selling livestock and trade goods now avoided Jerusalem like a plague, fearing their property would be seized by the Romans, which would be followed shortly by their own crucifixion.

It was not harvest time. There was little food on the ground. Without traders bringing in grain and meat, Jerusalem was essentially without a food supply.

The Judeans that had made the pilgrimage to Jerusalem for Passover were still in the city, trapped by the surrounding Roman army. Now that the Romans had cut the supply of food to the city to nearly nothing, people were starting to get hungry at an exponential rate.

Titus had now been outside Jerusalem for over a month, almost the entirety of which had been occupied with building his three forts. Other than the skirmish with the Sicarii his first day surveying the city, Titus had not engaged the Hebrews, spending his first efforts to intimidate them with his fortresses. Now he sent Josephus to see if he could talk them into surrender.

"Flavius Josephus, I believe this is where you take the lead," Titus said. "If they don't surrender and end this foolish rebellion, they'll all be slaughtered. Make sure to remind them of that."

"I will give them every sound argument. I will beseech them

at my own expense, but only God can determine whether they want to end this conflict peacefully," Josephus said.

Titus nodded.

"I came all the way back to Jerusalem for this moment, perhaps my God will shine wisdom down on the Judeans today."

Josephus, riding solo on horseback and wearing a Roman breastplate that Titus had insisted upon, held a thin wooden rod in one hand with a white flag at its end. He rode his horse in a slow but determined march towards the Damascus gate, stopping his beast some hundred yards away from the wall—out of harm's way.

Simon's Sicarii and Idumeans stood ready on the wall walk, bows in hand, resting in firing positions on top of the merlons.

Josephus dismounted from his horse, grabbed it by the reins, and turned it around. Then he slapped it hard on its ass.

"Yah!" Josephus yelled and sent the horse running back to the Roman line.

Josephus turned back around and closed his eyes to mentally prepare himself for the arduous task of dealing with his own people.

"I am Joseph, son of Matthias, the high priest! I wish only to speak," Josephus yelled out in Aramaic, the Judean native tongue.

The Judeans on the wall walk had no idea what Josephus was up to. Some fancied it a Roman deception, others raged that Josephus was a high traitor.

"Go back to Rome, Roman!" one Sicarii yelled out.

Josephus stood silently and gathered himself before thousands of Idumeans and Sicarii, standing on top of the wall.

"Bless me, Yahweh," he whispered to himself. "Let me honor You by being Your instrument that averts more bloodshed."

Josephus looked up to his audience and began to preach:

*O miserable creatures! You forget your real allies! And when did God, our Creator fail to avenge those that had done us wrong? How great a supporter you have profanely abused! Remember not the prodigious things done for your forefathers. How great their enemies were. Do you not remember the terrible wars this city won for you in times past?*

*You may be informed that you fight not only against the Romans but against God Himself!*

*Shall I mention the removal of our fathers into Egypt? They were used tyrannically and under the power of foreign kings for four hundred years. They might have defended themselves by war and fighting but did nothing except commit themselves to God. Who is there that does not know how Egypt was overrun with all sorts of wild beasts and consumed by every disease: the land went barren, the Nile turned to blood, and how the rest of the ten plagues followed upon one another.*

*Do you not remember how our fathers were released, under a guard, without any bloodshed and no danger, led forth by God to establish His Temple worship?*

*Again, when the Philistines carried off our sacred Ark, did not the whole nation of plunderers rue the day? Their private parts suppurating, their bowels prolapsed, they brought the Ark back with the hands that stole it, appeasing the Sanctuary with the sound of cymbals and timbrels and with peace offerings of every kind. It was God whose generalship won this victory for our fathers, because they placed no trust in their right arm or their weapons but committed to Him the decision of the issue.*

*When the Sennacherib, King of Assyria, brought all of Asia with him and encircled the city with his army, did he fall by the hands of our soldiers? Were not our king's hands lifted up to God in prayer, that an angel of God destroyed that prodigious army in one night? When the Assyrian king arose the next day he found a hundred and eighty-five thousand dead bodies. And then he and the remainder of his army fled!*

*You are also acquainted with the slavery we were under at Babylon, where the people were captives for seventy years and not made free again until God made Cyrus the gracious instrument in bringing it about. The Hebrews were set free by him and did again restore the worship at the Temple.*

*I can produce no example wherein our fathers were successful at war or fell short of success when, without war, they committed themselves to God.*

*For example, when the king of Babylon, Nebuchadnezzar, besieged this very city, and our King Zedekiah, not heeding the predictions made to him by Jeremiah the prophet— Zedekiah was at once taken prisoner and saw Jerusalem and the Temple demolished. Yet how much less were Zedekiah's transgressions than that of your present leaders?*

*But you! I am not able to describe what your wickedness deserves! You abuse me, throw darts at me. You who only exhorts to profit or save himself.*

*Need I mention more examples? What can it be that originally stirred up an army of Romans against our nation? Is it not the impiety of the inhabitants? Whence did our servitude to Rome commence? It was civil strife among our ancestors when the asinine brotherly rivalry of Aristobulus and Hyrcanus brought General Pompey against the city and God put beneath the Roman heel those who did not deserve to be free. After a three-month siege our Judean ancestors surrendered to Pompey though they had not sinned against the Sanctuary and law as you have done! And they were far better equipped for war than you!*

Josephus Preaches
Surrender to the Judeans

*Thus it was never intended that our nation should bear arms, and all wars have inevitably ended in defeat. It is the duty of those who dwell on the holy ground to commit all things to the judgement of God. You have not eschewed the secret sins, theft, treachery, adultery, fornication, and murder. The Temple has become a sink for the nation's dregs, and native hands have polluted the hallowed spot that even the Romans venerated from a distance, setting aside many of their own customs in regard for your law.*

*After all this, do you expect Him whom you have dishonored to be your ally? Are you indeed righteous worshippers? Is it with clean hands that you beseech your Creator?*

*The Romans are only demanding the customary tribute which our fathers paid to their fathers. When they obtain this, they will neither destroy Jerusalem nor lay a finger on your holy places. They will give you everything else, the freedom of your children, the security of your property, and the preservation of our holy law.*

*Again, God knows how to take immediate vengeance when there is need—thus on the very night the Assyrians pitched their camp by the city, He crushed them. So if He had judged our generation worthy of liberty or the Romans of chastisement, He would immediately have fallen upon them as He fell upon the Assyrians.*

*So I am sure the Almighty has quit your holy places and stands now on the side of your enemies. Do you think God can endure this wickedness in His house—God who sees each hidden thing and hears that which is cloaked in silence? You boast of your unspeakable crimes and daily vie with one another to see who can be the worst, as proud of your vices as if they were virtues!*

*In spite of it all, a way of salvation still remains if you will follow it, and the Almighty is ready to pardon those who confess and repent. Do not be obstinate fools! Throw away your weapons, take pity on your birthplace, at this moment plunging to ruin. Turn around and gaze at the beauty of what you are betraying. What a city! What a Temple! Does any man wish these things to fade away? Nothing better deserves to be kept safe than God's house, you inhuman, stony-hearted monsters! If the sight of these things leaves you unmoved, at least have pity upon your families, and let each man set before his eyes his own wife, children, and parents, certain to perish by famine or by war.*

*I know that danger threatens my own father, mother, and wife, a family of great noble heritage. Perhaps you think I mean only to save them and myself. Kill them not as they are innocents. But take my flesh instead as the price for your own salvation. I am ready to perish if that will show you wisdom.*

*For the sake of the generations of Judeans that will or will not be depending on your decision—surrender!*

As Josephus finished his great speech, tears ran down from his eyes. He fell to his knees, and his hands covered his face in genuine sorrow.

The thousands of Simon's men that lined the wall walk listening to Josephus stood in grave silence. They could not present an argument to rebut Josephus, who was right on every point and indictment. For fifteen minutes no one said another word. Some of the Idumeans turned their backs to Josephus and began to silently shed tears, believing their coming destruction was assured by God. Many Sicarii had indescribable rage boiling within them, being called out for the atrocities they knew they were guilty of committing.

Then Simon emerged at the top of the parapet, standing on a merlon.

"Josephus!" Simon shouted. "For your treason, you have cursed yourself and your family! To repent for this humiliation beyond humiliations, Matthias, patriarch of your house, will be executed!"

Matthias was brought out in chains and paraded on the wall walk for Josephus.

"Simon, don't you hurt my father. He is an innocent!" Josephus yelled.

"Put the noose around the old fool's head already," Simon ordered.

"If you surrender, I'll accept your terms," Josephus offered.

"Surrender? Matthias is a guilty collaborator. He is being lawfully executed! I've been especially hoping for such a moment." Simon turned to his hangman, "Well, what the hell are you waiting for? Toss him over the side!"

"I love you, Father!" Josephus screamed. "Forgive me!"

Josephus started running towards his father, unconsciously forgetting he was in the zone of danger.

"You have nothing to be forgiven for. I love you too, son," Matthias said.

A Sicarii kicked Matthias in his rear, sending him falling over the parapet. The rope pulled taut and Matthias' neck snapped.

"No! No! No! Simon, you bastard!" Josephus' run came to a screeching halt as he fell into the sand and began moaning like a dying animal.

He rent his clothes and took dirt from the ground and washed his face with the earth. He laid crying in a semi-fetal position.

"Josephus!" Simon cried out again. "The executions are not complete. Bring his bitch out!"

Mariamne, Josephus' ex-wife, bound in chains like Matthias before her, was escorted to the wall walk and lifted up onto the parapet.

"I'm sorry, Mariamne. Forgive me!" Josephus begged.

"Simon, you murderous coward!" he roared. "I offered my life, not my family, and that was only if you renounced this rebellion and surrendered—which you have no intention of doing!"

"You're right. I have no intention of renouncing the *redemption* of Jerusalem," Simon said. "Your family was tried and convicted of collaborating with the Romans. Every crime must be punished, Flavius Josephus."

"You monstrous foul tyrant!" Josephus screamed.

A second rope was secured around Mariamne's neck.

Simon motioned to his guards.

Mariamne, silently staring Josephus in the eyes, shed a solitary tear. Then she went flying over the side of the wall—her neck broke with a loud crack.

Josephus wailed but then grew silent and motionless at the sight of his mother on the wall walk.

"Did you think we forgot the whore that bore you, Josephus?" Simon taunted.

"Simon, please, I beg you, please, take my life for hers. Please! Take my life! For the sake of old friends!"

"Oh, I fully plan on taking your life, Josephus. After I watch your Roman heart break for its treason," Simon said. "Hang her!"

"Forgive me, Mother! I love you!" Josephus cried out.

"I love you too, my son," his mother replied with a warm smile.

Within a couple seconds, Josephus' mother had a noose tightened around her neck and was kicked to her death.

Josephus' father, ex-wife, and mother, all now dead—all hung next to each other against the stone wall of Jerusalem.

Josephus lay inconsolable in the dirt. But he was only fifty yards from the walls of the city, well within accurate range of arrows, spears, and slingshots. It was with the latter that a boy no older than fifteen years of age hurled a rock at Josephus, hitting him on the head. Josephus received a fractured skull which caused a concussion.

"Damn the Gods!" Titus yelled out. "Get him the hell out of there!"

Quickly a company of Titus' bodyguards rushed to Josephus, assembling in their protective tortoise formation and shielding him against further harm from the incoming Judean stones and arrows.

His injury, though severe, would only cause temporary pain and sensitivity to light. Josephus was lucky to neither die nor receive any permanent damage from the stone. It mostly caused Titus' heart to steel with fury.

Josephus had done everything in his power to save Jerusalem from itself. But the Judeans had added injury to insult in their refusal to accept Roman terms, cursing and stoning the messenger of peace.

Now Titus would starve the Judeans mad.

# Chapter 29:

# The Horrors of the Siege

**NOW THAT** Titus' force had stopped every beast and bit of grain from entering the city, the Judeans began to starve *en masse*. The blockade, though slow to take effect, grew in impact each day.

Since Titus' arrival outside Jerusalem, it had been a month since goats, sheep, grains, and other important foodstuffs had entered the city.

The Judeans had no choice but to compensate.

At first, the sheep previously only used for wool were slaughtered and eaten. The same went for the milking goats and cows. Then came the butchering of horses. Then came the dogs and cats. Still not satisfied and with fewer and fewer options, the Judeans—their ribs bulging through their chests and stomachs, began setting traps for rats. Finally the residents were reduced to eating their leather belts and sandals, and every blade of grass or tree leaf they came upon.

During the blockade, Titus sat on top of his fortress outside the walls of Jerusalem watching John and Simon's forces fight each other from their respective positions above and below the Temple Mount.

Though in command of the city, neither warring faction was impervious to starvation, and each became hungrier with the passing days. So starved, the Judean belligerents paused their hostilities to inflict yet more horror on the non-partisan residents of Jerusalem in a mad search for food.

John and Simon made a temporary truce. John agreed to stop firing projectiles down from the Temple Mount in exchange for a small gang of his bandits being permitted to raid the Upper Marketplace, which Simon still controlled. Simon agreed to stop assaulting the Temple Mount from below in return.

The full fury of the Judean factions was now unleashed on a population already suffering from shortages of meat, bread, and water.

John's bandits, who had been granted plundering rights by Simon, went house to house, building to building, as if they were a police force systematically searching for a violent maniac in their midst. If there was any fat on the bones of the common Judeans they came across during a raid, they were immediately accused of hoarding food—an act now made illegal by Simon and John's decree. Or the commoners might be accused of the more severe crime of receiving rations by collaborating with the Romans, which resulted in a death sentence.

■ ■ ■

**IN ANOTHER** part of the city, a group of ten Sicarii, cloaked in their black shawls and robes, broke down the doors to a residential household.

"That bitch is fat!" a Sicarii captain yelled out to his men as they came across a small family of two children, a middle-aged father, and his wife. "Where's the fucking food, you damn traitor? Show it or die!"

The father rose up, attempting to redirect the scorn of the Sicarii onto himself. "Please, take this half loaf of bread. It's all we have left. Just don't hurt my wife or my…"

Before the man could finish his plea he was struck in the face with a metal bar, separating his jaw from its socket and knocking him unconscious to the floor.

The Sicarii captain bit down into the half-loaf, making no effort to share with his comrades. Another Sicarii demanded a portion of the bread—threatening the captain much the same way the captain had threatened the female of the house.

After their small internal squabble, the Sicarii, still possessing an unsatisfiable hunger, turned their rage back to the wife.

The captain grabbed her by the hair and slammed her face onto the wooden dining table.

"Give me something. Give me something good and we'll leave without hurting your family further," the captain said softly into her left ear.

"The bread was the last piece of food we had in this world!" she replied in hysterical tears, more fearful of harm to her children than to herself.

"Kill the Judeaness whore and her children!" a Sicarii boy, not more than ten years of age, yelled out.

"Give her the herb!" another Sicarii youth, sprouting in his masculinity, proposed.

"Last chance," the captain said into the woman's ear, slapping her face with his free hand.

"Eat me!" she cried out.

"Wrong answer!" the captain screamed back and then violently smashed her face into the table again. "Boys, we'll give her the herb—maybe that will inspire her memory!"

Five Sicarii men took ahold of the mother and flung her flat onto her back on top of the table. The captain ripped her undergarments off while four other Sicarii held each of her extremities pinned in submission. The remainder of the Sicarii stood looking on like spectators in the Colosseum, dizzy with hunger and pleasure from the horror they were inflicting on the innocent woman. Then one of the Sicarii, carrying a burlap satchel over his shoulder, opened it up, and pulled out a large handful of oleander.

"Here, we have a gift for your cunt!" The Sicarii holding the poisonous herb shoved the entire handful into her vagina as if he were striking a blow in a fist fight.

"Rahhhhhhhhhhhhhh!"

Her scream pierced the walls of her house and echoed off the buildings blocks away in all directions. Blood pooled across the table and she passed out, half-naked, sprawled out like a helpless and wounded animal. Her two children cried almost as loudly as their mother had while the small mob of Sicarii laughed at their handiwork.

The youngest Sicarii went over to the youngest child and punched him in the face to even greater communal amusement.

The Sicarii completely ransacked the house to find no food, no gold, only a half jug of water, and an ounce of black tea.

The captain took the first drink of water, grabbing it without asking from the discovering Sicarii.

"I knew that bitch was hiding something," the captain said, being presented with the small jar of tea. He spit on the unconscious woman, and the Sicarii made their exit.

The father rose several hours later to find his wife dead from oleander poisoning. He wept for God to take him and his children as well.

This behavior on the part of the Sicarii was more than common. In fact, they would usually slaughter every last soul in a home they believed to be hiding food.

Seeing nearly every home brutalized, ransacked, and butchered to death moved many survivors to flee the city in favor of Roman care. Whether it meant execution, enslavement, or a chance to purchase their freedom made no difference to the Judeans.

The common Judeans still alive mostly had their gold, silver, copper, diamonds, and other items of value absconded with during the systematic pilfering by John and Simon.

One Judean, Seth, the high priest who had joined John's bandit crew for a time, became so sickened by the atrocities he witnessed that he instinctively fled Jerusalem to turn himself over to the Romans. But before he scaled the walls to defect, he swallowed three gold coins he had managed to save.

Knowing the city well, Seth slipped over the wall in the middle of the night when the Sicarii who were guarding that area were mostly drunk and asleep. He immediately presented himself to the first guard that he found. To his misfortune, he met a Syrian who was part of a mercenary company supporting the Roman initiative.

"Put your hands up! Up where I can see them!" the Syrian guard screamed as he came upon Seth.

Seth obeyed, content to receive any fate that came to him, though he hoped for a pardon from the Romans in exchange for information. Not that it was very valuable, but it was more than nothing—he knew where John and Simon's men were located, the design of the Temple, and the main features of its defensive capabilities.

Seth walked with his hands tied behind his back, guarded by the Syrian, towards the Roman fortress on the northern side of the city. But instead of walking into the fortress, the Syrian directed Seth into an ancillary tent encampment beside the fortress. It was not run by the Romans, but by the Arabs, the Syrians, and even some Egyptians.

Being pushed through the cloth opening of the ancillary tent, Seth immediately felt his skin crawl in a deep panic. A hundred sets of eyes turned to stare down the Judean high priest.

One of the commanders, sitting at the mess table, wore a gold silk robe that came down to his shins, a Yemenite dagger in its sheath, and a metal head cap wrapped with a red silk shawl that flowed down his back.

The Arab commander stood up and walked over to inspect Seth further, trying to determine if he was a pauper, as his appearance suggested, or if he was merely playing a Judean trick to keep his valuables safe.

"What's your name?" the Arab asked curtly.

"Seth, son of Saul," Seth replied humbly.

"You have money, yes?" the commander asked with a friendly tone.

"All I have is what is on my body," Seth replied.

"I not want trouble for you, yes? You give me the money and you can have drink and eat, yes." The Arab explained his extortion directly. "You not give money, we have problem, yes."

Seth could not produce the gold coins in his belly any sooner than his innards would permit him—he stuck to his story.

"I have nothing more than my body before you," Seth said, praying the Arab would agree he was poor and send him to the Roman detention center, now bustling with thousands of deserters just like him.

"Funny thing is, Judean, I no believe you, yes," the commander said. Then, speaking rapidly in Arabic, he ordered three men to rip Seth's clothes off so they could inspect every last inch of his body.

An Arab subordinate began moving Seth's arms up and down, looking in his arm pits for hidden treasure. Then his legs were moved forward and back to see if there was anything of value between his thighs. Finally Seth was thrown face first over the mess table and his ass cheeks were spread, his cavity opened, and his testicles fondled.

"Now you want to die, yes?" the Arab commander screamed as his underling finished the search to no avail. "Perhaps if I give you love, you'll give me money, yes."

"Wait! What are you doing? That is forbidden! Wait!" Seth yelled out.

But despite his pleas, the Arab had already begun to mount him. After several hard thrusts, Seth, being held down in total submission, cried out, "I have money! I have money! Please, stop and I'll give you all of it!"

"I knew you were hiding something, yes, yes!" the Arab said, pausing his assault to hear of the spoils he was to take. "Now tell me, Judean, where is the money, yes?"

"It's in my stomach. I ate three gold coins this morning," Seth explained. "Just give me a bit of food and water, and the coins will be yours before the morrow next."

The Arabs all erupted into laughter. The commander yelled out again in Arabic, informing his men to turn Seth over onto his back—they immediately tossed Seth around on the table, holding him in complete submission.

A Yemenite dagger made a grinding sound as it came out of the commander's sheath.

"Wait! No! No! God! No! Ahhh!"

But Seth's cries fell on deaf ears. The Arab gutted Seth from his pubis to his sternum. Seth's guts were mostly all removed before his soul left him. Now the priest's corpse lay open with a pile of intestines and a stomach beside him on the table. The commander again shouted in Arabic, and the poor soldier that had the foul duty of examining Seth's loins was now made to sift through every inch of his guts.

"Belah! Belah!" the commander cheered out as the first gold coin came out. "Acktar umin!" he demanded, and Seth's guts continued to be searched—another gold coin was soon found.

Finally all three gold coins were produced, but it was not until all of Seth's organs were sliced up and opened that the search desisted.

The story of Judeans hiding gold in their bellies spread like wildfire. Every Judean the Arabs were holding was now also vivisected. Within an hour, the two hundred Judeans in captivity under Arab guards all lay dead, their intestines mutilated in the dirt.

Not one more gold coin was found.

As the daybreak came and Titus arose, he received the report of the Arab slaughter. He had never been more furious. He grabbed his sword and dagger, taking no care to dress himself above the waist, and ran at full speed in his loincloth to find the perpetrators of the heinous crimes. Titus' bodyguards all followed in rapid succession, fearing the Arabs might try and kill him, being too stupid to know better than to strike General Titus.

Titus burst into the Arab tent. "Where are they? Where are the men responsible for these abominations!"

The first Arab to come face to face with Titus raised his hands slightly to his side, nonchalantly explaining he did not know.

Titus quickly slew him with his dagger, jabbing it directly up under his chin, through his mouth, and into his brain. Titus removed the dagger, dropping the man down to the ground, dead.

The next man that Titus came upon began to scream wildly in Arabic and pointed to the commander. Titus looked towards where the Arab was directing him and saw a thick coat of blood over the commander's golden clothes.

Titus ran in a mad sprint towards the commander, who now began to wet himself. Titus, holding his dagger in his right hand, moved it to his left and then brandished his gladius. Titus took a fully extended swing, instantly decapitating the commander, sending his metal cap dressed with the red silk shawl tumbling to the ground.

But Titus' rage had not yet been quenched. He continued slaying every Arab within his blade's reach. Finally running out of breath after collecting over twenty lives, Titus rested.

"Do you think the Hebrews will surrender if they hear we cut their bellies open for gold?" Titus, still mad with anger, screamed out. "When the assault begins, every last Arab will form the vanguard. If you don't care to see this conflict end peacefully, then you will die ending it violently!"

Titus threw his sword and dagger to the ground, spit on the dead body of the Arab commander, and made for the tent's exit. But before leaving he paused and turned back around to address the Arabs once more.

"And if every one of these Judeans' bodies is not given a proper burial by the day's end, my Romans will finish the job and then bury all of you!"

He briskly walked out of the tent encampment, even more bloody than the Arabs responsible for instigating the incident. Titus' bodyguards quickly followed behind, carrying Titus' weapons—all the men returned safely to the main Roman fortress.

■ ■ ■

JUST WHEN the atrocities in and around the city seemed to be at a surreal nadir, they continued to get worse.

The Sicarii had spent nearly an entire month eating the scraps of food taken from the helpless innocents unable to protect themselves or their property. But now, as nearly every single home had been ransacked and raided, even the Sicarii began to go mad with hunger.

When a man does not eat for many days on end, his mind degenerates into the obscene, the bizarre, the primal. So did the minds of the Sicarii.

Having no place left to find food and no way to force the Romans to end their blockade, they began to debase themselves in their deranged state. Any activity that could allow them to forget their aching bellies was taken up as if it were a relished pastime.

A company of a dozen Sicarii burst into an already-ransacked wealthy home, looking for food yet again, though they had not found any just a few days before. What they did find was a closet full of female clothing and cosmetics.

One of the Sicarii, delirious in his hunger, decided it would be amusing to try on the female clothing. So he did—then he also applied rouge to his cheeks and lips and mascara to his eyelashes.

Another Sicarii man saw the Sicarii dressed in female clothing, painted with makeup, and decided to join in on the peculiar activity.

Still rummaging through the house, one Sicarii found some perfume and started spraying the stuff on himself, on others, and into the air until there was no more left to be sprayed. The house both looked and smelled like a brothel full of cross-dressing male Sicarii youths.

Before long, the fumes of the perfume had taken hold. The entire company of Sicarii began dancing around the dinner table, holding hands—all dressed, painted, and smelling like women!

A traditional Judean song broke out:

> *Shalom aleichem, malachei hashareit,*
> *malachei elyon,*
> *mimelech mal'chei ham'lachim,*
> *hakadosh baruch hu.*

> *Boachem l'shalom, malachei hashalom,*
> *malachei elyon,*
> *mimelech mal'chei ham'lachim,*
> *hakadosh baruch hu.*

*Barchuni l'shalom, malachei hashalom,*
*malachei elyon,*
*mimelech mal'chei ham'lachim,*
*hakadosh baruch hu.*

*Tseit'chem l'shalom, malachei hashalom,*
*malachei elyon,*
*mimelech mal'chei ham'lachim,*
*hakadosh baruch hu.*

As the Sicarii continued dancing, the powerful odor of an entire bottle of perfume released into the air could be smelled a block away in each direction.

At the same time, John's bandits were on their daily patrol to wreak havoc on the poor residents of the Upper Marketplace, as permitted by Simon. Not finding much of anything edible or valuable so far in their scavenging, the bandits found themselves following the scent of the perfume, emanating from just a block away.

As they moved closer to the epicenter of the smell, John's bandits picked up speed, convinced a lovely naked woman lay nearby.

The bandits approached the house with the Sicarii men inside, all of them still dressed, painted, and smelling like women—the bandits' lust overtook them, and they began to rip the clothing off and assault each and every Sicarii, fully believing they were putting a female to their loins. The bandits fully saw the manhood of the stripped Sicarii, but their starving minds played a trick on them—they saw only women.

John's bandits were understandably mad with hunger and thirst due to the water shortage. They were also hungover from wine and deceived by female clothing, makeup, and perfume. The bandits mounted every Sicarii in both their mouths and rears.

Once John's men had satisfied themselves, they momentarily came to their senses. Seeing what they had done—with Sicarii manhood staring them all in the face, they instantly regressed into rabid animals.

Some fell over vomiting—though starving with an empty stomach, only a small glob of bile came out of their mouths, leaving them to dry-heave until their abdominal muscles cramped.

Most of John's men let out lion roars, raging at the violation the Sicarii had brought forth by allowing themselves to be raped.

After this terrorizing cry, the bandits grabbed every weapon in sight and began to slay the Sicarii in a grotesque-like fashion. No Sicarii was left standing or breathing; the lot were all cut to shreds, becoming nothing more than bone, blood, and meat— every person indistinguishable from one another.

Realizing what they had done, the bandits raced back to the Temple Mount, passing another horde of Sicarii that still upheld John and Simon's truce. The Sicarii assumed the bandits' tan robes, now blood-soaked, came from their permitted raiding in the Upper Marketplace.

It was not until the bandits were already safely back within the Temple's protection that other Sicarii came upon the twenty sacks of mangled Sicarii flesh. Immediately they realized John's bandits were the only possible and completely obvious perpetrators of the violence—one bandit had even lost his tunic in the melee and debauchery, racing back to the Temple Mount with only a bloody cloth to cover himself. The Sicarii leader picked up the tunic and brought it to Simon as evidence.

The truce between John and Simon was instantly nullified, and Simon once again made open war on John and vice versa. Immediately firestones began to be launched up and down the Temple Mount while arrows traveled in both directions again as well.

During all of this, Titus stood fast, watching the Judeans destroy themselves. From the lookout tower in his main fortress, he could clearly see the ongoing fight among the factions.

"Men fall dead off the Temple Mount from arrows and fire-stones fired by Simon while others perish below from the darts and rocks delivered from above by John," Titus observed. "Do the Judeans not know that Rome is here?"

"They just don't care. Their own hate overrides their senses," Josephus, standing next to Titus, replied.

Fireball stones, spears, and arrows rained up and down the Temple Mount for two days straight.

Titus used a sound military strategy in letting the enemy weaken itself. He still could not comprehend a people that would burn each other alive while the Roman army waited like a lurking vulture, ready to swoop in at the most opportune time.

The result of the continued battle between John and Simon was, predictably, a complete stalemate, resulting in only more deaths, wounds, and increased delirium. Hostilities between the factions again paused as men on both sides became too tired and weary to continue.

- - -

**THE PEOPLE** remaining alive in Jerusalem continued to literally starve to death.

One mother, Mary, and her little baby boy Shiloh were all that remained of a family of eleven. Her husband and three boys had been run through by John's bandits a month past. Her three daughters were raped and killed by the Sicarii a week past. This morning Mary's mother collapsed and died of a broken heart when she woke to find her husband, Mary's father, hanging from the kitchen ceiling by a rope.

Mary sat in a corner talking to her baby. "Everything will be fine, my little one. We will be with God soon."

Mary had not eaten so much as an ounce of bread in two weeks. She had lost over forty-five pounds in the months leading up to this moment. Her baby was inconsolable, for his mother's breasts no longer gave milk and had not for over a full week now.

She looked into Shiloh's eyes, both of them crying for the same reason: hunger, maddening and all-consuming hunger.

"Have no fear, little one," she said, so choked up her words were barely audible.

"You will be better off in the afterlife. I know God will be your keeper in the Kingdom of Heaven. Forgive me, Lord, for I have no power to stop myself."

A couple of blocks away a crazed and emaciated troupe of young Sicarii were walking down the back city streets. The oldest boy began attacking the youngest one, accusing him of hiding food. The elder ripped the young Sicarii's clothing off to find nothing but a thin sheet of skin stretched by a burgeoning rib cage.

"Do you smell that?" the oldest Sicarii asked, stopping his attack.

"I smell something too," another Sicarii member confirmed.

"It's coming from over there!" the oldest determined.

The entire group turned into an alley, following the billowing smell of cooking meat.

They came to a small wooden door that was locked from the inside. Too weak to even break the unimposing door down, they began climbing over each other to crawl through the dwelling's one square foot-wide open-air window.

The Sicarii fell onto the home's floor on top of each other as they all climbed hands first through the same clay opening.

Famine in Jerusalem

Mary sat at her dinner table, a plate in front of her. On her plate lay half a skeleton, its bones still sticky with small bits of tendons, skin, and fat on them.

On a platter in front of her plate was half of her roasted baby Shiloh, his hair fried off, eyes sunk in, and steam still rising from the cooked flesh.

"You boys can have the rest of Shiloh if you would like, though I'm quite sure I already had the better half," Mary said daintily and continued gnawing on the bones for every last morsel of meat she could extract.

Four of the boys fell over, heaving uncontrollably.

Three boys ran out of the house, screaming as if being chased by a demon.

Two boys picked up empty plates from Mary's kitchen and sat down at her table.

The word of this atrocity spread throughout the city like an unstoppable and deadly airborne virus. Hearing this, many Judeans curled up within themselves physically and metaphorically as if they had also committed such an abominable crime—some of them indeed had.

# Chapter 30:

# The Outer Wall Is Taken

**THE ROMANS** had been sitting outside Jerusalem for almost two months without engaging in warfare—there had only been the one small opening-day skirmish.

Since then, Titus had been waging a war of attrition, first attempting to starve out the Judeans in an effort to avoid slaughtering them with the sword. Additionally, he had studied the siege in 586 B.C. by Nebuchadnezzar and knew taking Jerusalem by force, even six hundred and fifty years later, would still be no easy proposition.

During this time, he hoped the reality of the Judeans' situation would become clearer and eventually undeniable with each hungering day. However, his hopes were only such, as the Judeans had no intentions of coming to terms with the Romans.

Seeking to further humiliate and antagonize the Romans into action was a small group of Sicarii involved in a secret mission overseen by Simon personally.

The Sicarii soldiers were stationed just inside Herod's gate, out of sight, on the northern side of the city. Suddenly, a dozen men, all wearing the uniforms of Roman soldiers, were marched, under duress, out of the city gate at the hands of the Sicarii. They were lined up in execution formation. An individual Sicarii guarded each condemned Roman with a dagger to the neck. The prisoners all had their tongues cut out so that they could not plead for their lives or divulge any information. Blood ran down the middle of each man's chin onto his uniform.

The shofar was blown, alerting the Romans within earshot of the Sicarii presence. The Romans watched their comrades in custody facing imminent execution at the hands of the Sicarii.

The sight drove the Romans mad, but they stayed stoic, fighting the temptation to instantaneously engage the Sicarii.

But before the Sicarii executed the Roman prisoners, they were first put to shame. A Sicarii wearing a blond wig, dressed and painted to look like a Roman whore, came out from Herod's gate. Catcalls and hisses abounded with his entrance. His clothes colorful and scant, the cross-dressing Sicarii walked up to each Roman and slapped his face, kneed his groin, and then spit or urinated on each captive.

Half the Tenth Legion, some twenty-five hundred men, watched intensely and unconsciously reached for their weapons. The Romans were completely transfixed by the Judean ploy, their blood boiling from this sharpest of Hebrew taunts.

"Judea is for Judeans!" the Sicarii all shouted out together.

Then they took their daggers and slit all the throats of those in Roman uniform—the onlooking Tenth Legion raged wild.

Without orders and without Roman precision, one, then two, then hundreds of Roman soldiers came barreling towards the Sicarii executioners, screaming a war cry of vengeance.

"Vindicta!" the Romans roared as they raced towards the Sicarii.

Sprinting to their dead comrades, the Romans discovered the men outfitted in the Roman cloth were not Roman at all. They were non-combatants—old and young Judeans, most with signs of long, unkempt beards recently and viciously hacked off at the chin.

The Sicarii, using the Roman soldier uniforms seized from the initial uprising several years ago, had disguised common Judean criminals whose bodies were available for execution. By the time the Romans had realized the folly of their haste, a force of over ten thousand Judeans emerged from the city gate and on top of the wall walk and parapet—all armed for battle.

The Romans had better weapons. The Judeans had better numbers. The Judeans fought with the fire of God. The Romans defended, embarrassed they had been fooled by the Judean cunning.

The battle was intense for an hour. Axes slammed into men's heads, splitting their skulls. Swords sliced through sternums. Fists found faces and hit again and again until one combatant was unconscious or dead.

The Roman Tenth Legion, that had leapt into battle unconsciously, fought with every ounce of strength to escape the snare they themselves had entered. Five hundred Romans lay dead next to fifty dead Sicarii.

It was an unquestionable victory for Simon, his Sicarii, and Jerusalem.

*  *  *

**THE SICARII** taunted the Romans mercilessly for falling victim to their sneaky ambush. For an entire day they stood precariously on the merlons of the parapet and bent over, showing their bare asses to the onlooking Romans, mocking and yelling lurid epithets the whole while. They even broke out sacred wine, raided from the holy Temple—the lot of them could be seen drunkenly roaming about the wall walk, singing, cursing the Romans, and laughing.

On the opposing side, the soldiers were greatly discouraged. They had been played. They had been beaten. They had been laughed at—and they now had to answer to an outraged Titus.

Inside the main Roman fortress, Titus stood before a table of his trusted advisors and military leaders.

"An entire legion devolves into madness at the sight of a false execution!" Titus yelled. "I should have the remainder of the men in the Tenth executed for dereliction!"

Titus frantically grabbed a small clay bust of Augustus sitting on a marble pedestal. With an agonized scream, he pitched it across the room into the fortress wall—shattering it.

"General, they had Roman uniforms on. They were being publicly humiliated and executed." Frachas attempted to calm the rage of his master.

"Quiet your tongue, tribune!" Titus ordered.

"The Judeans will never resubmit. We will have to slaughter them all, so we might as well get into the thick of it," Tiberius Alexander stated. "My men are ready to move on the city this minute, Lord Titus."

"Let my engines get started on the walls at the very least," the commander of the artillery, General Cestius, suggested.

Titus paused and looked out from his fortress to Jerusalem in great contemplation.

Impatience and anger twisted his thought process. Titus silently speculated that his attempt to diminish the lives lost through his many peace offerings to the Judeans was actually resulting in more Roman and Judean blood being spilt.

"I want the walls leveled, I want the city burning, and I want it now! Every hour that passes idly by with the Hebrews maintaining their rebellion is an affront to Rome, an affront to Caesar, and an affront to me!" Titus yelled. "General Cestius—ready the stone-throwers!"

"Your wish is my command, my lord," Cestius responded.

"It's time to remind the Hebrews that Rome still controls the world," Titus declared. "Get your companies ready. The assault on the wall begins at daybreak. Dismissed!"

**Execution of 'Romans' Stratagem by the Sicarii**

...

**"GOOD MORNING,** Cestius," Titus greeted him.

"Good morning, Lord General," Cestius replied.

"Well, let's get about it," Titus commanded.

"Yes, my lord. Deploy the stone-throwers! Prepare to attack!" Cestius yelled to his tribunes and centurions.

A hundred catapults were at the ready. The engines were deployed across most of the three main sides of Jerusalem's outer wall. The weakest sections of the wall were heavily targeted by the catapults—the strong places were left unchallenged.

The catapults were mostly uniform in size and weight capacity. Most of the stones thrown were about eighteen to twenty-four inches in diameter and weighed from about seventy-five to a hundred pounds.

The art of the artilleryman was to know the individual capability of the engine and match the engine with the stone it could be most effective with. Cestius was the best in the business and had thoroughly prepared for putting the engines into service against the walls of Jerusalem.

"Load catapults!" Cestius ordered, and his officers speedily spread the order down the line.

From Titus' view in his fortress tower, he could see thousands of Romans hustling about the desert, positioning projectile stones into catapult cradles.

"Oil up and ignite!" Cestius shouted, and a hundred balls of fire emerged around the city.

Cestius looked towards Titus overseeing the unfolding battle from his fortress tower. Titus nodded his head in approval.

"Fire!" Cestius roared.

"Fire!" was repeated through the lines.

The Siege of Jerusalem

In the folly concerning the wall-breachers, Titus had lost two thousand men and an enormous military allotment of armaments and wood. He had never before encountered such a setback in all his years of warfare.

Rage filled Titus' heart and eyes as he stood before his most trusted advisors in the war room inside the main Roman fortress. Tiberius Alexander, Frachas, Cestius, Domitian, Josephus, and a few other generals were in attendance.

"Speak!" Titus shouted.

"Let's ram through the gates. They are wood, not marble like the walls, brother," Domitian proposed.

"Brilliant!" Tiberius Alexander sarcastically rebuked him. "Have you learned nothing of what the Judeans do to wooden engines by the wall?"

"Speak to me in that manner again, general," Domitian replied coldly, "and I will see it is the last time you use your tongue."

"Domitian!" Titus roared. "The enemy is out there, not in here. Don't make me remind you of that fact again!"

Domitian shot Titus a murderous glance at his open chastisement.

"Tiberius Alexander, what say you to sending the rams?" Titus asked.

"It is worth the risk—we need only breach one gate. But I fear the Judean bastards will dump oil on the rams as they did on the breachers, obliterating them all. Perhaps the wooden gates will also catch and provide us entrance residually," Tiberius Alexander speculated.

"I'm inclined to agree with you, General Alexander. You are the field marshal, and you will lead the battering ram assault. Dismissed," Titus ordered.

The rams were essentially huge trunks of thick trees, each two feet in diameter. A bronze spike was forged into a cap that covered the head of the tree trunk, forming the ramming end. Attached to the trunk were handles at its midsection every two feet. Holding these handles, the soldiers would thrust the ram into the gate with every last ounce of energy their bodies could deliver.

The Romans brought with them advanced rams that hung from ropes inside a suspension chassis, creating the back-and-forth swinging action of a piston. This increased the force with which the ram's head plowed into the gate.

While the grips worked in unison to swing the ram into the gate, each had a Roman soldier dedicated to shielding him from arrows, spears, stones, oily fire, and whatever else the Judeans might use to defend with.

However, protecting the men and the ram from the overhead dousing of oil was nearly impossible. Even with a full tortoise defense, before most of the rams could be put into action, the soldiers operating them had either been killed by an arrow, spear, rock, or covered in boiling oil and set on fire, resulting in a torturous death.

Wooden logs sat before gate after gate, turning to ash as the breachers had done the day before. Not one gate was opened in the Roman offensive, but another few hundred soldiers had been lost.

"We can't break their walls. We can't breach them. We can't ram through their gates! What the hell is going on? Why is this such a problem? They are starving and fighting among each other for crumbs of bread in the streets, murdering each other behind those very walls we cannot overcome! Someone tell me something!" Titus roared.

"You are starving them out, my lord. The city swells still with sojourning souls trapped from the Feast of the Unleavened Bread and no food can enter. They can't survive much longer before they all start falling over dead," Frachas pointed out.

"I tried of letting them starve. They proved that was too good for them," Titus said.

"I have an idea. It's untested, of course, but it will cause the Hebrews hell," Cestius suggested.

"Continue, general," Titus said eagerly.

"The problem we had with the wall-breachers was that they all burned down because they were made of wood. Also, they were too short for Jerusalem's walls—they should have been higher so the men were not exposed to an oil attack as soon as the bridge was lowered," Cestius explained to a very intrigued Titus.

"I'd make a wall-breacher out of iron. Iron won't burn when covered with burning oil. And I'd make it at least fifty feet high, with multiple breaching bridges at different heights. I'd also arm it with turrets on the forward three sides. These improvements will give our brave warriors inside the engine an honest chance at succcess," Cestius said.

Titus was enamored, and his silence spoke louder than his words could.

"Cestius, I want you to oversee this project. How long before this new breacher might be deployed?" Titus inquired.

"We have all the materials we need. Maybe a week, depending how much metal we have to forge into beams," Cestius answered.

"Excellent," Titus commended him. "Get started on the iron breacher immediately. The rest of you, find a reason for me to be as impressed by you as I am with Cestius right now. Dismissed."

Frachas stayed behind after the exit of the other officers, maintaining a facial expression that openly declared he was beyond skeptical of this new plan to construct an iron breacher.

"Is there something wrong with your face, tribune?" Titus asked, exasperated even before receiving Frachas' first word.

"No, general, it's only that we haven't been successful with catapults, breachers, and battering rams—I don't think another

**The Romans Fail with the Battering Rams**

engine is the answer."

Titus stepped into Frachas' personal space and grabbed him by the collar of his tunic.

"Damn it, Frachas! I need you with me now. I need ideas, not criticism. We've been outside Jerusalem for over two months and have only losses to show for it!" Titus raged. "When you make a face, I see it, as do all my officers!"

Frachas immediately realized the error of his approach.

"Forgive me, my lord. I know the great weight that lies with your position. I will do my utmost to unburden you in any and all ways I can. I promise no further dissension from me outside a private meeting with you.

Titus, somewhat surprised by the quick obedience of his tribune, decided to let the conflict slide. "Good."

"And if it's ideas you are looking for, general," Frachas said as he made his way to the exit, "try bribing one Judean faction to ally with us—once we have control back inside the city, we can subjugate any remaining dissenting forces. It worked over a hundred years ago for General Pompey. Good night."

■ ■ ■

CESTIUS NOW looked more like a blacksmith than an officer, let alone a general. Every stitch of his armor was removed from his person, his sword belt exchanged for a tool belt.

"I want the height of this beast to be sixty feet tall. The design is simple; the complexity will come with adding the turrets and multiple bridges. Let's get the smelter cooking! We have lots of iron beams to make!" Cestius ordered.

Hundreds of soldiers-turned-metalworkers hurried about the outside of the main Roman fortress. Some were busy installing an oversize smelter. Many servants and slaves scavenged and hauled all the disposable metal that the smelter could absorb. Others gathered a stock of coal to heat the device.

Beam after beam, hour after hour—iron pillars were laid and forged.

As soon as the beams cooled, they were immediately put into use as part of the skeleton of Cestius' new iron breacher. Men working all day in the desert sun, wearing nothing but aprons, loincloths, bandanas, and sandals, hammered away at metal. The whole thing sounded like an impromptu percussion concert of epic proportions.

One ironworker led the rest, hammering the metal rivets at a rhythmic pace: *hard-tap, soft-tap, triple-hard-tap.*

The congregation of metal workers repeated the beat: *hard-tap, soft-tap, triple-hard-tap.*

But before long, the beat got stale, so the leader changed the rhythm to something with a bit of contrast: *double-soft-tap, triple-hard tap, double-soft-tap.*

It was not a great change, but it was enough to make the hours of hammering seem a little less monotonous.

The week had nearly passed and there had been no more direct Roman assaults against the city. They had spent the entire time building the iron breacher. The blockade continued despite the ceasing of projectile fire. The Judeans even went back to fighting with each other. John and Simon had resumed tepid hostilities resulting in a few more deaths on each side.

- - -

**THE ROMANS** were nearly done building their newest war machine.

"It's looking good," Titus said, observing the nearly complete, new iron breacher.

"The men are calling it the 'Nico,' sir," Cestius informed him.

"What does 'Nico' mean?" Titus asked.

"It's Hebrew for 'conquers all things,' or so the Judean slaves say," Cestius replied.

"I like that," Titus said. "How much longer until we can put it into action?"

"I'd say two days. We're nearly there now. The men are finishing up work on the turrets. The bridges are being installed. But this is the best part—come take a look at this!" Cestius beckoned. "I had it made special by the Hebrew slave glassmakers. It's a modified Archimedes Death Ray!"

The convex glass focus, circular in shape and six feet in diameter with about a width of a foot at its center, was attached to a metal brace from which the person operating the glass could easily adjust its position and angle. The brace was attached to a bronze pipe protruding from the top of the Nico.

Also on the top of the breacher was a parabolic gold mirror the same size as the focusing glass. The device used sunlight to operate: the gold mirror collected sunlight and beamed it directly into the glass lens, and the lens focused and directed the light into a laser beam of fire onto the designated enemy target.

"I've never seen one in action, though I've heard the rumors. Does it work?" Titus inquired.

"Why don't you see for yourself?" Cestius offered.

Titus nodded his head in agreement.

"Show General Titus what this monster can do. Sunlight!" Cestius yelled out.

A Roman soldier working as a grip removed the tarpaulin cover over the gold mirror and glass lens. He adjusted the angle of the mirror. Once it was properly aligned with the sun, *Voila!* A laser of death shot out of the glass!

The Roman operator cut a line of fire down into the earth. He focused the beam on a bale of hay, bursting it all into flames. Then the soldier used the laser to cut a Judean, freshly affixed upon a nearby cross, in half—ending his crucifixion early.

"My gods! I've seen enough," Titus said, overwhelmed, as he watched the Judean's guts slide out of his severed corpse.

"Ceasefire!" Cestius yelled out to his operators. "Cover it up!"

"Well done, Cestius! This will surely turn the tide!" Titus lauded him. "I'm certain of it."

Cestius was elated with the magnificence of his creation but more so with Titus' approval.

Josephus saw the military adaptation for what it was: a god-like advantage, known to him from a lifetime of reading scripture. His heart sank, for in his mind only God himself could now save the Judeans from total destruction, something He only did for the righteous—Jerusalem was a modern-day Sodom and Gomorrah.

Josephus was the only man in the Roman camp dismayed at the likely prospect of now winning the war—it might mean the death of his people. Horror spread with goosebumps across his body.

Standing next to him was Frachas, giddy with anticipation at releasing an iron-made, fire-breathing metal dragon on the Judeans.

"This beast will cut us a path to the Temple!" Frachas predicted joyously.

Josephus could not bring himself to respond and merely walked away silently to his quarters inside the Roman fortress.

The Nico was almost finished. Its wheels were installed. The turrets were welded into position securely. The bridges, one on the very top level and one on the main level, were finished.

The devilish iron machine, with one eye of glass and another of gold, towered sixty-five feet top to bottom—it truly did look like a metal beast of death.

Titus, his confidence restored, signaled the Nico to advance while he continued the aerial bombardment from the catapults. This time he had Cestius aim not for the impenetrable walls, but for the homes, residents, and soldiers on the parapet.

Hours passed and flaming stones continued flying through the air. The Nico advanced to the wall on the backs of a hundred Roman grips, pushing and pulling with all their might.

Judean arrows, stones, and spears hit and harmlessly bounced off the Nico as it moved forward.

The Nico continued its slow motion towards the wall.

"In firing range!" the tribune commanding the Nico yelled out.

The Roman soldiers on the Nico's turrets began their assault. The three turrets on the breacher were essentially small ledges with shields. There a soldier could fire an arrow or throw a javelin down on a man standing behind the parapet on the wall walk with ease, all while maintaining a level of protection.

One Roman soldier on the forward turret was essentially a stone-thrower—his job was literally to drop stones directly onto the heads of the enemy. Not considered sophisticated by Roman standards, this method was still employed as it continued to be very effective.

And then there was the gold-mirror-and-glass eye of death. It could cut men in half from fifty feet away. Its red laser terrified men as much as it tortured them. No Judean, since the Ark of the Covenant disappeared, had seen fire of the like. The weapon could kill twenty men a minute if the operator was working speedily and precisely, which he was.

The fire-glass was so terrifying that many Judeans ran from their posts, favoring being slain by their own commanders for desertion over facing death from the pillar of red light resembling the wrath of their Hebrew God.

"Get ready with the oil, men!" a Sicarii commander on the wall walk yelled out as the Nico closed in.

Dozens of Sicarii prepared to oil the Nico. The Roman lens operator focused his target on those men carrying buckets. One by one, the defending Sicarii burst into flames as their buckets of oil combusted from contact with the death ray.

The Nico continued its advance. It was nearly within breaching distance, less than ten yards out from the wall.

"Oil!" the Sicarii commander ordered his men.

A few unscathed Sicarii tossed buckets of boiling oil upon the Nico, wondering if they would find the same success when tossing oil on iron as they had on wood. A hand torch was tossed onto the oil-spattered bridge of the siege tower, igniting the crude. Flames engulfed the Nico, but the structure did not succumb—the iron was fire-resistant.

The Nico had made its way as far forward as it could go—approximately a yard separated the wall face from the Nico's iron. The wheels of the breacher were moored.

"Lower the top bridge!" the Roman tribune yelled from inside the Nico. "Lower the main bridge!"

The bridges from the top and main floors of the breacher tower quickly began to descend over the wall parapet.

"Charge!" the tribune screamed.

A company of Romans unleashed their war cry, sprinting forward, carrying their weapons high across the engine's bridge.

Fearless Judeans on the wall screamed back. Some defended with stones. Dozens more men behind the parapet shot their arrows. Others fought the Romans by throwing javelin after javelin towards the oncoming enemy.

The two forces collided and began to fight hand to hand. The dead and wounded fell from atop the bridge and wall, thirty feet down to the barren Jerusalem dirt.

The Judean defense force had been greatly weakened. The Roman force inside the Nico was protected by the iron giant's large metal shielding plates and by thick hanging hides laid against the inside walls of the Nico. The hides had been doused with water, partially to prevent smoke inhalation but mostly to protect men from the heat of the outside flames sure to come.

Cestius smiled as he watched the Nico engaging the wall on the northwestern side of Jerusalem. Blasting Judeans into a fiery oblivion, the Nico allowed the Roman companies to breach the wall.

"You see, Lord Titus! The day is ours!" Cestius boasted.

"It certainly seems so, but let's wait until we are feasting in the Temple before we celebrate its capture," Titus advised.

"Look, our men are breaching the city! You see!" Frachas yelled out, seeing Roman soldiers jumping from the bridge of the breacher over to the wall walk.

"Get the legions ready. We're going in through the front gate," Titus commanded.

The Nico had been successful in getting over a hundred Roman men up over the wall. In fact, so many men made it that the Romans had to work quickly to move another company of men through the breacher.

Ten thousand Roman soldiers assembled two hundred yards outside of the Damascus gate, ready to storm in. Romans continued entering the city through the Nico, navigating across its bridge and down the overrun wall into the thick of battle. These foreign soldiers now fighting inside the city made their way through the crooked and narrow streets of Jerusalem towards the inner-city side of the Damascus gate, doggedly fighting Simon's Sicarii and Idumeans the entire way.

## 'Nico' Shoots a Death Ray

Titus kept a steady eye on the gate doors. Suddenly they began to shake. The Romans who had breached the wall succeeded in making their way to the inside of the gate. The Sicarii and Idumeans tried to stop the Romans, but after an hour of slaughter, the great wooden gates were opened, and Titus' army was granted entry into the Holy City.

A mad dash of ten thousand Roman soldiers all converged at the entrance of the Damascus gate, now open and admitting—they soon found themselves in the Upper Marketplace.

Only a few mad homeless people continued moving about outside. It was barren, dark, quiet, and void. Simon's men had all fled.

One starving homeless man, removed from reality due to his hunger, approached a Roman officer. The squadron commander, now infiltrating the Upper Marketplace, looked at the old man.

"Can you spare a copper, my lord?" the homeless man begged, not realizing he was in the middle of what had become a hot war zone.

The Roman officer was kind and merely pushed the man to the ground with a gentle open palm.

Now that the outer wall was overrun and the Damascus gate open, the Judeans fell back to a position beyond the Upper Marketplace, the 'second wall.'

Securing their field advances, the Romans demurred for the rest of the night. They slept like newborn babies sporting devilish grins in the makeshift camp they had erected in the Upper Marketplace.

The Romans had conquered the great wall of Jerusalem and were rightfully proud—it had taken Nebuchadnezzar a year and a half. Titus did it in just over three months.

◀ ◀ ◀

**IN THE** middle of the night, there was an explosive crashing sound. It was from the Nico imploding and being consumed in a towering inferno. Never having heard anything like this terrible noise before, the Romans in the Upper Marketplace thought the Judeans were making a nighttime assault. The Romans jumped from their cots, some totally naked, convinced that the Judeans had broken their line. Sparing garments and sandals, they were concerned first and foremost with grabbing their swords and spears. The soldiers began threatening every comrade not known to themselves personally.

"What's the password?" was the cry heard around the camp that night. Only if a correct answer was given did the Romans calm themselves. Many forgot the password.

"I'm a fucking Roman! You idiot!" a soldier screamed in Latin, right before he heard the sound of a sword piercing his flesh.

Adrenaline rushed into every Roman's bloodstream in the camp.

Were the Judeans attacking? Who was killing who?

Fear outweighed decency, and three score Romans lay dead from fighting one another. It took only the sudden destruction of their great iron breacher to shatter the illusion that they were safe from attack.

Had the Judeans themselves been aware of what misfortune befell the Romans, they might have taken advantage of the situation, but they were as ignorant about the melee as were their enemy. In fact, the Judeans thought the sound of the Nico collapsing was an incoming attack on themselves.

All that had happened was that the iron structure of the Nico simply failed from the heat of the burning oil weakening the metal. The stress of the weight proved too great, and the Nico collapsed upon itself. The Judeans had not enacted another special stratagem or received any divine intervention as the Romans feared.

After much unnecessary turmoil and senseless bloodshed, Titus regained control of his soldiers from a makeshift pulpit next to the downed Nico.

"Romans! I order you all, upon pain of death, to drop your blades to the ground! We are not under attack! The Nico collapsed under its own weight. It is unfortunate, yes, but your senseless bloodshed is worse, a hundredfold. Now put this nonsense behind yourselves. Rejoice that we have taken north Jerusalem!" Titus yelled to thousands of ears in princely Latin.

Titus further ensured the men that no harm was threatening them, and that the final conquest was nigh. The men heard Titus' words but felt terror in their hearts, for they knew of times past when the God of Israel had plagued the mighty with unexplainable calamity.

After his speech to the troops, Titus convened with Josephus and Frachas.

"Every advance feels like a setback," Titus said.

"That's because it *is* a setback," Frachas confirmed. "We lost sixty men tonight by our own stupid hands."

"They are forcing me to destroy them!" Titus raged.

Frachas raised his wine goblet. "To destruction!" he toasted.

Only Frachas drank. Titus and Josephus held their goblets, unimpressed with Frachas' humor.

"There are only so many walls in Jerusalem they can hide behind. And I can get over all of them," Titus declared. "Get some rest. Tomorrow morning we get back to work."

# Chapter 31:

# The Great Ramp

**THE CITY** of Jerusalem looked much like a beehive with its multiple layers of protection. If any one wall was breached, the entirety of the city would not be lost.

The outer wall that the Romans had breached the day earlier was reinforced a couple of hundred yards in by a second city wall. In their conquest of the outer wall, they had gained access into the city as far as the Upper Marketplace. The second major wall blocked their access to Antonia Fortress and consequently the Temple.

Titus' army now used the marketplace as a staging ground to complete their campaign and thoroughly quash the Judean rebellion.

"This position is worthless, general," Tiberius Alexander said. "We have to take another wall before we can even get to Antonia Fortress. We could build another Nico if we had the metal—but we don't. I recommend a great ramp. It should be rather easy given the relatively flat land we have near the second wall on our side."

Titus thought about the proposition and took a moment to visualize it in his head.

"Make it happen," Titus ordered.

"It'll be under construction for a half-moon, but once it's ready, we'll break the Judeans fast, general!" Tiberius Alexander pronounced with assurance.

Tiberius Alexander was overly eager to prove his worth on the back of Cestius' great victory in taking the outer city wall by employing the iron breacher.

In the next week, Tiberius Alexander oversaw the construction of a great ramp so the army could easily march up and over the second wall.

The most troublesome part of the entire endeavor was the lack of wood. After the Roman fortresses were constructed outside of Jerusalem and the fleet of stone-throwers and breaching engines built, there was hardly a spare log to use for general repairs, let alone the quantity needed for constructing a great ramp.

Cedar again had to be caravanned in from Lebanon as all the wood within fifteen miles had been cut and spent. The delay due to waiting for the Lebanese wood became a point of tension in the camp.

As soon as the wood arrived, the Roman slaves were put to brutal work. Tiberius Alexander had ten thousand servants, slaves, and soldiers all employed with the backbreaking labor. Hundreds of oxen and horses were working just as hard, hauling carts full of earth, stone, and wood.

Before long, the foundations of a massive ramp were set, and the scaffolding was rising.

The ramp's purpose was simple but effective: build an earthwork that allowed legions of men to charge up over the second wall as easily as if it were no taller than their knees. From there the Romans could extend wooden bridges and walk over the parapet onto the wall walk.

The massive design of the ramp included many turret houses from which supporting bowmen and artillerymen could protect their charging soldiers seeking to breach.

Working so close to the wall of the inner city, many engineers were slain or put out of commission by the Judeans—despite their protection, they were ever susceptible to darts, oil baths, and projectiles. Some were even speared by javelin-throwers.

During the entire building process, the Judeans harassed the Roman workers. The Roman soldiers shielded their workers with a half-testudo at all times, but a few hundred soldiers, servants, and slaves were still killed during the building of the ramp. Hundreds of Romans acted as dedicated firemen, dousing the many fires the resisting force rained down during the ramp's construction.

The greatest triumph the Sicarii made while the Romans built the ramp was actually in the form of horse theft. The Romans believed that the Judeans were completely confined within the walls of Jerusalem. They failed to realize the Judeans had all sorts of secret ways to pass in and out the city, especially in the darkness and through underground tunnels.

So while the Roman soldiers let their horses graze about outside their fortress unattended at night as they feasted and drank wine heavily, the Judeans went out in small numbers and stole almost a hundred horses from the inebriated Romans.

"Someone is going to die for this," Titus said somberly when he heard of the latest Judean insult to his command. "Frachas, you're always looking for more responsibility. You get to choose which one of these poor excuses for a Roman soldier receives death."

Titus stomped away from a silent and sober Frachas, who unhappily went through the process of selecting a man to be executed.

Titus made every man that lost a horse watch as their Roman comrade was crucified.

"May that be a lesson to the lot of you! Get your shit together! A drunken Roman soldier often ends up a dishonored and crucified corpse," Titus screamed and then turned in for the night.

■ ■ ■

**"HE WANTS** to see you," Sadius said to John. "His force is greatly weakened by the Roman advances."

John sat on his dais inside the Temple, in the Holy of Holies. He was surrounded by Simon's Sicarii and Idumeans below the Temple Mount, who were surrounded by the Romans beyond.

"I may make Simon the king of Jerusalem by accident. He knows nothing of our latest stratagem, correct?" John asked.

"There are no signs he has any inkling of what we've been up to," Sadius replied.

"Good. I'll be able to negotiate from a position of power once he realizes it will be by my hand that he is delivered. Arrange a meeting," John ordered.

At sunrise the next day, John exited the Temple doors, having been guaranteed safe passage by Simon to Antonia Fortress. Simon's beloved wife took the place of a hostage to ensure John would be returned to the Temple alive.

"Shalom aleichem, John."

"Aleichem shalom, Simon,"

"Just so you understand, if my wife says so much as one hair has been touched on her body, I'll slay you even if I am slain the next moment. Other than that, we are not enemies today, we are comrades," Simon declared.

"I guaranteed her complete safety just as you have guaranteed mine. She will see no harm, only hospitality," John replied.

"Good. You see—they are nigh to breaching the inner wall. Look at them build that earthwork. In a week's time they will have crested the wall, scaled Antonia, and will be at the doors of the Temple waiting to crucify you just as soon as they are done with me," Simon said to John as they both looked down on the Roman effort.

"It certainly does look like you are in need of great assistance," John replied. "Simon, Simon, Simon—if we can come to terms, perhaps I'll be so kind as to explain how I will deliver you."

"What are you talking about?" Simon asked.

"Do you think I've been sitting in the Temple for these past months doing nothing but whoring, eating, and drinking wine?" John asked.

"I hear you are quite fond of torturing your captives," Simon quipped back.

"I've heard the same about you," John retorted.

Simon nodded fiendishly, proud of his brutality.

"I've been digging," John explained.

Simon stood stunned at this game-changing development, for he knew of the tunnels under Jerusalem.

"Solomon's tunnels provide passage to an area aligned almost directly underneath the Roman ramp. My men have been clearing a series of mineshafts some ten yards below the Earth's surface. I've stocked the mineshafts to the brim with loads of oil, pitch, and wood. At my command, their massive work will come crumbling down like the walls of Jericho!"

John laughed heartily while Simon contemplated the news.

"If we can come to terms, as I said, perhaps I'll be motivated to set the tunnels ablaze at the opportune moment, giving us a definitive victory over the Romans," John said nonchalantly, knowing he had complete power over Simon.

"What do you want, John?" Simon inquired, comprehending he had no choice but to accept any terms John offered.

"If you want the help of my mineshafts, you will have to swear allegiance to me in front of your men."

"You are trapped! And you expect me to kneel to you?" Simon shouted incredulously.

"Kneel to the invading heathens if you prefer, but don't ask me for the use of my tunnels when you are boxed into Antonia by the Romans on one side and by me on the Temple Mount on the other side," John countered.

Simon stood stoically silent.

John began to stomp off, seeing that not even salvation would alter Simon's loyalties.

"I'll have your wife returned at once," John barked as he walked away from Simon.

"Wait!" Simon yelled. "Let's talk some more on this. We can at least agree to tolerate each other more than the Romans, no? I will swear allegiance to you once the ramp has destroyed the Roman army. If that is not good enough for you, then don't ignite your mineshafts, and once those gentile bastards storm through my last man standing—they will be smoking you out of the Temple the next day!

"Testify," John demanded.

"Are you serious?" Simon replied.

"Do I not look serious?" John answered.

"No," Simon said.

"Testify or the deal is off! I want you to be able to feel what you will lose if you betray me," John yelled.

"You are an evil and strange man, John of Gischala."

Simon acquiesced and removed his loincloth.

John parted the front of his garb, exposing his testicles.

"Look me in the eye when you testify," John demanded.

Both men simultaneously took hold of one another's ballsacs with their left hands.

"Remember your pledge to swear allegiance," John said calmly, "for if you renege on me, you will surely lose your family jewels."

John squeezed Simon's sac hard. "Testify!"

"I testify before Almighty God," Simon barked. "Now let go of me!"

"Good. Very good," John said, and then removed his hand from Simon's crotch and patted him on the back like a friend.

Simon and John gazed down together upon the Roman bank. "They don't even know it's coming," John mused. "Poor devils," Simon added. They both burst into maniacal laughter.

▪ ▪ ▪

**"WE'RE NEARLY** there, my lord," Tiberius Alexander reported to Titus at the Roman fortress headquarters. "We should be able to launch an assault within the day."

"I want to take a look at the front line," Titus demanded.

Tiberius Alexander saw Titus' eagerness and nodded in compliance. "Follow me, my lord."

Titus and Tiberius Alexander, accompanied by guards, exited the Roman fortress. They made their way under the conquered Damascus gate and through the Upper Marketplace, now bustling with Roman soldiers. They inspected the ramp as they walked around the great structure.

"Take a look, my lord," Tiberius Alexander said. "The final planks were just laid. We can launch an assault at any moment now."

"This is good work, Tiberius Alexander. Are your men up for a drill?" Titus asked.

"Always, sir!" Tiberius Alexander rose to meet Titus' challenge.

"Sound a forward-assault alarm. I want to see how these men react on their feet," Titus said.

"With pleasure, my lord," Tiberius Alexander gleefully said as he passed the order for a drill down the line.

Roman tribunes and centurions began shouting orders. Then horns blasted a single, unending wail, waking and alerting the entire legion stationed by the inner wall.

The shofar sounded on the Judean side of the wall too. But unlike the Romans, the Judeans were not preparing to defend the wall. They were fleeing from it!

"What the hell are they doing?" Titus asked out loud.

"It looks like our alarm frightened them into a retreat," Tiberius Alexander said, standing beside Titus. "Lord General, shall we attack?"

Though Titus was only planning a drill, fate seemed to have intervened. He saw the huge opening behind the inner-city wall where, only moments before, the Judeans had stood on guard. His warrior-trained mind told him this was the moment he had been waiting for—a break in the Judean defense.

"Seizing this opportunity might well be one of the turning points in the conflict," Titus thought, but in the back of his mind he worried it was another Judean stratagem he could not presently understand.

"Send in the legions," Titus ordered. "This ends today!"

Tiberius Alexander relayed the order, and thousands of Romans made their way from the base of the great ramp and started their ascent towards the top of the inner-city wall.

*  *  *

**"THE ROMANS** are attacking!" Sadius yelled out as he burst into the Holy of Holies. "They are trying to breach the inner-city wall!"

John, passed out drunk, took no notice of the alarm and continued snoring. The concubines lying naked next to him laughed at Sadius' distress and continued eating grapes and dates from a silver platter.

"Get out, whores!" Sadius screamed and unsheathed his dagger.

The naked girls quickly lost their laughter, grabbed their garments from the floor, and exited.

"Forgive me, my lord," Sadius said to the still-sleeping John before slapping him across the face.

"Ahh!" John yelled as he awoke to Sadius staring at him. "What the hell is going on?"

"The Romans are attacking from their newly-constructed earthwork. A legion has begun breaching the inner-city wall! The men defending fled instantly as if commanded simultaneously to retreat. What are we to do?"

"Let there be light," John said. "And by light, I mean light the fucking tunnels!"

"Aye, my lord," Sadius acknowledged.

He quickly left John's side to pass the order down to his subterranean comrades.

Little did the Romans know that while they were constructing an enormous ramp to breach Antonia, the Judeans were hard at work below ground. John had ordered thousands of cubic yards of dirt excavated. He erected a series of wooden scaffolds below to prevent the mineshafts from collapsing on themselves. Three hundred yards of tunnels, barrels teeming with oil, pitch, rope, and dry wood lay underneath the foundation of the Roman ramp.

"Light the damn oil now!" Sadius commanded a troop of men responsible for the underground tunnels.

Quickly, John's men lit the wick that served as a fuse for the entire lot of incendiaries. Fire raced along the walls and floor of the mineshafts precisely as the men had planned.

"That's it. Out! Everyone out!" Sadius yelled. "We've only a few minutes before the barrels blow!"

The flames inside the tunnels grew. Smoke started percolating upward out of the ground around the base of the Roman ramp. The Judeans had been smart enough to build an airshaft, allowing the fire to continue growing for no want of oxygen.

A mass of ten thousand Romans marched from the ground up the great ramp towards the top of the inner-city wall.

A small Idumean force of three hundred, loyal to Simon to the death, kept fighting behind the parapet of the inner wall instead of retreating. The Roman force was overwhelming, but the Idumeans momentarily halted the Romans' advance.

In the tunnel under the ramp, barrels full of unrefined petroleum began to burst. Underground explosions, over a dozen in total, went off—each barrel causing the next one in the sequence to blow.

The ground began rumbling. All the Romans atop the ramp fell to their buttocks, pinned down by the shaking.

A piercing roar blasted from the epicenter of the mineshaft. For a moment, the ramp stopped shaking. The Romans, now on their backsides and faces, began to arise, believing it an earthquake.

A series of loud snapping sounds resonated from below the ground under the great Roman earthwork.

The ground beneath the ramp began a great implosion. Flames and smoke appeared where the wooden planks of the ramp had been only moments before.

A great cry from thousands of Roman lungs rang through the air. Their screams were replaced with the implosions of the bank crumbling below them. The ground opened, and almost the entire Fifth Legion was lost, swallowed whole, Old Testament-style—only smoke and fire returned up from the earth.

Titus saw everything from only yards away, nearly drawn into oblivion himself. His eyes instantly turned bloodshot, seeing thousands of his men die.

"Sound the retreat." Titus spoke softly and calmly, in a dazed trance. He retired for the night without speaking another word.

*  *  *

# The Great Ramp Implodes

**THE NEXT** morning, Titus, Frachas, Josephus, Tiberius Alexander, Cestius, and Domitian all sat in Titus' office, sadly discussing the latest setbacks.

"I've never encountered a people so crafty at warfare." Titus expressed his frustration.

"The latest effort is working," Cestius proclaimed. "After the first month, we were still outside the city walls. Now we tighten our grasp around the throat of Jerusalem, gaining new territory each day."

"Veritas to that!" Frachas chimed in.

"I believe on the whole, Cestius is correct," Tiberius Alexander said. "By collapsing the ramp, they also destroyed a huge section of their inner wall. Once the fires go out, we need only to build a bridge across the chasm and Antonia Fortress will be ours again. And once we own Antonia, the Temple and the end of this madness will be at hand."

"As a bombardier first, I have to agree," Cestius concurred. "We should also pound the face of the Antonia Fortress day and night with the stone-throwers."

"We stay focused on the mission," Titus ordered. "Build a bridge over the ramp's crater, keep up the projectile fire, and send in the firemen to put out the ramp fire. We will take Antonia within the next two days. Dismissed."

His officers' eyes bulged at the steep but not impossible demands of their general.

Titus' office emptied out, but before Josephus left, Titus put a hand on his shoulder.

"Josephus, I have some bad tidings. I received this scroll in the latest post from Rome. My father is willing to side however you wish," Titus said, handing Josephus the scroll. "I'm sorry, brother."

Titus left his own office so Josephus could privately study the document.

Josephus noticed the seal was broken on the letter. He wondered who and why someone would spy on him. The logical guess was Vespasian. Did his new father suspect his adopted son was a traitor, in league with the Judean rebels? Putting that thought out of his head, Josephus read the note—tears started falling from both his eyes.

*My dearest,*

*A few weeks after you left for Judea, an Egyptian gold trader called on me to do business on your behalf. He claimed to owe you a hundred gold talents, so I was obliged to accept the money in your name.*

*When we met, he was friendly and offered me wine. But this was a bad man, and he drugged my drink. When next I awoke, I lay naked, bleeding from my womanhood on the Egyptian's bed. I thought he meant to kill me, but after my pleading, he agreed to let me go as long as I didn't speak of it.*

*A month later, I knew I was carrying his child. I was ashamed. I couldn't have this man's baby. The whole world would slander me as a harlot and wrongly think you a fool.*

*I ended the baby. For my crime, God will never let me bear a child again.*

*I have petitioned Vespasian for a divorce and I beg you to consent.*

*Forgive me, Josephus. Forgive me. Forgive me.*

*—Violet*

After Josephus finished reading, he fell to his knees, raised his arms, and screamed into the sky, stopping short of cursing God. "Why, Lord, have you forsaken me with women?"

# Chapter 32:

# Battle of Antonia Fortress

**NEARLY FIVE** thousand Roman men lay burned and buried alive where the great ramp once stood. The sight was biblical. It was as if God Himself had opened up the earth with fire to bring destruction down on the Romans.

Every Roman still alive could see the towering flames from the collapsed ramp where a large section of the inner-city wall once stood.

Across the soldiers' faces, looks of terror, dejection, and apathy screamed silently. Many Romans seemed lost and carried on unconsciously. Some had completely snapped and caused scenes of panic, raving in front of the rest of the army.

The Romans were scared. Fear penetrated the ranks as whispers of the Hebrew God coming to the aid of the Judeans spread, though no one wanted to say a word about it to Titus. But the elder Flavius son, being keen and aware of the state of his men, felt their terror.

"I want to talk to the men," Titus said to Frachas, now employed as Titus' chief of staff.

"What will you say to them?" Frachas asked.

"Just make sure they assemble after mess tonight. Food makes the soldier alert and sensible," Titus ordered.

"Yes, general, consider it done," Frachas acknowledged.

Throughout the entire evening meal, the Roman soldiers were as solemn as if in a burial ground. There was no idle banter, no joking, no theorizing nor conspiring. Everyone was quiet.

"After you finish your meal, report to your assigned seating areas to hear a word from General Titus," Frachas yelled out—centurions spread the order down the line.

The Romans sat in an amphitheater arrangement so all could hear. Titus walked up to a lectern lit by torches, stepped up onto two crates, and began to preach:

"Men, brothers, Romans! This war is unlike any in the history of Rome. We face an enemy that would rather die than admit failure. An enemy that believes his God will deliver him, even once the blade has been pushed through his heart. Now the moment of truth is upon us. What you men do or fail to do in the next hours will determine your fate for the rest of your lives. Cower, hide, run, and you will do so until you take your last breath. Stand tall, fight, vanquish, and you will be celebrated as heroes of Rome for all time! Your children will scorn their father if he returns a coward. Your wives will commit adultery with your neighbor. You will be dead inside and know no peace forevermore."

"You are the greatest army in the history of Rome, supported by the greatest man ever to rise to Caesar. Have no fear in your officers or weapons. I have ensured they are all up to the task. Fear only yourself. Only by conscious choice can you be destroyed. Rome does not quit! I do not quit! Show these bastard Judeans that you do not quit either!"

Titus' heartfelt monologue was truthful, resonating with his men. Only a few moments before it had seemed as if Titus stood over a funeral—now it appeared he was nursing his men back to health with each inspiring word.

"We have nearly won this war. I repeat, the war is nearly won! We burned the countryside and smashed the small cities. We breached the great wall of Jerusalem! We have also collapsed the inner wall. All that stands in our way now is Antonia Fortress. Our fortress! Remember the slaughtered garrison did not have such an army to defend themselves. Avenge them!"

Cheers, roars, along with banging and stomping noises of rebounded determination rippled through the assembly.

"I will shortly call for the bravest man to step forward and prove himself. But first hear of the great place in the annals of Roman history and halls of Roman luxury he will receive for such bravery," Titus said.

"For all those who do not return from Antonia, I shall grant a family tribute, a commendation of valor, and speak gloriously of those men who are killed in the midst of their military bravery forever. And that patriot who first mounts the wall, I should blush for shame if I did not make him envied by the others with rewards I would bestow upon him. If such a man escapes with his life, he shall have the command of others that are now but his equals and a fat allotment of gold annually for life!"

The more pecuniarily-concerned soldiers' eyes instantly popped open wide, as did those seeking a rise in station.

"Who dares step forward into everlasting glory?"

For a few moments no one moved. Titus looked out to his Romans, but his men looked down to the ground. They had been inspired by his speech but could not muster the strength to jump towards their deaths.

Finally, after no Roman soldiers stepped forward, it was a Syrian that arose from the army. The Syrian was dark-skinned and short, but he moved with such confidence one would never have thought him a small man.

He strode up to Titus. "I serve thee and great Caesar. Let my victory bring me the great fortune you promise, and let my death result in my name being spoken of gloriously!"

"And what be your name, soldier?" Titus asked.

"Alius."

Alius whistled, and eleven other Syrians rose to their feet and followed him towards Antonia Fortress, walking carefully, one by one, around the crater created by the great subterranean explosion.

The dozen Syrians approached Antonia. They stared down the fury of Simon's Sicarii and Idumeans, taunting them as they approached the fortress.

"Are you lost?" one Sicarii mocked Alius' small force from two flights up and behind the stone wall of Antonia.

"Open the gate and surrender, and we will allow you to live," Alius commanded the guard above the main Antonia Fortress gate.

An amused couple of Hebrews returned enthusiastic laughs at this ambitious order.

"Last chance," Alius threatened.

The gate stayed locked—no one replied to Alius.

"Alright, men, let's have ourselves a climb!" Alius yelled out and then furiously removed his wall-climbing hand axes from his backpack.

Alius' men followed suit, and all twelve men began free scaling the Antonia Fortress, using their axes to claw into the face of the rock wall.

"Shoot them already!" a Sicarii commander yelled out.

Simon's forces began sending dozens of darts at the climbing Syrians.

Looking on at this spectacle, Titus was reinvigorated—these men were going to their deaths for Rome, glory, and the prize.

Alius ascended like a skillful climbing gecko up the fortress wall. He would zig towards one spot, flailing his axes and arms, and then zag to the next spot to defend himself from Sicarii arrows and stones. His pickaxes were more like extensions of his body than inanimate objects. He continued up past the second story of Antonia Fortress.

Intermittently he would have to turn his climbing axe into a killing axe as Sicarii tried to get at him from every direction. Many Hebrew resistance fighters who stuck their nosy heads out one of Antonia's windows received a pickaxe in the skull followed by a drop to the ground.

Alius received slashes and bruises but continued upward. No sword, arrow, or spear could find Alius' torso nor head. He continued climbing the fortress, creating a pile of lifeless bodies below him—already numbering nearly twenty Sicarii.

One by one, Alius' men, following their fearless leader, were picked off by the Sicarii. Eleven followers became six, all cut up like butchered animals.

Alius looked back at his fallen comrades.

"Ahhhhhhhhhh!" he raged and began swinging his pickaxe about the Sicarii in a most violent fashion as he continued to climb.

Alius made his way to the roof of the fortress. The Sicarii defending the southeast tower fled at Alius' mad breach. They all believed that the Romans were close to overrunning the entire fortress. If so much as one Roman had managed to scale the tower, the entirety of their force was feared to be directly behind.

Alius stood out from the edge of the tower, bragging of his accomplishment to Titus and the army. One hand holding onto a merlon to maintain his stance, his other hand waving to the Roman army, Alius shouted at the top of his lungs: "Vive Roma! Vive Caesar!"

A great cheer returned from the Roman soldiers, who became reinvigorated watching Alius' bravery.

Then the edge of the fortress parapet which Alius had placed his weight on gave way, and Alius fell nearly twenty stories down to the ground from the southwest tower of Antonia Fortress.

"Damn!" Titus screamed, watching the fall of his champion.

"Come, my lord," Frachas said, always seemingly close by.

Titus returned to the solitude inside his Roman fort and temporarily put Antonia out of mind.

For a day, there was no Roman action. The entirety of Jerusalem was quiet.

Titus cringed, thinking the entire effort was in vain, but it had not been. The sight of Alius' valor had given the entire Roman army the courage to resume the conflict with total resolve. The fear from the implosion of the great ramp was now all but forgotten.

■ ■ ■

**TITUS STOOD** looking at Antonia from his office in the Roman fortress headquarters, contemplating his next attack in the middle of the night.

Interrupting his attention was Josephus, knocking at his chamber door.

"General, I have an answer for your father," Josephus began.

"Josephus! It is always good to see you. You're up at this hour too, I see. Come, sit, and let's talk," Titus replied, pleasantly diverted by Josephus' presence. "Will you join me for wine?"

"That sounds nice," Josephus said.

"The benefits of being a Flavius." Titus grinned. "It's imported from Rome, not the piss the Hebrews make, no insult intended."

"None taken—I never thought the wine in Judea was that great either," Josephus replied, and the two began lightly laughing together.

Once the laughter broke, the two became solemn, knowing the difficult conversation they were about to broach.

"I want a divorce," Josephus declared.

"That's probably for the best," Titus added. "You want an heir to carry your family through the generations, not a barren woman that has been ruthlessly violated. You'd be known as a fool for the rest of your days even if she tells the truth of the whole matter."

"Just thinking about this makes me angry, and divorcing her is the best way to help me think of it less," Josephus confessed.

"If you like, when this war is over, I can send a company of men to hunt down the Egyptian and bring him before you, groveling in chains for whatever torturous pleasure inspires you."

"Thanks for the offer of Flavian justice, but I want to focus on forgetting about Violet and this entire business."

"Suit yourself," Titus replied.

Josephus and Titus sat quietly, sipping on wine, the weight of the world on both men in different ways.

"Thanks for the wine," Josephus said, beginning to stand up.

"Are you leaving me so quickly?" Titus asked.

"Surely you're busy with military preparations, general," Josephus queried respectfully.

"Yes, that I cannot deny."

"Then I will leave your company until later. Thank you again for helping me with… well, you know," Josephus said.

"I'm your brother. It was my duty," Titus replied. "Come, embrace me."

The two joined arms, and then Josephus left Titus' office.

■ ■ ■

**"I LOVE** the quiet time before a fight," Frachas said as he sipped on a cup of goat's milk.

"There is something special in the air. I can feel it," Tiberius Alexander declared.

"It's time to get this battle underway," Titus declared, his mind sharp, though a bit tired from being up late.

"I concur," Cestius added.

"As soon as you are ready, general, you may proceed." Titus authorized Tiberius Alexander to resume the forward assault of Antonia. "And, general, don't muck this up."

"Of course not, my lord. I'll see you on the Temple Mount," Tiberius Alexander said and jumped on his horse to command the advance.

The Romans, using their last scraps of wood, were able to build a bridge across the crater, providing ample passage for three soldiers standing abreast.

"The bridge is ready and free of enemy harassment, my lord," a junior officer informed Tiberius Alexander.

"Excellent. Time to unleash the hounds," Tiberius Alexander replied.

The Ninth Legion began storming across the wooden bridge—they were met with little resistance, only arrows which were mostly blocked by their Roman shields.

The Sicarii guards at the Antonia Fortress entrance abandoned their posts in order to seek shelter on the Temple Mount.

"Quick, slay the Hebrews before they escape to the Temple!" a centurion called out as he led the charge through the fortress.

The Romans had taken Antonia Fortress, and with nearly none of their own lost in the conquest.

Still, they were devoid of access to the Temple Mount.

A small bridge known as the 'Northwest Passage' connected Antonia Fortress and the Mount—it was now a no man's land.

Any soul venturing to this place would be instantly struck down by spears, arrows, stones, and boiling oil. This place was where the hostilities came to a tense standstill.

The remaining hostile force of Sicarii and Idumeans who had fled Antonia raced to the Temple Mount. The remaining Hebrews in rebellion were now forced to use their holy house as their last citadel. Simon commanded the remaining force of about ten thousand rebels stationed on the Mount. John stayed inside the Temple's inner sanctum, behind the locked great gold doors with the rest of his followers.

"Don't you want something sweet, Daddy?" a concubine said, grabbing John by his manhood.

Normally, John would have instantly begun to ravage the girl.

"Not now, whores! Out of my sight!"

John threw a dagger, almost hitting a concubine, then he turned to see about his underground escape operation.

"Give me some good news. How far are we, Sadius?" John asked.

"A hundred yards," Sadius replied solemnly. "Considering we are tunneling through solid rock—it could be much worse."

"We are being squeezed to death, Sadius! The Romans are nearly close enough to kiss us. I should kill someone for this disaster! We needed to be at two hundred yards—yesterday! Find some real pathetic clod and kill him in front of the rest of the miners. I want men digging until the skin has fallen off their fingers!" John ordered.

"Of course, my lord. I'll pick a good one to crucify," Sadius pledged.

Sadius went off with five guards and selected one of the older miners who had not shown much zest for his work.

"Him there!" Sadius pointed out to his henchman, who quickly took the older miner into custody.

"What have I done—Lord Sadius?" the miner inquired.

"You are charged with dereliction of duty by being a poor miner. You are condemned," Sadius proclaimed.

"What? You can't do this!" the old miner began to argue.

Then Sadius nodded to his guard, who gut-punched the old man into silence.

"I like you better when you talk less," Sadius said to the man. "You are an example for the rest of the workers. Those men that work hard are rewarded with continued life. Deal with your lot with some dignity." Sadius turned to his guards. "Take him to the crucifixion station, and make haste with this one—the Romans are closing in."

*  *  *

**BACK AT** Titus' fortress headquarters, his top officers were assembled.

"We have it! We have Antonia back!" Tiberius Alexander boasted.

"But not the Temple," Titus quipped, ending Tiberius Alexander's celebratory spirit. "When we have the Temple securely back under Roman control, I'll share your enthusiasm, general. Until then, we work."

"Now that they are completely surrounded and nearly captured, they might come to their senses. Maybe it's worth trying to talk to them again?" Josephus ventured to speculate.

"My intuition says they will only insult you more, but perhaps now they see that they are truly trapped, they might consent to be arrested peacefully. You may try to speak with them one last time," Titus responded. "But if they refuse this offer of peaceful surrender, they will be completely destroyed."

"I understand. You know I would give my life to end this slaughter," Josephus replied.

"That I do, but I'm only asking for you to give your words at the moment," Titus answered back.

Josephus walked out to the top of the roof platform of Antonia Fortress to address John and Simon's remaining resistance force, now all relegated to the Temple Mount due to the continued advance of the Romans.

"Hello, my Judean brothers! It is I, the high priest, Joseph, son of the late Matthias! Yes, Matthias the high priest was executed before these very walls by the murderous tyrant Simon," Josephus began in Aramaic. "You have surely kept this city wonderfully pure for God's sake! Ha!

"It is never dishonorable to repent and to mend what has been done amiss, even at the last moment. Who is there that does not know the writings of the ancient prophets, particularly the oracle whose prophecy is just now going to be fulfilled upon this miserable city? For they foretold that this city should be taken when the Judean slaughters his own countrymen. It is God, therefore, God Himself who is bringing on this fire to purge the city and the Temple by means of the Romans."

"You have one final chance at life! John, Simon, and every one of you allied with them, surrender completely and drop all arms, or the Romans will burn you all alive! The choice is yours," Josephus spoke.

"Traitor!" a Judean soldier allied with John yelled at Josephus.

"Son of Caesar!" a Sicarii yelled.

"Sell-out! The words may be in Aramaic, but they come from a Roman! Flavius Josephus!" an Idumean heckled.

The barrage of slurs kept raining down upon Josephus.

John looked out a window from his stronghold inside the Temple's inner sanctum directly at Josephus, standing tall atop the roof of Antonia Fortress. Their eyes met. John mildly smiled, exuding evil with his grin, telling Josephus he would rather be killed fighting to the last man than surrender to the Romans.

Simon was less obvious about his intentions and could be seen barking orders at his men in preparation for the Roman assault on the Temple Mount.

Again Josephus had failed to move the Judeans with his wise words and sound arguments.

Titus readied his soldiers.

As it stood, the Romans now held the whole of Antonia, but the Hebrews held the entirety of the Temple Mount. Lying in the middle was the Northwest Passage.

Titus now appeared on top of Antonia Fortress. But he was not there to talk—he waved on the frontal assault from Antonia Fortress through the Northwest Passage to the Temple Mount.

First came a wave of elite Roman forces approaching the Northwest Passage. Simon and John had anticipated that the Romans would launch an attack on the Temple this way and had already covered the top and sides of the corridor with a thick coat of pitch, adding every last piece of kindling they could find to the top of the bridge.

"Set it on fire!" Simon cried out.

A dozen Idumean bowmen positioned on the roof of the Temple portico, sporting burning arrows, sent them flying directly into the Northwest Passage. A half-company of Tiberius Alexander's fiercest Romans on the narrow passageway were caught in a towering inferno.

The Romans engulfed in flames now had to choose between burning to death or jumping off the passageway, over a hundred and fifty feet to the stones below. Soldiers did both.

Cries of agony came from those burning on the Northwest Passage while screams of fear came from those who jumped off to their deaths. A loud series of cracking and crunching sounds peppered the ears of all soldiers.

The fire grew in such intensity that parts of the Northwest Passage itself started to collapse. As the stones came loose, Romans lost their footings and fell. All but one Roman who hit the ground after the fall from the passageway died. The one Roman who survived broke both his arms, his legs, and his torso—he lay immobile on the ground, crying meekly at the sight of his departed comrades.

Finally the intensity of the fire overcame the Northwest Passage, and it completely collapsed. The Romans began to fall with the rubble to the ground. Fire and marble blocks mixed with flesh. It all came to a fast stillness a few moments later once all the stones from the collapsed passageway came to rest, and the broken bodies found their final positions in this world.

"Those bastard dogs will pay," Titus mumbled to himself. Then he stormed his way down from the lookout tower of his fortress and locked himself in his chambers.

*   *   *

**"ENTER AT** your own risk, Hebrew." One of the bodyguards assigned to protect the entrance to Titus' chamber stared Josephus in the eye sternly while giving the warning.

"I said no disturbances!" Titus shouted as Josephus opened the door to his office. Titus sat with his back to the door, unable to see who entered.

"I can't remember you ever calling me a disturbance before," Josephus said, attempting to ease Titus' anger.

"Oh, Josephus! Forgive me. I thought it was another bumbling centurion or a tribune or, worse yet, a general talking more nonsense that doesn't require my attention. I always have time for you. Come, sit, and drink," Titus offered in a friendly tone.

"I fear I'm not in the drinking mood," Josephus said somberly.

"Oh dear, this sounds serious. What's on your mind, brother?"

"I'm a Goddamn traitor. That's what," Josephus answered.

"Are you?" Titus asked in a thought-provoking way. "Have you not made every effort to spare your people from destruction? To spare the destruction of the Temple? Did you not face Rome's greatest general at Jotapata? Did you not kill tens of thousands of Romans as defender of the city? Shall I go on?"

"My people will not hear any argument from me no matter how sound. I live now on Rome's coin. I call myself Flavius Josephus. I call Caesar my father!"

"And so you do! So what? Does that make you a traitor? Your people are mad. Mad with war, starvation—mad with God! Who cares what those who defile the very holy house they swear to protect call you? You know what and who you are, Josephus. And your God, I venture, does as well. That, I say, should be enough to content your heart," Titus spoke to a stunned, silent Josephus.

"I think I'll have that drink now," Josephus said after a few moments of quietly staring into Titus' eyes.

"Of course," Titus said as he replenished a carafe of wine and then filled Josephus a goblet.

"There is nothing simple or easy about your life," Titus declared. "Let history be a judge of your character, and since history is written by the victors, and since we're going to win this war, your history can be whatever you want it to be. You're a scholar. Write it down. Write down everything you have seen, and let the generations of thousands of years from now determine if you are a traitor or a patriot."

Josephus took a gulp of his wine, transfixed by Titus' suggestion.

"Perhaps I will write it down. That's actually one of the best ideas you've ever given me," Josephus complimented him.

"And you burst into my chambers expecting bad ideas?" Titus said playfully.

"Thank you, brother," Josephus said as he embraced Titus with a Roman hug.

"Josephus, I'm ordering a full assault on the Temple Mount from all sides. The war ends tomorrow."

Josephus was unable to respond.

*· ·*

**THE ROMANS,** now masters again of Antonia, encircled the Temple Mount, applying maximum pressure. Tiberius Alexander deployed companies to every staircase, ladder, and back alley passageway, even from tunnels underneath the ground that led to stairwells rising to the main level of the Temple courts.

The Romans held off their assault until the morning, when Titus would personally direct the advance on the Temple Mount from atop Antonia Fortress.

Josephus locked himself in his personal chamber.

"I am trying to serve you, Lord. Why have you given me a tongue that can talk to so many, only to close the ears of all those to whom I speak?" he yelled.

"Am I damned? Have I mortally betrayed you? Why have you kept me alive only to watch everyone else die?"

Josephus began raging, beating his straw mattress, trying to expel his guilt over being a Roman Judean in the middle of a war between the two foes.

Mucus bubbles swelled from his nose. Every evil thought crossed through his mind. Josephus spied his dagger hanging on the wall. Perhaps he should murder Titus in his sleep and bask in the glorious crucifixion it would bring him. Or he could end his misery quicker by slitting his own throat. Being around armies now as long as he had, Josephus was no stranger to seeing soldiers commit suicide a number of ways. But all these thoughts soon ceased as he thought of all the commandments he would break in a fit of rebellious petulance.

As his mind whirled, Violet came back into his thoughts. Had she been violated as he was told? Was she one of those sexual vixens that enjoyed mating with anyone other than a Roman? Was God punishing him for taking Violet as his second wife in his desire to have children and satisfy his lust?

Josephus let these thoughts pass and focused on prayer, which had always brought him solace. He began reciting...

# PSALM 51

*Have mercy on me, O God, according to your steadfast love; according to your abundant mercy blot out my transgressions. Wash me thoroughly from my iniquity, and cleanse me from my sin. For I know my transgressions, and my sin is ever before me.*

*Against you, you alone, have I sinned, and done what is evil in your sight, so that you are justified in your sentence and blameless when you pass judgment. Indeed, I was born guilty, a sinner when my mother conceived me. You desire truth in the inward being; therefore teach me wisdom in my secret heart. Purge me with hyssop, and I shall be clean; wash me, and I shall be whiter than snow.*

*Let me hear joy and gladness; let the bones that you have crushed rejoice. Hide your face from my sins, and blot out all my iniquities. Create in me a clean heart, O God, and put a new and right spirit within me. Do not cast me away from your presence, and do not take your holy spirit from me.*

*Restore to me the joy of your salvation, and sustain in me a willing spirit. Then I will teach transgressors your ways, and sinners will return to you.*

*Deliver me from bloodshed, O God, O God of my salvation, and my tongue will sing aloud of your deliverance. O Lord, open my lips, and my mouth will declare your praise. For you have no delight in sacrifice; if I were to give a burnt offering, you would not be pleased.*

*The sacrifice acceptable to God is a broken spirit; a broken and contrite heart, O God, you will not despise. Do good to Zion in your good pleasure; rebuild the walls of Jerusalem, then you will delight in right sacrifices, in burnt offerings and whole burnt offerings; then bulls will be offered on your altar.*

By the time Josephus had finished this prayer, his spiritual consciousness had landed him back in the white space.

Josephus was once again blinded with bright white light.

"Joseph, son of Matthias," Elijah's unseen voice called out to Josephus.

"Elijah, praise God, you have returned to me," Josephus replied as if Elijah had already delivered him.

"I come to you now to set your mind and heart at peace. You have been tormented, not through your own failings but through your own virtue and successes. God sees you, child. He knows how valiantly you fought the Romans, how you faced death at every moment but stayed true to Him. He knows you seek the salvation of His Temple and His people. And He knows you suffer daily for all your good efforts. For your faith and good deeds, you will be blessed with a long and prosperous life. Now record what you have seen and will see concerning the Judean war with the Romans as a lesson for all time and posterity. It is your duty."

"I will, Elijah. I will record it all, for all time and posterity," Josephus resolved. "Praise be to God."

"Now that your soul is at peace, get on with your work. Do this great task, and you will be remembered through the ages for your writings and what thou didst witness."

The overpowering white light turned into the most perfect vision of Josephus' personal heaven.

"This is paradise," Josephus said softly.

"When your last day comes, fear not, for here is where thou wilt be delivered," Elijah said.

◾ ◾ ◾

"ADVANCE ON the Temple Mount," Titus ordered Tiberius Alexander. "Let's finish this."

"Aye, general," Tiberius Alexander answered. "Sound the advance!"

Twenty thousand Romans began suffocating the remaining ten thousand Judeans on the Temple Mount. Simon had his men erect a square to defend the mount from all sides, but the Roman force overwhelmed it.

"I want to see arrows in a crossfire! Push them back into the Court of Women!" Tiberius Alexander shouted out commands as the Romans tightened their grip on the Temple Mount.

For a day the Judeans stood tall, inflicting thousands of Roman casualties while receiving even more themselves.

Spears entered men at the oddest of angles. Arrows downed countless soldiers on both sides. Swords severed limbs.

Judean and Roman bodies started piling up, making it difficult to walk. So Titus ordered a wave of cavalry up the stairs to the top of the Mount. The horses, being able to jump on and over bodies, collapsed the Judean line.

Finally, the Romans closed in on the Mount from all directions.

Those on horseback slaughtered countless Sicarii and Idumeans as their nags could overtake a man on foot in mere moments. The Court of Gentiles was turned into a battlefield of intermixed corpses.

The Romans slaughtered half the resistance on the Mount before the remaining rebels turned tail and ran behind the gates into the Court of Women.

"Retreat inside the Temple," Simon quietly ordered his top officers, seeing the Romans emerge from all sides on the Temple Mount.

The remaining Sicarii force fought valiantly in the Court of Gentiles as they attempted to hold their defensive positions.

Inevitably, Simon's lines broke, and they raced to retreat once again, five thousand men approximately making it behind the gates of the Court of Women.

Many Sicarii had the gates closed in their faces before they could reach safety and became trapped fodder for the Romans following behind them.

"Wait! Keep the gates open. We're Hebrews!" a Sicarii yelled as he was locked out of the Court of Women, condemned to share the battlefield with the Roman army.

Titus, seeing his army stymied at the gate, ordered in the rams.

"Send in the damn battering rams—break down those gates," Titus ordered, commanding from atop Antonia.

A flagman from Antonia signaled Titus' orders to deploy the rams to Tiberius Alexander controlling the field from the Temple Mount.

"Lord Titus says advance with the rams!" an officer yelled out to Tiberius Alexander.

Dozens of Roman soldiers carried three gigantic battering rams with bronze-pointed heads affixed. For several hours the Romans attempted to ram the gates of the Court of Women. It proved completely ineffective—the gates were made of twenty-four-carat solid gold beams and were rather impervious to the Roman battering rams. The gold bent and dented slightly, but it would not break.

Titus, exasperated but on the verge of conquest, gave the order to set the Court of Women's gates on fire.

Tiberius Alexander personally saw to lighting the gates on fire. He used coals to create such a high temperature that the gold began bending like butter. The intense, kiln-like heat collapsed the gold gates onto the court.

"Ha! We have them now," Tiberius Alexander cheered as the gate fire roared.

Simon's Sicarii and Idumeans as well as John's bandits and Zealots watched the gates melt down from roaring flames, but instead of trying to put out the fire, half of them stood dumbfounded and demoralized, and the other half retreated inside the Temple.

It took an entire day for the flames to be finally quenched by the Romans so that they might resume their advance.

The remaining Judeans in rebellion, less than four thousand able-bodied men in total now, all hid behind the great doors of the Temple's inner sanctum.

- - -

**"WE HAVEN'T** finished tunneling!" John kicked a scaffold over in anger as he and Simon looked over the subterranean effort.

"It's your damn fault we're not done with the tunneling!" Simon yelled back.

"King Solomon dug so many tunnels, it could be months before the Romans find us, and by then, we'll have found a way out," John assured him.

"Solomon's tunnels go down. We need to go *up* to get out of Jerusalem, or we are going to get trapped within layers of the city," Simon retorted strongly.

"Keep digging, you useless fools!" John barked at the miners who had paused to view the argument between himself and Simon.

"The Romans are banging on the front door! Get us moving, John!" Simon barked.

With that insult, John pulled a dagger. Though he was much older than Simon and fat, he was still as fast as a cat. The blade pressed against Simon's throat before he could defend himself.

"Insult me again, and I'll cut you down, knowing full well your men will cut *me* down in consequence," John threatened, his eyes wide with rage.

"One time, John, one time, I will let you threaten me, but next time you better kill me, or you'll be the dead man," Simon replied coolly.

"Lord John! Lord John!" a miner called from deep down inside the tunnel. "We've just broken through to an old mineshaft. I think you have an escape, my lord!"

John and Simon looked at each other, their anger instantly disintegrated by renewed hope.

At the same moment they both said to each other, "Time to go."

# Chapter 33:

# The End of Jerusalem

**IT WAS** the ninth day in the eleventh month of the Hebrew calendar year 3,830, a day also known by the Judeans as Tisha B'Av. It was on this day over 650 years prior in 586 B.C. that Jerusalem was destroyed by the Babylonians.

The fighters still in revolt included John's Zealots and bandits, and Simon's remaining Sicarii and Idumeans. The ragged two-thousand-man force stood locked behind the grand, solid-gold doors of the inner Temple sanctum, waiting for the Romans' next move.

Titus was more concerned with saving the Temple than the rogues defending it. Instead of ordering the Temple destroyed on the spot, he called his top military leaders to advise on the matter.

"Burn the damn thing down and end this war, general!" Tiberius Alexander implored.

"I'm inclined to agree with the general, Lord Titus," Cestius said. "Have every stone broken. Never let the Judeans participate in this madness again."

"You know I want to see the place burn to the ground," Frachas added.

Turning to Tiberius Alexander, Titus said something that would render Josephus speechless: "General Alexander, I want every last Judean in the city found and slain. I want the Temple destroyed stone by stone and its treasures recovered. I want Antonia Fortress torn down to the ground too. And burn everything in the entire city—every last house, hut, and haystack. Jerusalem is ended!"

"There's up to a million people in the city, my lord," Tiberius Alexander reminded.

"Then there will be up to a million dead Judeans!" Titus proclaimed. "Kill them all and they will never rise again!"

"Aye, general," Tiberius Alexander said, fully comprehending the severity of Titus' order.

"You have your assignments. Dismissed," Titus said.

After the generals had dispersed, Josephus went up to Titus privately.

"Is there any other way?" Josephus asked.

"Is there?" Titus asked back. "Half a million Judeans are already dead from disease, war, and starvation. The other half are almost dead from the lack of food and will soon die anyway. What good is it to spare the dying men and women only to prolong their agony?"

"Death to all my people? Are you mad?" Josephus asked, his emotions bubbling up and out.

"You are Roman, Josephus! Your people are the Roman people now!"

"I'm also a Judean, a high priest, no less, and of royal descent. A million dead Judeans, Titus—that's really what you want on your head? Most of them are innocent civilians, just trying to live an honest life like a stonecutter or baker in Rome."

"Enough!" Titus yelled. "I'm sorry, Josephus. I have my orders too."

"Vespasian has ordered the death of all the Judeans?" Josephus asked.

"As I said—I have no choice."

"No choice? You command this entire army!" Josephus yelled back.

"Vespasian demands the Judeans be exterminated for their intransigence. Forgive me, brother, but it has to be done," Titus pleaded.

"Forgive you? You, whose life I saved multiple times? You, who I call brother? Who is only committing mass murder of an entire race, my race—you ask why I shouldn't forgive you?" Josephus' sarcasm smacked Titus in the face.

"That's not fair, Josephus," Titus rebutted.

"It's completely fair. Even if someone tells you to do something, you still have the choice whether to do it or not!" Josephus said.

He left Titus' quarters and tried to get rest, knowing the full horror the next day would bring. Of course, he could not sleep a wink.

*  *  *

**TITUS SENT** Tiberius Alexander about his work, and he systematically marched his men through every last nook and alleyway in Jerusalem. Those people found hiding begged for life until the Roman blades took it from them. It was common for Romans to execute Judeans with multiple blades all inserted simultaneously, then removing the blades in unison—dropping the dead corpse.

Mostly the Romans found houses full of people dead from famine or disease.

Bodies littered the streets. The majority of Judeans had been deceased for weeks, but many were recent deaths. The smell was so wretched Roman soldiers gagged at a regular frequency—officers covered their faces with piece of cloth soaked in spirits.

"What are you doing, tiro?" a seasoned centurion yelled out in the panic of the massacre.

"She's just a child," the young tiro replied.

"We kill everyone! General Titus' orders!" The centurion pressed past the tiro.

Raising his gladius, the centurion slew the girl with a slash to her throat.

"You may not like your duty, son, but you have to do it. I'll forget this time, but if I see you taking prisoners again, I'll report it and have you court-martialed. Do we understand each other?"

"Yes, centurion."

"Good. Now go. And good hunting. It's open season—try and enjoy yourself." The centurion patted the tiro on the back and ran back into the madness of Jerusalem's destruction.

The Judeans knew the Romans were coming, and they had prepared. Many bodies hung from ropes around their necks, placed there by their own doing, rather than suffering death at the hands of the pagan foreign invaders. It was not uncommon for a company of Romans to burst into a Judean house to find an entire family all dangling motionless next to each other.

"I'm going to be sick," a Roman soldier said at the sight of bodies whose faces had been eaten off by the starving rats.

Many Judeans remaining alive, seeing the Temple and the city burn while the Romans marched street to street, were content to be executed in a conveyor-belt-like fashion—not resisting, only asking for a quick death.

Josephus spent the day in the Roman fortress in his quarters, in solitude. Only with his fingers pressed hard against his ears could he shut out the screaming of Judeans being slaughtered across Jerusalem. Sometimes his mind heard the screams even with his ears firmly pressed closed.

Blade into flesh—red fluid spouted from human tissue. The Romans' savagery knew no bounds.

Listening of the wails of the dying for hours upon hours seemed to last a lifetime.

As the smoke lingered over Jerusalem from the fires the Romans had started, the day seemed to turn to night as the smoke screen made the sun appear more like a full moon. The Romans checked all the buildings and houses, slaying everyone they found. The babies were the luckiest for they knew not their fate. The adolescents were the least lucky for they could fully comprehend their situation yet remained powerless to affect it. They were also the most likely to be abused by the Romans recreationally.

That day, untold masses were slaughtered by the Romans—at its end, up to a million dead Judeans lined the streets and homes of Jerusalem.

Those Judeans with strength left, trying to remain free, burrowed into hiding spots. But the Romans brought dogs and sniffed out most of them, resulting in a death by mauling.

As Tiberius Alexander moved across the meager remains of the city, all of Jerusalem turned red with fire and blood. It was no longer only the Temple that was burning—it was the buildings, homes, walls, and human bodies. Every foul scent infused the air with such a stench the Romans choked as if inhaling poison gas.

Night had come, and Tiberius Alexander was now focused on flushing out the few thousand or so fleeing residents in the tunnels. Like an exterminator, methodically and systematically the Romans trudged through all the known tunnels under the Temple Mount. They forced Judeans to guide them at spearpoint to ensure they left no tunnel unsearched. Every few minutes it seemed pockets of Judeans were discovered and then summarily executed. The Romans, carrying torches, moved fast through the tunnels, with such speed it almost seemed they had prior knowledge of the subterranean design.

All of Jerusalem wept that day. Lightning struck both Romans and Judeans dead though no rain fell from the sky.

"Titus, for the sake of my God, for the sake of me—make Tiberius Alexander stop!" Josephus said hysterically, grasping Titus' legs like a common beggar.

"Josephus, get up. You're my brother, not a homeless madman," Titus responded.

"Even Nebuchadnezzar took slaves when he sacked the city. Titus, I beg you with every part of my soul—stop the summary slayings and take the Judeans as slaves," Josephus pleaded.

Titus hesitated.

"Your life debt will be forgiven for this exchange," Josephus tempted Titus.

"You are a crafty man with words, no doubt about it," Titus answered. "Squire!" he yelled, and then began scribbling on a piece of parchment. Titus closed and affixed his seal to the order.

A young squire hurriedly appeared at Titus' side.

"Go find Tiberius Alexander and give him this letter. Tell him General Titus orders all killings to stop immediately. The Judeans are to be taken as prisoners. Now go!"

The squire took the sealed note and ran off like a squirrel.

"Thank you," Josephus said.

"You're welcome," Titus replied. "What are brothers for? Right?"

"Right."

Some hundred thousand Judeans left alive in the city were rounded up and taken as slaves, happy to be under Roman protection versus being slaughtered on sight, which was more than ten times their kith's fate. Little did the new Judean slaves know that they would be luckier to end up in the mines of Egypt than sold into the Colosseum or other theaters as bait for the wild beasts and gladiators. The slaves were harshly cared for—many thousands died in Roman captivity before ever being delivered to an owner.

## Jerusalem is Destroyed

■ ■ ■

**EARLIER THAT** same morning, while Titus consulted his advisors, Roman soldiers on the Temple Mount were up to no good. Idleness always being one of Roman soldiers' greatest weaknesses, it often caused disorderly drinking and gaming.

One soldier, acting like an ignorant teenage child, began playing with the embers that were still red and white-hot from the smoldering Temple gates.

The prank was simple—scoop up a hot coal from the fire site in a wooden cup and place it on the crotch of a sleeping soldier.

This Roman went so far as to even lift the skirt of another soldier's loin covering to exact a more forthcoming hilarity.

As the soldier placed the reddish ember on a sleeping Roman's bare genitals, a shriek pierced all the ears on the Temple Mount.

"Ahh! Ahh! What the Hades? Ahh!" the Roman screamed out, swatting the embers off his male accessories.

A gang of spectators laughed at the burnt Roman's expense—the Roman soldier responsible laughed the hardest.

"Who the shit did this? Was it you?" the victimized Roman accused the man that had assaulted him.

The perpetrator began to run—the enraged Roman began to chase.

"You want to play with fire, you lowly tiro!" the mad legionnaire screamed.

The assaulter kept laughing so hard it nearly impeded his foot escape from the man he had violated.

The wronged Roman saw the still-smoldering gates as he chased his assailant. Making a small detour, he ran for the reddish embers and, using his leather sling shot, he began firing hot projectiles at the fleeing perpetrator.

The tiro running away had caught a case of the hiccups, his

laughter was so intense. His running speed was reduced to a slow jog as his laughter intermixed with spasms of his diaphragm.

The retaliating legionnaire picked up another ember with his sling. The piece of glowing coal was attached to a small piece of gold from the melted gates, creating enough weight to hurl the ember over a hundred yards.

His shot missed—the metal ember went flying way past the tiro, still laughing about his abominable prank. So far did the weight of the gold carry the burning ember—the projectile flew straight in through a window on the second floor of the Temple. The gold metal shard hit a drape and stuck in it with the glowing ember touching the fabric. The drape ignited, and fire quickly spread throughout the Temple.

The fire Titus was certain to order within hours or even minutes erupted on its own, seemingly by the hand of God.

The Temple fire continued to roar with increasing intensity. Cries of men burning inside the Temple could be heard across the Temple Mount. Men loyal to John and Simon started to flee the Temple by opening the locked solid-gold front doors rather than burn alive. A wall of Romans fifty men deep and a hundred across covered the entrance to the Temple. Every Judean who tried to escape the fire ran directly into the spears and swords of six thousand Romans of the Fifteenth Legion, eager to earn their glory in the war.

The fire roared. The intensity reached a level that the Judeans hiding behind the great doors, many covered in flames, ran chaotically out of the burning Temple right into the steel of the waiting Romans. A pile of burning and smoking bodies grew outside the great Temple doors.

With the doors ajar, the Romans breached the Temple—everyone was slain. Men, children, the elderly, priests, women, and even a few babies were cut to pieces.

In this mad scene, a blanket of dancing flames covered the ceiling of the Temple above while a six-inch-deep pool of blood covered the white marble floor of the Temple below.

Bodies lined the ground like they were an entire school of dead fish floating belly up in a lake of blood. Judean corpses lay burnt, dead, and stacked layer upon layer as people raced to cram into the yet-unburnt sections of the Temple.

*  *  *

**BY THE** time Titus was alerted to the Temple burning, it was already half up in flames. He ran out to the Temple and gave orders to put out the fire, but his men were in such a raucous, drunken state of celebration at the sight of the Hebrew Temple ablaze, no one heard him, though he was clearly shouting orders.

"Put the damn fire out!" Titus commanded.

The only response he heard was laughter.

"What the hell is wrong with all the men?" Titus asked.

"They're all drunk on vino and victory," Frachas replied.

Titus nodded in acceptance and smiled—he finally realized, at that moment, the war was over.

Seeing his men mostly drunk, unable to take orders, and celebrating what appeared to be the end of the war, he could not be angry. After all, Titus had already resolved to burn the Temple to the ground earlier in the day. He could relax now that the final Judean rebels were turning to ash within their holy Temple.

Titus and his men sat comfortably, watching and basking in a true Roman victory. The horrid screams of the last Judeans cooking alive brought laughter from the deepest part of their Roman hearts.

"Captain!" Titus yelled to a captain he spotted drinking with some centurions.

# The Temple is Destroyed

"Yes, general, sir!" the captain answered, instantly scared sober by attention from the son of Caesar.

"Tell me one gods-damned thing!" Titus shouted. "Why don't I have a goblet in my hand?" Titus' stoic scowl turned into a smiling prank. "Gotcha."

The captain, relieved that his general was not genuinely angry, began laughing at Titus' good humor and quickly found a spare vessel for Titus' wine.

"Congratulations, General Titus!" the captain said. "You've beaten the Judeans!"

"We've all beaten the Judeans, soldier!" Titus replied, and they clinked goblets together before drinking.

The Romans continued to guzzle wine while the Temple exhaled flames and a plume of smoke.

Fraternal Roman songs broke out and men danced drunkenly with glee.

*We are Romans, we are Romans!*
*Today we beat you, today we eat you!*
*We are Romans!*

*We are Romans, we are Romans!*
*Now you serve us, now you service us!*
*We are Romans!*

*We are Romans, we are Romans!*
*We bed your wives, tomorrow night it's your brides!*
*We are Romans!*

*We are Romans, we are Romans!*
*Now we take your gold, while we pillage and scold!*
*We are Romans!*

*We are Romans, we are Romans!*
*We'll conquer on, long after you're dead and gone!*
*We are Romans!*

■ ■ ■

**SIMON, JOHN,** Sadius, and Rabinus had quietly made their way underground in hope of a subterranean escape. Their success depended on King Solomon's tunnels. Luck was not on their side. They were trapped by a collapsed and impassable tunnel on one side and the Romans on the other. Their only advantage was time. The Romans would not pursue them until the Temple fire had been quenched. Simon, John, and the others waited underground, hoping the Romans would not be able to find them.

"God seems to have ordained our capture," Simon said, defeated by their circumstances. "Perhaps we could go back and try a different route?"

"This is the only route, unless you want to fight the entire Roman army!" John proclaimed.

"That's right," Sadius coolly interjected. "We're fucked."

■ ■ ■

**JOSEPHUS STOOD** on the Temple Mount watching the Temple burn to the ground. Frachas stood beside him.

"It was always going to come to this, you know," a drunken Frachas said, sipping on a cup of wine, then offering Josephus a sip, trying to unburden him.

Josephus of course refused the drink.

"I was shown it would come to this long ago, but that doesn't make it any easier," Josephus replied. "The Judeans are all dead—the Temple and the city are destroyed."

471

"The Judeans are not all dead. You are alive, and there are some Judeans left in the countryside—Titus has pardoned a hundred thousand." Frachas tried to lift Josephus' spirits.

Josephus grabbed Frachas by the collar with both hands and headbutted him, causing the wine goblet to fly out of Frachas' hand.

"Look, you ignorant fool! What do you see? What do you see everywhere? Dead Judeans!" Josephus screamed at the top of his lungs and then stormed off, cursing Frachas under his breath.

A stunned Frachas did not dare fight back. From his vantage, he could see an incomprehensible number of corpses—he had no way to tell how many. At that moment, Frachas finally understood a small part of Josephus' anguish.

- - -

IN A few days' time, the fire on the Temple Mount was fully extinguished by the Romans, but mostly it had burned itself out.

Titus was now keen on his trophies.

"I want the big gold candelabra taken back to Rome," Titus instructed Frachas, who was charged with assessing and re-appropriating the riches of the Temple.

"Yes, general," Frachas acknowledged and began taking notes.

"I want the coin and gems too."

"Of course, general," Frachas once again affirmed.

"I'm going to show my father more gold than he's ever seen," Titus declared.

"Consider it done, my lord," Frachas obsequiously replied.

Now a caravan of all things gold began trailing out of the still-smoldering Temple. The Romans had not even bothered to bury their own fallen, and of course not the Judean dead.

Domitian wandered around inside the Temple, taking any artifact he thought might be of value. Then he came upon a secret chamber of sacred Torah scrolls. These scrolls had so far been saved from the fire—they were written during the diaspora of Babylon—over six hundred years prior.

"Ahhhhhhhhhh!" Domitian moaned as he emptied his bladder all over the holy scriptures. "I just wanted to make sure the fire doesn't spread any further," he facetiously explained to the regular soldiers watching his defilement.

Still urinating, Domitian took his hip flask of wine and drank. "Come, join in, boys!" He beckoned to them.

Roman soldiers now stood in a line, all wetting the parchments of animal skins centuries old, laughing and passing around Domitian's flask.

Josephus, wandering through the Temple trying to salvage as much as possible, happened upon Domitian in the act of desecrating the Torah scrolls.

"What in God's name are you doing?" Josephus yelled. "Stop it, this moment!"

At the sight of Domitian and regular soldiers violating the sacred scrolls, a part of Josephus snapped—he threw a closed fist into Domitian's jaw.

Domitian fell to the ground.

"Seize him!" a stunned Domitian commanded his soldiers.

Josephus stood immobilized in Domitian's custody, four soldiers holding his person. Domitian took out his dagger.

"I could kill you where you stand—my only consequence would be an earful from my brother and father," he threatened.

"You would kill your brother for chastising you justly?"

"No! No! No!" Domitian shouted. "You are not my brother. You are a Hebrew and will always be a Hebrew! Titus, my father, the world may call you Flavius, but we share no blood and never will."

Domitian held his bejeweled golden dagger inches from Josephus' face.

"Pretty, isn't it," Domitian said.

"Very," Josephus replied.

"One thing I've learned throughout my life is that pretty things cause pain."

With a flick of his wrist, Domitian cut a small slice through the upper lobe of Josephus' ear, spilling blood down the side of his face.

"It'd be best our paths don't continue to cross, for the sake of your health. I do so care for your well-being, Hebrew," Domitian warned sarcastically and nodded to have Josephus released. "Oh, and if my brother asks about your ear, you'd best mention it was a grooming accident."

*  *  *

**AFTER SEVERAL** days of searching with dogs and a few Judean informants, the Romans stumbled upon Simon and John hiding in their small, dead-end tunnel.

"We know you're in there, Judeans!" one centurion yelled from beyond a large rock that Simon and John had moved in front of their tunnel passage to conceal and protect themselves.

"I want to surrender!" John yelled out. "It is John of Gischala! So long as Titus grants me life and food, I will surrender this instant!"

"Shut up, you delirious fool!" Simon yelled at John. "You haven't eaten in a week and you can't think straight."

"You said you are John of Gischala?" the Roman asked.

"Yes!" John joyously replied. "And Simon bar Giora is also here with me!"

"I said shut up, you fool!" Simon furiously yelled and then punched John in the face.

The two men began to pathetically fight each other, falling onto the mud-covered ground. Sadius, still loyal to John but realizing the game was over, simply sat back and watched the two kick, punch, scratch, bite, and claw at each other for a few moments while contemplating his life.

The Romans began to move the rock protecting the entrance, and Sadius grabbed his dagger. With one clean slice, he opened his carotid artery and collapsed among spurts of blood. Rabinus, seeing Sadius keel over from suicide, took Sadius' dagger and sliced his own carotid open as well.

After some effort, the Romans removed the large rock barricading the tunnel and took John and Simon alive—first having to drag them apart from fighting each other in the mud.

When Simon was forcefully escorted away, he was dressed in a white frock with a purple cloak. He continued to swear he was anyone other than himself, including King Agrippa—John kept contradicting Simon all the while, begging for food and life assurances.

Titus was informed of the capture of both men, who were put on the first outbound vessel and delivered to Rome for spectacle justice.

*  *  *

**OVER THE** next week, every last Judean found alive was put into a holding pen outside the city near Titus' main fortress. There were over one hundred thousand men, women, and children in Roman bondage. But there were over one million Israelites dead from the war.

"It is time to return to Rome—we stop at Caesarea and then sail home," Titus proclaimed. "Our celebration and our prize await us, Josephus. Maybe you'll even find a new woman?"

"I can't wait to meet my third ex-wife," Josephus joked sourly.

"Lighten up, Josephus. We're victorious. *You're* victorious!" Titus declared.

"Then why don't I feel victorious?" Josephus questioned.

"Josephus, I have only ever been for Rome, and even I don't feel completely victorious. War has an awful price. We have seen the horror of horrors—neither side can plead innocence. But we are men, and this is life, and we must go on. Come, our journey is not yet over. I'm going to be Caesar one day, or so a little bird told me," Titus said, giving Josephus a coy smile and a wink.

"You're not going to Masada?" Josephus asked.

"If a thousand crazy Hebrews want to hold out against Rome in Herod's greatest fortress, I'll let someone else build the ramp. This war, as far as Rome is concerned, is over," Titus said, embracing Josephus. "We have won."

*  *  *

**ROME'S GREAT** military machine began to move back towards the coast. Nothing was left of Jerusalem except small fires, rotted black corpses, bones, and ash. The Romans had been busy completely demolishing every last stone on the Temple Mount per Titus' orders. Only part of the retaining wall on the western side of the Temple remained as proof of its existence.

A Roman military train spanning some five miles in length slowly crept towards the Mediterranean Sea. At its very front rode Titus, Josephus, Frachas, Domitian, Tiberius Alexander, Cestius, and other high-ranking officers. Behind them traveled the lion's

476

share of the Roman soldiers. Then came the servants, and directly behind them, a hundred thousand Judeans in bondage.

The Tenth patrolled the rear, ensuring the slaves remained obedient. Many Judeans were slain en route—the Romans did not help those wounded, and if a Judean received a beating that broke a leg or hip and thus became unable to walk, the Romans would obligatorily cut the Judean down dead and leave the corpse to the desert.

As Titus entered Caesarea at the head of the Roman caravan, the city burst alive in a joyous celebration. Caesarea was the most Roman city in Judea. It was the one place in the Holy Land that never wavered in its allegiance to Rome.

Calm had finally washed over Titus. His great work was complete, and it was now time to enjoy himself. After all, he himself could have been slain multiple times during the campaign. He resigned himself to a week of drunkenness and debauchery.

"Fill it up to the top!" Titus jovially ordered the boy servant waiting on his wine. "Tomorrow night is my brother's birthday party—much wine is required to mentally prepare for such an event."

Josephus had spent the last week mourning for the dead and was in no mood to celebrate. Rome may have won the war, but Josephus saw himself as a failure. His words could not save the Judeans, the city, or the Temple. The guilt that lay on his shoulders was palpable to everyone that spoke to him.

All of Josephus' Roman friends shied away from him in the days following the destruction of the Temple, which was fine with Josephus, who wanted no part in Rome's postwar festivities. But Josephus never thought a birthday celebration would escalate into the bedlam that became Domitian's party.

# Chapter 34:

# Domitian's Birthday Party

**IT WAS** an early autumn morning in 70 A.D. when seemingly the entire Roman army, laid over in Caesarea for the voyage home, found itself occupied with pre-homecoming celebration preparations.

Domitian was turning eighteen, and as a son of Caesar coming into his own manhood, he demanded great festivities in his honor to commemorate the Roman victory over the Judeans. The fact that Domitian was barely a footnote in the war record caused him to overcompensate in his celebration's grandiosity.

"I want a cask of wine and a concubine for every man!" Domitian ordered Frachas, who was charged with making the celebratory arrangements.

"Of course, my lord," Frachas acknowledged.

"Use some of the Judeaness captives—they don't cost us anything. I also want a hog for every company. I want gold and silver coins at my disposal to shower upon the men. Have some young Judean slaves—both boys and girls, carrying buckets of coins at my beck and call."

Through it all, Frachas scribbled on a wax tablet to record Domitian's every demand.

"And I want games! I want to see the Judeans kill one another over a piece of meat, then I want to see the beasts of Judea eat the Judean victors!"

"I don't think they will take up arms against one another, my lord," Frachas said, expressing his concern over the feasibility of Domitian's orders.

"Burn a few hundred Judeans alive if they won't fight one another. Watch the rest take up swords against the others directly."

Frachas began visibly shaking, unable to write legibly as he was physically sickened by Domitian's party requests. Frachas was no stranger to killing, or even killing Judeans—but he knew there was something very wrong with Domitian's party demands.

"My lord, I don't know if General Titus will approve of all these requests," Frachas opined.

Domitian's smile instantly disappeared—he unconsciously pulled his dagger and placed it firmly against Frachas' neck, drawing a line of blood.

"Were you told to tell my brother about this? Do you forget who is the Flavius and who is the soldier? Shall my blade remind you?" Domitian screamed.

"I serve thee, Lord Flavius," Frachas submitted.

Domitian's rage vanished as fast as it had onset. A smile returned to his face—he pulled the blade back from Frachas' throat.

"That's all I wanted to hear," Domitian said. "If I find my celebration lacking in the least, I will also be celebrating your death."

He then walked away from Frachas whistling a Roman war chant.

Frachas, deeply shocked, nearly collapsed after Domitian was out of sight, having forgotten to breathe for nearly a full minute.

Then Josephus, making his way to see about the welfare of the hundred thousand Judeans in captivity, approached Frachas.

"Tribune, how are my people today? Are they receiving food and water? Medical attention?"

"Shut your stupid mouth, you dirty scheming Judean!" Frachas yelled and ran to seek solace in his private quarters.

"What the hell has gotten into him?" Josephus said out loud to himself.

*   *   *

**THE PARTY** preparations were being set.

The regular soldiers, unaware of Domitian's narcissistic and gore-laden lusts, were cheerfully relaxed, eagerly awaiting the beginning of their long-awaited celebration.

Titus sat in the governor's mansion engrossed in paperwork when Josephus came to talk to him.

"Greetings, brother," Josephus said softly, trying not to disrespectfully interrupt Titus at work.

"Greetings, Josephus. What can I do for you today?"

"Is there something amiss, brother?" Josephus asked.

"Amiss? Why? What could you possibly mean? The war is won! Before the sun sets, the most joyous festival in years is set to begin!"

"I realize all that, but I merely asked Frachas an innocuous question and he snapped as if he was accused of premeditated murder! He's never been one to hide his feelings, though he may not be able to verbalize them."

"Gossip, Josephus?" Titus replied.

"I'm not gossiping. I'm merely concerned that the man tasked with setting up this celebration seems to have gone mad."

"Frachas has never cared for my brother. I don't blame him for being frustrated by attempting to meet Domitian's demands."

"Perhaps the nature of the demands is the problem?" Josephus suggested.

"What do you want from me, Josephus? Are you asking me to cancel my brother's eighteenth birthday party which also commemorates our glory? That is not going to happen," an increasingly agitated Titus said.

"That's not what I'm saying, Titus. I'm merely concerned Domitian is up to something," Josephus rebutted.

"Of course he's up to something. It's Domitian! It's his birthday, and he wants the grandest party of all time—I'm sure he has directly or indirectly let Frachas know that his dissatisfaction or approval would greatly affect Frachas' station. He might have even threatened Frachas' life. You know how Domitian is," Titus said.

"Would you tell your brother that this party is just that, a party? I fear he may slaughter some of my people for a sick spectacle."

"That's enough!" Titus yelled and then banged on his desk. "Forgive me. I didn't mean to explode. Domitian knows the Judeans are my father's property, and they are to be presented to my father as such. Josephus, have some wine, relax, maybe even try to enjoy yourself tonight."

"Will you tell your brother there are to be no executions tonight, or is that request too much to ask of you?" Josephus pressed the issue.

Titus took a deep breath and acknowledged the probability that Domitian would use the Judean captives for his own demented fantasies.

"I will tell him no executions. Is there anything else?" Titus asked.

"No, and thank you," Josephus said, partially bowing his head with respect. "I'll see you at the party."

Josephus began to exit Titus' office.

"Wait!" Titus boomed out.

Josephus stopped, frozen—a terror coursed through his body. This was the first time Josephus had ever been afraid of Titus. The thought of Titus calling Josephus a traitor for wanting to help the Judeans immediately crossed his mind. Could Titus turn on his own adopted brother even though the war was over and won?

"Yes, brother?" Josephus submitted humbly, readying himself for anything from being verbally chided to being incarcerated and condemned.

"Do I not receive a familial embrace?" Titus said, holding out his arms for Josephus.

"Of course, my brother," Josephus replied.

After holding each other for a moment, they looked each other contentedly—Josephus exited.

Titus took out a scroll and began to write.

"Centurion! I have a message to be delivered to Domitian—post-haste!"

◾ ◾ ◾

**"GENERAL TITUS** requests your presence, my lord," the centurion said to Domitian and presented him a scroll sealed with Titus' stamp.

"What now?" Domitian asked. "I don't have time for scrolls. Tell Titus I'm busy setting up my party."

"General Titus expected you to say as much and informed me to tell you that if you do not see him before the sunset, there will be no party," the officer said as humbly as a messenger could.

This grabbed Domitian's attention—he quickly snatched the scroll out of the officer's hand. He broke its seal and then read the note.

"I'll see my brother now," Domitian replied.

◾ ◾ ◾

**"AH, GOOD!** Domitian has come," Titus said, welcoming his young brother into his office. "I need a few minutes with my brother—alone."

All the officers, counselors, and servants immediately exited. Titus, dressed in a toga, anticipating the night's festivities, opened his arms and greeted his brother with a big smile.

"Is this summons necessary, brother?" Domitian waved the scroll, getting directly to the point. "Am I under arrest?"

"Ha! Always the jokester. Sit and drink with me for a moment."

"Brother, this is really not the best time. The festivities begin in less than an hour," Domitian complained.

"Sit!" Titus said sternly but without yelling.

Domitian huffed but complied.

"What is it, brother?" Domitian asked.

"Tonight is to be a great celebration. It will be remembered for countless Roman generations. It is to be a happy event. I want you to tell me you are not going to execute any of the prisoners. They are property of my father."

"Don't you mean our father?" Domitian shot back.

"Yes, of course, our father," Titus replied.

"Your man Frachas has been telling you lies, hasn't he?" Domitian accused.

"Frachas and I have not said more than a greeting word to each other in several days. He is not to be touched, or you will feel his pain doubled. Understood?"

No reply came forth.

"Understood?" Titus shouted.

"Yes," Domitian answered.

"Now tell me you will not execute any of the Judeans," Titus demanded.

Domitian, flustered, not knowing how Titus came to hear of his intentions, spoke flippantly. "No executions. Are you happy?"

"Quite. Have a great party. That's all," Titus said. "You may go now."

Nodding his head, Domitian jumped up from his seat and exited Titus' office without so much as a friendly parting word or gesture.

He immediately traveled directly to Frachas to defecate his displeasure over Titus' fraternal oversight.

"You ratted me out to my brother, your best friend, you little worm—didn't you?" Domitian accused Frachas.

"I did nothing of the sort, my lord. I swear it!" Frachas immediately denied the claim while backpedaling on his feet, expecting Domitian to attempt to physically assault him.

"Of course you didn't say anything," Domitian sarcastically answered. "Titus had a dream from the Hebrew God that told him of my plans! If you weren't his childhood friend, I'd have you on the cross already!"

"Please, my lord!" Frachas begged while pressed up against a wall. "I am telling the truth!"

"You'd be more useful as fodder for the beasts than a tribune," Domitian told Frachas. "Do not burn any of the Judeans alive. But promise those who choose to fight voluntarily against one another grub, gold, gems, and girls. And promise death by crucifixion to those who decline."

"Yes, my lord," Frachas acquiesced most pathetically.

"See you at the festivities," Domitian said and abruptly stormed off to his next destination.

*■ ■ ■*

**THE CRISP** cracks of the snare drum, the deep thuds of the bass, and the call of the horns set the mood for Domitian's birthday party.

The familiar savory smells of roasted pig joined forces with burning incense and hot cakes. But the scent which intoxicated the Roman regulars most was that of young but ripened female Judeans—a few hundred of whom had been bathed in luxurious oils and lotions, and dressed in the finest linens Caesarea could find for them. These girls were to be for the soldiers. Domitian knew the deep desires of Romans could not be satisfied with gold alone.

Adjacent to the amphitheater was the dining hall where hundreds of tables sat, all fully stocked with wine and bread. Legions of men flocked about, then sat with their individual companies.

Huge spits of cooked meat were presented, and the feasting began. A Roman could only thoroughly enjoy sport and shows after the stomach was fully satisfied. Tonight, 'excess' was the mantra. Of all the tens of thousands of Roman soldiers drinking and gorging themselves on the endless supply of food—more than a few hundred indulged in their fondness for vomitoriums. Some soldiers partook in the practice right in the middle of the assembled dinner, creating the foulest stench, accompanied by drunken laughter.

After an hour of the soldiers forcing wine and meat down their throats, the spectacle part of the celebration was set to begin. The Romans rose from their eating tables and filtered into the amphitheater.

The assembled officers and geriatric bureaucrats of Caesarea had the choicest of seats—behind them sat the regular Roman forces.

"Let the festivities begin!" Domitian shouted from the center stage of the Herodian theater, clinging onto his gold goblet, spilling wine with his every gesture.

Upon hearing Domitian's pronouncement, all of the Romans assembled rose and gave a hailing cheer.

He grabbed a young Judean slave holding a bucket of coins, reached his hand into the bucket, and rained down money on the soldiers. Men leaped into the air, spilling their beverages in a mad dash to grab each gold piece.

"Don't fight. There's enough Judean gold for every Roman!" Domitian preached while sending handfuls of silver and gold pieces to entire seating sections of the amphitheater.

The regular Roman soldiers went wild for Domitian's showmanship.

Next, Domitian welcomed a female dance company to the stage—he further helped himself to their breasts and buttocks with his open hand, to the hoots and hollers of the watching soldiers.

The Romans laughed with joy and slung insults demonstrating their masculinity at the dancers—the dancing had not even started yet.

Titus sat in the first row, front and center, with a golden table before him. Josephus and Frachas sat next to him on opposite sides.

"Your brother certainly has a way with women." Josephus gently voiced his displeasure.

"Don't I know it," Titus muttered. "Just drink your wine and smile. It will be over soon enough."

"Yes, of course," Josephus replied.

Titus was already drinking his fill, attempting to numb himself, not caring to remember Domitian's wantonness this night. But Domitian was a Flavius, and thus Titus was bound to condone all his misdeeds—his homecoming would not be celebrated if he brought Domitian back in chains or a box.

Amid the dance routine, Titus' eye was caught by the same buxom girl who had seduced him in Caesarea after the Roman victory at Jotapata some years past. Josephus saw Titus give the dancer that look that a man gives a woman when he desires her flesh.

The dancing finished.

A mock play with a dozen dwarfs began. Half were dressed in Roman uniforms; the other half donned the black 'Sicarii' sheets. Then the 'Siege of Jerusalem' ensued with the dwarfs pretending to kill one another, ripping off fake limbs, and using sausage links to pretend to disembowel their 'enemies.' The dwarfs even faux-crucified themselves on crosses appropriately sized for the short actors—they feigned mortal wailing as they were being falsely nailed to the wooden beams, all for the assembly's entertainment.

"Where is the damn wine steward?" Titus angrily griped as the evening went on.

"I'll see about it," Frachas said and began to rise from his seat.

"No," Titus barked. "I'll go find the steward myself."

Titus' insistence on finding the wine was actually an excuse to remove himself from Domitian's party, not because he was having a poor time, but because he wanted to see about his dancing female friend.

Not a minute after Titus' exit, Domitian's hand came to rest uncomfortably on Frachas' shoulder.

"Where is my Judean war?" Domitian asked with a sinister rage.

"I'm sorry, my lord. I don't understand," Frachas answered.

Domitian slapped Frachas across the face.

"Come, come, you toad. The dancing and playing are over—now it's time for my Judean war! Where are the men that have volunteered for battle?"

"About that, my lord, I thought General Titus prohibited executions tonight?" Frachas humbly countered.

"Men voluntarily fighting is not an execution, you mindless stooge! Now, if I don't see the Judeans fighting one another, I'll see you fighting all of them! Off you go—wait! Mention one word to my brother, and I'll be sure your death comes only after you beg for it."

Frachas jumped out of his chair and made his way to the holding pen of Judean captives.

"Josephus, I'm sure you are going to particularly enjoy the next round of festivities," Domitian said with an evil grin.

"I think I'll pass, my lord," Josephus answered and attempted to stand, but Domitian's bodyguard pushed him back into his seat.

"No, no, no. You are going to enjoy this, every moment of it," said Domitian.

He then helped himself to Titus' chair.

"Your brother is going to be back soon, and even you must answer to him," Josephus said.

Domitian slapped Josephus across the face.

"Do you want another one?"

"No, my lord," Josephus said.

"Then keep your crafty Judean mouth shut!"

*  *  *

"**HERE THEY** come!" Domitian boasted, seeing two columns of five hundred Judean captives each hustle towards the stage. "My Roman brothers," a now-fully-inebriated Domitian shouted, throwing yet more coins into the audience, "tonight we commemorate the victory over the Judean dogs with a reenactment of the Judean war!"

Drunken cheers erupted from the soldiers, now delightfully delirious with every effort Domitian made to please them.

A line of five hundred Judeans wearing only red armbands and red loincloths represented the Romans—they stood to the left side of the great amphitheater. An equal Judean force with black armbands and loincloths stood on the right side of the stage, representing the Judeans. A company of Roman soldiers quickly distributed all sorts of handheld weapons of war, equally to both sides.

Drums beat at an increasing pace, and every soldier in attendance reveled in the coming savagery that was uniquely Roman.

"Let the war begin!" Domitian shouted.

He looked behind him, and the Judeans on both sides remained standing still, paralyzed with fear.

"I said fight!" Domitian screamed. He grabbed a spear from a soldier standing next to him and javelined a random Judean wearing a black armband. "Fight, or I will spear you next!" he threatened the prisoner beside the Judean he had just slain.

The Judeans began to destroy one another.

Domitian laughed and gulped his wine. Josephus, sitting as a prisoner in his seat, closed his eyes and cried at the screams of his fellow Judeans dying for Domitian's amusement.

"I'm going to be sick. Let go of me!" Josephus yelled at Domitian's bodyguard, who was still forcing Josephus to stay in his seat.

"You can go when my lord Domitian says you can go!"

That same moment, Josephus unloaded his feast into the bodyguard's face, blinding him with bile.

Josephus, now released, hurried off to find Titus.

"General Titus! General Titus! Where are you?" he screamed as he searched the most obvious places he thought Titus might have disappeared to, first checking the wine station.

Josephus suddenly saw a vision flash through his mind of Titus in his bed with the buxom dancer. Of course, Titus was mid-coitus. The amphitheater was a small hike from Titus' mansion, and a vomit-covered Josephus moved his feet as fast as they would permit him to.

"Halt!" a bodyguard said, protecting the entrance to Titus' mansion.

Josephus revealed his jeweled family ring and was waved ahead.

"Titus! Titus! Titus!" Josephus called out with all his lung capacity.

"What the hell?" Titus muttered, his head between his woman's bosoms. "This better be good or I might teach the messenger a lesson about privacy."

Josephus continued wailing, "Titus!"

"Yes, yes! I'm here. What the Hades is going on?" Titus responded, one hand holding onto a sword, the other hand attempting to clothe himself awkwardly.

"Domitian is murdering hundreds, thousands, maybe every last Judean taken captive!" Josephus screamed.

"Damn it! Shit! I'm on my way, brother!"

*  *  *

**BY THE** time Josephus and Titus had returned to the amphitheater, Domitian had been busy coordinating the evolution of his spectacle. All one thousand Hebrews involved in the reenactment of the Judean war had been slaughtered. The 'Romans' won the battle, and then Domitian released wild beasts on the 'victors.' Domitian saw his men enjoying the slaughter at the hands of the beasts even more than the mock war. He decided to maul another thousand unfortunate Hebrew captives to death.

Making the Judeans kill one another in simulated battle and then setting the wild animals of Africa on others *still* was not quite enough for Domitian. He further decided to take another five hundred Judeans and put them to the fire: alive!

It was too time-consuming to tie each prisoner to a spit. Domitian had his soldiers slice the Judeans' Achilles tendons, hobbling them but not killing them. Then a great fire was built around the mass of immobilized captives, thrown on top of each other in a massive pile.

Titus and Josephus looked upon the amphitheater, now a giant funeral pyre. The screams of the dying crackled and popped until finally only the smell of their flesh lingered in the air.

At the sight of his fellow Judeans aflame, Josephus rent his clothes, grabbed the sandy Caesarean dirt, and rubbed it uncontrollably over his face as he himself screamed like a writhing animal.

Titus, watching the tens of thousands of Romans cheer on Domitian and the abominable spectacle, began to cry. It was one of the few times he shed a public tear in his entire life.

Yelling at a staff officer, Titus said, "Get Josephus out of here! Get him a drink and watch him sleep this night. If he hurts himself, I will hurt you doubly! Now take him away!"

Josephus remained sobbing uncontrollably on the ground as a mother wails over the death of a newborn babe.

"Josephus, you must go. I'll take care of Domitian!"

"Take care of him? Like you promised you would earlier today? You pathetic wretch! I should have never saved you from the Greeks!"

Josephus approached Titus, rage emanating from his eyes. A staff officer, fearing for Titus' safety, took a baton and struck Josephus across the face, knocking him unconscious.

"Damn it all to hell! Did I tell you to touch my brother?" Titus screamed at the staff officer. Before he realized what had become of his rage, Titus was pulling his gladius from the officer's chest, unable to remember pushing it in.

▰ ▰ ▰

**THE NEXT** days were muted. Guilt, rage, and depression all lingered over Titus and Josephus. They saw each other but did little more than acknowledge each other's presence.

The Romans were busy with preparations for their homecoming to the capital.

Hour after hour, the Romans packed their trophies into their fleet of vessels. The surviving Judeans, now slaves, were whisked into cramped stalls, chained to one another in the bellies of the ships. The Roman soldiers took every opportunity to dehumanize the captives.

The Judean females were casually raped. The Judean men were obligatorily beaten. Only leftover scraps of Roman meals were given for food. Many died from dehydration as water was usually dispensed only once daily, if at all.

Titus and Josephus stood atop the Roman flagship, the *Little Caesar*, as the ships began to set sail back from whence they came.

"Do we understand each other, brother?" Titus asked Josephus.

"I don't know. I will need time, a long time to heal. But we are still brothers."

# Chapter 35:

# The Return to Rome

**POOR SAILING** weather kept the Roman army in Caesarea for the rest of the season. By the time the army returned to the capital across the Mediterranean the following year in 71 A.D., Vespasian had been working for several months on the festivities, celebrations, feasts, and spectacles to commemorate the greatest victory in modern Roman history.

For Titus' parade, every ornament was hung up. Everyone wore their finest uniforms with each medal and pip polished.

The sky rained white and red rose petals—women and girls stood on the city balconies and tossed entire baskets of the stuff. Inches of petals accumulated on the ground before being crushed under the feet of the next marching column.

Legion after legion of Roman soldiers marched in formation through the main Roman route before Vespasian, sitting on his golden dais at the top of red carpeted marble steps.

The trumpeters continued their military tunes unendingly as the procession of troops, captives, and booty required the entire first half of the day.

Titus, Josephus, Frachas, Tiberius Alexander, Cestius, and Domitian rode next to each other in golden chariots drawn by magnificent white Arabian steeds. The greatest honor went probably to Frachas who, though a tribune, was the lowest-ranking soldier among them—Josephus being a non-combatant.

Vespasian stood up from his throne as the company headed by his sons approached. Upon seeing Vespasian rise, Titus halted the progression of the horses.

Vespasian lifted his arms to silence his subjects, then began to speak. "Three cheers for Flavius Titus!"

"Titus! Titus! Titus!" the citizens of Rome cheered.

It was the greatest moment of Titus' life, and he was not yet Caesar.

"And three cheers for Flavius Josephus!" Vespasian said to Josephus' great astonishment.

Before Josephus could show pride or shame, all of Rome was sending their acclamation his way.

"Josephus! Josephus! Josephus!" the Romans chanted.

His exploits were well known throughout the empire, from originally facing Vespasian in battle at Jotapata to saving Titus' life (and Vespasian's technically, though in a much different manner) to conquering the Colosseum and finally coming home from war, victorious with Rome.

Josephus raised his right arm in acknowledgement to Vespasian. There was no smile on his face, nor was there a frown.

The hundreds of thousands of Romans in attendance went mad. For a few moments, there was such vocal ecstasy that not a person at the parade could understand a single word from the closest person next to them. Everything was screams and cries of joy.

The terrible civil war and 'Year of the Four Emperors' was over. Now a great victory over the Judeans had bolstered their spirits. The Roman citizens and soldiers felt the deep peace one feels in those few special moments during a lifetime when everything seems to be going right.

The parade continued with the presentation of the Judean scoundrels. Cheers intermixed with jeers at the criminals being hauled naked in chains through the streets of Rome. Simon and

Victory Parade in Rome

John were the captives of honor, and special attention was paid to each of them.

After enduring being pelted with withered cabbages, rotten eggs, and feces on his walk of shame, Simon bar Giora received the lighter sentence of being thrown off the Tarpeian Rock. The height of the fall being only eighty feet, some men did not die instantly, but rumor has it that on impact, Simon's head hit the rock directly, exploding like a watermelon being dropped.

After John's equally public and degrading shaming, he was judged more harshly and sentenced to life in Roman captivity. This meant he received minimal care, only enough to prevent him from dying. Titus had John starved so that he went from his large husky frame to a frail old pauper in a year's time. The best Roman jailors trained in the harshest treatment were assigned to John. He was beaten and starved for food every remaining day of his life. The guards were given a fat bonus for every year he stayed alive and in discomfort. Rumor is he lived another half-life and had a finger or toe taken on every anniversary of his imprisonment.

■ ■ ■

**NOW THAT** the day's spectacle parade was over, the great celebratory feast at the emperor's palace began. Titus, Frachas, Josephus, Tiberius Alexander, Cestius, Domitian, and even Vespasian got drunk on hard Roman spirits, double-distilled. Songs were sung. Courtesans danced, and men fell asleep in their seats as they should at a good party.

Frachas made a particular ass of himself by having sex with two boys inside the palace. Luckily for Frachas, Vespasian was so drunk and cheerful about the future of Rome, if he did take notice of Frachas that night, he looked the other way and entirely forgot about it.

As best friend to Titus, Frachas enjoyed a somewhat undeserved increase in status and station over the years that followed. He served Vespasian and Titus faithfully for the rest of their lives. After Titus' passing, Frachas all but faded from Roman society, being disliked by Domitian his entire life. He was content to live out his days consumed by hedonism, drinking many of his waking hours away with male prostitutes less than half his age. He mounted his gladius from his days fighting in Judea on the mantle of his state-provided mansion, never to be used again.

Alcohol and busty women always got the virile Titus in a lustful mood. Sexual tension mounting and sufficiently inebriated, Titus took a busty courtesan to his bed—he could never resist a beautiful full bosom.

In the years to come, he would continue as his father's right hand. In less than a decade, Titus would rise to Caesar after Vespasian's peaceful passing—though he would only serve two years before his own demise from common illness, setting the stage for Domitian's tyrannical reign. Titus would be remembered for the glorious time of stability and prosperity during the Flavian Dynasty.

Still enjoying the after-party but needing to relieve himself after drinking far too much wine, Josephus made his way to a bush in the emperor's garden. He opened his garment and urinated. After he finished and fixed his clothes, Josephus walked over to the running fountain to wash his hands.

As he looked at the Roman god of war, the fountain's centerpiece, he thought of the commandment prohibiting the worship of false idols and smiled, knowing full well all the Roman gods were false and rather ridiculous.

Now clean, Josephus sat on a marble bench in Vespasian's garden and looked out at the stars.

"Thy wonders are endless, my Lord," Josephus said softly to God. "I commit myself to write the histories as I have seen them, as commanded by Elijah."

Then a shooting star caught his eye. It flew right towards the North Star and then stopped, hovering in the sky. A ring of white light flashed out from it, three times quickly in repetition. Then the star vanished—Josephus smiled.

"Baruch Hashem," Josephus said as he looked at the night-time heavens. "I do not believe you would have let me survive, let alone flourish, if I had done wrong in this world," Josephus said softly.

At the same moment, a white dove landed on Josephus' head and pooped.

# Epilogue

**JOSEPHUS SAT** at his writing desk. Pieces of parchment covered in Greek words were stacked hundreds of layers high to his left and right. In between those tall piles was one sheet of paper—it was blank. He picked up his feather quill and dipped it into a jar of black ink.

He was an old man now. Every part of his body had changed since the time he addressed the Judeans outside the walls of Jerusalem. His hair was all but gone, and the little that remained on the sides of his head was snow white. Brittle silver hairs protruded from his nose and ears. His skin was wrinkled across his entire body, his bosom drooped low, and his gut bulged from a life subsidized by the state.

Josephus was hard of hearing now, and his eyesight was not what it used to be, but he still had total control of his faculties.

"I have completed my account of the histories of the Judeans," he wrote. "Please send me a scribe fluent in Greek so that my work may be copied and circulated to the Roman people, preserving it for posterity. Your servant, Flavius Josephus."

He took some powder, sprinkled it over his ink marks, then blew it free.

Josephus' life was now full of luxury, even more so than when he was a high priest. His home had been given to him by Vespasian, and he lived well on an annual pension of a hundred gold talents—a sum so large he had to buy a strongbox just to hold all the gold he could not spend. He had a dozen servants who worked around the clock for him, including a butcher, a cook, a gardener, and various other manservants.

He married four times and he divorced three times, true love always seeming to elude him, though his last two wives did bear him children. His days and nights mirrored themselves, both being fraught with torturous loneliness. Though a small army of people was commissioned to care for Josephus' every need, he was as distant to them as if they were paupers, panhandling on a street corner.

Josephus wanted for nothing, every evening feasting and drinking. He could have afforded two courtesans a night, but now, touching a woman physically only reminded him how painfully distant he was spiritually and romantically from true love.

His bed was empty of other persons—his wife slept in another wing of the mansion. Only Bella, his cat, comforted Josephus at night. But even Bella was symbolic of his failures with women as she cared only for his warmth and food, never sharing a symbiotic moment longer than it suited her needs.

Josephus rolled up his letter, first making sure to secure the paper from both ends with a string. He took a lit candle resting next to the scroll, picked up a stick of red wax and put it to the flame. Once it was dripping, he secured the string and paper with the melted wax, all under the seal of his Flavian-crested ring. Josephus then blew on the wax to make sure it hardened into a solid form.

"Boy!" Josephus yelled and waited, annoyed, for his young manservant to enter his office chamber. "Take this to the printer's house. Tell him the scribe is going to need lots of ink."

"This minute, my lord," the manservant said.

Josephus placed a gold talent in the boy's hand. The boy stood looking at the gold piece, wide-eyed.

"Well, go," Josephus said sternly.

The boy put the coin in his waistcoat pocket and grabbed the scroll from Josephus' hand before running out of the chamber, slamming the large wooden door on his way out.

Josephus sighed at the loud bang caused by the slamming door. Then he took a fresh sheet of paper from the stack on the far section of his writing desk, beside the candle. He placed the sheet in front of him and sat back, pondering his words.

Josephus dipped his quill in the black ink and wrote, "*Antiquitates Judaicae*, by Flavius Josephus."

As Josephus finished his great work of translating the Old Testament into Greek for the gentile world, he sat back in his chair and took a deep breath with his eyes closed.

When he opened his eyelids, a copy of his first book, *Bellum Judaicum* or *The Judean War*, was directly in his line of sight.

Josephus' mind began speaking to himself. "I wonder if anyone will remember what happened in Jerusalem generations from now. I wonder if they will read my history long after I am dead. What they will say of me? Will any of it be true?"

B. Michael Antler

## Josephus, the Historian

CPSIA information can be obtained
at www.ICGtesting.com
Printed in the USA
BVHW030335211120
593667BV00001B/2/J